TAKING THE DREAM SPINNER

TAKING THE DREAM SPINNER

A MATT "ACE" BLACK NOVEL

Thomas Belisle

LUMINARE PRESS

WWW.LUMINAREPRESS.COM

Visit the author's website at
www.thomasbelisleauthor.com

Luminare Press
442 Charnelton St.
Eugene, OR 97401
www.luminarepress.com

LCCN: 2021906923
ISBN: 978-1-64388-679-4

Dedicated to
Veterans of the United States Armed Forces

Special Acknowledgement to the US Navy SEAL Teams

ALSO BY THOMAS BELISLE

Raptor Bloom

Chapter 1

June 2018

The bright flash in the southwestern sky of Azerbaijan cut through the otherwise sterile curtain of darkness. It was followed in milliseconds by a muffled boom, like distant thunder from the summer's usual nighttime storms. The gray-bearded shepherd glanced upward, hoping to gauge how much time he had before the rain came. His herd of sheep and goats was used to the nightly interruptions in the sparse landscape. As he coaxed them toward their small corral for the night, he looked up again. There was no storm approaching.

He saw a trail of glowing debris coming from what he presumed was a stricken aircraft falling toward the ground. He watched in stunned silence. Upon hearing the muted thump of the doomed plane's impact on the damp wadi, he knew that if it was an aircraft, there would be little hope for survivors. The night returned to its sullen, silent darkness, but not before his herd reacted to the unusual noise. The animals tried to scatter, but his well-trained Caucasian mountain dog quickly channeled them toward the security of their pen.

The old man hesitated for a moment before deciding what to do next. His large dog would protect the herd while he investigated the disturbance to his otherwise peaceful night. The ride through the barren landscape in his small horse-drawn wooden wagon would take about fifteen minutes. While he knew the land well, the night posed hidden dangers to a careless traveler. He had survived in the rugged environment for years by being careful. There were no second chances, no help for him if his wagon wheel caught an unseen rut carved into the narrow dirt path during the summer rains. He could not risk getting stuck, or worse, tumbling into a ditch. His gut instincts had kept him alive for years, and he chose not to ignore them.

As he approached the impact site, he smelled the pungent smoke from the smoldering wreckage and could see the still-glowing scattered remains of the small passenger jet in the evening's shallow moonlight. He wandered carefully, avoiding the pools of aviation fuel and stepping through the charred bits of unrecognizable aircraft pieces. The shepherd found bodies strewn about the disturbed desert soil. He checked for a pulse on the unfortunate victims—all men. There was no sign of life in the three he found close to the wreckage—all were clearly dead, burns visible even in the darkness, limbs missing.

He almost didn't notice the fourth man as he headed back to his wagon. Suspended awkwardly amongst the broken limbs of one of the few olive trees that managed to grow in the desolate area was the twisted shape of another body. A tree branch had penetrated the man's left shoulder. His left arm and right leg were clearly broken, appearing awkwardly bent and mangled among the branches. He reached up to check the pulse of what he expected to be a lifeless form. The man was barely breathing.

The shepherd was hesitant at first. There was a chance that if he tried to remove the nearly lifeless victim from the olive tree's branches, he might bring the man's existence to an abrupt end. But he had to try. There was *no* hope for the crash victim's survival if he did nothing. The old man was surprisingly strong despite his age—strength gained through adversity and the need to survive in the often hostile and unforgiving Azerbaijani countryside. He cut the tree branch that had punctured the man's shoulder and carefully lifted the suspended man from the tree.

He carried him to his cart, trying his best to avoid inducing further injury. After placing the battered man on the weathered, straw-covered wooden wagon bed, he bound the shoulder wound with part of his own tunic, braced the broken arm and leg with olive tree branches and twine, and covered the man with an old wool blanket. The now very tired Azerbaijani immediately set out in the general direction of Salyan, hoping to reach the nearest small medical clinic in time to do some good. He doubted the injured man would live through the twenty-mile trip.

Chapter 2

July 2018

The nightmares and cold sweats haunted Matt Black, the unwanted visions creeping slowly into his subconscious during his deepest sleep, repeating themselves every night. They didn't start as a horrific dream. They began first like a rush of adrenaline. He found himself strapped securely in the cockpit of his fighter aircraft. He had targeted an enemy aircraft during the heat of an air battle in the sky over Iran. His missile had found its mark.

But then, the excitement of a combat kill quickly changed, shocking him into believing the unthinkable. His aircraft had been hit by an Iranian missile, and he was trapped inside the flaming wreckage of a violently gyrating out-of-control aircraft as it plummeted from the sky.

Centrifugal forces from the corkscrewing, fatally wounded warbird pinned him against his ejection seat. He felt like a massive weight was on top of him. No matter how hard he tried, his arms and hands wouldn't respond, making it impossible to reach the ejection handle. He had only seconds left to get out of his F-22 Raptor stealth fighter before it crossed the coast line and slammed into the dark sea.

He strained to control his hands, willing them to reach for the yellow handle positioned against the front cushion of his ejection seat. He caught flashing glimpses of the Persian Gulf rushing up to greet him. It was ready to welcome his premature death. To join others who had been casualties of previous battles, their bones lying scattered on the seabed floor.

His heart pounded, feeling like it was exploding from his chest, as he tried to control his panic. He wasn't going to make it. He was gasping for air through the damaged oxygen hose connected to his helmet. Then, somehow, his hands grasped the handle. Would the ejection seat even work in his crippled aircraft after the surface-to-air missile warhead had ripped the Raptor apart?

A final glance—the dark sea was ready to engulf him and end his life. *Pull the handle*, his brain screamed. The sea's blackness raced toward him, his Raptor inverted, the canopy seconds away from impacting the water.

He gasped, taking one last breath as he used every ounce of strength to pull the yellow ejection handle upward. Then, nothing. He squeezed his eyes tightly closed, hoping to avoid seeing the inevitable. The open arms of death waited to embrace him.

"Wake up, Matt!" shouted Julie, shaking him as she tried to draw her husband out of the nightly horror show he had been burdened with since his return home from the Middle East.

He bolted upright in his bed, covered in sweat, his heart pounding. He had relived his brush with death in the sky over Iran for the umpteenth time. He looked around the darkened room, saw his wife next to him, staring at him. She was barely visible in the slivers of moonlight slipping through the window blinds.

"I'm okay. I just wish these crazy nightmares would stop. I don't know why I keep reliving what happened, especially twisting the ending to what could have happened but didn't."

"You need to talk with a doctor about these nightly episodes. I'm afraid they're going to affect your health—your heart is pounding, racing crazily whenever I wake you from these horrible dreams."

"I've got to work my own way out of this, Jules. I don't need some quack in the medical community grounding me for some psychological reason he dug out of a textbook. I know that none of this affects my ability to fly."

Captain Matt "Ace" Black had, in fact, been shot out of the sky while leading combat missions against Iran in his F-22 Raptor. But the ending had clearly not resulted in his death. He'd managed to eject from the doomed aircraft. He could still remember looking up at his billowing parachute as he floated down toward the warm water of the Persian Gulf. He remembered struggling to free himself from his chute before it pulled him underwater—trying not to panic, relying on his training. He had been rescued within an hour of his watery immersion and cleared to resume combat after a short recovery period.

Back in the battle, he had continued to clear the sky over Iran of several enemy aircraft. One of them had been a small military passenger jet carrying a man named Khalil Ruffa, who had been trying to escape the country's destruction. Intelligence sources had later determined that the radicalized Syrian had likely met his fate.

Now, one month after the short war in Iran had ended, Matt was home in Virginia. He still harbored plenty of anger for the Syrian who had earned Matt's friendship during the time when Khalil led the engineering teams who'd modified the F-22 Raptor. But Khalil Ruffa had stolen top-secret technology and provided it to America's enemies. He had subsequently sabotaged the Raptor fleet by corrupting its software. As a result, he had compromised the powerful capability of America's premier stealth aircraft.

Matt still couldn't believe that a man like Khalil had been given so much—citizenship in the United States, a first-rate education, and a top job in one of the country's most sensitive highly classified industries—but had thrown it all away. Khalil had become a traitor to the United States. His actions linked him with the leading sponsor of terror in the world—Iran. And it had almost cost Matt his life.

He looked at his beautiful wife next to him. She was already dozing off again, returning to the peaceful slumber she had been in before Matt's painful recurring nightmare had interrupted the night's stillness. He thought about getting out of bed now that he was wide awake. His heart had stopped pounding, and he was beginning to relax. He looked at the clock. Too early for coffee, so he figured he might as well try to do something productive. An early morning run in the pre-dawn darkness usually helped clear his head and calm him down. He gave Julie a soft kiss, grabbed his running shorts, Air Force Academy T-shirt, socks and sneakers, quickly dressed and headed toward the front door.

Exercise wasn't a chore for Ace. It was part of his life. A fitness nut used to an almost daily regimen of aerobic exercise and weight lifting, he hadn't gained a pound since graduating from the Academy and had simply added to the muscle his well-tuned body sported.

As he sprinted down the damp, dimly lit streets that surrounded his home in Yorktown, Virginia, his head cleared. The mist hung in the air, creating a surreal environment as he blasted through it on the deserted roadways, the halos of humid air surrounding each streetlight beckoning him as he approached and passed by.

He thought briefly about the Syrian as he picked up his pace. How relatively easy it had been for one man to have had such a disastrous impact on him, his country and the world. He shook the thoughts from his head and concentrated on his run. After all, before he returned home from his combat duty, he had been assured that his missile had indeed knocked out an enemy jet escaping from the defeated rogue Iranian regime. The traitor, Khalil Ruffa, was presumed to have been on it, a casualty of war.

Chapter 3

Azerbaijan

The patient's eyes twitched, fluttered ever so slightly. Subtle, nearly imperceptible movements at first. Indications of a body coming back to life. The fact that he was even alive, almost inconceivable. The odds of surviving the horrific aircraft crash, infinitesimal. Yet somehow, he had cheated death. It wasn't his first time.

He was being closely watched. Cared for. Treated the best way possible with the limited rudimentary medical resources the clinic had to offer in the desolate area. Given the scarcity of any form of intensive care capability there, prayers had been said for him when he had been brought in. It was, at least, *something* that they could offer. Few of the staff, if you could call them that, believed he would ever recover given his battered condition.

Khalil slowly peeled back the layers from the unconscious state he had been in. Neurons within his brain began firing erratically. As his body repaired itself, the connections within his neuronal structure knitted themselves together, working as intended, electrical impulses providing the critical messaging needed for a body to function normally. There was more eye movement beneath his closed lids. He became aware of his own strained breathing—and then the pain, seeming to emanate from every inch of his damaged frame. He turned his head slowly to the right, just enough to convince the medical staff that he would wake soon.

He opened one eye, then the other. His mind tried to comprehend what he saw through his blurry vision. And what he was feeling. He was on his back. Where was he? In some sort of room with a few pieces of what appeared to be medical equipment nearby. A tube extended from a bag hanging on a metal stand near him, fluid coursing into his arm. His eyes slowly cleared. He could see daylight spilling through the partially open canvas door flap. The bright sunlight outside was further blocked by the dark corrugated metal cover that served as the roof over the small wood-framed clinic.

"He is awake, doctor," a female voice blurted out. "It's a miracle!"

Khalil was confused. The voice was not familiar. Nor was the place that his eyes managed to gradually bring into focus. *Some sort of medical facility, a hospital?* He looked at the balding, bespectacled man in the white smock approaching him. *A doctor?*

"Welcome back to the world. How do you feel?" the physician asked as he checked his patient's pulse.

"What is this place?" Khalil nearly choked on the words, his dry throat rudely expelling a raspy sound from a voice that had been silenced for the past three weeks.

The doctor placed a wet cloth to Khalil's lips, careful not to induce an involuntary gag reflex with too much liquid. The injured man's tongue tried desperately to capture the cool droplets to soothe his parched throat.

"You are at the Danbi clinic. We are the only medical facility for about fifty miles. We don't have much here, but it appears that it was enough to keep you alive."

"Where am I? What country am I in?" Khalil questioned, his voice becoming a little stronger.

"Azerbaijan. You were brought here by a shepherd who saved your life. You were very badly injured—there was not much hope that you would survive. You stopped breathing shortly after arriving here, but we managed to get your heart beating again. I did the best I could to tend to your injuries. I haven't treated anyone before with such severe trauma and managed to live. Yet somehow, Allah has blessed you with another chance at life." He paused as Khalil appeared to process the information about his condition.

"What is your name?" the doctor asked.

Khalil hesitated, not sure if he should divulge his real name. In his weakened state, he told him.

He looked at the repairs done to him. The cast on his left arm. The crude pins protruding just below the knee of his immobilized right leg. As he focused on the pins in his elevated lower limb, he became aware of the pain, his stare triggering his brain's acknowledgment of the primitive but effective surgery that had taken place. He tried to take a deep breath and felt a stabbing sensation in his chest. He touched what felt like a large bandage on his shoulder with his free hand and winced.

"Most of your ribs were fractured. They will take time to heal, along with the rest of your injuries," the doctor cautioned. "Your leg had compound breaks, and I was forced to use pins to secure the bones. If I had not done that, you likely would have never walked normally once you recovered. Even so, the injury may prevent you from ever achieving full mobility. Your skull also appeared to have been fractured, although I can't determine how severely without an x-ray—a capability we don't have here."

"You said a shepherd brought me here. How? From where?"

"The shepherd carried you away from an airplane crash site several kilometers from here. The others on the aircraft were not so lucky. I was told that they were clearly dead."

Khalil became silent. Others? Crash site? He touched his forehead, then the large bandage covering the sutures in his head, trying desperately to clear his foggy memory. Things slowly solidified in his brain. Fragments of thoughts. Bits of disconnected information. He vaguely remembered being on an airplane. Something had happened while he was on it—maybe an explosion? He wasn't sure. He remembered nothing more about the airplane or any other passenger.

"The army has been looking for you. At least I think it is you whom they have asked about. We hid you. We told them nothing."

Khalil jerked up in the bed. He immediately regretted the abrupt movement and was instantly jolted by excruciating pain. It felt like a searing bolt of lightning raced up his leg and into his back. His chest felt like a spike had been driven into it and his head seemed like it was about to explode. He winced, his body revolting against the ill-advised movement, his brain informing him of the need for more rest, time to heal.

But the pain jolted more memories. His escape from Iran. That was why he had been on the plane. He didn't remember the crash. The moment the aircraft had fallen from the sky. Or why it had crashed. He wondered who the others on the doomed plane had been.

"Why did you help me? Why did you not turn me in to the army?"

"From the scraps of Iranian Army uniforms the shepherd brought to me, I presumed you all were trying to escape the carnage there. The fact that *you* somehow survived is a message from God—that you are destined to do more with your life. Turning you in would have served no real purpose."

Khalil nodded, his memory gradually coming back. A few random thoughts were connecting into something meaningful about why he was in Azerbaijan. Perhaps this was a planned escape route.

"We can protect you here and keep you from being discovered. The army comes here on very predictable dates. There are places nearby where we can hide you, where you will not be found."

Khalil tried to sit up again but nearly passed out. The doctor could see he was in excruciating pain and offered him the strongest medication he had—paracetamol, otherwise known as Tylenol. Khalil didn't answer. He was fading into unconsciousness again, the pain shutting down his ability to remain awake, and allowing an escape from the agony he was experiencing.

"Should I give him the drug?" the medical attendant asked the doctor.

"Let him sleep, but monitor him closely. When he wakes again, we will see what level of pain he is in. For now, rest is the best thing for him."

Deep in sleep, Khalil's brain began stitching together the past memories. His parents and brothers had been killed in Syria when he was a child. An American fighter bomber attack on his village had been the cause—the pilot who had led the attack was a man named Alec Black. Khalil and his young sister had somehow survived. They had been rescued by their uncle, who had brought them to England first and then to the United States. The final tragedy in his life had happened when his sister had been accidentally killed on a Dallas street. Her death had followed many years of mental trauma following a vicious attack while she had attended a Texas high school. For Khalil, it was the culmination of heartbreaking life events that had turned his anger into hatred for America—and made him the perfect candidate for manipulation by a cleric in a Texas mosque and for Khalil's subsequent radicalization.

When he eventually awoke, the pieces of his past would solidify in his mind and become a call to action.

Chapter 4

June 2023

United States Air Force Major Matt "Ace" Black shuffled the papers across his desk at Joint Base Langley-Eustis in Hampton, Virginia. The job was painful for him as a relatively new major. He was "flying" a desk. He was out of the cockpit—out of the environment where he felt truly alive. In fact, escaping the bonds of earth in an advanced fighter jet made him believe he was superhuman, possessing not just the gift of flight but the awesome power of the warbird he piloted, which became a natural extension of his own body.

The base was not new to him. It was a return trip. He had been stationed here in 2016 as a combat pilot with the call sign "Ace," flying the F-22 Raptor stealth fighter. The three-plus years he had spent at the sprawling base had a special meaning for him. He flew the most powerful aircraft in the world here. This was where he had met the love of his life, Julie, and it was the place where his three children had been born.

He was doing his time, as many officers called it, a prerequisite to continuing his advancement in rank and responsibility. His job was to help develop the next generation of advanced technology for the Air Force. In the end, if he couldn't be flying, this was still a great gig until he could claw his way back into a jet.

When he escaped the monotony of the headquarters' briefing rooms and managed to get to the base fitness center, he had a chance for at *least* a solid physical release. And some time to reminisce about how he had gotten to where he was. He would often think back on what had transpired over the past five years and his combat time in the Raptor.

———————•———————

The war in the sky over Iran was a distant memory, but he could still remember the highlights. The utter enjoyment of piloting America's premier stealth fighter. Testing his skill against an adversary. The thrill of combat. The excitement of winning in battle, in life-or-death confrontations. He could also never forget nearly getting killed, shot down by an Iranian surface-to-air missile while he'd led combat forces to prevent a rogue ayatollah from starting a potential nuclear holocaust. The time might have slipped away, but the memories were still there.

When Ace had returned from his wartime stint, he'd already had military orders to proceed to his next assignment—the Air Command and Staff College in Montgomery, Alabama. The one-year break from flying operations was a refreshing change that included plenty of social interactions with U.S. and international military students.

Ace had been greatly disappointed at graduation when he'd received notification of an assignment to South Korea in another nonflying job. He would be assisting the South Korean armed forces in procuring new weapon systems from the United States and coordinating joint U.S.–South Korean military training exercises supporting counterterrorism operations. While there, he'd developed a strong working relationship with a United States Navy Sea Air Land (SEAL) team. Ace quickly bonded professionally with the team's leader, a powerfully built frogman who shared the same sense of commitment to helping an important U.S. ally. Their relationship had grown especially tight when *off* duty in the smoky Busan steakhouse bars.

When not working, Ace had kept his fitness in top form, spending a considerable amount of time learning the fine art of tae kwon do. He had also picked up some advanced techniques used by the Israeli Defense Forces that would serve him well later in life.

THOMAS BELISLE

Two years in Korea had ended on a high note. He had almost exploded with excitement hearing he was headed to F-22 refresher training, and then on to Nellis AFB outside Las Vegas, Nevada, for an assignment at the USAF Weapons School. As an instructor at the desert base, he'd helped Raptor pilots fine-tune their combat skills. That assignment was pretty unusual for a senior captain, but his success leading combat missions in Syria and Iran had secured his place at the premier fighter pilot base.

He had been selected for promotion to the rank of major while there, just before heading to his current assignment—back to his old Virginia stomping grounds.

———•———

"Hey, boys, I'm calling it a day," Ace announced to his office staff. It was Friday, and the week had seemed like it would never end. Now he was eager to get home and begin packing for his vacation.

He and the family were heading south to Port Canaveral in Florida. This trip had been in the planning stages for months. It was a celebration of his wedding anniversary with his beautiful wife, Julie and their three children—Claire, age seven, and the twins, Roman and Nick, who had just turned six years old. They were all ecstatic to be hopping on a large luxury cruise ship bound for the sunny Caribbean.

He spotted his car quickly, the shiny vintage Grabber Blue paint distinctively marking its location. He backed out of the parking space in the overcrowded asphalt car lot and pulled out onto the street. The throaty rumble of the 375-horsepower, 429-cubic-inch V-8 engine of his 1970 Boss Mustang angrily announced his departure. Ace had restored his deceased father's car years before and kept it in prime operating condition. He did his best to keep the straining beast under the twenty-five-mile-per-hour speed limit.

Ace headed around the east end of the airfield runway on the perimeter road, slowing to admire the two F-22 Raptors streaking skyward for an evening mission. The circuitous route took him by the

Back River waterway and past what used to be the Lighter-than-Air part of Langley Air Force Base's history, when helium-filled dirigibles had been flown there in the 1920s and '30s. That area had now been replaced with military support facilities and homes for Air Force families who chose to live on the base. He continued his drive, proceeding past the base's Eaglewood Golf Course, through the entry gate to the NASA Langley Research Center, and finally toward Yorktown, to the home he had purchased in the historic colonial region.

When he arrived at his house, it looked like a tornado had torn through the children's rooms. Clothes littered the floor, pulled from bureau drawers in a futile attempt by the kids to choose what they thought was needed for the trip. Julie, looked a bit frazzled as she tried to restore order and ensure they took only what they *really* needed for their early Saturday morning departure.

"Jules. What's going on here? Thought you'd have the kids packed and ready by now. This place looks like a disaster. You know we've got to head south tomorrow morning pretty early. It's a long drive to get to Cocoa Beach."

The look he got from Julie stopped him in his tracks.

"Yes, Matt, I know!" she pronounced a bit too loudly. "But *you* weren't exactly *here* to help out today. I thought you were coming home a lot earlier."

She was not smiling. He'd seen the dreaded look before, her displeasure at both his comments and his late arrival clearly showing.

"I know. Sorry. I was inundated with requirements this morning that had to get taken care of before I could leave."

"Well, it's not as bad as it looks." She was beginning to calm down. "The kids are pretty much ready. Just need to check their suitcases one last time." She looked back at him and gave him the slightest smile. He breathed a sigh of relief as she continued. "I'm more than ready for a nice break from here."

"Me too, baby." He grabbed her around the waist and twirled her around, finishing with a tender kiss. "Let's get this packing frenzy over with and head out to get something to eat."

Julie smiled even more, relieved. Tomorrow, they would be on their way, providing her a well-needed escape from the day-to-day grind, and an opportunity to spend some time with her parents, who were joining them on the cruise ship. Matt's mother, Cathy, would be meeting them as well.

Other *surprise* guests would help make the cruise vacation truly memorable for Matt.

Chapter 5

n the five years that followed the war in Iran, Khalil had stayed openly camouflaged in Tajikistan. When he had regained his health after the crash, he had linked up with Mustafa al-Alawi, a radical sheikh in the Ar Qetar mosque in Baku. The imam was linked to a terrorist cell in the Tajik countryside and had already communicated with the group's leader in Dushanbe. Khalil had been secreted across the Caspian Sea, through Turkmenistan, Uzbekistan, and across the border into Tajikistan, to eventually arrive at his destination in the Tajik capital, Dushanbe.

The rugged country was well chosen for the Syrian's new home—extreme landscape, limited transportation and communication networks, and a cultural mix of Tajiks, Uzbeks, and Russians.

With over nine-tenths of the country mountainous—its highest peak over twenty-four thousand feet—the topography kept all but the locals from being there. Most of the population resided not in the few major cities but in many hundreds of small quishlags, towns of up to four hundred homes in the valley areas, and in smaller numbers in the steep mountain regions.

In stark contrast, Dushanbe, the country's largest city and capital, had a distinctly European flair—modern buildings, streets, museums, cafés, and education centers. Additionally, its concentration of technical excellence suited Khalil perfectly. He was just one of thousands of other professionals blending in, nearly invisible among the one million other city inhabitants.

Khalil often thought about his work at Omega, the world-class software development and integration company. He had been their best, their brightest engineer. He had managed a United States government contract to upgrade America's F-22 Raptor stealth fighter aircraft but had given the Air Force a bit more than what they had paid for.

When the United States military had begun their attack on the Iran, Khalil trusted his efforts to sabotage the Raptor's software would cripple their stealth capability and strike a mighty blow against them. He had hoped also to exact some retribution for his personal family tragedies—from the Americans who had taken everything from him.

In the end, his efforts had not been successful. He had failed. Iran's nuclear ambitions, which had depended on the Raptor's defeat, had collapsed under the weight of overwhelming American firepower. The F-22s had dominated the battle once their corrupted software had been fixed, flying with impunity and the protection of stealth, which had ultimately led to the regime's demise.

After five years, he still wondered. Did the Americans know he was alive? How would they know? They must have known he was in Iran before the carnage had begun—that he had slipped out of the United States after completing his traitorous actions in Omega. They might have believed he had been in the ayatollah's underground command center, which was subsequently reduced to rubble by American bombs. How would they know he had not perished there along with the Ayatollah? Did they know he had escaped just before the bunker had been destroyed? That he had managed to flee the country on a small military passenger aircraft? How would they have even known he was on that ill-fated plane that had been blown from the sky, probably by an American fighter jet? Nobody could possibly believe there were any survivors—even if it was known that he had been on the aircraft.

His name had changed. Khalil Ruffa was now Khalil Atta. His appearance was distinctly different from before the crash—partly due to normal aging, partly from what he had endured. Several scars on his face, over his left eye and on his right cheekbone, gave him a hardened appearance. It reminded him of the battle-tested warriors from his homeland in Syria during the days when the radical Islamic group Black Dawn had reigned. His hair was a bit longer now and he sported a trimmed beard, a different look from when he had worked as a software design engineer at Omega.

The accommodations provided for him on the outskirts of the capital city had been adequate. Nothing fancy. Just the basics required to live a modest life. A one-bedroom apartment with a kitchen and a bathroom. The nondescript building was quiet. His neighbors kept to themselves, and few noticed or acknowledged him or one another as they passed. They paid little attention to Khalil, and most seemed indifferent to the comings and goings of any of the small apartment complex dwellers.

Khalil's sponsorship by the radical Panja cell leader Farad Asmaradov, and the group's covert ties to one of Tajikistan's leading universities, the Academy of Sciences in central Dushanbe, placed the Syrian right where he needed to be. A perfect fit for a man with incredible intellect and unprecedented software skills. The school's advanced computer laboratory provided the precise environment to leverage his skills, which were destined to support Asmaradov's future extremist endeavors.

The terrorist kingpin had built a reputation for sponsoring and planning deadly strikes in major cities throughout the region. He was known for the stealthy nature of his attacks, striking without warning in heavily populated, minimally defended places. *Soft targets.*

He had earned the name "Viper" from those who feared him, and from his deadly attacks, similar to the strikes made by his reptilian namesake. A wanted man in most of Europe, the Caucasus, and Central Asia, he was number one on the United States' high-value target list. However, Asmaradov was number one in Russia for a very different reason. Vladimir Putonov, the country's president, had very strong ties to the Viper and was the primary source of funding for the terrorist's escapades. Putonov had his reasons for his cash injections, possibly for a major future endeavor.

The Viper knew the history that came with the Syrian—his critical link to Iran's failed plan to unite the Persian Gulf nations in a holy caliphate years before. It had almost succeeded.

In spite of the failure, Khalil still had great potential, still had the fire in his belly, the *will* in his heart. The gray-bearded cell leader recognized him as a committed soldier, dedicated to radical ideals and willing to put his life on the line to execute a mission. The Viper knew that Khalil would be integral to a daring plan already in its formative stages.

Chapter 6

The Syrian engineer had been given his direction by Asmaradov. He was requested—strongly encouraged—to apply his skills to a very specific project. Within the academy's computer lab, Khalil had developed and tested the myriad ways to breach the ultra-secure networks of large integrated ship systems. Reference to a specific ship type—freighter, tanker, passenger vessel—was masked, initially. The Viper was hesitant to provide any further information, part of his quest to keep secret the final details until the time was right. Khalil would become aware that the target was indeed a cruise ship.

The plan was complicated and extremely detailed. It would rely on precise execution, and depend on insiders, embedded years earlier into the cruise ship industry—specifically, into Pleasure Cruise Lines. It also depended on penetrating multiple levels of security on a cruise ship. Khalil was about to gain the critical insight that would make his task much more executable.

The logistics of moving people into key positions was also crucial to success—laying the groundwork over time for their subsequent assignment to work on the targeted ship, and placing them in position to pull off one of the greatest terror attacks ever seen on the high seas.

Asmaradov had acquired the ship's blueprints—CAD construction plans and electronic wiring diagrams—following a substantial cash payment generated from the radical cell's generous benefactor in Moscow. A pliable Pleasure Cruise Lines engineering supervisor had the requisite access to obtain them and had been more than willing to provide them for the right amount of money. Most significantly, the Viper had obtained through his Russian supporters the one crucial element needed to achieve success in the upcoming mission—the ship's software program.

The Bulgarian company, AI Global Software Ltd., located in Sofia, had produced the latest hybrid autonomous software technology that had been acquired by Pleasure Cruise Lines and installed in their fleet of ships. The specialized state-of-the-art software enabled control of all ship systems through a central computer hub. Putonov's deep reach into Bulgaria's political leadership, including leverage over energy holdings in Gazprom, gave him the influence to covertly acquire the software for a purpose it had never been designed for. The *Dream Spinner* was one of the ships that had been the beneficiary of the software. Now in possession critical control element for his upcoming mission, Asmaradov had chosen his specific target.

The Viper's bold plan would make a political statement to the western world. It would escalate his terror activities to the next level—induce fear that no one was safe anywhere. While he was not fond of making any connection to a superpower, Russia was a useful tool to his end objectives. He believed that disrupting the Tajik government's growing attraction to the Americans and moving it back to a more pro-Russian alignment would hopefully stifle efforts to clamp down on radical cells like his that freely operated in the rugged landscape. Putonov was more than agreeable to stoke the fire of radicalism in Tajikistan any way he could if it helped further his geopolitical objectives in the strategic Central Asian location.

The plan would hopefully achieve another, more personal goal of Asmaradov—gaining release of a top mastermind of terrorism and two others from the United States prison in Guantanamo Bay, Cuba.

The plan was bold. Not since 1985 had a cruise ship been successfully hijacked, its passengers held hostage and threatened with death if terrorist demands were not met. The *Achille Lauro*, a vessel of Italian origin, had been overtaken off the coast of Egypt by members of the Palestine Liberation Front. The hijacking had resulted in the brutal death of passenger Leon Klinghoffer, before the ship was freed. The Viper had an entirely different expected outcome for his planned endeavor.

He had put in place nearly all elements needed for success. The last few would require timing, speed, and maybe a little luck. He had faith in the last element. He had engineered his own luck by careful preparation and intense commitment by all participants. He knew that he was born for this plan, this mission.

Asmaradov counted on Khalil's incredible software skills to pull off the daring effort. The advanced software technology in cruise ships controlled all of the electronically integrated operational functions of the vessels. If one could take control of the electronics that powered the ship, one could control the ship's ultimate destiny. The task would be made easier by the acquisition of the key elements needed for Khalil to develop a way to effectively penetrate and control the ship. But there was still plenty of risk.

The talented Syrian would have to devise a way to hack into the *Dream Spinner*'s secure mainframe electronic control system—no easy task. First, there had to be a way to get on board and be accepted as a member of the ship's crew.

Then, he would need to penetrate the heart of what controlled the ship. Even with the advantage of having the CAD blueprints and software program, the fully integrated, protected electronic systems likely had redundant safeguards he might not know about until he tried to penetrate the system while on board the ship. Clearly it would not be as difficult a task as the one Khalil had performed when he'd hacked the F-22 Raptor's central computer. The level of technology in the stealthy fighter aircraft far surpassed the still significant advances made to cruise ship electronic systems. But there was always the chance that he would be discovered by the *Dream Spinner*'s crew.

Additionally, the level of coordination, timing, subterfuge, and perhaps violence that would be required made this entire gambit a risky operation. A handful of Tajik nationals, now Islamic State–inspired radicals embedded into the ship's crew, would still have to gain control of nearly all of the officers and crew members.

Asmaradov knew the plan required more than the personnel he'd pre-positioned on the ship. They could surely handle the hacking of the ship's systems, and perhaps the initial subterfuge and the confusion, to set up what was going to be required next—the violence. But there would need to be a way to import those who would deliver that violence. Also, how were the explosives and weapons going to be brought on board to carry out the task in spite of the tight security in port? Had the Viper planned for that too, at the right time and place?

As the time grew near for the event the Viper hoped would shock the world, Asmaradov had called a secret meeting of his key Panja cell members. He had explained the importance of planning, precisely executing his strategy, and being prepared to give one's life for his cause, but no specifics had been provided. Most of those present had wondered what the true mission was.

"I understand that we are to be part of a major plan to strike at the United States," Khalil had said to Asmaradov. "I believe we all are fully committed to executing your wishes. But when will we know what the plan really is? I presume, since I have been working on ship systems, the plan involves a ship? What specific kind of ship? And when will we know when the plan will be prosecuted?"

The cold, dead eyes with the penetrating stare set Khalil aback.

"Patience is a virtue," Asmaradov responded. "You will know at the right time, a time of my choosing. Have faith, my brother."

Asmaradov made some final comments. "The seeds of the plan have been germinating for several years and will soon produce the bounty we await. We will successfully execute the most significant attack in decades. Key long-term actions have been taking place over this time to position the right people in the right places to support this mission. They lie in wait for the time when we will begin our jihad."

Khalil apologized for challenging the Viper. He was acutely aware of the others around him, their questioning gazes focused in his direction. Some had concerned looks on their faces, wondering why he dared question Asmaradov. Why he had been pressing their leader for answers.

Asmaradov concluded, "The blow we will strike on the United States will be burned into the eyes of the Western world for years to come."

Before the meeting ended, the Viper called Khalil to his side.

"I want you to meet your partner for the upcoming mission."

An attractive woman stepped forward and extended her hand to Khalil. He introduced himself with a firm handshake.

"Banu Sayeed," she said.

She needed no introduction to him. The skilled assassin knew the Syrian, even though she had never personally met him before. And she knew what she had done in Ohio years before to prevent him from being discovered for his treasonous activities. She had been responsible for the abduction of one of Khalil's Omega engineers, Steve Brooks, who had inadvertently witnessed Khalil tampering with classified F-22 Raptor software, and for the subsequent disposal of the engineer's body in the deep recesses of Ohio's Monongahela National Forest. She had followed her orders—all in the name of hiding Iran's sinister plot to compromise one of America's vital weapon systems.

The meeting ended and Khalil walked away. Recollections of the failed caliphate in Iran had him wondering. That, too, had been intended to bring the U.S. to its knees—but it had failed. Iran had underestimated the United States and its capability to react quickly to a crisis. But then again, maybe part of the failure had been a lapse in planning for all contingencies by the Ayatollah. Certainly not the result of his own actions. Maybe this time, it would be different.

He wondered what the real mission was. He would find out very soon.

As summer approached, the Viper's warriors had dispersed. Some headed to a port on the eastern coast of the United States, in Central Florida. Others traveled a bit further south to an island about seventy miles off the southernmost point of Key West.

Chapter 7

Day 1

Ace backed the big SUV out of their driveway in the early morning darkness, intent on putting some miles on the car while the kids were still tired enough to sleep for a few hours. He could at least count on some quiet time for a little while. He hoped the long drive to Port Canaveral was going to be pretty much uneventful. What was he thinking? He was going to be in a car for thirteen hours with his wife and three young kids.

Hours later and miles down the highway, Ace was busy settling the constant arguments over who was touching whom, who was making weird sounds, and trying to resolve pretty much every other conceivable conflict three cooped-up kids could engage in. At least they had their iPads to keep themselves occupied for some of the time with movies uploaded the day before.

Ace was grateful for the stops at the interstate highway rest areas. They gave his family time to stretch their legs and let him clear his throbbing head. The fast-food stops satisfied the kids' seemingly endless appetites when the snacks they had brought with them ran out, and also provided a break from the confines of the car.

Ace gutted it out on the drive, wanting to make it all the way from Yorktown, Virginia, to the hotel near the port in one day. The nearly eight hundred mile drive was a better option for him than stopping at a hotel along the way. He could rest the next day on the cruise ship, sipping a cold brew while stretched out on one of the countless reclining lounge chairs on deck.

After what seemed like an eternity, their freeway exit from Interstate 95 approached in the waning daylight. Ace checked his watch.

Crap, he thought. *It's almost seven o'clock. It's a wonder the kids aren't screaming for dinner.*

He pulled in to a nearby fast food joint—burgers and fries were not what he preferred, but it was quick. A half-hour later, they arrived at their hotel just a few miles from the port. The family immediately settled into the large suite he had booked. Claire got the spare bed and the twins shared the fold-out couch. They were all pretty tired from their early morning departure and were sound asleep before nine o'clock.

The sunlight poured through the partially closed window shades, the bright beams stabbing Ace's eyes and awakening him after a deep sleep. It was still a bit early for the rest of his brood. The kids likely wouldn't rise anytime soon. He crawled out of bed, threw on some clothes and headed to the lobby for a jolt of coffee. He noted that the daily newspaper had the usual array of U.S. and international reports, including a terrorist bombing in Pakistan at a Peshawar marketplace. Four American journalists killed. *Still plenty of radical-inspired terror around the world.*

Their boarding time was not until one o'clock, so there was no real rush to get out of the hotel early, and late checkout had been approved. When he got back to the room, the creatures were stirring. He gave Julie a tender kiss and then headed to shave and shower. Once the group had dressed, the family headed to the hotel lobby breakfast area.

They had some time to kill before proceeding to the ship, so after eating, they drove down the coastal road toward Cocoa Beach. By late morning, the traffic was already heavy as they approached the main thoroughfare that led to the famous beach. After driving around for fifteen minutes, Ace finally found a parking spot, and the group hiked a few hundred yards to the beach. The kids wanted to put their feet in the white sand as soon as they saw it.

The children were on an emotional high—they pulled off their sneakers and socks, then ran onto the sand and down toward the warm Atlantic water. The surf was mild this morning, the beach pristine except for the seaweed left stranded from the earlier high tide. Ace and Julie strolled behind the kids, enjoying the sight of their frolicking children having fun splashing around in the light surf. They relished the short prelude to the cruise, their walk in the surf, before heading back to the car.

"Okay, guys. Wipe the sand off your feet. I don't want it all over my car," Julie pleaded.

"Good luck with that," Ace chuckled.

They drove past some of the iconic Cocoa Beach landmarks and turned toward the hotel. It was time to clean up a bit, pick up their bags, and then proceed to the cruise ship.

Chapter 8

"Okay kids. Time to go," Ace said as he tried to usher the family out of their hotel room.

The kids needed no encouragement. "I can't wait to get on the ship," shouted Claire excitedly.

Ace loaded his crew in the large white SUV, along with all the luggage they would bring on board. He made the short drive toward the terminal area and found the sign he was looking for. The large cruise liner *Dream Spinner* was located at Terminal 8. He pulled the big SUV onto the access road that would take them there, and immediately found themselves in a long parade of cars waiting to proceed through what looked like a series of checkpoints.

Ace nodded to himself, remembering reading about the security threat reports before leaving Langley. The tempo of anti-American activities generated by radical organizations had picked up around the world, and especially wherever U.S. forces and citizens were living or traveling. Recent intelligence indicated that it was just a matter of time before the U.S. homeland was hit again. There had been some unverified reports of threats from Central Asian–affiliated militants, but nothing that might indicate an attack was imminent or any specific place was a target.

His thoughts were interrupted by the armed security officer who tapped on his car window. Ace lowered the glass.

"Hello, Officer."

"Sir, I need to see your identification and boarding documents." He took a close look at Ace and then through the window at the other passengers. "Please roll down the passenger windows as well."

Ace did as he was directed. He pulled out his driver's license and documents and handed them over. The officer caught a glimpse of Ace's military ID when he pulled out his license.

After a careful review, they were waved forward.

"Thanks for your service. Have a nice cruise."

"I appreciate your dedication to keeping this place safe," Ace replied.

As he pulled the car slowly forward, he noticed that there were a few more checkpoints to go through, the route to the terminal curving around cement barricades intended to keep the traffic moving slowly. Ace presumed the threat reports he heard about might explain the enhanced security measures being taken in a place where literally thousands of people were congregating. One checkpoint had two armed Homeland Security officers and another holding a long pole with a mirror affixed to the end. As Ace was directed to stop, the man with the mirror walked around the car, checking the undercarriage for anything that shouldn't be there.

"Daddy, what are they looking for?" asked Claire. "They all have guns."

Roman piped up, "I think it's pretty cool!"

Ace looked at Julie first, then turned his head to the back seat.

"Honey, they're just making sure that the right people get to board the boat. They want you to have a terrific time when you get on the *Dream Spinner*."

Julie looked back at him with a frown. Ace gave her a forced grin in return. Every effort was being made to ensure the safety of all passengers on their upcoming vacation.

After three security stops, they cleared a final checkpoint and drove up to the baggage unloading area. By now, every carload of people in front of them was eager to get on the ship. They stopped briefly to pass their suitcases to the handlers, who then loaded them onto large baggage carts.

"You guys wait by the terminal door while I park the car."

They all climbed out, grabbing the items they would hand-carry on board. Julie grabbed the children's backpacks and her small roll-aboard suitcase. Then she asked Claire to hold her brothers' hands and closely follow her toward the terminal door. She led her small herd to a clear spot to wait for her husband.

Ace quickly drove to the nearest open parking spot, pulled in and turned off the ignition. He grabbed his backpack and hat and jogged his way back to the terminal. The crowd had grown, but after a bit of searching, he found his family and they walked into the passenger welcome area.

As they waited in line to get to the check-in counters, Ace noticed that cruises still attracted plenty of people from around the world. The colorful clothes bespoke the fun all of them hoped to have in the coming days. Most of the passengers looked like they were from *anytown* America. Others were clearly from outside the U.S.

He overheard at least five different languages being spoken by the eager tourists—French, Spanish, Chinese, possibly a Central Asian language, and Arabic. *Lots of diversity on this boat*, he thought to himself. There were wide ranges of folks of all ages, from babies to grandparents. A few passengers in wheelchairs. A group of muscular young men, dark-skinned, most with beards, looked like an athletic team celebrating the end of a successful season.

There were plenty of passengers from the Far East, taking advantage of America's ability to provide them a first-rate vacation. After traveling from halfway around the world, they had likely visited Disney World and Universal Studios before boarding the ship, wanting to make the most of their trip. Mouse ears perched on top of a couple children's heads confirmed that thought.

He glanced to his left, recognizing the language being spoken— at least a few words he remembered from his international classmates when he'd attended school at Maxwell Air Force Base. A few men, maybe brothers. No women with them, or kids. Interesting. His focus was interrupted when he was asked to step to the counter.

Despite all the paperwork he had already electronically transmitted from home, he was getting a bit frustrated having to do it all over again at the check-in counter. He controlled his growing irritation, constantly reminding himself that he was on vacation. After the family got their photos taken and obtained their boarding passes and cruise cards, they lined up at the security stations, where everything they were bringing on the ship was scanned. Each passenger was scanned for anything that might be prohibited on board.

Finally, they proceeded up the gangway, where they were greeted by smiling cruise staff members who encouraged all arriving passengers to take a photograph that would memorialize their cruise. And of course, it would be offered for purchase on board, if they wanted it. The kids and Julie insisted that the photo be taken. By now, Ace was sweaty from the beach walk, the baggage handling, the jog from the parking lot, and the hassle over documents at the check-in counter. The last thing he wanted was yet *another* delay before grabbing a cold beer. But he gave in to the pleas from his children.

"Sure, let's all take a picture, he said grudgingly." He put on the best smile he could.

Their group then encountered yet another screening area for the hand-carried bags they had each brought with them. While Ace had become a little irritated with all the security checks, he knew it was essential for the overall safety of the passengers. People often brought some crazy stuff on vacation, and he was glad that all manner of contraband was being confiscated by the security staff and piled up in a large bin.

"We made it," Ace shouted to his family. "Now the fun begins!"

"Let's drop our stuff in the rooms first," Julie said. "Do you think they're ready?"

"Yeah, great idea. The rooms are supposed to be ready by now."

They followed the herd of other passengers from the lower deck toward the elevator. It was a mass of irritated, sweaty adults and whining kids waiting to take the easy way up to their deck.

"Let's take the stairs. Are you kids up for a little exercise?"

"Matt, I don't think the children can make the climb up several staircases."

"Sure they can. I'll carry them up if I have to," he bragged. "I'm not going to wait a half hour for the elevators to clear out."

Surprisingly, the kids scrambled up the stairs with no problem. But when they reached Aloha Deck 8, they were all glad there were no more stairs to climb. They walked down the colorful carpeted corridor until they found the two staterooms Ace had booked, which had an adjoining inner door between them. Although he'd had to assure the cruise staff that an adult would stay in each room, the kids would occupy the larger suite-sized room with beds for them all. The adjoining door would stay propped open for the usual migration of at least one child with a nightmare, a late-night question, or just the need to snuggle up.

They quickly checked the rooms and dumped their stuff. Ace was hungry from the workout he felt like he had gotten just getting his family situated on the ship.

"Let's get some chow. Anyone else interested?"

The kids unanimously shouted their concurrence. Julie checked her cell phone for the texts she was waiting for.

"Give me about five more minutes and I'll be ready," she stalled.

A few minutes later, Julie said, "Let's go."

As they left the room, they were immediately greeted by family.

"Daddy," shouted Nick. "There's Grandma and Grandpa!"

"Hey, Mom, Dad. Did you just get here?" Julie asked her parents.

"Yes," replied Jack Stevens. "Just made the short drive from Delray Beach up to Cape Canaveral. Only took us a couple of hours."

The kids ran to their grandparents and enjoyed a warm embrace.

"My mom is supposed to be getting here anytime as well," Ace remarked as he gave them both a warm embrace. "She flew into Orlando this morning and is taking the shuttle here."

"That's great," said Julie's mom, Gemma. "We're so glad she's going to join us."

As if it was choreographed, Matt felt a tap on his shoulder. He turned and Fred "Flamer" Lightner gave him a big man-hug.

"Flamer! What the heck are you doing here?" Ace shouted, rather stunned to see his old friend.

"Hey, man, I thought you'd be happy to see us," he said as Flamer's wife, Colene, pushed her way past him to give Ace a friendly hug.

"Julie wanted this to be a surprise for you. She's the guilty party that arranged this whole thing!"

"Where's Sean?" Ace asked his buddy, referring to Flamer's son.

"Believe it or not, he's at a two-week vacation camp in the woods outside Eglin Air Force Base. So, my bride and I have this time to ourselves. We couldn't pass up *this* cruise opportunity."

"I can't believe they gave you the time off," Ace commented, referring to the Air Force Test Center at the expansive Eglin air base where Flamer was one of the pilots helping develop and test the newest armament for fighter aircraft.

"Hey, buddy. I'm *with* you there. I'm a pretty important guy. Who knows what kind of disaster will happen with me gone? I'm not sure they'll survive without me," he laughed.

Colene elbowed him in the ribs. "Enough bragging. Let's get this party started."

"Well, this is just perfect. We're going to have one helluva time," said Ace. "And we've got some catching up to do."

He and Flamer had trained together at Langley during Ace's first Raptor assignment years before. They had flown in combat, both in Syria and Iran. They knew the taste of battle, and the cost. While they had kept in touch, the Air Force had sent them down separate paths in the intervening years. This was their first opportunity to link up and bust each other's chops. The two fighter pilots were determined to make the most of their reunion.

Chapter 9

"Holy mackerel. Everybody on board seems to have the same idea and are here to eat," Ace exclaimed, a bit disappointed in finding himself again immersed in a crowded sea of humanity.

"Well, we're all hungry, so let's just get in line," Julie responded.

The dining area was packed with passengers. Most of the guests were simply hungry after hours of traveling, waiting in lines, and checking into their cabins. They surged around the extensive buffet area, the large counters filled with an assortment of tempting snacks, fast food and formal lunch fare. From the looks of things, no one was going to be disappointed.

They got through the lines as quickly as possible, wrangled a table amidst the frenzied crowd, and finally sat down. Ace saw his mother enter the dining area, waved her over to the table, and after the requisite hugs and kisses, the vacationing group was complete. As they ate, they all talked about the terrific opportunities that awaited them on board the massive ship.

Ace had grabbed the information packet from his stateroom and perused it between bites. The *Dream Spinner* was one of the newest state-of-the-art luxury ships in the Pleasure Cruise Lines inventory. Produced by the famed Meyer Werft shipbuilders in Papenburg, Germany, its current port of registry was Nassau, Bahamas. The mammoth vessel had fourteen decks and was over one thousand feet long and one hundred and twenty feet in breadth. Two giant General Electric gas turbines generated thirty-four thousand horsepower apiece, producing the powerful thrust that moved the big ship swiftly through the water.

The operating crew was nine hundred strong, including one hundred officers.

The ship had the capacity to carry three thousand, three hundred guests in style, including penthouses, suites, and balcony and non-balcony rooms. Guests occupied staterooms from Decks 3 to 12. Nearly all of the hardworking ship's crew were in spartan cabins designed for double, triple, or quadruple occupancy on Decks 0 and 1, below the waterline, and 2, just above it. These lower decks also housed the engine control room, electrical and mechanical shops, provisioning areas containing refrigerated and general storerooms, massive laundry facilities, and garbage-handling areas.

Entertainment was first rate. Like most cruise lines, the *Dream Spinner* offered Broadway-style shows performed by talented crew members, supported by orchestras with musicians that could compete with some of the best in the United States. There was also the usual complement of performances by magicians, ventriloquists, and acrobats, and of course, game shows.

Ace knew that some shows, in particular, were intended to suck unsuspecting audience members into coming up on stage to make absolute fools of themselves. He'd keep a low profile during those performances.

"Check this out, Jules," he said, pointing to the brochure details explaining the options for non-stop fun. She leaned against his shoulder as he pointed out each opportunity.

There was an exceptional array of amenities to occupy a vacationer's time—a rock climbing wall, several swimming, slide and surf pools, including one specifically designed for the safety of small children, a large video arcade and games area, a jogging track, basketball courts, and finally, for those passengers who hadn't *just* boarded the ship to eat—a large fitness center. *Note to self*, Ace thought. *Need to spend some time there for my daily workout.*

Additionally, the *Dream Spinner* provided an entertainment option that only Pleasure Cruise Lines offered—a skeet shooting range off the stern of the boat. It used environmentally friendly, biodegradable rice-composite skeet targets that would dissolve in the ocean. The shotguns were secured there within the adjacent ship's armory. Like the skeet targets, the shotgun shells were loaded with a specially designed composition of biodegradable pellet materiel, keeping the entire operation out of the crosshairs of any environmental complaint.

"Flamer. I was counting on spending time at the range. Time to prove who is the better shot!"

"Very funny buddy. I can out-shoot you any day of the week."

"Well, we better get the contest underway before you start drinking," he laughed. "But then again, it may actually improve your aim!"

"Bring in on, brother," he asserted. "We can celebrate my victory with a great meal and some premium whiskey."

The *Dream Spinner* was also renowned for its cuisine—the food was Michelin-rated as some of the finest in the world. There was truly something for virtually any appetite. The best chefs from around the world had been recruited to develop menus that would leave lasting memories of the gastronomical delights.

Ace was especially looking forward to dining at the Chop House about midway through the cruise. It was the premier steak dining facility on the high seas, and Ace couldn't wait for that evening to come.

At the top of the list for Matt and Julie was some first-rate snorkeling at some of the best Caribbean dive sites. The *Dream Spinner*'s itinerary would take them on a circuitous route south from Port Canaveral, past the Bahamas, off the coast of Cuba and down to Aruba, Curaçao, and Bonaire. Ace had gotten hooked on snorkeling and scuba diving while training on the F-22 at Tyndall AFB near Panama City, Florida. The clear Gulf of Mexico waters boasted some phenomenal coral reefs and shipwrecks that opened up a new world of beauty to explore. Ace couldn't wait to get to Bonaire, home to some of the best available diving in the Caribbean.

After they finished lunch, most of the group decided to go back to their rooms to unpack, since the crew had finished delivering all passenger bags.

Claire, Roman and Nick, were eager to check out the entertainment meant just for them. Their grandfather, Jack, led them on an exploration of the pools, water slides, game rooms, movie theaters, and of course, the ice cream shops with endless servings.

"Jules. I'm going to reconnoiter this ship for the best places to hang out," Ace remarked.

He wanted to get a head start on learning how the ship was laid out. Easier now before every one of the passengers decided to do the same. Most of them were still eating a late lunch or getting situated in their rooms.

"Well, don't be too long. After all, this is our anniversary vacation. I want to spend plenty of *extra* quality time with you," she said with a sexy smile.

"Don't worry, baby. I'll be back soon," he said with a grin.

Ace paced the decks on his own while his family and friends unpacked. As he walked, he gazed over the polished teak rail at the activity going on below, at the flurry of actions taking place to move the final provisions and other equipment onto the ship. He looked across the terminal area toward the arrival zone, the parking lots. The cars entering the *Dream Spinner* area had dwindled to one or two last-minute arrivals—it was getting close to departure time.

He checked his watch and then hustled up to Deck 14 to join his family and friends. They had agreed to meet and watch the *Dream Spinner* pull out of Port Canaveral. Ace saw them after snaking his way through the crowded deck. It seemed like every other passenger on the ship had the same idea. The departure was obviously a popular venue. He elbowed his way to the deck rail to meet them. The biggest problem now was finding a bartender to get him and Flamer a beer!

While his buddy tried desperately to take care of that problem, Ace noticed, in the distance across the terminal entry route, that the Homeland Security officers were still at each checkpoint. So were the other heavily armed men who wore nondescript clothing.

Not U.S. military. Maybe nongovernmental security forces hired to supplement DHS. They had been thorough, he noted, in their zeal to ensure people entering the security exclusion zone had a right to be there. They hadn't seemed to turn anyone away, though—a good thing, hopefully. And the multiple checks of each person and their bags in the terminal—definitely a good thing.

He noticed large pallets of provisions still being rolled toward the loading area near the bow. *Wonder how that stuff gets checked,* he thought. *You could hide some really nasty things deep inside that cargo, if you wanted to.* He shook his head, convincing himself that the intense passenger baggage check had likely been replicated on literally everything coming on board.

Chapter 10

Ace looked at his watch, then over the deck rail at what was going on below. He wondered about the scheduled departure time. It was supposed to be just about fifteen minutes away, but the boat was going nowhere based on what he saw. The dock area was clear of passengers, and the suitcases and other cargo had been loaded. But the gangway structure was still in place, and it didn't appear that anyone was in a hurry to move it away.

"Guess we're not getting out of this port on time," Ace commented to Flamer. "But it probably doesn't matter much. These ships can make up for the delay once they get underway."

"Hey, buddy, they can take all the time they want. I'm on vacation now, and nothing is going to bother me—as long as I have plenty of alcohol to lubricate my body." He drained the rest of the tasty Florida Lager and started looking for one of the busy waiters to reload his glass.

The delay was not caused by late passengers or a maintenance problem with the ship. It was caused by a more insidious, carefully planned action. Farad Asmaradov had orchestrated a last-minute change in the ship's senior officers. He had infiltrated key administrative functions within the Pleasure Cruise Lines headquarters and now had his own people embedded there, including in the crew scheduling department.

The urgent notification from the cruise ship headquarters had caught the *Dream Spinner*'s captain by surprise. Three key officers—the captain, the chief engineer, and the chief of security—had been advised that their operating licenses had expired, and they could not proceed with the departure from Port Canaveral.

The captain had objected vehemently, claiming all of their credentials were current. But the call he'd subsequently made to the scheduling department had confirmed that the required paperwork appeared expired. While the scheduler agreed to investigate whether there had been an administrative error, the three senior officers would need to depart the ship. They were advised that it would only take a few days to sort out the problem, and that they should proceed to Cocoa Beach, check in to a hotel and await orders. Another Pleasure Cruise Lines ship was due into Port Canaveral in four days. By then, their credentials would be verified and they would crew that vessel. Meanwhile, they were encouraged to enjoy the beach area. Replacements had been sent when the expired licenses had been discovered—the officers would arrive at any moment.

The notification sent to the *Dream Spinner* as it sat berthed in Port Canaveral was a bit unusual. Often, changes to key crew members occurred at the last minute. But it was odd that three key senior officers would be changed at once—that had never happened before.

"Check that out, Flamer," Ace remarked as he pointed down to the dock. "Wonder what's going on down there?"

A large black sedan with dark tinted windows pull up toward the gangway entrance. When it stopped, three men exited the car, grabbed their bags from the trunk, and walked toward the ship. They all wore senior officer uniforms. Before they reached the entry area, an equal number of men dressed in similar uniforms exited the ship and proceeded toward the automobile. They acknowledged each other awkwardly as they passed. The exiting captain stopped before he reached the sedan. He looked back at the replacement officers as they boarded. He didn't recognize the captain that had taken his place. Odd. He knew all of the senior officers that piloted the large vessels within his company. He would make another call to Pleasure Cruise Lines about the oddity, perhaps to one of the security officials.

As the replacement crew finished boarding, the frustrated officers leaving the ship took their seats in the sedan. At least they would get some time off on the company's dime and enjoy the white sands of Cocoa Beach. The captain pulled the cell phone from his pocket and prepared to make a concerned call about the unfamiliar replacements.

The darkened car windows made it impossible for anyone outside the automobile to see what happened next. The muffled sounds of three suppressed Makarov automatic pistol shots ended the lives of the three officers. The sedan pulled away from the terminal and was not stopped as it left Port Canaveral, since only incoming traffic was screened by security agents. There was little chance that anyone else from Pleasure Cruises would notice their absence for at least four days—too late to impact the Viper's deadly plan. The black sedan sped toward the interstate highway with its lifeless cargo.

Once the three new officers were on board, the covered gangway retracted and was pulled away from the ship. The *Dream Spinner* appeared ready to sail upon the new captain's orders.

The swap-out of the *Dream Spinner*'s captain and senior officers was critical to the success of the Viper's plan. Captain Hafez Zoyatov was now ready to assume command of the ship—and help prosecute the deadly actions that were to come.

Inside the bridge, Zoyatov gathered the staff to explain what had happened. When he was notified to travel posthaste to Port Canaveral to command the *Dream Spinner*, he had requested two trusted officers who had sailed with him previously, should accompany him.

His explanation got push-back from the ship's first officer, who claimed the changes were unprecedented. It was not so much the issue of the captain being replaced—once in a while, that happened. But bringing two additional senior officers with him was clearly way out of the ordinary, and not how the company usually operated.

"Gentlemen, I am just following the company's orders. They obliged me, given the last-minute change to this cruise."

The official message transmitted by Pleasure Cruise Lines seemed to satisfy the first officer, at least for the moment.

The new captain had one more action to complete before sailing. He went through the standard pre-departure review of the ship's critical systems. With his back shielding anyone from viewing what he was doing, he slipped the small flash drive from his pocket and inserted it into the navigation system computer. The virus in the small device was downloaded in seconds. He quickly removed the drive and tucked it back in his pocket.

As Zoyatov ran a self-test of the vessel's electronic navigation and communication systems, spurious faults interrupted the program. The problems would clearly impact their ability to effectively navigate the ship on the high seas. He brought the issue to the attention of the first officer. The stunned second-in-command challenged Zoyatov's claims, insisting that the systems were operating perfectly when the ship had arrived in port.

"There is no problem with our navigation system. Show me the faults you claim are there."

The new captain pointed to the monitor and replied, "See for yourself. If you think the system is problem free, then I question your competence."

The first officer angrily stared at the monitor and couldn't believe what he saw.

Zoyatov continued. "The ship is my responsibility, and mine alone if problems are encountered while we are underway. I will get this fixed immediately."

He then made a short phone call. When he was finished, he was confronted again by the first officer.

"Captain, we can't afford a delay in leaving port. We have an electrician on board who can take a look at the problem."

"The problem requires a specialist in the navigation software. There will be no delay. I have already communicated with the cruise line. There happens to be a communications and software engineer in the port area servicing another vessel who will be here shortly to address the problem."

Zoyatov reminded the bridge staff that a navigation system failure while underway could lead to a disaster for the passengers and a major embarrassment for the *Dream Spinner*'s parent company. The impact could cause the loss of millions of dollars in future sales, and potentially, from lawsuits brought on by dissatisfied passengers.

He would not set sail until the engineer boarded to address the system shortfalls—a man recruited and trained by Farad Asmaradov. Zoyatov directed the gangway be reconnected to the ship. Within two hours, a bearded man boarded the cruise liner. He brought his laptop computer and a small suitcase of tools and test equipment. He was also accompanied by a dark-haired beauty who appeared to be his assistant.

The specialist spent thirty minutes working on the system faults.

"I have put a temporary patch into the software to fix the problems that are popping up. However, they may occur again. Your system needs more work than I can do in this short time."

"Very well," Zoyatov replied. Per Asmaradov's plans, he continued. "The company indicated that if you could not solve our problem, you should accompany us on this cruise. If the faults recur, you can address them to prevent any impact on our scheduled itinerary. We can provide you both with a stateroom and there are plenty of spare uniforms to keep you clothed and comfortable during the next eight days."

With the situation now fully under his control, Captain Hafez Zoyatov made a brief announcement to the passengers, introducing himself, and explaining the delay in departing Port Canaveral as the gangway was pulled away. The issue had been resolved. Then, he directed his beverage staff to provide complementary drinks to all passengers for the inconvenience. The *Dream Spinner* was now ready to depart. He encouraged all guests to enjoy the sunny late-afternoon weather and watch the large cruise ship pull away from the busy port.

Ace, his family and friends were more than ready to enjoy the departure. The kids were excited, never having been on an ocean cruise before, and were enthralled by what they saw as the ship begin its gradual movement into the narrow channel. Ace quickly sipped the last of his beer before the oppressive Florida heat and humidity made it undrinkable. He ordered another one, and then watched envious Floridians waving from Jetty Park as the *Dream Spinner* slipped into the Atlantic.

The rest of the day seemed to fly by, first with dinner, and then a welcome celebration in both major entertainment areas, the Centrum, and on the top deck. As it approached eleven o'clock, the tired group retired to their rooms for the night.

As Ace was brushing his teeth, he reflected on what he had observed since boarding the ship. The intensive security controls implemented on passengers and their baggage. The loading of the large pallets purportedly containing provisions for the cruise— hopefully also screened for contraband. The interesting mix of international guests on board. The crew changes. The curious black sedan with the dark windows. The technical problems that had delayed their departure.

His fighter pilot senses were always on the alert—but sometimes made him over-think what he was seeing.

Chapter 11

Day 2

The soft knock on the cabin door woke Ace. He looked at the digital display on the end table. Six o'clock. Coffee. He rolled off the bed in the darkened room and carefully walked around it toward the door, tensing up as he tried to avoid jamming his toe into a bed frame leg in the tight confines of the stateroom. He quietly opened the door, expecting the delivery.

"Sir, good morning." The smiling cabin steward had a tray of coffee and some pastries, per the order Ace had filled out and hung on the outside door handle the night before.

"Thanks, Juan. I'll take the tray. My wife is still sleeping and I don't want to wake her."

"Certainly, sir." Juan held the door open with his foot while handing the tray to Ace. "Is there anything else I can do for you?" he whispered.

"No, thanks. I appreciate it."

Once his steward had left, Ace grabbed the hot carafe of coffee and a cup and slowly parted the dark drapes. The sun was below the horizon, only a soft orange glow in the darkness as it began its gradual ascension. He quietly slid the glass door open and stepped gingerly onto the balcony. It was slightly damp from the morning mist that hung lightly in the air. He set the coffee down on the small table, not wanting any of the emerging morning light to eventually come spilling into his cabin. He pulled the drapes across the opening and then slid the glass door closed.

He sat down on one of the two white plastic balcony chairs and poured the steaming liquid into his cup. Sipping the dark brew, he watched the orange-hued sun continue to rise slowly—so beautiful even in the light mist, emerging over the dark, flat ocean's edge. He leaned toward the balcony rail and was greeted by the salty spray that seemed to explode from the wake produced by the ship's steel hull as it plowed through the water. As he looked down toward the churning ocean below, he could just make out two dolphins breaking the water's surface, racing alongside the ship, both clearly hoping to enjoy an easy breakfast of the fish escaping the turmoil of the *Dream Spinner*'s expanding wake.

This is the life. He felt more completely relaxed than he had been in years. He loved the smell of the ocean in the morning air. The sea state was nearly flat, except for the violent white surf spilling from the *Dream Spinner*'s wake as the ship cut through the dark blue water. He felt no wind other than what was generated by the ship cruising south toward their first stop. The temperature was perfect—about sixty degrees at this time of the morning. The coffee wasn't the best, but it would do.

In the adjoining room, he heard no sound of movement. The kids were apparently still sleeping. That would change soon as hunger would rouse them. For now, Ace enjoyed the solitude, the quiet peace the balcony offered. He knew that the day would soon get busy, loaded with activity and entertainment for the kids and adults alike.

Two hours later, he had shaved and showered. Julie was also up and getting ready for breakfast. The noise through the adjoining doorway was evidence that the kids were up and getting restless. Cartoons blared, drowning out the children's chatter.

Once everyone was dressed, they headed to the Windjammer dining room a little before nine o'clock and met the rest of their gathering. The maître d' guided them to a large table, and in a flurry, the kids jockeyed for adjacent seats. A few of the adults ordered from the breakfast menu, while Ace led the kids to the endless display of goodies arrayed on the counter. The pastry area hosted every manner of sugary rolls, doughnuts and croissants intended to entice the children, along with their father's favorite, cinnamon-raisin bread.

After the kids had filled their plates, Ace decided on a fresh-cooked made-to-order omelet. As he approached the station, an attractive auburn-haired young lady wearing a chef's hat greeted him. Her name tag read "Aleksandra" and her country of origin, Ukraine. She was one of many *Dream Spinner* crew members representing countries from around the globe. Most found working on a cruise ship a great way to earn some money and see the world while getting free room and board.

"Hi," Ace said to her as he returned her bright smile. "Those omelets you just cooked look great. Can you whip me up one as well?"

"Certainly. What would you like?"

"I'd like some onions, bacon, tomatoes, mushrooms, jalapeños, and cheese, and if you don't mind, brown it up a bit."

"You chose great ingredients!" she exclaimed. "I'll have this ready for you in just a few minutes."

"Have you worked on cruise ships for a long time?" he asked as the omelet pan sizzled.

"Yes, I have. This is my third year. I find it fascinating to travel around the world—it's a terrific opportunity. This is my first trip to the Caribbean."

"You haven't been cooking all that time, have you?" Ace asked.

"No, of course not. I rotate through a variety of jobs. It helps keep me interested and I learn new things."

"Well, at least that should keep you from being bored—and it looks to me like you're enjoying yourself."

As she turned the omelet in the pan, she said to him, "You look like a military man."

It caught him a bit off guard. "Why do you say that?"

"I can usually tell. Your haircut, you are clearly very fit, and you have that look."

"What look is that?" he said with a smile.

"You have a serious look, very sure of yourself, very confident. That is what military men look like. And not overweight," she laughed.

Ace just smiled. *Interesting,* he thought. *Seems an odd comment over an omelet.*

"Here you go," she said, handing the large browned concoction across the counter to Ace.

"Thanks. I appreciate it." He headed back to the table and saw that everyone was ferociously devouring their breakfasts.

Roman was trying to stuff two doughnuts in his mouth at the same time, an obvious challenge to his twin brother, Nick, who wasted no time in attempting to do the same thing.

"Don't choke on that," Ace chided. "How about one doughnut at a time. It'll taste better too."

Julie chimed in. "Boys, stop that. Behave yourselves. You look like a couple of crazy kids, and your father's right—you're going to choke on all that food."

"They'll be okay," he said. "After all, they're on vacation."

"Well, they're embarrassing me."

Jack didn't help. "Watch this," the boy's grandfather said before he stuffed an entire large pastry into his mouth.

That prompted loud laughter from the children.

His wife, Gemma, was not amused. "That's a great example for your grandkids," she said with a frown.

Everyone around the table then just burst out laughing.

Ace worked his way through half of the omelet, then asked what was on the agenda for the morning.

You'd have thought he started a riot. The near-simultaneous shouts across the table from both kids and adults alike indicated there was no real agreement about anything that was going to happen after breakfast. Ace smiled, thinking it was better that way. They were on vacation. Do whatever you want, whenever you want.

The kids were old enough to be signed over to the well-trained chaperones of the children's entertainment staff. A wide variety of tailored activities, games, and movies would keep the kids safely occupied for a few hours while parents could enjoy some alone time.

The ladies were heading to the Orchid Spa for a massage. They'd booked the works, insisting that this opportunity was not to be missed. They would be there for at least three hours. The men had other ideas. Like heading to the back of the boat and shooting some skeet.

Ace thought it was pretty unusual that passengers were actually allowed to handle and fire weapons aboard the cruise ship. He knew that there must be some pretty stringent controls over the shotguns and ammo. After all, nobody wanted a crazy inebriated passenger to get wild ideas about shooting up the ship after losing at the casino's poker table.

Chapter 12

The *Dream Spinner*'s skeet shooting operation encompassed the Deck 5 stern. Built with safety in mind, it had a large overhanging roof to ensure that there was no chance of any pellets going vertical and potentially threatening other passengers. The shotguns were twelve- and sixteen-gauge autoloading semiautomatics specially outfitted with suppressors to muffle the gunshots. Sound-absorbing walls surrounded the two shooting cells, and two large fans directed the sound outward, away from the ship.

The opportunity for bragging rights was about to begin. Ace had plenty of experience with shotguns from when his father used to take him hunting for pheasant, dove and other birds. But it had been many years since he hunted with him. When his father had been blown out of the Syrian sky by a surface-to-air missile in 2003, those good times had ended.

Julie's father, Jack, had been an Army Ranger during his time in the military. He clearly knew how to shoot. But, again, that was a long time ago when he served combat tours in Afghanistan. Flamer was the novice with a shotgun. He needed some tutoring to ensure he didn't shoot himself or anyone else.

The weapons and ammunition locked in the adjacent ship's armory were brought to the range by security officers and placed at the shooting stations.

The instructor at the range was a British chap who, like many of the crew members, also had side jobs supporting other entertainment venues on the ship. He stood by to offer assistance to first-time skeet shooters. Ace immediately bonded with Mark "Buzz"

Caster. The brawny Brit had spent some time in Her Majesty's Royal Marines and was a crack shot. He also had a fantastic singing voice that made him one of the key members of the nightly *Dream Spinner*'s show circuit.

"Welcome, mates," Caster started, his slight cockney accent clearly still enough to identify him as British, "allow me to show you the ropes here. As you might imagine, shooting skeet from a cruise ship is an exclusive with Pleasure Cruises. No other company offers this kind of excitement for our guests. In order to keep things safe for you and the passengers on board who don't want to get shot by you, allow me to demonstrate." He waited for a reaction to his attempt to generate a bit of humor. Nobody laughed but Flamer.

"Please watch me carefully and try to closely replicate my routine when it comes your time to shoot."

With that intro, Buzz picked up a twelve-gauge shotgun and loaded two rounds, chambering the first shell. Standing at the shooting station, he assumed the correct position for taking on his first target. He depressed a peddle on the floor, and a red disc flew straight out from its launcher. Buzz waited a second or two and quickly dispatched it, splintering the disc into fragments. He depressed the peddle again, and a second disc flew from the launcher, this time crossing the stern. Buzz nailed it with his second shell.

"Okay, men, are you ready? Who is first on the firing line?" he asked.

All three of the eager shooters were impressed. Buzz was clearly an expert. Ace stepped up to the shooting position first. Two hours later, it was over.

Ace got his share of targets, hitting about seventy-five percent of them. Julie's dad hit nearly all of them, missing only two. He hadn't lost his touch or his aim. Flamer hit less than half of his but blamed the wind, the ship's slightly pitching stern, the distractions from a few of the ocean's whitecaps, and the laughter of those around him. But he knew that no matter what the outcome, there was some premium Scotch whiskey to be had later at the lounge on the upper deck.

When the men had finished, they thanked the Brit for his help and promised to look for him on the entertainment stage during the ship's nightly productions.

"We'll keep a sharp eye out for you tonight," said Ace. "I guess you'll be the one in tights and lace, right?" he laughed.

"That's a funny one, mate. I'll make sure I single you blokes out from the audience and prepare a special surprise for you on stage," he laughed back.

"Just kidding, Buzz. Glad to see you Brits have a sense of humor."

"Cheers, boys. Enjoy your cruise, and I'll see you round the ship," Buzz finished, shaking each of their hands.

The men headed back to their staterooms, making sure they showered to clean any toxic gunpowder residue from their bodies. After banging his elbows about ten times in the closet-sized shower stall, Ace finished drying off, threw on some clothes and put his dirty clothing in a plastic laundry bag. The ship provided a free service to anyone using the range to wash their gunpowder-contaminated clothes for free. The three men eventually joined up and decided to explore the *Dream Spinner*.

While they walked, Ace checked his coupon for the start time of his "All Access Tour" of the ship. He had signed up for the specialized excursion, that was limited to only a few passengers. It included the bridge, the engine control room, the dining room and main kitchen, provisioning areas, storerooms, and laundry, and took them past some of the spartan crew quarters below the waterline. Since Ace had a couple of hours before it started, the men decided to get a bite to eat before they parted ways for the afternoon.

Flamer's post-lunch plans involved lounging on one of the breezy upper decks, lathered up with sunscreen lotion, sporting his Maui Jim sunglasses, and reading one of the two thriller novels he had brought with him. Julie's dad was heading to the casino. He wasn't normally a gambler but wanted to try his luck at the poker table for a few minutes.

Ace began his search for the children. They were already going nonstop, hitting every entertainment activity they could engage in with the ship's staff. First on their agenda—the expansive swimming pools, all geared to accommodate children of every age. The attentive staff who managed the Kids' Club made sure that the children stayed safe and kept a close eye on every child. The water slide was the boys' current choice.

Ace wandered over to the pool area and saw Roman and Nick trying their skill in the twisting slide chutes. Each of them was attempting to go as fast as he could to get to the bottom. A lifeguard was standing close by in the pool in case any youngster needed help. No assistance was needed for Roman! He seemed to relish speeding down the slippery chute and making the biggest splash that he could at the bottom. His brother, Nick, was waiting his turn to show that he was just as fast—and brave.

Ace stood by the rail overlooking the pool for about thirty minutes and just smiled in awe. He was proud of the way his two young sons were developing—both of them fearless, willing to try just about anything new and conquer it.

Nick saw his dad and yelled out, "Dad, wait a minute and watch me. I bet I can get to the bottom faster than Roman!"

"I don't know about that," he shouted back. "Roman looks like he's got this sport down pat. But I know you'll give it everything you've got to show him who's best."

Nick shot down the water-lined plastic chute and made a large splash at the bottom. With a big smile, he looked over at his father for some acknowledgment.

"Great job, Nick. You two guys tied, I think. You were both pretty fast."

That didn't satisfy the two brothers, who immediately started arguing with each other over who was fastest.

He looked around for his daughter. She was supposed to be keeping an eye on her brothers. "Where's Claire?"

"She's over at the arcade with some of the other girls she met," said Roman.

Ace knew that the trusty chaperones were with her.

He had momentarily forgotten about the ladies and their plans for the day. He wondered where the women were. They should have finished their spa treatment by now.

"How about your mother, Mema, Grandma and Mrs. Lightner?"

"They came by to watch us for a few minutes. Then they took off."

"When you're done here, ask the staff to help you go find your sister. You kids need to stay together if you can, and keep tabs on each other."

He wasn't overly worried about his children with the heavy contingent of trained chaperones. In spite of their age, his kids were all level-headed and smart and had plenty of common sense. They had been raised to be aware of their surroundings and sensitized to things that might get them in trouble. Still, kids were kids!

Ace looked at his watch. He had only thirty minutes to get down to the assembly area for the tour. He didn't want to miss a minute of the in-depth look at the cruise ship's operations.

Chapter 13

J ack knew that Ace would be tied up for a few hours and had told him that he would keep watch on the kids. He left the casino and walked briskly to the pool deck. Jack found them and took over admiration of two young boys having the time of their lives. Both Roman and Nick were excited to see their grandpa. Each of them now tried their best to impress him with their antics and bravery in the pool. Jack just smiled. He thought to himself that this time with his grandkids couldn't get much better. Nothing could possibly spoil this cruise.

When Ace arrived at the central administration area on Deck 5, it was packed with passengers. Some were booking excursions for the upcoming island stops. Others were trying to straighten out their accounts with the purser. And a few were just chronic complainers— nothing would satisfy them when it came to their accommodations, the food, the ship, or the staff.

He saw the tour guide holding a small sign indicating the assembly area. Ace was one of only twelve guests lucky enough to snag one of the limited slots for this very detailed and restricted itinerary. While some of the tour stops held little interest for him, two were technological wonders he hoped would broaden his knowledge—the bridge and the engine control room.

For the first two hours, he learned about how the ship served up over ten thousand meals a day in the dining rooms, restaurants and cafés, and how the food made its way from the lower deck provisioning locations via elevators directly to the kitchens. The food preparation areas were a maze of stainless steel grills, tables, refrigerators, and storage units, with plenty of surveillance cameras to keep track of anything that might go awry. The choreography demonstrated by the busy waiters, cooks and managers was impressive.

Then they wound their way through a tight corridor, restricted to crew members only, and then down a small steel staircase that led them to the Deck 2 laundry facilities. It seemed like a hellhole to Ace—hot, humid, and noisy from the massive washer and dryer operations that tried to keep up with the passengers' needs. He felt sorry for the sweat-covered staff as they worked amidst a mountain of white sheets and linen.

A few minutes later, they entered the provisioning area. It was a relief from the sauna-like laundry, with cool air coursing through the storage room hallways. A number of locked sliding steel doors sheltered everything—meats, seafood, produce, and liquor. Stacks of nonperishable food were arrayed neatly across the deck on steel pallets, adjacent to the access door that allowed small forklifts to bring the stores onto the ship through the starboard entry point. As in the kitchen area, security cameras were positioned everywhere, including inside the storage rooms.

Finally, to Ace's relief, the group headed toward his primary areas of interest. The engine control room was also on Deck 2, only a few minutes' walk down a narrow twisting pathway toward the *Dream Spinner*'s stern.

As he walked through the tight corridor, Ace thought about the pallets in the provisioning area and what he had seen earlier while they'd prepared to pull out of the port. About how tight security was for passengers getting on the ship. He had wondered about the cargo. The huge pallets could have almost anything buried deep underneath the canned food stocks—hidden from any security check. He didn't believe he was overthinking the possibility of concealed contraband. But he had been around long enough to know that, if someone knew there were gaps in security, the likelihood of secreting prohibited items on board was significantly increased.

His suspicious thoughts were interrupted once they arrived at their destination, their access blocked by an armed security guard.

"You will all have to empty your pockets and remove your hats. You will be checked by the security guard before entering the engine control room," the tour guide directed.

The guard electronically scanned each passenger one by one, then asked them to step toward the steel entry door. He picked up a telephone from the box by the door and waited for a response. Within the engine control room, the chief engineer gave the go-ahead to enter by punching in a code on his console. The electromechanical lock could be heard opening, allowing entry.

As they walked in, the hum emanating from the myriad electronic displays engulfed them. Computer terminals were positioned near each bank of monitors, and in the center of the room, an additional large circular display held engineering diagrams of all aspects of the ship's propulsion and control system, as well as fire suppression, bilge pumps, and all emergency electric power. Another diagram depicted the status of the massive watertight compartments meant to ensure the ship's buoyancy.

They were met by the chief engineer, Drako Kratec, and three additional assistant engineers clad in white jumpsuits. Kratec, one of the two senior officers who boarded the ship with Captain Zoyatov, began.

"Welcome, my friends," he said rather loudly, hoping to be overheard above the droning electronic buzz. "I would like to discuss the systems that make this great ship what it is—one of the best in the world."

He proceeded to explain the walls of blue-and-white multifunction displays that surrounded the room. Kratec had been well trained before the assignment aboard the *Dream Spinner*. An experienced Russian cruise ship officer, he had thoroughly familiarized himself with the technical plans for the *Dream Spinner*, plans covertly obtained via Asmaradov's extensive preparations for the deadly mission.

"As you can see, our terminals have actual video feeds from each of our large gas turbine engines, from the steam turbines that power the electricity, and from the other key systems that power the utilities that our passengers rely on. Other monitors show the data coming from the performance of the two twenty-foot-diameter five-blade propellers, and from the four bow thrusters and stabilizers. We also control and track the emergency generator, the bulkhead valves, and other key systems."

He paused. "The other displays from our various camera feeds provide a complete view of the outside of the ship—the bow and stern, port and starboard sides." As the guests admired the technology surrounding them, he continued.

"This room has a number of phones that are direct lines to the bridge, our electromechanical and machine shop engineers, and of course, our security chief."

"So, from here, you basically control the ship?" asked one of the passengers.

"Well, control is directed by the bridge, but it is executed right here," replied the chief engineer, pointing to the main switchboard controls.

"Security seems pretty tight," Ace remarked.

"Yes, of course. This is the heart of the *Dream Spinner*. As they say, he who commands the engine control room controls the ship." His penetrating stare swept across the group.

The look that Drako Kratec had in his eyes when he made the statement did not seem to arouse any particular reaction from the other guests, but it made the hair on the back of Ace's neck stand up. The aviator had seen that kind of intense look before. One that sometimes transmitted different meanings. Sometimes it was a look of absolute confidence in one's ability to handle any crisis. Occasionally, it carried a different message, one that embodied a devious, perhaps deadly meaning. Ace shook his head. Again, he was letting his imagination get away from him.

Ace was completely fascinated by what he saw around him. It reminded him of how much he missed being on the operational side of things. The engine control room was clearly where the action was happening on *Dream Spinner*, and it reminded him of the excitement he felt when he strapped into the cockpit of an F-22 Raptor.

He was impressed. He spent several minutes talking with the three white-suited engineers and then spoke briefly with the chief engineer. Drako Kratec proudly boasted of the ship's capability. Ace couldn't help but pick up on the accent again. Russian? Central Asian? *Interesting.*

As he walked around the room, Ace took a close look at the ship's detailed deck plans on display. He saw the location of corridors and stairways not visible on the colorful main passenger deck displays that helped guide the vacationers around the ship. This particular display showed the closed-off hallways and rooms intended only for crew access, allowing the ship's staff to stay out of the paying passengers' way. It also depicted the elevator systems all over the ship, including the one used to move food from Deck 2 to the kitchens.

"Okay, folks, time to head up to the final stop, the bridge," directed the tour group leader. They exited the engine control room, walked down a long corridor, found the elevator, and headed toward Deck 10.

After stepping off the elevator, they walked through another maze of hallways and past the communications center before arriving at an unmarked door. Once everyone had gathered, the leader picked up the phone hanging by the door and asked for entry. The door opened, and the group was ushered into another room occupied by an armed guard. The security officer, Cho Lee Kwan, was also there, having boarded the ship with Zoyatov and Kratec. His name tag indicated that Asia was his country of origin. He observed the screening of the passengers.

Ace looked into his eyes, and then at the name tag. *Interesting. Looks like he could be Korean.*

When the screening was completed, an additional call was made to gain entry to the bridge.

Ace immediately noticed how quiet it was, quite a change from the noisy engine control room. The bridge had an unobstructed view of the bow, starboard, and port sides. Cameras provided video feed surveillance of the stern. Fifteen-foot walkways extending perpendicularly outward like arms from each side of the central bridge enabled the officers to view all the way down each side of the ship to the waterline.

The senior ship's officer, Captain Hafez Zoyatov, welcomed them and motioned to follow him as he explained the bridge functions. As in the engine control room, there were dozens of computer displays, eight of the monitors mounted on the walls near the ceiling and several others along the consoles themselves that were viewable from the seats in the enclosed central cockpit area. The captain's chair was positioned in the optimal position within the cockpit and was forward of two additional chairs for two other key crew members—the first officer and navigator. The cockpit was separated from the rest of the bridge by a three-foot barrier.

Looking at the controls and instruments, Ace was impressed by how modern and advanced everything was—it was a glass cockpit, almost like the one in the premier fighter aircraft he used to fly. Old-style analog displays found in many older cruise ships were replaced by new, multifunction glass touch-screens that also included voice command capability. He saw controls for executing every critical function, from propulsion to steering with a joystick controller, and for performing emergency procedures like closing watertight doors when needed.

There wasn't a lot of chitchat going on. Serious business here. Everyone had a job to do and wasn't going to be distracted by the tour group. It was clear to him that Captain Zoyatov ran a tight ship. Disciplined. Formal. Direct. Deliberate actions were being taken by the entire bridge staff.

The only thing that kept gnawing at him was the accents. Like the chief engineer, Zoyatov spoke with a decidedly Russian or Central Asian accent.

Maybe the Dream Spinner *is staffed with experts who came from that part of the world. Parts of Central Asia and especially Russia have large maritime industries.* He shook his head. *Overthinking this.*

Ace walked to the expansive window overlooking the bow. Two decks below was a large green-painted helicopter pad.

Must be for emergencies that might arise.

He noted that it was surrounded by a metal chain fence and was posted as one of the many restricted access areas on the *Dream Spinner*, allowing entry to only specific crew members.

The tour officially ended after the bridge visit. The group headed their separate ways, and Ace decided to go find his bride. While he wandered through the *Dream Spinner's* colorful, ornately decorated walkways in the central portion of the ship, he thought about the tour he had taken. His near-photographic memory enabled him to easily revisit every detail of the tour in his head—the paths he had taken, the information he had absorbed, the critical systems he had seen. It reassured him, at least a little bit, that the cruise was being led by a very experienced staff of senior professionals.

Even if *most* of them seemed to speak with a Central Asian accent.

Chapter 14

The president of Tajikistan, Ivan Mikolayev, was among the longest-serving leaders in Central Asia. The former autonomous republic had gained its independence from the Soviet Union after the Berlin Wall had fallen and Moscow's hold on much of the region had been broken. During the turmoil from internal power struggles and civil wars across the rugged landscape, Mikolayev had grabbed the reins of power in 1994. While he led an independent country, the republic still had Russia's long tentacles reaching deep inside his government. Vladimir Putonov was determined to keep Mikolayev closely tied to Moscow and do his best to maintain a major foothold in the strategic location.

Tajikistan, by reason of geography, had limited natural resources and a weak economy. Less than seven percent of the land was suitable for growing crops due to the country's mountainous terrain—certainly not enough to feed its population. This made the country dependent on its neighbors, some of whom had interests that were far from noble.

Russia, in particular, provided steady cash flow, military armament, and economic support to Mikolayev's government. In return, Putonov was provided basing rights in the northern part of the country. Additionally, the offsetting Russian dependence on the illicit opium and heroin streaming across the border from Afghanistan helped further balance the scales. A predictable consequence of the rampant drug trafficking was widespread corruption, expanding criminal activities, and unchecked violence from radical elements who controlled selected portions of the territory.

In spite of Putonov's close relationship with Mikolayev, the Tajik president saw opportunity and benefits in building a strong allegiance with the United States. Over the past three years, economic aid, infrastructure support, and counterterrorism training for his armed forces had been the primary deliverables. The latter helped Mikolayev try to control key parts of the Tajik territory and promote a semblance of stability. The aid was essential, in the Tajik president's mind, to keeping the delicate balance he maintained between peace and civil unrest.

In return, the U.S. sought the potential use of Tajik territory to stage American troops and equipment in the volatile region. The recent aid also came with one particular hook, one that ran contrary to the Tajik president's desires—that he conduct legitimate open and free elections. This one element could be the eventual eviction order for Mikolayev, and the end of his lengthy dynastic run as the country's ruler. He was in no hurry to leave the opulent gold-domed Palace of Nations, also known as the White House in Dushanbe, where he resided.

Ivan Mikolayev wasn't the only one concerned about too radical a change in the status quo. The chief of his military forces, General Dimitri Voitek, had a lot to lose if the Americans made too big an impression on Mikolayev. Voitek's personal coffers had been fattened over the years by a steady cash flow from certain drug kingpins in Afghanistan. As his wealth increased exponentially over time—the money secreted into accounts in Switzerland—his military forces looked the other way as the stream of illicit drugs crossed the border. His future wealth was clearly at risk if the Americans managed to shut the door on the transiting drugs.

The country's newfound alliance with the West also did not sit well with many of the radical elements who sought to keep the region in a state of turmoil, as it had been under Russian control. Terrorist groups operated indiscriminately and with near-absolute impunity in the fifty-five thousand square miles of rugged, inhospitable terrain.

Farad Asmaradov took full advantage of the territory's protective landscape and lack of political will. He had built his reputation on violence, brutality, and terror. As leader of the Panja cell, he had been responsible for attacks across Central Asia and Eastern Europe.

His strong ties to Moscow kept him flush with the cash needed to keep a standing army of militants well trained and equipped. There was no shortage of former Russian bloc soldiers, expatriate commandos, and those who had the skills to build advanced improvised explosive devices. This left Asmaradov with the resources to focus his attacks—and hatred—on the West.

Putonov was determined to keep strong links to Tajikistan, even if it meant using Mikolayev, Voitek and Asmaradov to help cement that relationship and hopefully terminate the growing American influence.

Terror had been successfully used as a catalyst for change in countries around the world for years. When applied in vulnerable locations, it created panic among the affected population, caused its citizens to doubt the ability of those governing them to provide adequate protection, and sometimes resulted in political changes.

Asmaradov had been given a bold challenge by Russia to be the vehicle for change in Tajikistan. If he was successful, he would give the American Congress a strong enough reason to turn away from Mikolayev and withdraw their support for an expanded U.S. presence in Central Asia. That would clear the way for Putonov to expand his current footprint and influence—and provide Russia a clear geostrategic position in the critical region.

Chapter 15

Ace found Julie strolling with Colene near the glass-enclosed solarium. Its greenery and colorful flowers helped passengers forget, at least for a minute, that they were on a cruise ship.

"Where are the old folks?" he asked, somewhat jokingly. He heard footsteps behind him and quickly turned around, only to find his in-laws and mother giving him an incredulous look.

"Who the heck are you calling old?" demanded Julie's dad.

Red-faced, he tried to recover his composure. "I was just kidding. I just meant that you all might be tired and were taking a nap." As soon as the words left his mouth, he regretted them. "I didn't mean that either!" He was digging the hole deeper and deeper.

All three of the senior adults started laughing hysterically. They didn't often get the best of Matt, but this was one of those times, and they were enjoying it.

"We're heading to the Fantail Lounge on Deck 14. If you behave yourself, we'll let you join us old people," quipped Gemma.

"Flamer volunteered to keep an eye on all the kids for a bit," Julie jumped in, trying to change the subject and extricate her husband from the uncomfortable position he found himself in. "He'll join us after he leaves them at the theater with the children's center chaperones for the afternoon show."

"Guess he's feeling a little guilty about not having our son with us on the cruise. But I know Sean's having a good time at camp," replied Colene.

"Sounds great," Ace said, still trying to recover from his ill-timed comments.

As if to offer him a modicum of comfort, Jack lightly slapped him on his back and laughed. "Hang in there, young man. Wisdom comes with age, and an acute sense of one's surroundings," he chuckled. "I thought as an aviator, you always 'checked six' for bogeys," he added.

They took the escalator to the lounge and grabbed some seats that faced the larger viewing windows. The rapidly expanding frothy wake coming from the large propellers provided ample evidence of the *Dream Spinner*'s speed as it moved smartly through the dark blue water.

The bar attendant came over to take their orders. Ace was surprised when he immediately recognized her as the same young lady who had made his breakfast omelet.

"Aleksandra. I didn't know you worked up here as well. Do they pay you more for doing all these different jobs?" he laughed.

"Hello again. No, but I enjoy this job better than making egg breakfasts." The attractive Ukrainian took the drink orders and headed back to the bar.

Ace forgot to ask for some pretzels to munch on and walked over toward Aleksandra. As she waited for the bartender to prepare the drinks, she turned as he approached.

"You know, you *really do* look like a military guy. I am a pretty good judge of people, since I literally get to meet hundreds on each cruise."

There's that comment again. "Hey, I could be a peanut salesman. In the U.S., all peanut salesmen look like me. We have to be pretty fit to lift those big, heavy bags of goobers." He smiled at her.

She shook her head and laughed softly. "What's a goober?"

"That's what we call peanuts in the States."

"So, what do you do in the military? Are you a Marine? No, maybe Army?"

He glanced at the bartender busily making the drinks at the other end of the bar and then looked back at her.

"Okay, you got me. I'm not a peanut salesman. I'm a diaper manufacturer. I had to get into the business when my wife kept having more babies. Thought it might be cheaper in the long run to get the diapers wholesale, you know?" He looked straight into her eyes.

She didn't laugh. "I just want you to know we appreciate the American military. They have the finest fighting force on earth, and some of the most advanced technology."

His brain was now starting to signal to him that things weren't quite right with the entire conversation. He wasn't sure what to make of this young woman.

"You sure ask a lot of interesting questions," he said. "Were you familiar with the military in Ukraine? Did you have a brother or father that served there?"

Her facial expression changed instantly. "Yes, my father lost his life in 2014 when the Russian Army forcefully occupied our country. It was during a terrible period of political unrest."

"I'm sorry to hear that, Aleksandra. That must have been very hard for you as a child."

"It was horrible. After he was killed, my mother did her best to keep us fed. But it was difficult. I'm in this job to help pay her back for all the sacrifices she made for me."

"I'm certain she appreciates all that you're doing for her."

"The support your country provided to Ukraine since then has helped us overcome the isolation imposed by the Russians. My country will never forget it."

"Hey, the United States is always ready to help when they see persecution happening."

Aleksandra smiled.

"I'll bring some pretzels with the drinks."

Ace headed back to the plush couches and armchairs. *That was an interesting conversation from an egg flipper/bar attendant.* Was she probing a bit too deeply? Or maybe it was just her way of trying to bond with her guests. Whatever was going on, it came across as a bit suspicious, a bit weird.

The drinks and snacks arrived just about the time Flamer wandered in. He turned to the bartender and shouted, "Make mine a top-shelf eighteen-year-old Scotch, a double, neat, and put it on that fighter pilot's tab," he pointed to Ace.

"No problem, Flamer. I've got this. But you'll definitely pick up *your* share. Especially when we hit the cigar and whiskey lounge later on in this voyage." He elbowed his buddy and said in a low voice, "Go easy on the fighter pilot references. No reason to advertise that."

The good-natured ribbing continued back and forth until the rest of the group could barely stand it.

"You two are a trip," Cathy Black said to the two soon-to-be inebriated aviators. "You better not get too sloshed before dinner. There's plenty of day and night activities left to enjoy."

Julie and Colene looked at each other and then at their husbands. They nodded their agreement in unison.

Surprisingly, at this late-afternoon hour, the lounge was pretty empty. Yet it was the perfect place to kick back, enjoy some libations, and spend some adult time with family and friends. They had at least another hour before picking up the kids at the theater. Then they could rest a bit before cleaning up for dinner and the evening entertainment in the *Dream Spinner*'s biggest theater, the Centrum. The night's venue was a Broadway-style show featuring the very talented *Dream Spinner* entertainers.

As the group broke up, Aleksandra came over to Ace.

"I didn't mean to ask so many questions. I like Americans. Especially military guys—and fighter pilots."

Ace was about to respond to what she said but thought better of it. "Thanks for taking good care of us. I'll see you at breakfast!"

On the way back to the room, he elbowed Flamer. "Hey, buddy. Let me fill you in on the weird conversation I had with our bar attendant."

As he explained what happened, Flamer just listened. He didn't comment but wondered if it was just idle conversation from a good-looking bar wench.

Ace's fighter pilot sixth sense told him that something was just not quite right.

Chapter 16

Day 3

The *Dream Spinner* dropped its two-ton anchor before dawn just about a mile from the private island. Most passengers never felt the ship slow and stop, anchoring itself in the coral-hued water. Pleasure Cruises had leased the small cay from the Bahamian owner years back and turned it into their first stop out of Port Canaveral.

The shallow water approaching the island's shores required the ship's orange-and-white tenders, otherwise known as lifeboats, to be used to ferry eager passengers for a day of fun and surf. In the shallow morning light, the ship's crew prepared the tenders for the surge in guests who would be heading to the Deck 2 retractable gangway in a couple hours.

The absence of the ship's movement began to stir the Black family. Julie woke first and snuggled against her husband. He opened his eyes slowly.

"What time is it?" he asked, enjoying her embrace.

"It's seven o'clock. You forgot to order your coffee last night, so apparently you just kept on sleeping instead of getting up early like you usually do."

"Crap, we've got to get up and get ready for our beach day on the island," he said and crawled out of the bed.

As Julie pulled herself from the bed, she remembered a conversation she had the night before with Flamer's wife. "Matt, did you hear about any passengers getting sick last night after dinner?"

"Hmm? What did you say about people getting sick?"

"Colene told me that she heard some ship's officers talking about it when we came out of the show."

"Didn't hear anything about that."

Ace hoped it wasn't a gastrointestinal virus that had occasionally plagued other ships over the past couple of years. That would wreak havoc on a vessel this large. Nothing was worse than being confined with a bunch of people who were vomiting and experiencing raging diarrhea. If it *was* true, he expected to see plenty of antibacterial hand sanitizer positioned in containers around the ship, and an aggressive crew insisting it be used by everyone.

"Well, I hope that no one in our group is sick."

He walked to the open adjoining room doorway and peered at the sleeping children.

"Okay, guys, time to get up. Today is a big day."

As the kids began to crawl from their beds, he remarked to Julie, "I think the first tender heads to the island at nine o'clock, and I'd like to eat before we go."

She wasn't so sure about eating breakfast after the rumors of sickness after dinner. But for now, she was willing to give the ship's food the benefit of the doubt.

After a quick breakfast, they assembled at the departure deck and waited their turn to board the tenders. Each boat was constructed of reinforced aluminum and fiberglass, and could seat one hundred and fifty passengers in an emergency. The ferry process provided practice for the crew in safely lowering the boats to the water, rehearsing boarding procedures, and operating the powerful lifeboat engines.

They found seats on the white metal benches close to the open windows. The smell of ocean spray and the pungent odor of diesel fuel wafted through the tender's cabin. Once all passengers had boarded, the door was closed and the lifeboat slowly pulled away from the *Dream Spinner*. It picked up speed and pitched slightly in the water's low chop as the noisy diesel engine drowned out any attempt at conversation. As they approached the small harbor, the water was calm, nearly flat, making maneuvering to the dock almost effortless.

When the tender was tied off, the passengers pushed their way toward the exit. The kids literally jumped from their seats, eager to get to the beach.

"Whoa there. Slow down, guys. We'll all get a chance to get off and start enjoying this island," Ace remarked.

Julie grabbed Claire's hand while Ace took control of the boys to make sure there were no problems as they were walking off. The *Dream Spinner*'s staff was standing by to help anyone needing assistance, and to keep folks from falling off the small weathered wooden dock.

Ace was determined not to waste a minute of vacation time, even on an island that didn't really have much to offer. The passengers could enjoy a thousand feet of pristine white beach sand, a large tiki bar serving liquid refreshments and grilled food, and vendors encouraging the tourists to buy souvenirs made in China. It also had a wide array of beachside cabanas for folks to simply relax and enjoy the soft sea breeze blowing in from the south, closely following the Gulf Stream's track. A small hut offered inner tubes, snorkeling equipment, and rubber rafts to be enjoyed in the crystal-clear aqua water. About fifty yards out from the beach, a small coral reef offered some great underwater viewing for intrepid snorkelers.

The kids were more excited than the adults. They were ready to explore the beach area on the small island sanctuary, splash around in the warm Atlantic water, and have as much fun as possible digging holes, looking for shells, and generally just having a great time. Most of the adults were more than content to lounge on the beach with a good book, and perhaps later sip some ice-cold Caribbean beer. Other, more ambitious beachgoers grabbed snorkel gear and swam out to the small reef.

After they secured a few blue canvas-covered sun shelters for the entire group, Ace and Flamer decided to get a little exercise.

"Let's take a hike around this little cay," Flamer exclaimed. "It'll be good to work up a sweat before we park our butts on the sand. I checked the map and I think we can make it completely around in about an hour."

He got no objection from Ace. "Sounds like a plan, Flamer."

Kicking off their sandals, they headed down the white, sandy shoreline and past the natural foliage barrier that bordered the official beach area.

"Don't suppose we're going to get in trouble for exploring," said Flamer. It was more a statement than a question. "I didn't see any signs prohibiting it."

"Hey, don't worry about it. We can ask for forgiveness later."

As they stepped around the tropical shrubbery, they noted that the shoreline narrowed but left them just enough sand to walk comfortably without sandals.

As they began their trek, they noted that, aside from the advertised beach area, the island was heavily forested, with little indication of being populated. There were a few openings in the lush vegetation, the sea oats bent over by either wild animals or maybe other adventurous explorers.

"Man, this island is pretty deserted," Flamer remarked. "If it wasn't for that nice beach area, there'd be no reason to even stop at this place."

After the two fighter pilots had hiked for twenty minutes, they came upon a small group of buildings set back off the shoreline, nearly hidden by the dense tropical foliage. As they got closer, they noticed something very interesting. The buildings were surrounded by a chain-link fence topped with concertina wire. There appeared to be a gate secured by a heavy-gauge padlock. Inside the fence, a camera was mounted atop a tall pole near one of the buildings, its lens aimed at the gate.

As Ace walked over to the fence, the camera seemed to move slightly in his direction. A small red light on it began blinking. Ace noted that the fence also looked like it had been wired to detect any attempt to cut through it, or foolishly climb it.

"Flamer, check this out. This is a pretty secure operation out in the middle of nowhere. Wonder what's so important inside those buildings?"

"Don't get too close. We may be pressing our luck by just *being* here. And from the blinking eye on that camera, I think we're being recorded, or watched on a live video feed."

A path, apparently used infrequently due to the undisturbed sand, led from the gate to the first building. Whatever was kept inside didn't appear to be in high demand based on the overgrown sea oats encroaching on the fence.

Ace began exploring the fence line. He walked as far back as he could before being blocked by the dense foliage, then jogged back to where Flamer waited. As they moved toward the far left side of the fenced area, they noticed that a concrete path extended from another locked gate in the fence. It led straight down to the water, where a rudimentary concrete dock had been built. A loading dock, possibly, they both surmised. But for what?

"This is pretty odd, Flamer. Why would anyone store shit out here? Especially on the opposite side of the island from where the tourist stuff is located?"

"Maybe it's to keep people away from here. People like us!"

"It's very strange."

As they walked away from the dock, Ace stopped. Something caught his attention. He looked down and spied something just barely protruding from the mix of wet sand, shells and seaweed. Its tarnished brass color stood in contrast among the more naturally occurring debris. He reached down and picked it up.

"Look at this. It's a cartridge for a rifle. Looks almost like the size of a 5.56-millimeter round, but maybe just slightly smaller."

"What the heck would that thing be doing here? I'm not getting any good vibes about this."

"Me either. Must have been dropped by whoever was loading or unloading stuff here." He paused a moment before continuing. "But I guess whatever someone's been storing in this place must be important enough to be guarded by folks carrying automatic weapons."

"Well, whatever it is, we ought to boogie out of here before our faces become plastered on the screen of the guy watching us from that camera and the gendarmes come swarming after us," Flamer exclaimed.

With that, they picked up the pace to get around the north end of the island and back to their families.

When Flamer and Ace arrived back at the sun shelters, they noticed that everyone had definitely gotten into relaxation mode. Julie was lying flat on her stomach, lathered with sunscreen and hoping to work on her tan. Colene was coming back from the tiki bar with some Caribbean spiced grilled chicken to munch on and a large plastic cup with a frozen pink cocktail topped by a small umbrella. The kids were now playing a game of tag in the light ankle-deep surf. The grandparents lay in the shade of their cabanas, apparently napping.

The two wanderers smelled the Caribbean chicken and immediately made haste to grab some for themselves, along with a couple bottles of cold beer. That got Ace's attention. It was the national beer of Cuba. Why would they stock Cuban beer here? Once they got what they needed, they headed to the cabanas to kick back a bit and enjoy the rest of the day. Food, beer, and a snooze—a perfect agenda for the day. As the beach party waned and the vacationers had satisfied their desire for sunshine, it was time to head back to the ship.

As the golden sun dropped lower on the horizon, they caught the tender back. The ride was a bit rougher since the wind had picked up and the sea was noticeably choppy. Once on board the *Dream Spinner*, the plan was to clean up and then go to the dining room around seven o'clock. The primary post-dinner activity was another show in the Centrum. Ace had also twisted Flamer's arm to get him to go with a slightly different plan—to visit the cigar and whiskey bar after the show. That didn't take much convincing.

They all enjoyed a spectacular dinner in the Windjammer dining room. Steak and lobster topped the evening's menu, and nearly all of them went for it. Dessert was Baked Alaska, followed by cappuccino for the adults and milkshakes for the kids.

The evening show was one of the major productions done by the *Dream Spinner* singers and dancers, supported by their world-class orchestra. The men looked for Buzz Caster, their skeet instructor, hoping to chide the Brit if they could get his attention. They didn't see him, which was fortunate given Caster's promise to drag them up on the stage. While Ace and Flamer were all in on doing what the group wanted, the show wasn't exactly what they had in mind for entertainment. However, they sat patiently with their families and enjoyed as much as they could while silently hoping it would end early.

They dispersed following the evening show, the two fighter pilots making a beeline for their planned destination—the Cask and Stogie lounge on Deck 6. The mahogany-paneled lounge had top-shelf premium liquor and also a large walk-in humidor with every imaginable cigar brand. They found a couple of flavorful Cuban cigars and then grabbed a table.

"This calls for some whiskey," declared Ace. "On you, of course," he added, encouraging Flamer to break out his *Dream Spinner* cruise card and pass it to the waitress taking their order.

Flamer scrunched up his face and reluctantly pulled his card out.

"How about some premium Scotch?" He looked at the waitress and asked her if they had any.

"Of course. What vintage would you like?" she asked. "We have twelve and eighteen-year-old Scotch."

Ace grinned. "Eighteen, of course."

Flamer groaned. "You know, there are plenty of days left on this cruise for payback. Wait till *you* see what *I* order next!"

As the two sipped their fragrant amber-hued spirits, Ace couldn't get something out of his mind—their hike around the small island. He thought it was pretty weird to come across the ultra-secured fenced area on the small cay. He wasn't sure what *that* level of protection could be for. Surely it wasn't for ships' provisions. All cruise ships stocked enough for up to thirty days at sea—or more.

Something just didn't add up. Who owned that facility? What was in it? Who was monitoring it? Were the contents tied in any way to the cruise line company? And what about that rifle cartridge? And then there was the Cuban beer.

As they both took a slow draw from their fragrant cigars, Ace stood up and looked out the window into the darkness. The last tender had long since brought the remaining passengers aboard. Piercing the blackness outside the ship, a flashing light appeared in the distance. It looked like a boat was coming around the left side of the island, not from the beach. Another tender? Carrying what, or whom? But it was nearing ten o'clock at night. What was a tender doing in the darkness approaching the *Dream Spinner*? Perhaps it was the cleanup crew coming back from the island. Making sure it was prepared for the next cruise ship to enjoy. But this late?

The two aviators settled in for a few more glasses of the tasty Scotch and then decided to go back to their staterooms.

The *Dream Spinner* pulled out of the private island hideaway late in the night, having given the passengers a nice long day to enjoy their first stop.

The guests had no idea how their *dream* vacation was going to suddenly transition into their *worst* nightmare.

Chapter 17

The *Dream Spinner* had charted a course out of Port Canaveral heading south-southeast through the Straits of Florida. After stopping at the private island, the ship proceeded toward Cuba, paralleling the deeper waters of the Great Bahama Banks. It sailed south through the Santaren Channel, into the Nicholas Channel just north of Cuba, and eventually into the Old Bahama Channel.

The planned route to their ultimate vacation destinations would take them past the eastern tip of Cuba, turning southwest through the Windward Passage toward the western side of Haiti and then finally southeast to their first stop in Aruba. A full day there would be followed by a short cruise to Curaçao, and then Bonaire, and finally to the last two stops, St. Lucia and Antigua. A two-day voyage back to Port Canaveral would finish the cruise. From all appearances, it was intended to be a picture-perfect itinerary for all the passengers.

———————•———————

Captain Zoyatov had been a ship captain for many years, cutting his teeth first on a variety of oceangoing vessels with Russian and Greek flags—including cruise ships—but mostly working where he was directed by his Russian handlers. Moscow had maintained covert links within the myriad transportation carriers around the world to ensure they had leverage when they needed it. Pleasure Cruise Lines was one of the current beneficiaries of Moscow's financial support. The link to the cruise line was Hafez Zoyatov's ticket on board.

Zoyatov had been one of several ship captains who enjoyed the benefits that came from carrying out Russian-sponsored missions over the past decade, receiving the substantial cash rewards that came from pulling them off successfully. Up to now, none of them had involved any hostile action—this mission was his first involving a Pleasure Cruise Lines ship.

This one was going to be different, and he knew it. Taking a cruise ship hostage, a hijacking, was going to be viewed by the world as a major terrorist attack. He had some serious qualms about the assignment he had been given after learning the details, even though he hadn't been made aware of *all* of them and about *how* the mission was to end. Based on the plan, Zoyatov did know that things were likely to get pretty nasty on board once the ship's normal activities became significantly impacted.

Passengers would start to panic once major onboard activities that they had paid a premium to enjoy were violently disrupted. But there was also real potential for a small insurrection to occur depending upon how the passengers and crew reacted. And Zoyatov might not be able to keep it from happening. Then, his team would have to maintain full control of the boat and proceed as planned.

Zoyatov was smart enough to know that the United States was predictable when it came to its citizens being taken hostage. Depending upon how the U.S. president reacted to the ship's take-over, a military response could descend upon the *Dream Spinner* very quickly. If that happened and the terrorist leader's plan failed, he wondered whether he could avoid any personal danger. Could he survive the ordeal by using his smarts, his cunning?

Meanwhile, he would proceed as he had been directed. The captain believed that he was in charge of the mission's execution—at least, that was what Asmaradov had *told* him. It was now time for him to affirm the Viper's planned actions with the key players of the upcoming dangerous mission.

He met with his onboard collaborators in his secure stateroom on the afternoon of the second day. The chief engineer, Drako

Kratec, his security chief, Cho Lee Kwan, and of course his new communications and information technology officer, Khalil Atta, were all present. Khalil's assistant, Banu aka Kelly Sayeed was absent. The provisioning manager showed up a few minutes late.

Drako Kratec had a crucial role when it came to the ship's propulsion, its speed, and handling all of the critical functions managed through the engine control room. It included everything from potable water servicing the passenger cabins to the electricity produced by the steam generator. He understood what he had to do and when, and how to respond quickly if things began to go badly—like an American military assault on the ship.

Cho Lee Kwan had a major part as well. He had to ensure that members of his security forces reacted instantly and appropriately. At some point, he had to be prepared to quell an offensive response external to the ship, and also handle any internal resistance posed by passengers or crew members—or even members of his own security team. And to deliver the right level of violence if it was required. He knew he would have some help to do both—more support for him was coming soon.

Khalil had replaced the primary communications officer shortly after coming on board. He had also built the flash drive used by Zoyatov to corrupt the ship's navigation computer. Zoyatov had reassigned the confused officer to other duties. With complete oversight of the ship's important area, Khalil was there to enable and disable anything controlled by its massive electronic network. He would, at some point, control all communications entering or leaving the ship. He also had the skill to bypass systems, activate and deactivate all cameras and loudspeakers, and control watertight doors, air conditioning and heat to cabins, and other critical functions.

Hafez also didn't know much about Banu Sayeed—who she *really* was or why she was on board—only that she claimed to be Khalil's assistant. He didn't know she was an experienced Iranian combat fighter. She used the name Kelly, the same alias she had used in past missions. She was there to ensure Asmaradov's strategy didn't go awry—as it pertained to Khalil Atta.

The provisioning manager was key to controlling any external access into the ship through the loading doors and safeguarding any sensitive cargo that might come on board in the near future.

Zoyatov didn't really control much of anything in reality, other than piloting the ship on a course planned by the Viper. Other militants already embedded on the ship as ordinary crew members, and even the group who had come on board with him at Port Canaveral, were taking orders straight from Asmaradov. And from Khalil Atta.

Unknown to the others, Khalil was the singular individual on board who knew the entire plan in store for the *Dream Spinner*, especially how the hijacking would ultimately conclude. That part of the plan would be kept secret from the others for the time being, and particularly from Hafez Zoyatov.

For now, Captain Zoyatov was proceeding as though he was piloting any other cruise ship on a normal vacation voyage. It was "ops normal" as far as the passengers and crew were concerned.

But *normal* was about to end.

Chapter 18

Day 4

The passengers' slumber was jolted by an announcement from the captain. Ace sat up in bed when he heard the in-room intercom repeat three times, "May I have your attention, please?"

He gently nudged Julie and told her to wake up. *The woman could sleep through a train wreck,* he thought.

"Jules. They're making some kind of announcement. Must be important if they're waking everyone up this early in the morning."

She slowly turned over and blinked the sleepiness from her eyes.

"This is Captain Zoyatov. I have an important announcement for all of our guests. As you may have heard, we had some passengers become ill the night before last. My medical staff has cared for them in our ship's infirmary, but those affected are not responding to treatment. Their condition is now critical, and I regret to inform you of an urgent and immediate destination change to allow them to disembark and obtain hospital care." The captain paused.

"We are making arrangements to proceed to the closest port that can provide the requisite care, and we will inform you when we have finalized our intended stop. I want to assure you that their illness does not appear to be contagious, nor caused by a problem in our food supply, from what we can determine. But we will be taking additional precautions in every area of the ship to ensure your safety. Thank you."

Julie was now wide awake. "Wow. What we heard before about some people getting sick was true. Wonder what caused it? Do you think they brought their illness with them when they boarded in Port Canaveral? Did they eat some spoiled food the first night on board? You know, just because the captain thinks the food didn't cause the illness doesn't mean it didn't."

"Well, we were all eating from the same trough in the dining room the first night, and on the island. None of us got sick. I bet they brought it with them from wherever they came from before boarding. You know, it only takes one infected person to pass on something pretty nasty—regardless of what the captain says about it not being contagious."

"It must be pretty serious if we're going to divert to another port," said Julie. "I hope whatever they got *isn't* contagious, in spite of what the captain said."

The appearance of one of their children peeking through the adjoining room's open doorway occurred moments after the end of the captain's broadcast. Claire walked in first, followed by the two boys.

"What's happening, Daddy?" she asked, rubbing the sleep from her eyes. She walked over to her mother and wrapped her arms around her, receiving a comforting hug in return.

"It's nothing, really," said Ace, trying to downplay the unintended stop the ship was going to make. "Go back to bed, or play some games in your room. You can also check the TV for something interesting to watch."

Needing no further encouragement, the children left, and minutes later, the sounds of cartoons disrupted any chance of them going back to sleep. At their age, cartoons reigned as mindless fun.

"Sometimes this happens," he said to Julie. "I know the cruise ship has plans in place to handle whatever comes up." Then he tried to be a bit more positive. "Look on the bright side. We're going to sail to a mysterious port that wasn't on our itinerary. This could really be exciting!"

Two hours later, as the family was preparing to head out for breakfast, the next announcement came over the ship's intercom.

"May I have your attention, please? This is Captain Zoyatov. We have approval to offload our critically ill passengers at Santiago de

Cuba. We will arrive there in three hours." The captain paused. "No other passengers will be allowed off the ship. This is not an authorized tour stop. We will remain in port long enough to disembark the sick passengers and take on some additional provisions." Again, a pause.

Cuba, Ace thought to himself. *That's pretty weird given our current policy on visits there. Must be pretty urgent to get these sick folks off this boat.*

"I can assure you that your safety is our primary concern. You may see some medical personnel boarding our ship to inspect the cabins of those passengers who were ill. This is only a precaution, to verify that there are no indications of anything that might expose our remaining passengers to what caused their illness. Please do not be alarmed by their presence."

Captain Zoyatov continued, "Once that is complete, we will promptly set sail for our original destination, Oranjestad, Aruba."

"Also, our food is safe. We have determined that our dining room food, and all of our food provided throughout the ship, did not contribute in any way to the illness experienced by the sick passengers. So, I encourage you to continue enjoying our premier dining experience."

Julie piped up. "I don't know if I'm buying *that* line. It seems like the food *has* to be the problem. I don't know if I want to touch *any* of their food."

"Jules, there is no way the ship is going to encourage people to keep eating from potentially contaminated food. I believe the captain."

"If they didn't get sick from the dining room food, then how did they become ill?" she asked.

"Who knows, Jules? Hey, at least we can keep eating! After all, that's a big reason to cruise. Nonstop eating," he said with a laugh.

Ace thought the captain's words were somewhat reassuring, since he was already hungry. He told the kids to get ready if they wanted to go to the dining room with him. Julie had lost her appetite.

Claire walked back into their room and climbed up on the bed.

"I'm ready to go eat," she said, clearly not concerned about the food.

"Good. We'll head to the dining room in a couple of minutes," Ace said.

"Where's Cuba" the inquisitive young girl asked.

"It's an island just south of the Florida Keys," he responded.

"I think it's pretty cool that we get to go to Cuba," said Ace, trying to stay upbeat. "I wonder if we'll see any of the old cars that I've read about. Cuba is supposed to be loaded with them."

Claire looked at her dad. "I'll bet they're not as cool as your Boss Mustang."

"Well, the cars in Cuba are much older than my Stang. Most of them don't even have the original parts. The Cubans have figured out a way to keep them running, though. I agree with you—my Boss Mustang is the best. But the Cuban cars are pretty cool too."

He thought about it for a minute. "We probably won't get to see them, though. You heard the captain. We can't get off of the boat. So, unless we can see the cars from where we dock, we may be out of luck."

The phone rang and Julie picked it up. It was her mother, Gemma, worried about what she'd heard. Julie spent a few minutes calming her down. Gemma was a bit of a hypochondriac. One of her biggest fears was getting infected on a cruise ship and being trapped—no escape, no way to see her own doctor. Jack wasn't worried, but that hadn't satisfied her.

"Don't worry, Mom. I heard that the ship is scrubbing everything down and taking the necessary precautions to prevent any possibility of spreading whatever might have caused the illnesses. If Dad isn't worried, then you shouldn't be concerned either."

Chapter 19

A s Captain Zoyatov sailed into the Windward Passage that separated Cuba from Haiti, he directed the ship's navigator to proceed on a westbound heading toward the port of Santiago de Cuba. A pilot boat would meet them outside the narrow, twisting entryway that led into a larger bay where cruise ship and freighter berths were located.

He had made contact with Cuban authorities, at least with the key contact he had been instructed to call per the Viper's plan. A few officers on the *Dream Spinner*'s bridge were surprised at how quickly authorization was given to dock at Cuba's second-largest port after Havana. A few of them talked openly about how strange this was, given the shutdown of cruise ship traffic in the past six months due to a diplomatic squabble between the U.S. and Cuban governments. They also questioned why the captain had chosen Cuba instead of an equally close location in Port-au-Prince. Haiti was already on the approved list of ports servicing tourists from the United States.

Zoyatov overheard the discussions and called them together in the bridge cockpit area.

"Based on the serious condition of these passengers and the need for urgent care, Cuba offers the best opportunity for immediate treatment. Haiti does not possess the intensive care equipment nor qualified medical personnel necessary to deal with this type of sickness, or this number of critically ill guests."

He received a few nods of agreement, but others were still a bit skeptical. They knew the ship could have even turned back toward

Florida and docked in Miami. Why had the captain not considered that option?

Two hours later, the *Dream Spinner* approached the entry channel to Santiago de Cuba. The harbormaster's boat was already racing toward them. Zoyatov reduced his speed and gave orders to prepare to board the Cuban harbormaster through the external bulkhead door on Deck 2.

The red pilot boat with its white cabin and two large top-mounted radar antennas moved toward the cruise ship. A Cuban flag flapped in the breeze from a small mast on the stern. Two black smokestacks belched a sooty dark gray cloud that seemed to hang in a distorted form above the boat in spite of the breeze, fouling the clear air off the coast. Large tires festooned its sides to ensure gentle contact with any vessel it came close to. As the boat approached the cruise ship, two men in the cockpit waved to the *Dream Spinner*'s captain who was staring from the bridge glass window. The harbormaster slowly came alongside the massive cruise ship and positioned his boat by the open hull door.

Once the Cuban was on board, accompanied by an armed individual wearing a military uniform, they were escorted to the bridge. Zoyatov met them and had a brief private discussion. The harbormaster then began giving the orders to navigate through the passage toward their intended berth.

It took about an hour for the ship to slowly make its way through the inlet. While it was maneuvering, a Cuban Marine Police boat shadowed the cruise ship. The small silver fast-attack boat's cabin had two men inside, while outside, two other policemen stood by the twin .50-caliber machine guns mounted on the boat's deck, prepared to use the guns if it became necessary.

"Holy crap," shouted Flamer from the deck rail as he and Ace watched the police boat move closer to the *Dream Spinner*. "Check out the armament on that baby. You *gotta* know we are in Cuban waters."

"Well, I guess they haven't seen too many cruise ships recently. Maybe they're just being a bit cautious."

"Do you think it's a little odd that we are docking in Cuba?"

"Yeah. But we really don't know the level of urgency to get the sick passengers off the boat. Maybe some are so critical that this was the best and quickest option."

"Well, you can count me out when it comes to the Cuban version of medical care. Communism doesn't breed high-end medicine. I can't imagine that it's all *that* advanced. Hopefully, the passengers will be okay."

As they approached the pier, the harbormaster relinquished controls to Zoyatov to maneuver the massive ship into its berth. As the ship nestled against the large rubber fenders that hung from the sides of the concrete dock, passengers lined the rails of virtually every deck and stateroom balcony to witness the final mooring. The burly stevedores muscled the large lines from the *Dream Spinner* and secured the big cruise ship to the black steel quay bollards on the pier.

The greeting that met the passengers appeared far from friendly. A line of olive-green Cuban military vehicles were positioned up and down the pier. Several had machine guns mounted on them, with soldiers manning the weapons.

A number of ambulances were also visible on the gray concrete pier, along with a dark green bus. Once the ship had completed disembarkation preparations, the sick passengers were quickly moved from the ship's medical center where they had been quarantined. Nearly half of them required stretchers to carry them off.

Once the last of the patients were removed, Captain Zoyatov made another announcement.

"May I have your attention, please? As you may have witnessed, our sick guests are now on their way to the nearest hospital that has the requisite medical support. We will do our best to keep you advised of their status throughout the remainder of our voyage."

"Meanwhile, strictly as a precaution, we will have a Cuban decontamination team come on board to do a final inspection of our ship and help us verify that we can continue our cruise safely. They will be taking samples with swabs and other test equipment.

The samples will need to be tested at a laboratory ashore to provide the verification we need. This process will happen as quickly as possible. I ask your patience and indulgence. We do this for your safety. Thank you."

Ace was now standing next to Julie in their stateroom, listening to the announcement.

"It's so sad about those poor people," she said. "They're going to be left in a Cuban hospital while we go on vacationing. I hope somebody is notifying the American embassy, if it still exists in Havana."

"Jules. I'm sure that the right notifications are being made."

"I heard a rumor that they were all from Deck 3. I think there are only a few staterooms there. The cheap ones, with no windows. I wonder if that had anything to do with why they got sick?"

Julie had actually hit on how the passengers on Deck 3 had become ill. The Viper had obtained a deadly substance developed in a specialized Moscow laboratory—a lab that researched ways to militarize toxins. The passengers had, in fact, been targeted specifically in those staterooms, to ensure they would become critically ill. It had been pretty simple to execute.

The toxin had been used to contaminate the things that passengers touch most in their cabins—the phone, the door handles, the light switches, the TV remote, the drawers where they placed their clothes and other items. But especially on things that would, at some point, touch a guest's mouth—the glasses in the cabin and bathroom, and on the complimentary bottles of water.

The poison could not be spread from person to person. It infected an individual by short-term contact only and was quickly absorbed by the skin. Once it was absorbed, it could not be further transmitted by human contact with anyone else. That prevented it from being spread throughout the ship. The reasons for targeting Deck 3 would emerge in the coming hours and days. Unfortunately, the four stewards that tended to the cabins on that deck became casualties as well, having touched virtually everything in the staterooms. They, too, were evacuated from the ship.

Ace wondered about what was happening ashore. Why had the military shown up with enough forces to handle a small conflict? Now that the sick passengers were offloaded, why weren't the military forces leaving? Granted, it was Cuba—a dictatorship ruled the island nation with an iron fist. Was he overthinking the whole situation? Looking for some sinister plot that wasn't there?

With the *Dream Spinner* docked, usually the casino and onboard shopping areas were closed down. But the captain made an exception. Since passengers couldn't leave the ship, all entertainment and shopping venues were opened to keep the tourists pacified until the ship got back underway. It was best to provide distractions for the guests and keep them from asking too many questions.

As evening came, the *Dream Spinner* was still docked. The ship's medical staff had received the "results" from testing and inspection of the food stocks. They were told that the illness was not caused by contamination of the ship's food. Based on that, the medical staff insisted that food had been illegally brought on board by the passengers on Deck 3 and had likely been shared among themselves. Supporting that conclusion, the Cuban medical staff claimed they had found evidence of the contamination in the cabins and had removed it. The rooms were subsequently decontaminated.

The *actual* cause of the illness was never shared with the passengers. The Cuban medical laboratory had not been completely honest with their findings. They knew full well, even before testing, that what had infected the passengers was a strain of saxitoxin called clostridium botulinum. The rapid-acting shellfish-based poison had done its job.

Captain Zoyatov made an announcement to his passengers, explaining the laboratory's fabricated conclusion—that the illness affecting the passengers had been induced by their own food brought on board.

"We have completed a thorough cleaning of their rooms and that entire deck. As a further precaution, we are completing another detailed inspection of all our food provisions, just to be sure there are no *other* areas of concern. Also, you may see some additional cargo coming on board while we are docked. This includes some added precautionary cleaning supplies to ensure we can keep the *Dream Spinner* safe for all our valued guests."

Ace thought about how certain the Cubans could be that they had contained whatever had made the passengers ill. They had said it was food. How sure could they be that the sickness came from the food brought on board? It was also pretty farfetched to believe all thirty passengers on Deck 3 had shared the contaminated food. Could it have actually come from the food stored on the ship? Was the captain hiding that fact to prevent a major panic in the dining areas? And what about the captain's announcement of needing to bring on added cleaning materials? If the contaminants had been removed or neutralized, and the ship checked and verified to be free of anything that would make passengers ill, then why was there a need for added cleaning supplies?

They had all eaten lunch a couple of hours ago. Had they all eaten contaminated food? At this point, Julie was pretty worried. She was sure she and the kids were going to get sick as well. And her mother—she was nearly hysterical with fear of becoming deathly ill. Ace did his best to calm them down, along with encouragement from Jack. Nearly all of them were a bit conflicted about going to dinner later—mainly out of fear from what *might* be in the food. But skipping a meal was a hard sell with the kids. They all discussed whether it made sense to go but finally decided that they had already eaten plenty of food on board and never had any problem.

Later, Ace was on Deck 8 with Flamer, sipping a cold beer and watching the sun move lower on the western horizon. Its rays cast shadows formed by their interruption by colorful buildings set back on the small rise in the port area.

"Flamer, I heard something pretty interesting. Rumor has it that the sick passengers aren't staying in Santiago de Cuba. I heard a couple crew members say that they're getting whisked away to a major hospital facility in Holguin, over eighty-eight miles from where we dock. You know what the name of that hospital is? The Vladimir Ilyich Lenin University Hospital. How's that for an introduction into communist medicine?"

"Well, hopefully that place has the treatment those poor folks need. Plus, I think it will be closer to our embassy in Havana. It might make it easier for them to get some good old US assistance."

As darkness began to encompass the pier, they saw two canvas-topped vehicles pull up to the ship. In the dim light, they stared at the activity going on toward the bow storage door. Covered pallets were brought onto the ship. Interestingly, the pallets coming on board were accompanied by several armed Cuban soldiers. The entire process took about an hour and a half.

Why do they have armed soldiers guarding the pallets? Hope that stuff was checked thoroughly for contraband before coming on board, Ace thought as he stepped from his balcony back into the stateroom. *Gotta stop overthinking this. But it is pretty strange.*

It was rapidly approaching the dinner hour. Ace took a quick shower, dressed in casual slacks and his favorite floral design shirt, and made sure his brood was ready to go. But his mind just wouldn't let go of how odd the day's entire scenario was.

Chapter 20

n spite of the captain's assurances that the food was safe, most of the diners jabbed inquisitively at just about everything on their plates. Suspicious looks. Sometimes holding the food up on their fork, as if they could see the contaminant that had brought the illness to the boat. Ace was confident in the thorough cleaning operation, and in the ship's staff. At this point, he knew that if anything, the cleanliness and food preparation discipline was going to be extreme—the cruise line couldn't afford any more bad press.

After dinner, the women and kids planned on going to the acrobatics show in the large theater area. Ace, Flamer and Julie's dad decided they weren't really up for a show. Instead, they headed for the casino to try out their luck.

In spite of the large air handlers attempt to clear the air of smoke in the casino, the smell of cigarettes hung like a dirty curtain as they walked in. It aggravated Ace. He hated the foul odor that stuck to his clothes. But tonight, he had committed to hang out with the boys.

Flamer planted himself at the poker table. He figured he was smart enough to make a few bucks while enjoying the free drinks given to guests willing to bet their luck at the tables.

Jack decided to entertain himself at the craps table. He had played it occasionally over the years and had been lucky, most of the time coming out ahead.

Ace wasn't a gambler—he only liked to bet on himself—a sure thing! But he didn't want to abandon the men and suffer through an acrobatic show in the Centrum, jammed in among the mass of guests resting their full stomachs after dinner.

He watched Flamer for a few minutes and then excused himself. He had forgotten his iPhone back in the room and wanted to capture a few casino pictures for posterity. After all, he knew Flamer would most likely lose his shirt to the dealer, and Ace wanted some shareable evidence of a fighter pilot in tears.

He walked out of the casino and strolled toward his cabin. The long hallway wound its way down the starboard side of the ship, the colorful red-and-green carpet emblazoned with seahorse and conch shell images. The hallway walls were adorned with seascape photos and many pictures from ports the *Dream Spinner* had visited around the world.

He walked past a few unmarked doors intended only for crew access. One of them was slightly ajar as he approached it. He overheard some loud voices. An argument. Not in English—but then again, most of the crew members were from foreign countries. Not unusual that they might revert to their own language when talking or arguing amongst themselves. *Interesting language.* Sounded a bit like a Central Asian language. Maybe Kazakh, Uzbek, Kyrgyz, or Tajik. He slowed his pace. Heard what sounded like the word *Dushanbe.*

That's in Tajikistan, he thought as he kept on walking down the corridor.

When he got to his stateroom, Ace swiped his card on the door lock and went in. He found his iPhone, slipped it into his pocket, and headed out. As he approached within fifty feet of the crew door where he had overheard the argument, it opened and two stocky black-bearded men wearing crew uniforms exited. They made brief eye contact with Ace, then turned and quickly walked away from him.

Something else was off. Their uniforms. Not neatly pressed. And another thing Ace noticed. Neither one of them had a name tag pinned to their uniform.

Another interesting observation popped into Ace's mind. Of all the crew he had seen over the past few days, none had had beards.

All were clean-cut—a few manicured mustaches, but no beards. As the two crew members reached a main hallway, one of them turned back to Ace. Just a brief two-second stare. A questioning look on his face, in his eyes.

What was that all about?

When Ace arrived back in the casino, he was just in time to witness his buddy Flamer making a big bet on what he presumed was a sure hand. Four others were playing at the table. All were looking at Flamer, wondering if he was bluffing. Two folded. One of the remaining two raised the bet, pushing the chips to the table limit. The other player quickly dropped out. Flamer looked into the eyes of the gentleman who he believed was betting that he'd fold. An old guy, well dressed, manicured nails, meticulous haircut—probably a successful executive.

Flamer glanced at Ace. Winked at him. He stayed in, betting that his hand was going to be a winner.

The beautiful, petite blonde with the obvious boob job walked over and put her hand on the old man's shoulder. He looked up at her and smiled. She gave him a soft kiss on his cheek.

Flamer was temporarily distracted by the young lady until the balding man with the close-cropped gray mustache turned over his remaining cards. Flamer's face blanched as if all the blood had drained from it. He was stunned at the straight flush staring at him.

"Shit!" he shouted, flipping his cards over, showing his full house. "Well, this just sucks," he said as Ace snapped a picture with his iPhone camera.

"Smile, buddy," Ace grinned. "It's only money. I won't tell Colene if you don't."

"Bite me," he blurted out. He pushed his chair away from the table and headed out of the casino with Ace toward the nearest bar. Julie's father had already walked back to his room to get some sleep.

The two fighter pilots sat on the barstools in their favorite cigar and whiskey joint on board, the Cask and Stogie. It was Ace's turn to buy, especially since he had witnessed his buddy Flamer shot down in flames, no pun intended, at the poker table. A stiff drink would do the trick. And, of course, some premium Cuban leaf.

"I can't believe my hand didn't take it. When you lose with a king-ten full house, something is just plain wrong." He shook his head, still bothered by his hefty bet and loss of a couple hundred dollars.

"I mean, what are the chances that a straight flush could be dealt with five players?" Flamer paused. "And can you believe that old dude stayed in with the bet on the table like that? I thought he was bluffing. He was too well dressed, kind of looked like some city slicker. And did you see the hot blonde that was young enough to be his daughter? Give me a break!"

"Don't know, buddy. Lesson learned. Expect the unexpected. I think he 'slickered' you!" Ace chuckled as he took a slow drag from the expensive cigar. It was about the top of his cigar pricepoint, offered in the bar at thirty bucks a pop.

"This is quite smooth. No real bite to it."

Flamer was barely listening. Instead, he was concentrating on the fine Scotch he swirled in his glass. "Yeah, it's a pretty good cigar," he said, drawing in a short puff, exhaling slowly, and then taking a sip of his drink. "But it would have tasted a hell of a lot better if I had won that hand! But then again, that was quite a nice rack. If I had to lose, at least I was opposite a vision of loveliness," he said sarcastically.

Ace felt it better to let him stew a bit. No need for any more consolation. He looked around the nearly deserted pub. Only two other people chose to enjoy the cozy mahogany-paneled surroundings. The ship had done it up right. A sporting motif. A boar's head mounted inside over the entry door. A steelhead salmon displayed over the bar. Some antique muskets bolted to the wall. A coat of arms hanging near the dartboard.

He glanced at the doorway. Through the decorative cut-glass panels, he saw a few passengers stroll by. Probably heading back to their cabins for the night. The acrobatic show had ended a couple of hours ago, and it was approaching one o'clock in the morning. He and Flamer would finish their stogies and tasty amber liquid, then head to their own staterooms.

As he continued to watch the late-night guests pass by, he saw a bearded crew member stop in front of the pub and say something to another man. Ace was jolted from his seat as he stared at a face that was curiously familiar. The face behind the beard looked a lot like the man who had tried to cripple the Raptor fleet years before. The man who had nearly enabled Iran to establish their nuclear program in the Persian Gulf.

That's impossible. That can't be who I think it is. That dude looks like Khalil Ruffa! That traitor has to be dead! Ace knew the man he was looking at, if he really was Khalil, had disappeared during the final battle in Iran and hadn't been seen since.

As he continued to stare at them, the two men briskly walked off. Ace tried to make sense of what he had seen. *Probably too much Scotch.* He was going to say something to Flamer but convinced himself that his mind was playing games. It had been a long day. Time to walk back to their rooms and get some sleep.

Just before his head hit the pillow, Ace felt the rumble of the *Dream Spinner*'s bow thrusters as the big ship prepared to ease its way from the pier.

————————•————————

The bearded man Ace had seen outside the Cask and Stogie had walked away, down the curving passageway that led to the communications center. He had a job to do.

Khalil prepared to make a key change to the ship's automatic identification system. Mandatory in all passenger vessels, the AIS provided information on the identity, position, course and speed of the ship to its monitoring center. In the case of the *Dream Spinner*, that monitoring center was at the headquarters of Pleasure Cruise Lines.

He had everything he needed to take the software program he had written in the Tajikistan lab in Dushanbe and adapt it to interface with the *Dream Spinner*'s software—which he had already gained control over.

The new program, once activated by Khalil, would essentially show anyone monitoring the *Dream Spinner*'s track that it was on course to its original plan—in this case, Aruba. The subterfuge was needed only for a short time, long enough for the cruise ship to move to its new location far from Aruba. Once it was in position for Asmaradov to begin his plan's execution, it wouldn't matter if the ship's true location was discovered.

Chapter 21

Day 5

While Ace and Flamer had been enjoying their visit to the Cask and Stogie, in the silent darkness of the dimly lit pier, Cuba's military forces had been at work. Only a few passengers strolled the decks at that time before turning in, others looking out over the deck rails at the dwindling city lights while polishing off the last of their drinks. They likely didn't notice the bubbles breaking the surface of the water alongside the ship.

Members of the Cuban military forces, naval marines, had slipped into the water hundreds of yards from the *Dream Spinner*'s mooring position. They swam toward the ship with a very special cargo. Per Farad Asmaradov's plan, they carefully attached a number of odd shapes to the ship's hull below the waterline.

The most advanced Russian-made Limpet-type explosive mines, capable of acoustic, proximity, and timer activation, were positioned against very specific watertight compartments, their intent obvious—to defeat the safety features built into the ship that would keep it afloat in the event of a hull breach. The mines also contained anti-removal triggers to thwart any attempt to pull them off the ship.

After the explosive devices were attached, the Cuban marines ringed the hull with an active and passive homing proximity radar system designed to detect anything that approached the vessel on the sea's surface. This added level of defense was intended to warn Captain Zoyatov of any attempted surface-level approach to the *Dream Spinner*.

While the underwater activity took place, two dozen heavily armed Russian-trained Tajik militants were secreted onto the *Dream Spinner*. Their boarding was masked by the ship's provisioning manager and the chief of security. The militants had been the last to come through the Deck 2 bulkhead doorway and were led directly to the empty staterooms on Deck 3. The area containing the "contaminated" cabins at the forward-most point on that deck had been blocked off from all access as a further safety precaution. It would eliminate the possibility of any attempt to proceed through the area by a lost passenger or nosey crew member. Few if any passengers transited that deck anyway, since there was nothing to see their but staterooms. Additionally, after the *contamination* was claimed to have been found in that area, nobody wanted to go anywhere near that deck. The militants would be easily hidden with little chance of discovery.

The harbormaster successfully guided the large cruise ship out of the narrow waterway and then departed the *Dream Spinner*, clambering back onto the small pilot boat. The Marine Police boat shadowed the cruise ship briefly until the *Dream Spinner* was ten miles out and then left. The cruise ship then proceeded due east along Cuba's coastline and past Guantanamo Bay before it finally began its turn south. The route would take them past the long finger of land extending from the westernmost tip of Haiti. Then the *Dream Spinner* would chart a course on its advertised route, a southeast bearing toward Aruba.

Khalil was busy in the communications center. He had successfully penetrated the ship's electronic brains, its primary bank of computers and processors, and was carefully applying the bypass mechanisms that would enable him to control virtually all the ship's functions and jam, at will, all communications in or out of the ship. He had little problem getting the privacy he needed. His assistant, the only other computer system engineer on the ship, was not going to get in the way of Khalil's tasks. The young man had mysteriously disappeared from the boat while in the port of Santiago de Cuba. A

THOMAS BELISLE

"family emergency" was the manufactured reason Khalil provided to anyone who asked.

The Syrian was extremely careful to avoid any obvious tampering with critical ship's functions that might be detected too early. All of these systems needed to operate as designed until the time was right—the time when Khalil would take control. Most important, he knew that communications in and out of the ship would have to be tightly controlled once the mission began its critical phase. At that time, passengers and crew members would find themselves unable to use any kind of cell phone, iPad or computer, regardless of its capability. The internet system across the ship would be shut down. Even ship-to-shore emergency communication would be limited to the captain and a few other key people.

As far as the explosives rigged around the ship's hull, Khalil had been fully read in on them, including their design and every aspect of their operation. After all, he had helped build the electronic network necessary to activate them, and planned to do just that after they had left the port of Santiago de Cuba and were at sea. He could also activate the timers, setting the mines to explode if the situation demanded it, and if need be, deactivate the timers, something he never intended to do once they were set. He had planned for every possible scenario.

Khalil had been getting plenty of encouragement from Kelly, his assistant, to make sure everything was ready to execute the Viper's plan. While he didn't think he needed any prompting, he appreciated what the young woman brought to the table. He knew that her skills as an assassin would likely come in handy when things got crazy aboard the *Dream Spinner*. She could handle herself in pretty much any contingency, having been trained as one of the few female commandos in Iran's Islamic Republican Guard Corps.

Beyond being a highly trained combat warrior, she made sure that Khalil had a way to relieve his stress. His appetite for sex was insatiable and had not waned much over the years since the aircraft crash. Kelly knew what he liked and made sure he got it. A *happy*

Khalil helped ensure she could manipulate him in any way, if it came down to that.

Of course, Khalil didn't realize that Kelly was primarily there to make sure he stayed focused on completing the mission. Asmaradov ensured that she knew as much as Khalil about the *Dream Spinner's* fate. The Viper trusted Khalil to a point—but in the end, the Syrian had a history of failing to execute once before. The highly trained Iranian commando would ensure Khalil finished the job this time, no matter what the costs.

On the bridge, Captain Zoyatov was making final preparations for the execution of the daring plan to take the *Dream Spinner*. But he needed an excuse to eliminate as many officers as possible who might get in his way.

One by one, he singled them out, dispatching them on errands. One to take an important document to the engine control room on Deck 2. Another to his stateroom to retrieve his glasses he had left on his credenza. And one to the communications center to pick up a codebook. The bridge required two officers at all times. The usual complement was five. When only Zoyatov and the navigator remained, the captain made his move.

He secured the entry door with the specially designed braces he had been given to prevent anyone from entering, including the remaining bridge officers. He pulled the concealed 9mm semiautomatic pistol from under his uniform coat. It had been smuggled to him by the harbormaster who had guided the ship out of the Cuban port.

The captain confronted the navigator at gunpoint. He really didn't want to shoot him—yet.

"Captain, what are you doing?" the stunned officer shouted. "Have you lost your mind?"

"Stay quiet if you want to keep on breathing," threatened Zoyatov.

He ordered the man to lie on his stomach, hands behind his back. Zoyatov tied him up with zip ties and then secured him to one of the chairs.

"What's happening here? You've locked out the remaining bridge officers. This is crazy!"

"I told you to quiet down," ordered Zoyatov.

"Your actions are going to put this ship at risk. It is, in effect, mutiny!"

After trying to gain reentry to the bridge, the frustrated and now very angry officers who had been locked out headed to where they expected to get immediate help. They sought out the security chief, Cho Lee Kwan, and described what had happened—that Zoyatov had sent them on errands, and when they had reported back, their entry was blocked. Their keys would not grant them access, nor would Zoyatov answer the phone.

Cho guided them to his office, insisting that they meet privately so as not to alarm other crew members or passengers. They were greeted by two armed men, weapons pointed at them. The stunned bridge officers were then locked in a small containment cell, otherwise known as the brig. They wouldn't be there long before they disappeared permanently from the cruise ship.

Shortly after four o'clock in the morning, the *Dream Spinner* altered its course. The track it was taking to Aruba changed to a heading of due east toward the periphery of the Venezuela Basin. The destination was northeast of Aruba, in deep water, nearly a mile from the Caribbean Sea's surface to the dark depths of the ocean floor.

On the bridge, the captain called Khalil and gave the go-ahead to activate the corrupted AIS program. With a single click of the mouse on his laptop, Khalil initiated it. The vessel would now appear to the monitoring office at the cruise ship headquarters that all was as it should be. The *actual* route change would go unnoticed. The time would come soon enough when the true location of *Dream Spinner* was discovered.

Soon, when routine communications with the cruise ship were blocked, the level of interest in the ship's status would accelerate quickly. Aircraft would be involved to try and locate them. Other ship traffic would be advised to be on the lookout for them and to report any findings.

But the *Dream Spinner* was headed to specific latitude and longitude coordinates that were clearly outside the normal sea lanes of both commercial and passenger traffic. Hopefully, that would buy Zoyatov some time. His boss, Farad Asmaradov, counted on it.

At this point, nearly all the elements of the Viper's plan were in place. So far, the cruise ship passengers had no idea about what was going to happen.

Chapter 22

efore dawn, the provisioning manager had pulled the weapons and explosives from their concealed positions inside the large pallets brought on board at the Cuban port. He had waited for the only two-hour block of time when his staff was not working so that he would not be discovered. The militants occupying the Deck 3 staterooms assembled in the large open Deck 2 storage area, and each was provided the weapons they would soon use on the *Dream Spinner*. Among the deadly cargo were a handful of man-portable shoulder-fired Strela-3 surface-to-air missile launchers.

Besides the radical group who had boarded in Cuba, there were additional embedded Panja cell members on the *Dream Spinner*. All had been groomed carefully within the cruise industry and eventually migrated their way onto the current ship. They occupied a wide array of jobs, mixing in with the rank-and-file crew. Through various means—surreptitious meetings in more private areas of the ship, covert message passing, and secure communications—all of the embedded cell members were completely tied into the Viper's plan and execution timeline. The total terrorist force on the *Dream Spinner* was now forty-four strong.

Together, they could commandeer the ship, control the passengers and crew and, at least for the short term, hold off any potential external assault. That last part, repelling an attack to rescue the ship, was essential until the demands were met—or so they were told.

Cho Lee Kwan and only two other trusted members of his security team had to ensure that the remaining twenty security personnel didn't try to stop the ship's takeover. Cho resolved to eliminate the risk of their interference.

He summoned his team to the training area they used on Deck 2. The large open spaces used to maneuver pallets of provisions were ideal for practicing the skills used to subdue and control unruly passengers. When they arrived, Cho ushered them into one of the large storerooms. He indicated he had a sensitive communication from Pleasure Cruise Lines about a threat to the ship and wanted to be sure that they weren't overheard by any other crew members who might be passing by the usually busy area. Khalil had temporarily disabled the cameras in that area to keep the next deadly actions from being revealed.

Once inside the room, Cho quickly exited and locked the door, leaving the stunned security members inside. The gas canister planted under one of the large pallets activated seconds later and quickly incapacitated the team members before eventually killing them. Their bodies were subsequently tossed out of the anchor opening in the morning darkness.

Meanwhile, Drako Kratec planned to eliminate any potential barrier to his mission as well. His three assistant engineering technicians were trained to manage and operate everything in the engine control room and could override almost anything Kratec tried to do. They had to be dealt with.

He dispatched two of them to the main mechanical equipment room to troubleshoot a fabricated problem. When they arrived there to look for the anomaly, they opened the metal panel that enclosed the integrated switchboard controls and began troubleshooting the systems. They never saw nor heard the two Tajik militants approach from behind. They were quickly garroted. Their bodies, like those of the dead security team members, were tossed overboard. The darkness and sounds of the waves breaking across the bow masked the splashes of their bodies as they hit the warm seawater.

Kratec believed he had effectively recruited the remaining assistant engineer to the Viper's cause. There was a degree of trust, of risk involved, but for now, Kratec would let him live.

In the early morning hours before there was any real likelihood of bumping into passengers, the Tajik gunmen left their Deck 3 staterooms and dispersed around the ship. Their weapons were cleverly concealed in some of the most common items seen on board. The smaller assault weapons were hidden in everything from backpacks to the colorful shopping bags used in nearly all of the ship's stores. The larger weapons and explosives were a bit more difficult to conceal. Some were rolled inside exercise mats from the fitness center, others in the large beach towels available at the three large swimming pools. The shoulder-fired missiles were, for now, left secured in the Deck 3 staterooms. They would soon see some action.

———•———

The rumble of the *Dream Spinner*'s powerful diesel engines and motion of the ship woke Ace. He looked at his watch—a little after four o'clock in the morning. He looked at his watch again. The compass showed they were heading due east. He wondered briefly about why they were headed in that direction. But he needed a bit more shut-eye. Meanwhile, the vessel continued its journey east toward the rising sun.

Less than two hours later, Ace woke up again. He felt the ship's movement—the seas were a bit rougher. His brain kept telling him that something was off, although he didn't know what. A few things had happened to the *Dream Spinner* during the night that were hidden from most of the crew, and definitely from *all* of the passengers.

When he rolled out of bed, it was just past six o'clock. He had forgotten, again, to order his morning coffee from the steward. Rubbing the sleep from his eyes, and perhaps the effects of the Scotch from the late night in the pub, he pulled on his sweatpants, threw on a T-shirt, and slipped on his sandals. He did his best to keep noise to a minimum as he opened the cabin door and shut it quietly. He walked down the deserted hallway toward the stairs that led to the upper deck, where coffee was served each morning.

No elevator for him. A little exercise was just what he needed to get his blood flowing.

He moved outside to the coffee bar by the pool. He expected to have the sun peeking at him over the port-side rail as it rose from the east. It wasn't. He was puzzled. Maybe there was some weather the captain was trying to avoid on the original route, perhaps to dodge a rain squall or shipping traffic. The ship should be cruising nearly due south toward Aruba by now. Instead, it still appeared to be headed east. It just didn't make sense.

Ace refocused his attention on the large silver container, grabbed a tall mug and filled it. No cream or sugar. Black. The way it was supposed to be. Coffee-flavored coffee. He found a deck chair near the railing and sat down. Not many passengers were up yet. Probably still a bit nervous from the health scare. There were a few crew members with hoses, buckets of disinfectant, and long-handled brushes. They were spraying down the teakwood decks, wiping the rails, cleaning tables and chairs, and making the area ready for guests.

Usually, a ship's officer or two were walking the deck at this hour, headed to their morning posting. Not today. Ace grabbed a refill of coffee and picked up a cinnamon bun for his wife. As he walked down the stairs at almost six thirty, a few guests wandered about, likely for the same reason he was. He opened his cabin door and found Julie just waking up.

"Get enough sleep, Jules?" he asked. "Brought you a little something."

She smiled as she saw the sugary treat. "Thanks, Matt. Did you bring my coffee too?"

"Oh crap. I'll run back upstairs and get you some."

"Never mind. The cinnamon bun is enough."

"Sorry, baby. I'll remember tonight to schedule our morning coffee delivery."

He pulled the drapes open to let in some morning light and then spent a few minutes trying to bring his laptop computer online. Ace had bought the internet package to help him stay informed while at sea. He waited a few moments for the computer to awaken.

As he tried to open his screen and view new mail, he got a prompt he wasn't expecting. *No signal.* He checked the settings to be certain that he had the right IP address. It was correct.

"Hmm. No signal. It was working great over the last couple of days," he said to Julie. "Wonder what's going on?"

Ace picked up the phone by the bed and tried to contact the passenger service desk. The ringtone repeated itself seven or eight times—nobody answered. He hung up, picked up the phone again and dialed the number for his stateroom steward. He got the same result. Continuous ringing, with no answer. He hung up once again and then tried to connect with the purser desk. Same result.

"Jules, this is pretty weird. Nobody seems to answer, no matter what number I dial."

"They're probably having some kind of central problem on board with the phone lines. Give it some time and try again," she said.

Little did either one of them know that their ability to communicate, other than by face-to-face means, had ended.

Chapter 23

The bridge was eerily quiet. The navigator was silent, sleeping in the chair he had been secured to earlier. The ship's captain was on schedule, on course—albeit not the one advertised in the *Dream Spinner*'s cruise brochure.

Captain Zoyatov reached his destination in the south-central Caribbean shortly before seven o'clock that morning. The ship's corrupted AIS would still be broadcasting a signal indicating the *Dream Spinner* was on course to Aruba. The captain would soon begin a random track that encompassed about eighty square miles. He had ordered the navigator at gunpoint to program the indiscriminate course that, by design, would remain unpredictable to the Americans who might eventually try to intercept the ship. The track would never leave their primary deepwater location. Everything was ready, according to plan. The armed militants had positioned themselves strategically around the ship. One more step was needed before his radical boss, Farad Asmaradov, made his demands to the United States president.

Those passengers still asleep were awakened by Captain Zoyatov's announcement. Most guests assumed it was the usual daily update on the upcoming port stop and events planned for the day.

But this announcement wasn't at all what they expected. A ship's drill would start in thirty minutes. The captain requested that all passengers who might already be out and about should return to their staterooms and prepare themselves to respond to their designated muster stations on the *Dream Spinner*.

Most passengers had yet to head out to breakfast, since the dining rooms began serving at eight o'clock. Some early birds had headed to the cafeteria but had been turned away by posted signs indicating a one-hour delay to sanitize the area. Still, nearly everyone hearing the announcement was surprised. It was a bit unusual to have a muster drill this late into a cruise.

Ace stuck his head through the doorway of the adjoining cabin. "Hey, kids. Up and at 'em. You heard the announcement. Get some clothes on, and get ready for the drill."

He was instantly rewarded with the children's sleepy objections, all of whom felt it was *way* too early to get up.

"What's going on, Matt?" Julie asked. "Why is this happening now? Is there something wrong on the boat we don't know about?"

"Don't worry. I'm not sure what the reason is, but it can't be too serious." He looked out the balcony window. Still heading east.

They all hustled to throw on some clothes, made quick bathroom visits, and prepared to leave their staterooms for the unexpected morning interruption.

When the three loud blasts from the ship's siren blared throughout the intercom system across the cruise ship, Ace's family, along with all the other passengers, began filing out of their cabins and proceeded to their designated muster assembly areas. They had been told to leave their life jackets in the rooms—a notification that comforted many who were wondering if there was a serious situation evolving. But curiously, they had been told to bring their passports.

The *Dream Spinner* was large enough that all passengers could assemble inside enclosed areas like the Centrum, the theaters, and the various lounges around the ship. Nobody would need to assemble outside in any of the open-air deck areas. This was going to be crucial to the Panja cell, and their ability to control the passengers during the early stages of the ship's takeover.

Ace managed to join up with his group in spite of the crowds funneling toward the Centrum. Flamer was not too happy with the disruption to his morning routine, nor was Colene. Cathy Black and Julie's parents were moving a bit slowly, their morning rest time taken from them. They found a vacant row near the side of the expansive room and took their seats. There was plenty of grumbling in the crowded theater.

When it was evident that the passengers were mustered, the doors to their assembly areas were closed. Staterooms were quickly scanned by the in-room motion detectors and any remaining folks ushered to their respective assembly locations.

A man dressed as a *Dream Spinner* officer walked onto the Centrum stage, microphone in hand.

"Ladies and gentlemen, thank you for your cooperation and participation. The captain believed it important to have an unscheduled drill to test the readiness of the crew and passengers. First and foremost, there is no problem or threat to our ship. All systems are functioning optimally." He smiled as he looked across the crowd.

"Please listen to our ship's captain, Hafez Zoyatov, who has a message for you all."

Zoyatov began, his voice coming through the loudspeakers in each of the muster assembly areas throughout the ship.

"As you know, there have been some cruise ship incidents in the past, around the world. One, you may recall, involved an Italian ship running aground. The crew there had not been prepared, and the results were tragic." He paused. "You can be assured that no Pleasure Cruise Lines vessels have ever been involved in that kind of mishap. But in the interest of safety, we ask for your cooperation during this drill. We take our responsibilities very seriously and will do everything we can to make your cruise safe and memorable. This test is similar to what is required now on all cruise ships." His last comment, of course, was a lie.

Zoyatov hoped that his explanation for the out-of-character muster drill, and his reassurance of their safety, would calm the passengers. From the murmuring going on in virtually every crowded room, it was apparent that things were far from calm. The guests had no real idea about what was coming next.

"Clearly, you have responded well to the test. I thank you again for your cooperation." He paused.

"You may also be wondering why you were asked to bring your passports. After the unscheduled stop in Cuba, we have been asked to reverify the status of all passengers. Please hand your passports to the crew members coming down the aisles. Your documents will be electronically scanned and quickly returned to you."

Flamer looked at Ace. "Buddy, I ain't liking this at all. This doesn't even make any sense. They know exactly who is on board based on the check they did of our passports when we stepped *onto* this ship, and from the passenger ID cruise cards we all carry. I'm not inclined to go along with this. I smell a rat!"

Ace nodded. He could hear the crowd reacting the same way. Most people were cooperating, but enough in the crowd were definitely not interested.

"Please, ladies and gentlemen. I insist on your cooperation. All passports must be collected," the ship's officer on the stage pleaded.

A couple men on the opposite side of the Centrum got up from their seats, passports in hand, and began pushing their way out of their row, intent on leaving the room.

The piercing rifle shot startled everyone and froze the two men in their tracks. A bearded man stepped onto the stage, shouldered his assault weapon and fired a second warning shot into the ceiling. The loud reports echoed throughout the room until they were drowned out by the screams of frightened, cowering passengers.

Ace had reacted instantly to the first shot, his warrior instinct kicking in. He pushed Julie down behind the seat in front of her and reached for his kids, doing the same to them. He motioned for his mother to get down behind the seat as well. Flamer, his wife, and the kids' grandparents followed suit. Many people screamed. The two men who had been intent on leaving immediately went back to their seats.

"Sit down and stay silent," commanded the armed militant as he tried to be heard over cries from the women and children. "Do as you were instructed, and no one will be harmed. Give your passports to the attendant at the end of your row. And pass your cell phones as well. Now!"

Nearly everyone in the room looked at each other. Most of them were slow to reach into their pocket or purse for their phones. Several passengers tried to tap out a message of distress, and some tried to make a call. None were successful, their phones reflecting a "no signal" indication, courtesy of Khalil's actions that had disabled all means of external communication from the ship.

"Do not try to use your phones!" screamed the armed man on the stage. "Pass them immediately to the crew collecting them."

Any hesitation passengers felt about releasing their passports and phones was instantly overcome by the sight of the assault rifle barrel sweeping across the crowd.

The items were quickly collected and carried out of the Centrum. A similar activity was happening in every other muster location on the *Dream Spinner*.

"Daddy, I'm scared," whimpered Claire to her father. Her voice trembled slightly, but she was holding it together. The boys just stared over the back of the seats in front of them at the man with the assault rifle.

"It'll be okay, honey," he replied. "We'll figure out what's happening soon."

When Julie looked at him, the terror in her eyes was something that Ace had never seen from her before. She knew that things were not going to be *anywhere* close to okay. Something awful was happening, and she was doing her best to keep it together, fearful about what was going to happen next.

Chapter 24

The United States National Security Agency plays a key role in providing the president intelligence and cybersecurity necessary to keep tabs on all manner of nefarious activity around the globe. It was not a coincidence that the Agency picked up a curious electronic emanation coming from the Central Caribbean. What made it *particularly* curious was that the transmission appeared to have been *meant* to be seen by the United States intelligence gatherers. The Viper had seen to that, facilitated by the actions of one particular Syrian on board the *Dream Spinner*.

Khalil had transmitted the message, knowing full well the keywords that were screened electronically, around the clock, from all signals and communication intelligence gathered by the top-secret agency. He also knew that the message he was sending would quickly end up in the hands of the most powerful man on the planet.

Within hours of the message interception, the president of the United States, David Foreman, was advised to tune in to a special closed-circuit broadcast meant only for him and his staff. They gathered early in the Situation Room of the White House. Foreman sat at the end of the large brown conference table, all twelve chairs around it occupied. His communications director in the Watch Room had prepared to receive the broadcast on the big screen mounted on the wall at the opposite end of the table from Foreman. The red light flashed on the input channel, and the image of the world's number one terrorist came to life.

"Is this a live broadcast?" the president whispered. "Find out where this is being transmitted from. We need to pinpoint his location."

"We're already on it, Mr. President," replied the NSA director, who had arrived minutes before the broadcast had begun.

"President Foreman, I am Farad Asmaradov, leader of the Panja cell. I know your intelligence staff knows who I am and what I represent."

The president looked at his national security director. The director nodded and motioned to an aide to pull up the file on Asmaradov.

"Right now, a cruise ship carrying over three thousand passengers, most of them American, is being held captive. It is being controlled by my Panja patriots. Currently, there is no danger to any American on board." He paused.

President Foreman motioned to his intelligence director, who had already begun making a secure call to try and validate what the terrorist leader claimed.

"Their safety will be assured as long as you comply with my demands. Within the next forty-eight hours, you are to release Victor Chernov from the American prison at Guantanamo Bay. Along with Chernov, you will release Ismail Soleimann and Zafir Heydar and turn them over to Cuban authorities."

"If for any reason they are not released within this timeline, the safety of your American citizens will not be assured. Also, if any attempt is made to assault the cruise ship, it will be sunk. You can believe that the ship is rigged with explosive charges that I will detonate if any offensive actions are taken by you. My Panja warriors are fully prepared to sacrifice their lives, and the lives of all those on the ship, if need be."

He paused again. "I will contact you in twenty-four hours. At that time, you will provide me with your assurance of the transaction."

The terrorist leader finished his prepared statements with a warning.

"If you try to approach the vessel, either from the air or from under the sea, you will regret it. As I have assured you, the passengers are currently safe. But that will not last if you take any actions to approach the ship. Their blood will be on your hands."

Asmaradov terminated the broadcast.

President Foreman looked stunned, but only for a moment.

"This is preposterous. I'll not have a terrorist dictate anything to me *or* this country. Get me everything we have on Asmaradov," he demanded.

Foreman also knew exactly who Victor Chernov was. He was in Gitmo, right where he needed to be.

"And I will not release Chernov. His capture two years ago was the biggest success we've had in a long time, eliminating one of the leading instigators of terror in the world."

The national security director had been passed a message.

"Sir, we've identified the cruise ship. It's the *Dream Spinner*, a Pleasure Cruise Lines vessel. It was sailing en route to Aruba yesterday. There haven't been any reported distress signals or any other indications that something is wrong on that ship."

"Where did its voyage begin?" The president was already thinking ahead about plans the U.S. had developed for just this kind of contingency.

"Mr. President, it began at Port Canaveral in Florida and had made a stop at their company's private island. Then, while en route to Aruba, they made an unusual course change, diverting to Santiago de Cuba. It was an unintended, unplanned stop that was made to offload some critically ill passengers."

"Get the JCS chairman in here ASAP," Foreman said, referring to the chairman of the Joint Chiefs of Staff, a four-star Navy admiral. "Also the SecDef."

"Right away, Mr. President. The chairman will be here in ten minutes. We gave him a call shortly before the video began."

"Sir, the *Dream Spinner*'s automatic identification system indicates it's approaching the harbor at Aruba. But we have verified that the ship is clearly not there."

"What are you saying? That, somehow, the system has been tampered with, perhaps some kind of spoofing to make the ship appear to be where it's not?"

"That may be one plausible explanation."

"We've got to pinpoint the ship's actual location. I know the Caribbean is a big place, but you can't just hide a ship the size of the *Dream Spinner* on the open seas!"

"Mr. President, we can have airborne assets begin a sector-by-sector sweep of the south-central Caribbean immediately. Additionally, we've got Navy ships that can also support the search. Finally, we can put out an immediate emergency broadcast to all vessels to report any sighting of the *Dream Spinner*."

Out of breath, the chairman hustled into the Situation Room and approached the president. He had been briefed via secure phone while on the way.

"Mr. President, I've already scrambled two of our maritime reconnaissance aircraft, our P-8s, to immediately begin a search for the ship. If it's floating, we'll find it. I can also have the Air Force and Space Force put some additional overhead assets in place to help the search—satellites, B-52s doing maritime patrols. And we'll use the Navy RQ-4 Global Hawk UAV to do a wide-area search," the JCS chairman stated. Foreman nodded at him.

"Great. I remember having been briefed some time ago on a contingency plan for this kind of situation. I believe it was mainly for freighters, or oil tankers or the like. I would like an updated brief in one hour that's tailored to the *Dream Spinner*. I know that doesn't give you much time, but every minute counts until we gain release of the ship and our American citizens."

"Mr. President, we do have contingency plans developed for a number of scenarios. Over the past two decades, it became clear that the maritime environment presented some unique challenges. Our specialized combat forces cut their teeth off the Somali coast years back in rescuing freighters that had been captured by pirates. Since then, our SEAL counterterrorism teams have trained on a wide number of potential missions ranging from securing anything that floats to oil rigs to coastal facilities. A cruise ship scenario was one of the anticipated missions."

THOMAS BELISLE

"So you're telling me that if I give the order, we can take back this ship?"

"Yes, Mr. President. We can handle it."

"Let's hear the contingency plan first, but have our counterterrorism forces ready to go."

"Yes, Mr. President. I'll take my leave and get my team ready to brief you."

Foreman turned to his staff. "I'd like a detailed brief on Asmaradov, Chernov, Soleimann, and Heydar immediately. I'm not inclined to release anyone at Gitmo. But we need to be prepared for all options."

The NSA director had anticipated the request and walked over with a file on Asmaradov. He handed it to President Foreman.

"Mr. President, Asmaradov, also known as the Viper, is one of the world's major terrorists. He operates out of the Central Asian region and has networks of militants linked to his radical Panja cell positioned throughout that area. They've been responsible for executing attacks not just in that region but also in both Central and Eastern Europe. This is the first time that he appears to have reached out to commit an atrocity near our shores."

Foreman paged through the file, staring at the grainy photographs that had been acquired of the Viper. He also looked at pictures of the destruction attributed to Asmaradov. He couldn't look at them for long while containing his growing anger.

"Sir, we believe there's reasonably solid information from a variety of human intelligence sources that Asmaradov has been operating in and out of Tajikistan for years. Our ambassador in Dushanbe has intel pulled in by the CIA chief of station there that seems to acknowledge that fact but hasn't been able to pin down an actual location for him. But the situation in that country has been unstable for years, as you know. It's also a breeding ground for crime, radical elements, and plenty of drug trade."

"Also, keep in mind that Russia has plenty of influence there. Tajikistan, along with five other Central Asian post-Soviet states, is linked to Putonov under their Collective Security Treaty Organization. While we don't officially acknowledge that treaty, we've got to tread carefully in Vladimir's backyard of power projection."

"I want our intelligence to zero in on Asmaradov. I know we have assets throughout that region. Press them to dig deep and get me something I can use."

The president left the Situation Room and headed back to the Oval Office.

His next action was going to be a phone call to the president of Tajikistan.

Chapter 25

Minutes later, the secure phone line connected President Foreman and the Tajik president, Ivan Mikolayev. General Dimitri Voitek was present with Mikolayev for the call.

After the obligatory introductory comments, Foreman discussed the *Dream Spinner*'s hostage crisis to the level of detail he had at the moment. And he discussed the terrorist, Farad Asmaradov, who he suspected had made Tajikistan his home.

Foreman tried to leverage some help at the most likely location where Asmaradov was hiding. He felt that, based on the steadily increasing levels of U.S. security assistance that had been provided to Tajikistan over the past years and the continued promise of more, he might get the support he needed to pinpoint the Viper.

At first, Mikolayev vehemently denied Foreman's assertion that the Viper was in Tajikistan. His chief of the military, Voitek, nodded his agreement. The Tajik leader insisted that there was no evidence supporting that assertion. Additionally, he assured Foreman that he would certainly know if the terrorist was within his borders. Voitek stayed silent—he was well aware of Asmaradov—but the terrorist was not an impediment to his personal wealth accumulation strategy. Mikolayev indicated that his military and police forces had been successful at reducing terrorism within his country, but, like everywhere else in Central Asia, the borders were porous and difficult to control.

"Look, Ivan. I need more from you than denial and your apparent reluctance to find Asmaradov and help me resolve this crisis. You have military forces that can pursue him. Hunt him down. I have given your Special Forces the specific kind of counterterrorism training needed to do exactly that. Not to mention the significant financial stimulation needed to fight the out-of-control illegal narcotics trade. The weapons and training I provided to your country, to you, to bolster your defense capability, to help secure your borders and protect your sovereignty, must stand for something."

"President Foreman, I will do what I can. But as you know, my country is as difficult to manage as my neighbor, Afghanistan. The rugged territory is a challenge to police and control. There are a thousand places where a man like Asmaradov can hide and operate, presuming he is *actually* in my country. And there are an equal number of radical and criminal elements that are willing to help him. My military is not large enough yet to bring the kind of order to Tajikistan that our people deserve."

There was silence on the line at both ends.

"Someday, we will be able to do what you ask. But it may be, in this case, best to comply with Asmaradov's demands to ensure the safety of the ship. Even if I could find him, from what you have told me, there is not sufficient time before he does something tragic, something horrible to the ship and passengers." He was silent for a moment.

"I believe Asmaradov will reciprocate with the release of the hostages if you meet his demands. After they are safe, we can pursue Asmaradov."

Foreman was about ready to blow a gasket. While Mikolayev couldn't see Foreman's face, it was turning a dark shade of red from anger over the Tajik president's recalcitrance to do pretty much anything.

"Ivan, there will be consequences for you and your country if this terrorist bastard harms a single American citizen. You've allowed him to operate freely in your country for years and done nothing. Now, I'm asking you—no, *telling* you—to do something!"

The Tajik president did not respond.

Foreman slammed the phone down, ending the call.

General Voitek kept his smile hidden from Mikolayev. The situation was proceeding as he and his Russian supporters had hoped. The general wanted the crisis to play itself out. If the Americans suffered a tragic blow by the hijacking, so be it. More turmoil linked to the Tajik president would make the U.S. think twice about their relationship with Mikolayev and discourage them from making any more inroads into Tajikistan.

President Foreman tried to weigh his remaining options. Unfortunately, the Tajik leader had not been much help. His country had been unable to control Farad Asmaradov for the past few years. Possibly because the terror cell leader had an incredibly large following, an effective network of protection, and perhaps some significant political leverage within Mikolayev's government.

It looked like the only way to handle the Viper was to come up with a viable plan. One that would protect American lives on the *Dream Spinner*. And one that would send a message that the United States would never acquiesce to terrorist demands.

President Foreman had faced his challenges in the first two years of his presidency. Earthquakes, devastating hurricanes, unprecedented flooding, and raging wildfires—all had required him to exercise the broad powers of the federal government to help the victims of these natural disasters. The worst man-induced challenge he had dealt with was facing down the portly young NK dictator with the unique hairstyle from launching projectiles and missiles into the waters surrounding the hermit kingdom. Threats to South Korea and Japan were not taken lightly. After intelligence indicated that North Korea had effectively demonstrated the ability to send an intercontinental ballistic missile far enough to reach the United States, Foreman had used his military and political influence, and the promise of economic support, to stem the launches.

This situation was different. Not since 9/11 had Americans in this number been threatened with potential death by terrorists. Foreman wasn't about to let this be *his* 9/11.

The president of the United States sat in the Situation Room, contemplating the contingency plan to rescue the ship's hostages. It was bold, and it relied predominantly on the use of Navy assets to pull it off. And, of course, some advanced technology that was suitable for just this kind of situation.

There were risks to the passengers that would have to be minimized to the extent possible. But in the end, if the order was given to assault the ship, then the fog of combat and ever-changing dynamics of the minute-by-minute execution sometimes resulted in unintended casualties. Foreman understood that there were no guarantees.

Now, a frustrated American president considered the use of his military forces. They would be made ready to execute within the next thirty-six hours. He believed his actions were necessary—no, essential—to rescue the passengers. That was, presuming the ship was located and he could have all the pieces in place to take back the hijacked vessel before Asmaradov's time limit expired.

"Tell me more about these terrorists in custody at Gitmo," directed Foreman.

"Yes, Mr. President," the NSA director responded. "The three men are some pretty bad guys. Victor Chernov, as you know, was captured two years ago in a raid our Navy SEALs conducted in Baku, Azerbaijan. They hit the purported safe house where Chernov was staying, killed most of the militants who tried to defend their boss, and finally grabbed him. He was exfiltrated through Turkey and whisked to our interrogation facility in Gitmo. He's been there ever since. With his capture, the worldwide terror network that he controlled was brought to a standstill. As a result, there haven't been any attacks on Americans, or for that matter, anyone else, attributed to him or his particular cause."

"Soleimann and Heydar aren't much better. After we grabbed Chernov, the rats started running scared. They made some mistakes in their haste to survive, and our intel sources found them both. We snatched them before they knew what was happening. Heydar was the money man for Chernov. Soleimann was the guy responsible for designing the nasty explosive bombs that took so many lives. Both of these guys have been at Gitmo for over a year."

"But what's the connection to Asmaradov? These guys were tied to a completely different radical cell operating out of Afghanistan years ago. Why is Asmaradov so interested in them?"

"My guess is that the Viper knows the benefit they can bring to his Panja cell and his radical causes," replied the national security director.

"Okay, got it. I surely don't want these three released. But we should go through the motions of preparing to let these scumbags out of jail. We need Asmaradov to believe we're complying with his demands. When we link up with him in twenty-four hours, I want to at *least* be able to reassure him that we value our American citizens more than these prisoners."

"Mr. President, getting our forces in place in the south-central Caribbean is going to take some time. We'll pull out the stops to be ready before the deadline. But it's going to be close," the chairman of the JCS stated.

Foreman countered, "Then we've got to stall a bit, if possible, to ensure our forces are ready to take back that ship." He paused. "It's got to be plausible. Something that Asmaradov will believe. Something that he could verify if he had to. I don't want that bastard to get the feeling that we're up to something and respond by executing passengers."

Chapter 26

Aboard the *Dream Spinner*, things were going downhill fast. Three hours had elapsed since the passengers had been herded into their muster areas, previously known as entertainment centers and now known as their prison cells. No matter which area the vacationers were trapped in, all were terrified about what was happening. Many needed to use the bathrooms and had to be escorted by collaborating crew members. None had eaten anything, and hunger sometimes made people do stupid things.

The militant group ordered every cabin to be searched. All laptops, iPads or similar devices were to be collected. Safes in the closets were opened and checked for communication devices, which were confiscated if found.

Khalil Atta was busy reaffirming the blocks he'd placed in all communication nodes. Any means of voice or digital transmission would fail. It wouldn't matter what was used or where on the boat an attempt might be made to communicate any information, any requests for help. The system was dead. Controlled by him and him alone. Khalil knew that he had to prevent any information, like the location of the terrorists on board and the type of weapons they carried, from reaching the Americans. That kind of information would be extremely valuable and would most assuredly be used in any planned assault to free the ship.

The central bank of integrated electronics, the system that controlled the key ship functions, had already been compromised by Khalil. Only he, the chief engineer, and Captain Zoyatov could control the vessel from any of their respective locations. And only

Khalil could override both of them. If circumstances required it, he could singularly control the *Dream Spinner*.

At this point, the ship was ready for Asmaradov to execute his plan—the Viper's forces were in place, ready to defend the ship, *or scuttle it.*

Khalil opened the door to the communications room, and the men who had collected the passports and phones came in.

"Put the phones in that large box," he said, pointing to the corner. "Separate the American passports from the international passports. Place the U.S. passports over here."

The two men began sorting through the piles of documents. About two-thirds were American. Blue passports. Close to two thousand.

"Separate men and women, and children under sixteen years of age. I want to see the men," Khalil said. "Check birthdays. Any men over sixty years old, throw back into the box with the women and children." He then told them to sort the remaining documents alphabetically.

Once that had been done, Khalil pulled up the program on the ship's computer that had the scanned information for all passengers on board. He had created it to collate the passengers by age. He further culled all passengers who had used a military discount for their fare and passengers who had used a military title on their documents, either retired or still serving. This category of passengers would be the troublemakers. They were the ones most likely to resist, those who might foolishly try to stop the inevitable. They were the ones that needed to be dealt with *before* they became a problem.

Khalil quickly cross-checked the electronic files against the actual passports. He flipped the pages, looking at the stamps of entry, the visas. He worked alphabetically through the names. He suddenly stopped. He stared at the electronic file, and then the dark blue passport. The name was Matthew Thomas Black. A familiar face on the passport picture stared back at him.

Can this be? He focused on the face. The man had aged a few years, but it was the same man. It was Captain Matt Black! The fighter pilot, the son of the man who had murdered his father, his family, years before.

Khalil sat back in his chair. He was stunned, then surprised at his own reaction. He was calm. Time had suppressed his feelings, his hatred for this man. He continued to stare at the passport photo. *What are the chances?* Then he smiled to himself. *How perfect is this?* After all these years, he would finish the job he had started—one he had previously failed at completing. Matt Black would never leave the *Dream Spinner* alive.

He pulled up the ship's electronic documents for his nemesis. He noted that Matt's wife and three kids were traveling with him. He made a note of their cabin numbers. Also linked to his reservation were other names—Cathy Black, and Julie's parents. Khalil smiled even more broadly. He forgot for a few moments why he was on the *Dream Spinner*.

His mission had nothing to do with exacting revenge. It had everything to do with propagating causes he believed in. It had to do with applying the skills he had been blessed with, guided by the hand of Allah. He had an obligation to Asmaradov, a moral contract, to use his talent to remove the stain made by Western culture.

In the case of the *Dream Spinner*, it was to support a cause funded and propagated by Moscow. He really didn't care for the Slavic people, the Russians. Or necessarily believe in the cause they pursued in Tajikistan. They were, in the end, just another tool to be used in his quest to wreak as much havoc and death on the Americans as possible.

Khalil felt a hand on his shoulder. Kelly had joined him in the communications center. She looked down at the passport he was holding tightly in his hand. The passport with the face of Matt Black imprinted on it. She did not know who the American was, whether he was a person of significance, or perhaps a threat.

"Who is this man? Do you recognize him?"

"Yes. He is one who has a special meaning to me." He briefly told her about what had transpired years before. She listened as he told her of the unbelievable chance encounter with the girl's father—and their history. She thought about the astronomical odds that Khalil would meet the one man he hated most—on this ship! The man who had foiled the entire plan to advance Ayatollah Batani's Caliphate. The son of the man who had slaughtered his family. She understood the hatred Khalil carried. She also knew that in the end, the man would die. Along with his daughter. And the rest of his family. And nearly everyone else on board the *Dream Spinner*. She nodded and understood that there was deep-seated hatred in Khalil for this man.

Nonetheless, she had to keep Khalil focused.

"Are you finished identifying all of the men who pose a threat to our mission?" She looked into his eyes. "You can deal with this other American at the appropriate time."

He nodded his understanding. "Yes, I'm just about finished. Five more minutes." *I'll definitely deal with Ace Black at the appropriate time—a time of my choosing.*

Chapter 27

The United States Marine Corps King Air UC-12W utility aircraft was on its way home from a mission in Bogota, Colombia, and was proceeding to an interim stop in San Juan, Puerto Rico. It had gone to the South American country to deliver a diplomatic pouch to the American consulate and to provide a briefing on joint counterdrug operations to the Ministry of National Defense.

The trip across the Caribbean was nearly a six-hour flight, not an issue for an aircraft configured for extended range. The aircrew had been settling in for the long flight across a broad expanse of the Caribbean, first heading north, well inside the Colombian border with Venezuela. They were careful, since nothing would delight the Venezuelan dictator more than to bring down an American aircraft that had violated his territory. There was enough unrest near and across the border into Colombia that the crew wasn't taking any chances. In the event that they were targeted, the aircraft countermeasures system had been armed. Once they cleared the South American landmass, they turned northeast toward San Juan.

The crew was aware of the NOTAM, the abbreviation for "Notice to Airmen," to be on the lookout for the *Dream Spinner*. The three-man crew was surprised to hear of the hijacked cruise liner. The young captain piloting the aircraft decided to take a quick look en route—while staying within the safe limits of his fuel load—to help in any way he could with the effort to locate the ship.

The King Air had been equipped with the newest small-scale inverse synthetic aperture radar—an advanced capability that the Marines had added to enhance their combat mission suite. It provided the small turboprop a means to produce high-resolution surface images.

The pilot had plotted a slight course change to take him a bit further east over the deep water of the Central Caribbean. The slight course adjustment might provide the best chance to sight the captive vessel.

"Got some radar hits off our nose. One is pretty large. Let's take a look," the copilot announced.

The twin-engine turboprop aircraft descended to about one thousand feet as it closed on the large radar return.

"Look, that appears to be a cruise ship about five miles out, about our three o'clock position."

The aircraft banked, putting itself on a heading straight toward the vessel. It approached within a mile and began gradually descending.

On board the *Dream Spinner*, a Tajik militant standing on the fantail deck had acquired the heat signature of the small aircraft on his Strela-3 missile launcher. The weapon system was a potent threat to low-flying aircraft. He depressed the trigger.

Suddenly, the copilot shouted a warning.

"Holy shit, is that a missile tracking toward us from that ship?" He saw the smoke plume from the missile as it streaked upward from the sea surface.

"We've been targeted," shouted the pilot. "Let's get the hell out of here."

The experienced Marine Corps aviator immediately began tactical evasive maneuvers to depart the potential kill zone. As the aircraft banked away from the stern of the *Dream Spinner*, the deadly missile raced toward it, adjusting its track to the pilot's maneuvers.

"Countermeasures, now," shouted the pilot. He didn't need to direct it as the aircraft system had sensed the incoming missile and expelled chaff and flares. The aircraft aggressively maneuvered to escape, approaching the design limits of its capability.

The infrared heat-seeking missile closed quickly on the plane. As it zeroed in on the hot engine nacelle, the high-explosive blast fragmentation warhead detonated near the right wing, tearing it off.

"Mayday, mayday!" the pilot shouted over his radio as he struggled to control the non-flyable aircraft. Flames from the ignited fuel in the ruptured wing tank engulfed the critically damaged plane as it began falling from the sky, gyrating crazily, its aerodynamic shape destroyed. The pilot looked quickly at his copilot, slumped over the useless controls. The right cockpit window had been blown apart, and the blast fragments from the warhead had apparently killed the copilot instantly.

The Marine Corps aviator fought valiantly to control his stricken bird, but his efforts were futile. His aircraft spiraled down toward the water and violently impacted the dark sea with all on board.

Chapter 28

"Mr. President, we just received a report of a Marine Corps aircraft accident in the Caribbean. It looks like it was hit by hostile fire and went down. We believe it may have been taken down by a shoulder-fired missile, possibly from the *Dream Spinner*. Our airborne sensors picked up a missile launch from a lone vessel in the southern Caribbean, in an area referred to as the Venezuela Basin. That's where the aircraft went down. The ship appears to be about two hundred miles from the closest landmass, off the northeastern coast of South America—due north of Caracas, Venezuela."

"Can we confirm it's the *Dream Spinner*?" President Foreman asked his JCS chairman.

"We are confirming it now. The imagery we have indicates it's a cruise ship. It appears to be operating in a random track pattern."

"So, you're telling me that it's not headed to any particular location?"

"It doesn't appear so, Mr. President. But it's too early to tell. The seemingly random course changes aren't really telling us anything. If it is the *Dream Spinner*, it may be part of Asmaradov's plan to make it more difficult for us to plan any kind of assault."

Foreman didn't care much for that answer.

"Sir, we just got confirmation—it *is* the *Dream Spinner*," replied the JCS chairman.

Foreman stared down at the table, his hands folded.

"Do we know if there were any survivors from the crash?"

"We've dispatched search-and-rescue assets to the area. Hopefully, we'll spot something."

"Damn it," he shouted at the admiral and staff in general. "I'm not sure what Asmaradov will do when he finds out his guys shot down an aircraft. He may think we're getting too close to the ship, and *that* may prompt him to do something worse, like kill a bunch of passengers just to make a point." The president was about ready to boil over.

"If it's true the missile was fired from the cruise ship, who knows what other potent weapons capability Asmaradov put on it. I've gotta believe that he has the means to destroy the *Dream Spinner*—and likely put up a hell of a fight when we execute our assault to take back the ship."

His staff nodded their agreement.

"I don't want any of our assets getting close to the ship until I give the word. For now, it looks like we know the location of the *Dream Spinner*. Meanwhile, keep everyone from flying anywhere near that vessel. But I want the assault plans on the front burner, ready to execute on my order."

"Yes, sir, Mr. President," the senior military advisor responded.

"How is the preparation going at Gitmo for release of the terrorist bastards?" asked Foreman.

"Mr. President. Are we prepared to start succumbing to terrorist demands, to negotiate with them—trade lives for lives? We don't really have any assurance that Asmaradov will actually release the ship once we free the prisoners at Gitmo." The chairman of the Joint Chiefs clearly wanted to execute the military option and get the situation under his control and not leave control in the hands of the Viper.

"It's a shitty situation to be in, and it's a gamble either way. There's no absolute assurance that our assault will be successful, or prevent loss of any innocent lives on that boat. We don't have eyes on that ship to tell us how many militants there are, where they're positioned, how well armed they are, and how they may have rigged the *Dream Spinner* to sink it if it comes to that." Foreman glanced around the room, looking for feedback from his staff. Only silence.

He continued. "We can insist on specific terms for the Gitmo prisoner release, an assurance that the militants holding the *Dream Spinner* are removed from the ship concurrent with the three terrorists being released in Cuba."

"We should be ready to put that on the table during Asmaradov's next communication with us. We've got another twelve hours before we link back up with him, presuming he keeps to the timeline for his demands," said the NSA director.

He continued. "Sir, on the comment about having eyes on the *Dream Spinner* to help us, we've checked the manifest. One of our CIA operatives is actually on the ship, taking what she probably hoped would be a well-deserved vacation. Her name is Martha Cook. I also know there are a number of active-duty military on board as well. We've got to figure out a way to use these potential assets to our advantage—and quickly." He paused. "That could make the difference between success or failure."

"Right. Get on it."

The chairman then provided an update on the readiness of the assault forces preparing for the worst-case scenario. A hostage rescue force had been rapidly assembled and would be airlifted to a Navy aircraft carrier.

"Mr. President. We've requested, through diplomatic channels and some key industry partners, the builder's blueprints and any modifications that might have been done to the *Dream Spinner*. We should have them shortly and can factor that into the operational plans for our upcoming mission. The SEALs will definitely appreciate getting that kind of detailed data to adjust their tactical operation."

"Great. Thanks for getting in front of that," Foreman responded to the chairman.

The USS *John F. Kennedy*, CVN-79, had been off the Virginia coast participating in a Composite Training Unit Exercise, a standard preparation for their upcoming deployment. Part of the Atlantic Fleet, the aircraft carrier had been conducting operations with a host of *Arleigh Burke*–class guided-missile destroyers up and down the East Coast when it had gotten the call to proceed posthaste to Jacksonville, Florida.

In Virginia Beach, at Joint Expeditionary Base Little Creek–Fort Story, the SEAL counterterrorism team had been directed to immediately proceed to the airfield, where they would board a CV-22 Osprey aircraft that would airlift them to the USS *John F. Kennedy*.

Once the SEALs were on board the nuclear-powered carrier with their gear, the ship intended to move at full speed toward Puerto Rico with its escort ships, then down past the U.S. Virgin Islands. It would take up a position about thirty miles to the north of the *Dream Spinner*'s general position. A nuclear attack submarine was also moving toward the area to support the upcoming mission.

The USS *Grayback III (SSGN-5326)* was third in the line of submarines that carried the *Grayback* name. The first had performed magnificently during World War II, sinking a number of enemy ships before it had met the same fate and been sunk itself. The *Grayback II* was its successor and had been in operational status until its decommissioning in 1984, then used as a target and sunk. The *Grayback III* was the newest nuclear-powered submarine specifically designed to support special operations forces, especially the Navy SEAL teams.

"How long before the SEALs could mount an assault?" asked the president.

"Sir, we'll have all the resources we need in place within twenty-four hours. Then, it will just take the execute order from you." The chairman of the JCS paused. "The SEAL team could reach the *Dream Spinner* shortly after that."

Foreman nodded his head in acknowledgment and turned to his National Security Agency director.

"Is there anything we can do to gain some extra time from Asmaradov? That's cutting it awful close to the deadline for prisoner release." He looked around the room at the serious faces of his staff.

"We've got to plan for the unexpected. This shithead Asmaradov is apt to do just about anything if he suspects we aren't being straight with him on his demands."

Foreman looked down at the pictures of the three Gitmo terrorists on his conference table, and then at the JCS chairman. He continued.

"I also presume that your SEALs would dearly appreciate the cover of darkness to initiate the assault. That pushes the timeline right up to the stops of the forty-eight-hour deadline."

"I've got an idea that might work," the NSA director offered. "There are no communications coming out of Gitmo from any of the captives. What if we feign an infectious illness on our number one bad guy, Chernov? Indicate to Asmaradov that Chernov caught it from a recent ISIS inductee who was brought to Gitmo. We can tell Asmaradov that Chernov is transitioning off a ventilator within the next couple of days and can then be moved."

"That might work. But whatever we throw at Asmaradov, it's got to be good enough that he believes it. If he suspects we're throwing bullshit his way to stall, there's no telling what he'll do," said Foreman. "We still suspect that the Viper is not on the cruise ship but still in his Tajik hideaway, right?"

Nods of concurrence across the conference table.

"If he's not on the *Dream Spinner*, he might just consider sacrificing the ship and his 'martyrs' for his cause. He might just view the *Dream Spinner*'s destruction as a massive blow to the United States. Hell, he might be planning to destroy the ship *regardless* of the prisoner release."

Chapter 29

O ver the course of just a few hours, the *Dream Spinner* had transitioned from a pleasure cruise ship loaded with raucous vacationers to a virtual prison, its passengers now held captive by a violent Central Asian terrorist cell.

The women, children, elderly and disabled passengers were being released by their captives and ordered back to their staterooms, escorted by crew members. The men remained secured in the muster areas under armed guard.

When Ace Black had heard Jack's name called, he'd breathed a sigh of relief. Apparently, Julie's father had met some kind of threshold for age and been granted release back to his stateroom. The captive men in the Centrum now numbered about two hundred. Ace thought that nearly all of those remaining appeared to be between about twenty and sixty years old.

He and Flamer had shifted in their seats to move next to each other as the older men had passed in front of them to head out of the room.

"What the heck do you think is happening here," Flamer whispered to Ace.

"Well, it's clear that whoever is holding this ship is focusing on keeping able-bodied men in this room. I suspect it's happening the same in the other muster stations. There could be a few reasons for that. The biggest one I can think of is that we pose some kind of threat to this bunch of terrorists. If they keep us captive in these muster areas, they likely believe they can control us better and reduce any chance we might try to oppose them."

"I'm not sure what kind of threat *you're* thinking about," noted Flamer. "*They* have the weapons. *We* don't!"

"Regardless of that, we greatly outnumber them. At some point, we could rush them, maybe overpower them, grab their weapons. Of course, there would be some casualties. And I'm not certain we could ever get the opportunity to talk it up between the fittest guys in here and gain their support to do something like that. But who knows. That might be the best and *only* option at some point." He paused.

"I suspect they're going to be careful with how they control us—maybe keep us from grouping together." Ace had a very serious look on his face.

"Flamer, we've got to figure out what the real agenda is on this ship. Once we know that, we can decide what we're going to do about it. But whatever the purpose of all of this is, it's not good, and I believe it's going to get pretty nasty before it gets better."

"I just hope this isn't a one-way cruise—I paid for a round trip," Flamer said, trying to lighten the tension. "Haven't heard of a cruise ship takeover before, at least not for a long time. And *that* one did not end well, if my memory serves me."

"Yeah. Keep the faith, brother. I don't believe any of the past ship hijackings resulted in many casualties. Most involved a few unfortunate deaths, but not much more."

"But that was before 9/11. The era of mass casualties began when it was brought over to our country, up close and personal. Who knows what the real purpose of this takeover is? I'm not crazy about a scenario like September 11, 2001, if that's where this is heading."

"You could be right, Flamer. My guess is there are quite a few of these armed dudes on board. How else could they handle all the muster stations? Also, I've gotta believe that some of the ship's crew are involved. It looks like they're helping out, escorting the passengers to the cabins, picking up our phones and passports. But they might be under threat, just like the rest of us."

He thought about how a hijacking like this could be pulled off.

"They've got to have some experienced senior help to run this ship. Maybe the captain. Probably a few other key positions. They would have to understand the ship's operations. Also, it would be difficult to control a vessel of this size without thirty or forty armed guys. Remember, we've got over three thousand passengers and nine hundred or so crew members on board—and a hell of a lot of territory covering fourteen decks. It would take a lot of people to effectively control the *Dream Spinner*."

Ace thought for a few moments, wondering about how the cruise had started. "I'm guessing that this was planned some time ago. Too many weird things were popping up. I don't know if you noticed, but our welcome package shows a picture of a different captain than the one we have. We saw three officers coming aboard just before departure in Port Canaveral. And then there was the diversion to Cuba to offload passengers who suddenly, overnight, became violently ill. But aside from those passengers, nobody else is sick. And why Cuba? We could have turned around and stopped in Miami. Cuba isn't even currently open to tourists as far as I know. That's gotta be where these terrorists got on board, along with their weapons."

Flamer agreed with his buddy as he carefully watched the armed militant on the stage.

"Also, some of the odd actions by crew members raised a bit of a red flag with me. Like the cute omelet cooker who also served drinks to us in the upper deck bar. She asked *way* too many questions that didn't line up with what you'd expect from crew members. She pressed me on being in the military. Questioned what I did there."

Flamer responded, "I don't know about Aleksandra. She just looked like a pretty hot bar wench to me." He smiled.

"And I swear I overheard what sounded like a Central Asian language, maybe even some Russian being spoken by the crew. But that may not be totally out of the ordinary, considering the number of countries the crew members come from."

He thought about what he was going to say next. "You want to know something else that's really weird? When we were pounding down Scotch and smoking our stogies in the bar the other night, I swear I saw a dude that I believed I'd never see again. You remember that traitor, Khalil Ruffa?"

Flamer had been listening intently, silently as Ace rambled on, but when he mentioned Khalil, he snapped his head toward his buddy.

"What?" he exclaimed a bit too loudly.

"Quiet down. I likely imagined it was him. He looked a bit different. Had long hair and a beard. But the distinctiveness of his face sure hit home. He was talking with another crew member. But think about it. If it truly *was* him, this whole mess we're in is starting to add up. Interesting also that all of a sudden, there's no internet, no email or voice connectivity. Nothing works. That smells a lot like the kind of stuff Khalil could control." He paused. "If he could hack into the F-22 Raptor, this should be a piece of cake for him."

"If this was planned like you're saying, then we are in a world of hurt," commented Flamer.

"By now, I gotta also hope that our country knows some bad shit is going down on this cruise ship. It doesn't take long for bad news to spread. If our president knows, hopefully he's already formulating plans to end this."

Ace thought about that for a moment. Might there be some demands being made already by some lunatic terrorist leader? Does Cuba play into this at all? It's got to all be connected, somehow.

"At least our wives and kids got released back to the staterooms. That should reduce the level of worry somewhat. But I'm sure they'll stress out about those of us who didn't get released," Ace commented.

"Sooner or later, I suspect that these gunmen are going to tell us something about what's going to happen next," Flamer added.

"You, on the side!" shouted the armed man on the stage. "No talking!"

He swung his weapon toward Ace and Flamer and took aim. The Centrum grew very quiet.

Asmaradov believed he had planned for every contingency. One of the more difficult aspects of taking over a ship as large as the *Dream Spinner* was controlling the large crew. He had figured out a reasonably logical way to control the passengers. Separate the men from their families. Keep the men confined in just a few central locations, under guard. Both the families and the captive men had been warned that any attempt to leave their rooms or muster areas would result in them being shot.

There clearly were never going to be enough militants to guard a massive crew that had literally hundreds of jobs aboard the *Dream Spinner*. They could be a formidable problem if they chose to take back their ship. Asmaradov's solution was simple. Get rid of their jobs and confine nearly all the crew to their cabins. The same rules applied. You leave your room, you get shot.

But there was one category of crew that needed to keep working. The kitchen staff and those who supported them, the provisioning staff. They could be managed by the radical Panja warriors. It was much easier to control cooks and servers in the kitchen and dining areas, and the small number of provisioning workers on Deck 2, than the entire crew.

The meal variety and quality changed as well. At this point, the militants holding the ship were only interested in basic meals sufficient to keep their captives alive. Passengers would be escorted in multiple shifts to the dining areas, their time to consume their meals extremely limited. The crew members would have their food delivered on large carts to a central area on their decks. They would be supervised, under armed guard, as they exited their rooms, got their food, and went back inside.

For now, Asmaradov had the control he desired—and the compliance of the *Dream Spinner* passengers and crew. So far, threats made by the militants were enough. Consequently, the *Dream Spinner* looked much like a ghost ship. All entertainment areas, specialty restaurants, the casino, fitness center, library, pools, laundry—literally everything was shut down. Hallways were empty, as were the shops and central meeting areas. Grand pianos were silent.

The fearful guests did their best to obey their captors, knowing that entry into any of the now-desolate areas made them an easy target for a bullet.

None of the passengers had eaten since they had been herded first into the muster areas, and then most of them into their staterooms. The militants began the ritual that would be replicated for the next few days. Passengers in staterooms were escorted in groups to the main dining rooms on Decks 4 and 5. The men in the muster stations were escorted similarly to the massive cafeteria on Deck 10. There was no chance that either group would intermingle. The seemingly forced march to eat was always going to be under armed guard and tightly controlled.

As the day drew to a close, a few passengers confined in the Centrum had other thoughts—faith that a hostage rescue plan was being formulated. And what they needed to do themselves to end the crisis.

Chapter 30

Day 6

The best of plans sometimes fail for odd reasons. There is an old adage—*anything that can go wrong will go wrong*. Off the coast of Florida, the Navy aircraft carrier USS *John F. Kennedy* had intended to move quickly in the direction of the *Dream Spinner* within hours of the president's order. That didn't happen.

The carrier experienced a minor technical issue in one of the two nuclear reactors that powered the massive ship. There was no real danger to the crew, but the problem had to be resolved before beginning the rescue mission. As a result, valuable time was lost, putting at risk the ability of an assault to take place before the terrorist deadline was met.

Once the technical problem had been remedied, the carrier, designated Strike Group 8, proceeded with its complement of escorts—one cruiser and three destroyers—to their intended position in the Central Caribbean. The USS *Bainbridge*, DDG-96, one of the guided-missile destroyers, would have a particularly important role in the hostage rescue to come. At their current rate of speed, the strike group would not be in the *Dream Spinner*'s area until shortly *after* the time expired to meet Asmaradov's demands.

Captain Kenneth Bell had been the commanding officer aboard the USS *John F. Kennedy* for almost two years. He had cut his teeth in a variety of jobs throughout his career, rose in rank, and eventually captured one of the most prestigious positions a Navy officer can get. He had seen his share of action in his twenty-three-year career. Most recently, he had supported combat operations in the battle with Iran in 2018. But this was his first cruise ship hostage recovery operation.

The current mission didn't necessarily need the level of firepower inherent in the massive aircraft carrier and its escort ships. The *Kennedy* was a powerful floating array of advanced weapons capability, hosting over eighty combat aircraft, a massive number of Sea Sparrow surface-to-air missiles and smaller infrared homing antiaircraft missiles, the MK-15 Phalanx close-in weapon system, and M2 .50 caliber machine guns.

Bell had already recovered the CV-22 Osprey on deck and brought on board the SEAL counterterrorism team flown in from Virginia Beach. The augmented platoon of SEALs led by two officers and one master chief had already begun preparing for the assault they knew was coming. Once they arrived at their intended position in the south-central Caribbean, an additional vessel would join them.

The USS *Grayback III* had finished a recent mission off the coast of Africa and was back in port. It was quickly configured with two Shallow Water Combat Submersibles (SWCS), a type of SEAL swimmer delivery vehicle (SDV). In essence, the SDVs were small specially equipped submarines that were secured in two dry deck shelters on the rear deck of the *Grayback III* and used to covertly move the frogmen silently through the water toward their target.

The carrier represented a formidable opponent to any challenger. Along with the *Bainbridge* and *Grayback III*, they were enough to overcome any surprises that Asmaradov might have waiting on the *Dream Spinner*, and certainly enough to handle the terrorists on board.

President Foreman was not a nervous man. A person doesn't get elected to lead the free world by giving off vibes that make people wonder about what he'll do under pressure. But this situation was a bit different. It was unpredictable in terms of potential outcomes. And if he guessed wrong, then many lives were at stake.

He had been briefed about the aircraft carrier's maintenance problem that kept it from immediately departing from Jacksonville and was not at all pleased. He hoped it would be in position to support a rescue operation before the deadline he had been given by the terrorist leader. It was going to be very close. The delaying action with Asmaradov was the answer.

"Explain to me again how we can buy more time? How is this action going to play out?"

"Mr. President, we've isolated Chernov in the hospital area at Gitmo. He's been heavily sedated, and our makeup guys have been at work doctoring his appearance to make him look pale and feverish. We have put in place some medical equipment that will display false readings, intended to mimic what a critically ill patient might display." He paused.

"When we pull up the video for your call with Asmaradov, we should be able to give him a close-up look at his 'sick' counterpart. We think it will convince him that we need at least another thirty-six hours to stabilize the patient for transport out of Gitmo. We'll try to convince Asmaradov that Chernov's life is at risk if we move him earlier."

"We don't think Asmaradov will insist on the release of the other two before Chernov. But if he does, we can live with that. If Asmaradov buys the ruse, it will give us some time to get our forces in place to support the rescue."

"I'm not too happy with the carrier's delay. The one time I needed a rapid response, I didn't get it. Now, we've got to get that fuckin' terrorist to agree to the added time. If he balks at it, we may have a real tragedy unfold on board that cruise ship."

"Yes, sir, but the delay did buy us some time to get the SEALs moved from the carrier to the SDVs on the *Grayback III*," the JCS chairman replied. "We'll be ready when it's time to execute."

Chapter 31

t had been a long night on the *Dream Spinner*, especially for the men held captive in the muster areas. Any chances for a decent slumber while in the Centrum were diminished by the upright auditorium chairs and bright overhead lights beaming down on the now very tired men.

When dawn broke on the sixth day of the cruise, there appeared to be some relief regarding the feeding schedule. The first day of captivity, the men were fed only twice. But the militant group believed that trapped, hungry men were desperate men, and less likely to be controlled. Three meals a day became the standard. They began escorting them in small groups to the buffet lines in the Deck 10 dining area.

The men were only allowed ten minutes to get their food and eat it. Then, the armed guards escorted them back to the confinement areas. The captive men never saw their loved ones and worried about their families in spite of the militants' insistence that they were safe.

"My back is killing me, Ace. I can't deal with sleeping upright in a chair. This shit has gotta end soon."

"Hey, buddy, be careful what you wish for. Right now, we're not really being harmed, and it doesn't appear that any of the passengers they released to the staterooms have been harmed either. But I'm betting that something has to change the scenario in the next day or so. There has to be a point to the ship's takeover. There must be some demands being made."

"Yeah, but I sure would like to know how my wife is doing. I'm betting you've got the same concerns, Ace."

"You're not kidding about that. But I know that Julie is a pretty capable, resourceful woman. There's not much that she can't handle, although nobody expected *this* kind of situation. I gotta believe she's keeping everything under control. Especially keeping the kids calm, or at least trying her best."

"Do you think these people are going to let us get back to our families at some point?"

"Don't know. I suspect we're not going anywhere until some significant event plays out. Maybe it'll be linked to some set of demands the damn terrorists are after. If they think they're going to get what they want, that might be the trigger event to release us."

"I hope you're right. But I'm a bit leery about you using the term 'trigger event' when some bearded terrorist has his finger on the trigger of a weapon pointed right at us. But you're right. Who the hell knows what that event might really be?"

"You know, I've not seen the dudes guarding us ever do a count of how many passengers there are in the Centrum. And they haven't insisted we group together, which would make it much easier to notice if someone managed to slip out of here."

"Ace! Are you out of your fuckin' mind? What are you thinking? That there might be a way to sneak out of here? How's that going to work? The lights are on constantly. The two guards seem to be watching us all pretty closely, but clearly, maybe not all the time. Even if you could get out of here, then what?"

"You mean when *we* get out of here," replied Ace.

Flamer just stared back at him in disbelief.

Ace went on. "I'm not yet sure what the plan is when we make a break for it. But I don't really want to leave all the decisions up to these radicals. You know, the advantage goes to the one who takes the offensive *first*, especially if it's a surprise, and if it can be done quietly—and effectively."

Their whispering was interrupted by the sound of a guard approaching them from the rear. He had a passport in his hand and was clearly looking for one particular individual.

"You." He pointed his finger at Ace and compared the passport photo to the man sitting before him. "Stand up. Come with me."

Ace was going to object when he saw the guard on the stage again leveling a weapon in his direction. Flamer was about to say something, but Ace waved him off.

"I'll be back."

He proceeded with his armed escort to the back of the Centrum and out the rear door. He was led through the photo gallery, past some small shops, and into the library, then ordered to sit down. The guard took up a position by the door, his weapon at the ready.

Moments later, a figure walked through the library entrance. Standing in front of Ace was the bearded man he had seen at the cigar and whiskey bar. It was Khalil. The Syrian stared at Ace, waiting for some acknowledgment, some measure of recognition from his past adversary.

Ace didn't get up. He thought about what to say. "I heard you were dead," he said with no emotion but clearly expressing his disappointment.

Khalil continued to stare at him. "I am far from dead. You Americans tried your best to kill me, and you failed. Now, I have returned to deliver a special message to all of you."

Ace looked closely at his old nemesis. He could see the hatred in his eyes. He wondered about the Syrian's comment—*deliver a special message?*

Khalil began, "You have not changed much. You have grown a bit older. And I presume you are still persecuting those whom your country hates—the Muslim faithful who wish only for a better world, one without your American filth and corruption."

"Hey, Khalil. My country doesn't hate Muslims or anybody else. In fact, Muslims, along with all other culturally and religiously diverse people, form an important and integral part of our population. The diversity makes us who we are. A strong, united country. The hate comes from people like you. And from the rest of your band of crazies that have hijacked this ship."

"That is the kind of response I presumed I would get from you. You people never change. You enjoy the luxuries most of the world never experiences. This cruise, the liquor you drink, the other excesses you Americans indulge in. And all the while, the suffering you impose on those less fortunate continues unabated."

Ace just shook his head. He thought about the missile that should have ended this particular terrorist's life. Why it hadn't was still a mystery, a miracle. Not a good miracle, in his mind.

"What the heck is going on here?" he asked Khalil. "What's the purpose of taking over this ship? Are you leading this whole effort? What is it that you people think you're going to get out of this?"

Khalil flashed a sinister smile.

"There are things at work that are for the greater good. You would never understand. Just as your country never understood the need for Iran to pursue its own destiny without your interference."

"Hold on there, Khalil. Letting a rogue ayatollah threaten the world with nuclear weapons is not the kind of destiny that would have brought peace to anyone. In fact, it would have had the opposite effect. It would have only caused more suffering."

"You and your arrogant country will never understand what was really at stake—what Ayatollah Batani hoped to accomplish in the Persian Gulf. He, at least, was doing what needed to be done to unite my brothers, the faithful."

"Hey, man. It's you who was deluded into thinking that nuclear weapons were a path to unity. And your delusion made you commit treason when you stole the F-22's top-secret technology and provided it to an enemy of the United States. I always thought you were a pretty smart guy. Guess I was wrong!"

Khalil's jaw tightened. His rage grew, seeming to ooze from every pore of his body as he listened to the man he hated—now mocking him. He forced himself to calm down, knowing he was being baited by Black, and thinking about how this new episode with his nemesis would play out.

"Well, Matthew "Ace" Black," he said mockingly, with emphasis on the aviator's call sign, "you will taste your own death soon, but not before you experience the same kind of suffering and pain that I felt when your father executed my family. You will soon understand how it feels to lose those you love."

With that comment, Khalil left the library, ordering the armed guard to escort Ace back to the Centrum.

On the walk back, Ace wondered about what Khalil meant with his threatening words—*that I will experience pain. Is he planning on killing my family? Or satisfying his rage by torturing and killing me?*

As he walked back to the Centrum, Ace knew one thing for certain. Khalil was capable of just about anything, given his previous traitorous actions against the United States and his complicity with the radical Iranian regime. At some point, he would impose more suffering on the ship's innocent passengers.

When he got back to his seat in the Centrum, he leaned over to Flamer and let him know what had happened in his meeting with Khalil.

"It was pretty weird, Flamer. The stinking traitor to our country has risen from the ashes. I think he's one of the primary dudes running this hostage operation. Never thought I'd see that bastard again."

"Well, you know, I didn't believe you when you said you'd seen him that night we were sipping our Scotch. But I guess you were right."

"There are some other things that all seem to be falling into place now. First, there was the switch-out of the captain before we sailed. Then, remember that fenced area on the island? The one ringed with barbed wire and security cameras? The rifle cartridge in the sand?"

"Yeah, I do. Are you thinking there's a connection?"

"You bet. Also, remember me telling you about the lifeboat arriving at our ship late the night we were supposed to leave that island? Well, I think that was how some of the weapons and militants got on our cruise ship."

"Makes sense," said Flamer.

"And then the strange activity going on at the pier in Santiago de Cuba. More opportunity to sneak weapons, explosives, and terrorists onto the ship."

Ace paused as he thought through everything he had just said. It was all leading up to more than what it appeared. The hostage situation was likely being controlled by someone other than Khalil, to extract demands, probably from the United States.

He strongly suspected that their current predicament was not going to end peacefully.

"There's going to be more of this shitstorm coming to the *Dream Spinner*. I just know it."

Ace wasn't going to simply wait for things to get past the point of no return. He had to do something—soon.

Chapter 32

nside the combat information center on the aircraft carrier USS *John F. Kennedy*, the course plotted by the navigator was getting keen interest. The carrier, accompanied by its escorts, including the *Bainbridge* destroyer, had followed the quickest course to the *Dream Spinner*'s presumed location, moving at maximum speed. The distance to their staging position was about four hundred miles, thirteen hours sailing time from Jacksonville. Once they arrived there, the carrier would stand by for the execution order. The *Grayback III* would also be in position to support the planned rescue operation.

Meanwhile, there was time for Captain Kenneth Bell to receive the detailed assault brief.

"Skipper, we have the SEAL team leadership in the briefing room, ready to provide the update on Operation Clean Sweep," the executive officer reported. The room was a command-and-control portal tailored for just these types of readiness briefings. The code name "Clean Sweep" had been assigned to the operation to free the *Dream Spinner* once the order was given to execute.

Lieutenant Commander Mark "Shorty" Robinson was a seasoned United States Navy SEAL, a veteran of multiple combat actions. He had earned his nickname due to his size. At five feet two inches, he might not have appeared to be an imposing figure. But Shorty was a textbook alpha male and possessed the strength most other men admired and desired. With him was a second officer, a lieutenant.

"Captain on deck," announced the Chief Petty Officer as Bell entered the combat information center. The captain took his seat and looked toward Shorty. Also present from Robinson's team were the lieutenant, a master chief, and two SEAL platoon squad leaders.

"Take your seats, gentlemen. Lieutenant Commander Robinson, proceed."

"Skipper. First, let me offer my thanks for quickly getting us accommodated on your carrier. We're not used to such plush surroundings." He smiled. "But it's much appreciated. Likewise, the space you've provided for our gear is perfect. We'll have no problem getting ready for an assault on the *Dream Spinner.*"

The SEALs had been billeted in the Air Wing Ready Room, not the usual place to put transient combat warriors, but they wouldn't be there long. Their gear was stowed in the hangar bay.

"You and your team are our guests. Don't hesitate to let me or my XO know if you need anything in your spin-up," Captain Bell said. He then asked Shorty to proceed with the briefing.

The SEAL team leader began with a detailed discussion covering all aspects of the assault plan, including ingress operations from underwater and the air, the kind of tactics his operators intended to employ to maximize surprise, and the things that can make a great plan go south pretty fast. In spite of the best planning by the SEALs, terrorists were unpredictable in their behavior. The operators would have to adapt and overcome. One particular unpredictable consideration was already forming well off the coast of Africa—a tropical storm. They would have to deal with that potential as well in their assault planning.

"Essentially, we're planning a split assault. Alpha Squad will ingress to the *Dream Spinner* underwater. Bravo Squad will parachute onto the top deck of the cruise ship. We'll move quickly and leverage the darkness to our advantage."

"Before I get too deeply into the briefing, can your XO get me an update on one thing that might be pretty valuable to our operation? Prior to arriving here, we requested a copy of the *Dream Spinner's* construction drawings, blueprints, or at least the schematics for the layout of this particular class of ship. Normally, if there was time, we'd use an actual cruise ship to rehearse our assault plan. Clearly, that wasn't possible. We have trained previously on a cruise ship, so it will be somewhat similar. I understand some strings are being pulled to get detailed information on the Dream Spinner from the German shipbuilding company. I believe the information is on the way?"

"It is," Captain Bell assured him. "The plans should arrive soon on an F-18 Hornet that's inbound to the *JFK*. As soon as the jet hits the deck, we'll get the documents right to you."

"Great, Skipper. Appreciate the help."

"We've been advised that there's a CIA operative on board the *Dream Spinner*. If there's a way to contact that person, we're hoping to get some additional key pieces of information before we execute."

"What information is that?" asked Captain Bell.

"If the operative can somehow determine the likely number of terrorists on board, where they might be positioned, the kind of weapons they are carrying, if they have NVGs—night vision goggles—and so forth, it would be great. I know that it's an almost impossible wish list, and the timeline is so tight right now that I'm presuming it may not be possible. If we don't get any of it, or just a few pieces of it, we'll improvise. That's what SEALs do." Shorty paused for a moment.

"Given the timeline for the demands being made by the terrorist cell leader—who, by the way, is not believed to be on board—we'll be ready to move our squads to their assault locations pretty quickly once we get the final go-ahead from our command authorities."

Shorty paused. "Alpha will board the USS *Grayback III*. I understand the sub is currently within a few miles of our position. That boat is Alpha Squad's ride to get close to the *Dream Spinner* undetected."

"Bravo will board the CV-22 Osprey on your deck and stand ready for the order to go. Depending on when we get the execute order, they'll be taking advantage of the near-moonless night to optimize their airborne approach to the cruise ship. Unless the radicals on board happen to be looking in the right direction and have night vision goggles, there's little chance our guys will be seen."

Captain Bell nodded his understanding. "Let me ask you something. Do you think there's a strong possibility of civilian casualties? That's a lot of territory to cover for your SEALs."

"We'll do our best to minimize injury to innocent passengers—and take down every terrorist holding a weapon. Given that we're planning on hitting them in the hours after midnight, most passengers will hopefully be tucked away in their staterooms."

"Sir," the XO interjected. "The Hornet is on final approach. He should be on the deck in a few minutes with the *Dream Spinner*'s deck plans."

The sea state was a bit rough as the sleek jet raced toward the pitching deck of the aircraft carrier. But the fighter pilot was pretty experienced in landing his twin-engine aircraft on what appeared as a postage-stamp-sized area for him to essentially do a controlled crash landing. Timing had to be precise, as did his first contact with the deck, positioned to catch the massive steel arresting cable with his jet's tailhook.

"The Hornet is safely down," said the XO.

"Excellent. Thanks. Is that it?" Bell asked Shorty Robinson.

"Yes, sir. We'll be ready to go in a few hours once we have time to review the ship's layout. Maybe we'll also get lucky and receive some information from the CIA operative on board the *Dream Spinner*."

The meeting ended and the SEAL commander and his squad leaders headed back to their assembly area. The cruise ship's deck plans would be waiting for them.

The SEAL master chief talked with Shorty as they followed the circuitous pathway through the carrier's massive steel corridors.

"Boss, you know we are going to be hanging it out a bit on this op. Even with the deck plans, there's a lot of territory to cover, and plenty of hiding places for these terrorist nutballs to leverage their own surprises on our guys."

"The deck plans are pretty important. We've got to spend the next couple of hours making sure we understand the most likely

THOMAS BELISLE

places the militants are positioned, then adjust strategy to move through the cruise ship," Shorty remarked.

"What do you think the chances are that the CIA operative can get us what we need in time to use it to our advantage?" The master chief wasn't overly worried about the added information but knew it would cut the risk for his operators.

"I suspect Washington and Langley are already in contact with her. The spooks have their ways of getting connected with their folks whenever and wherever they are in the world. Whether we get the info or not, our guys are ready to take these bastards out—and try to minimize the civilian casualties."

"I know. I suspect the element of surprise, speed and brute force we throw at these radicals will tilt the odds in our favor."

Shorty hoped he was right about the last comment.

Chapter 33

"**M**r. President, the link is up and ready for the two-way video communication with Asmaradov." The NSA director waited for President Foreman to take his seat in the White House Situation Room.

"Okay. Are we ready to import the feed from Guantanamo? I want to make sure it's clear enough for Asmaradov to see what's happening there when we tee up the need for more time."

"Yes, Mr. President. It's ready to go."

Moments later, the video came to life on the large screen. In the past, previous presidents had used the capability to do everything from monitoring, in real time, covert combat actions like the capture of Osama bin Laden to having face-to-face conversations with key world leaders in the effort to deescalate a crisis. Until now, it had never been used for the purpose of negotiating with a terrorist. It would run contrary to current long-standing United States policy of never negotiating with terrorists. But the most powerful country in the world always found a way to gain the upper hand and bring the world's radicals to justice—one way or another.

Foreman knew this full well. But he also knew that, for now, the lunatic Panja faction leader had the upper hand. He had the *Dream Spinner* captive. For now, the Viper was holding the trump cards. But Foreman was intent on making sure the terrorist's current tactical advantage didn't last.

President Foreman looked into the face of Farad Asmaradov. After a second or two, the terrorist leader spoke.

"You have made a big mistake, Foreman. I warned you not to approach the *Dream Spinner*. Because of your foolish actions, one of your aircraft was destroyed. If my people view any other overt actions by you, I will begin executing passengers."

"I promise you, I did not plan or direct any action against that ship. The aircraft was on a routine flight to Puerto Rico when it overflew the *Dream Spinner*. Your actions were uncalled for, and extreme."

"A warning unheeded is a death sentence," replied Asmaradov. "I presume you are prepared to meet my demands on the release of the Guantanamo prisoners."

"We are working toward the release of the three individuals being held at Cuba, as you have requested. There is one small complication that we're trying to resolve."

"What complication?" demanded Asmaradov, the anger evident in his tone.

"As you may know, Victor Chernov has been recovering from a sickness that he contracted a week ago." Foreman knew that Asmaradov had no way of knowing this. "He likely contracted it from an Islamic State captive that was extradited from Iraq by our military and brought to Guantanamo."

"I don't believe you, Foreman. You lie. Your stalling will only bring death to passengers on the cruise ship."

"It's not a lie. I'm prepared to link this video to the critical care unit at Guantanamo Bay, where Chernov is currently being kept in an induced coma due to the intensive medical treatment the doctors have him undergoing. They believe Chernov's medical state should improve markedly in the next thirty-six hours, at which time he would be ambulatory. He could be safely moved at that time from our charge to the Cuban medical staff."

"That is long past the deadline I gave you, Foreman. I believe we are done talking, and you will face the consequences."

"Wait! I'm telling you the truth. What will it take to verify Chernov's condition and convince you?"

The president wasn't sure if Asmaradov was so angry that he was about to terminate the video connection. If that happened, the plan to buy some time would have failed miserably, possibly causing the death of many passengers on the *Dream Spinner*. The silence continued for nearly a minute before Asmaradov spoke.

"If you think I'm going to take your word for his medical status, you are mistaken. I want Soleimann and Heydar to be brought to Chernov's bedside. I want to question them myself."

"We certainly can arrange that," the president replied. "It will only take about thirty minutes, maybe less, to get your people over to our hospital unit." Foreman didn't want the line to go dead and perhaps not come back up. "Are you willing to wait for the verification? We'll move as quickly as possible."

"I will close the video feed and bring it back on line in thirty minutes. You should be prepared for the consequences if this delay is a sham or hoax."

"I assure you, it's not," Foreman lied. "You will see for yourself that Chernov isn't capable of surviving a move from our hospital at the present time. I'm sure your people will attest to that when they see him."

Foreman's comments seemed to be working, at least for the moment. Maybe he'd pulled it off. Then he made a comment that shocked his staff.

"I want to warn you now, Asmaradov. I'm doing exactly as you have asked. If you want to risk moving Chernov and he dies as a result of your decision, that's on you. I'm confident he can be moved in the timeline my medical staff indicated. Additionally, if, in the meantime, any American passengers on that cruise ship are harmed in any way, there's nowhere on this planet where you will be safe."

The video feed locked up before he could say another word.

The president's team in the Situation Room was stunned by what he had said. While it was true, the timing was clearly off. Some believed that making such a threat to Asmaradov was not productive and might result in disaster.

THOMAS BELISLE

President Foreman looked around the room, found his NSA director, and sought some assurance about the plan.

"We have only one shot at getting this right. If for any reason Asmaradov doesn't believe what he sees, then who the hell knows what will happen next on board the *Dream Spinner*."

"Mr. President, it will work. First, there's no way that Soleimann and Heydar know about Chernov or his condition. He's kept in a separate, isolated area with no visitors and no communication. So the story we've concocted will work. The two militants will believe what they see when they get to the ICU. Chernov will be unresponsive, in an induced coma, on a ventilator. The medical equipment around his bed should be more than convincing."

"Sir, we've already sent our folks to retrieve Soleimann and Heydar. We should be ready to boot up the video before thirty minutes," a staff member interjected.

"If things go to shit quickly, how soon will we be able to mount an assault on the *Dream Spinner*?"

"Within twelve hours," replied the JCS chairman.

———————•———————

The video came to life thirty minutes later. Asmaradov observed a spilt screen. One was the Situation Room. The other was the ICU at Guantanamo Bay. Both he and President Foreman observed Chernov, the camera focusing on his bed, with the other two terrorists at his side.

"Ismail," Asmaradov said. "How is my brother? Is he as sick as the Americans indicate? Try to revive him."

The doctor present immediately objected. "We can't begin to revive him for at least another twelve hours. As you can see, the intravenous medication is coursing through him, and the ventilator is keeping him breathing while we eliminate the horrible infection he contracted."

Ismail Soleimann looked toward the camera. "Farad, our brother appears very sick. I see beads of sweat on his forehead. His color is bad. I don't think it's possible to awaken him right now." Heydar nodded his concurrence.

The ruse was working.

Asmaradov spoke to Foreman. "I will grant you no more than twenty-four hours, and then you will move Chernov from your prison and turn him over to my Cuban friends." He paused.

"But you will release Soleimann and Heydar immediately. They will inform me when you release Chernov. I must be certain that you are not trying to stall in order to take some foolish actions on the *Dream Spinner*. That would be a big mistake on your part."

"We will keep our end of the bargain. You need to keep yours. How will I know that you aren't going to harm the *Dream Spinner*'s passengers after Chernov is released? How will you get your militant force off the ship?"

"At the time of his release, I will advise you of the cruise ship's destination. It will berth at a location where I know my people will be protected. Once they have disembarked, the ship will be free to return to the United States." This time, the Viper was the one doing the lying.

"Agreed," President Foreman said. The video link abruptly ended before he could say another word.

The president looked at the clock on the wall. The countdown timer had been activated when the original demands had been met. There were now six hours remaining before the original deadline. They had hopefully bought another twenty-four hours of time. But when dealing with terrorists, the president knew that anything could change, usually for the worse. He didn't trust Asmaradov for a moment, nor the terrorist's promises of keeping up his end of the bargain.

Chapter 34

The strike group reached their planned staging position, and the *Dream Spinner* was clearly painted on the radar display in the *Kennedy*'s combat information center. At a little over thirty miles, the carrier was over the horizon, not visible from the cruise ship with the naked eye.

The *Dream Spinner*'s radar would surely see the dots of any ship traffic in the surrounding expanse of the south-central Caribbean. Most would be at similar distances transiting east to west, or west to east. The USS *John F. Kennedy* and the *Bainbridge* continued moving carefully. They mimicked the commercial traffic so as not to appear as if they were approaching the cruise ship, nor shadowing the *Dream Spinner*'s random track. They would stay close enough to execute the mission when it came time to do so. The remaining escort ships positioned themselves to support them if necessary.

The USS *Bainbridge* was not an ordinary destroyer. It held a special cache of new technology provided by DARPA, the Defense Advanced Research Projects Agency. For years, the United States had conducted research to pursue nonkinetic means for disabling an enemy vessel. Whether it was a small attack boat or large cruise ship, the intent was to quickly neutralize a combatant without inflicting undue casualties. The new technology was tailor-made for this particular mission and was to be an integral part of the SEAL counterterrorism team's strategy of concealment, surprise and shock.

All the elements of the tactical military strategy were coming together nicely. When it came to power projection, speed, and technology, the United States had few equals in the world. Besides the

Kennedy and its entourage, another Navy ship was en route to the staging area that had a large contingent of United States Marines on board. They would be available, if needed, to help restore order on the *Dream Spinner* after the assault by the SEALs.

Lieutenant Commander Robinson was eager to get the execute order. He presumed if he got it, it would be tonight or the following night. Likely, early in the morning. He had his team prepared, and at this point, they were ready and eager to engage the enemy. Standing silently ready to support the SEALs, at a depth of one hundred feet, was the USS *Grayback III*.

Martha Cook wasted no time finding her concealed satellite phone that she had brought onto the *Dream Spinner*. All good CIA operatives made sure that they were prepared for any circumstance—and Martha was one of their best. She carefully unscrewed the nearly invisible seam on her thermos bottom and pulled the phone out. The clever design allowed about two inches of coffee visible through the clear top. She stepped out of her cabin and onto the stateroom balcony. Her room was not above or below any of the open deck walkways—there was little chance of any of the captors hearing the conversation she was preparing to have.

She got a strong signal from a low earth orbit, special communications satellite, and punched in the number she knew so well. Her call was answered on the second ring. The CIA's Langley, Virginia headquarters where she worked was operating around the clock.

They were keenly interested in the daily updates she had been providing regarding the ongoing hostage situation aboard the *Dream Spinner*. She had passed as much information as she could gather in her few days of captivity. It wasn't much, but it was better than nothing, given that all other forms of communication had been shut down on the ship, and passenger movement severely restricted.

The CIA operative at least confirmed that the passengers were currently safe and confined in their staterooms. That was, except for most of the men. She explained where they were being held. She couldn't provide a reason, except to presume it had something to do with their ability to resist their captors. Martha described the weapons she had observed being carried by the militants. She wasn't aware of anything else in that regard.

She also indicated she would try to get a definitive number of terrorists and their positions on the ship. She wasn't yet sure *how* she was going to do it, but she would find out as much as she could in her daily journeys to the dining room—hopefully without tipping off any militants about what she was up to. While Martha was very resourceful, as were all CIA operatives who had received some of the best counterterrorism training in the world, it was a daunting task.

Langley requested she make contact with them again in three hours. They would likely have a few more tasks for her after consultation with the White House.

Chapter 35

Khalil had a couple things on his mind. The first was ensuring he executed the mission Asmaradov had given him—he had fully committed to the cause. But Khalil now had something to do that was a bit more personal. Once he had found Ace Black on the ship, years of repressed feelings had swelled in him. Unpaid debts were foremost among them. It was his intent to remedy that, and he had already decided his next move.

He dispatched a trusted comrade to keep an eye on the stateroom belonging to the Black family. The two rooms in question were occupied by Julie Black and her children, Nick, Roman, and Claire. The plan was simple. At the first opportunity, grab one of the children and bring the child to Khalil. The move would be an ugly attempt by Khalil to exact some mental pain and anguish from his old adversary, Ace Black.

It didn't take long for one of the kids to make the mistake of leaving the stateroom. Claire Black slipped out of her cabin while her mother was in the bathroom. The young child was determined to see her grandmother, only a few doors down the hallway. It should have been a brief, safe walk. But it might as well have been a long trek across the ship. The danger was waiting.

She didn't pay any attention to the man dressed as a cabin steward as he walked down the hallway.

She was quickly grabbed, silenced by a hand over her mouth, and taken up several decks to the communications center, where Khalil waited. There, the crying child was bound and gagged in a quiet corner of the room.

Minutes after Claire was taken, Julie emerged from the bathroom. Roman was waiting, and told his mother that Claire had gone to see her grandmother. Julie, in a panic, immediately called her mother to make sure her daughter arrived. When she found out that Claire wasn't there, she became hysterical. She opened the door to her stateroom, and ran up and down the empty hallway before returning to her room. Jack Stevens, Claire's grandfather, exploded with anger and worry when Julie told him what had happened. He expected the worst. Jack left his room and raced down the hallway, all the way to the end of the ship. Nobody stopped him. He headed back the other way and almost made it to the opposite end when he was confronted by an armed militant who stepped out of the exit opening to the aft stairway.

"Halt," he yelled at Jack, pointing his AK-47 directly at him. Jack raised his hands over his head quickly. "Return to your room. No people allowed here."

"I'm just looking for my granddaughter. Have you seen a young girl in the hallway?"

"Get back to your room, now!" the guard said, this time taking aim at Jack's chest.

"Okay. I'm going."

The guard followed Jack down the hallway, and watched him enter his stateroom.

Inside, Jack turned to his wife. He shook his head. "There's no sign of her." He hugged Gemma and said softly, "I'll find her. God help me, I'll find her if it's the last thing I do." The former Army Ranger began formulating a rescue plan in his head.

———————•———————

Things had turned ugly in the late afternoon aboard the *Dream Spinner*. A couple of young men had experienced enough of their confinement and believed it was time for them to try and overpower their captor in the Spinnaker Lounge. While they had initially been able to tackle the terrorist when his back was turned, the militant's counterpart, hidden in the back of the lounge, had shot both of them with bursts of fire from his assault rifle. In the melee, the gunfire had also killed the other guard.

In the lounge, the remaining men cowered under the tables and behind the overstuffed chairs.

"Get to your seats!" ordered the guard holding the still-smoking rifle. A couple militants ran into the lounge to put an end to any further resistance. Noting that things were under control, they took the bodies of the two young men and the dead guard from the room and tossed them over the side of the ship into the Caribbean.

In each muster area, and across the ship, the shocking announcement came over the ship's intercom.

"This is Captain Zoyatov. Unfortunately, there has been a tragic accident on board. A couple of foolish passengers tried to take the weapon away from one of their guards. As a result, the two men are dead. I must warn you all. If any attempt is made to resist in any way, the result will be similar to what happened to these two passengers."

This set in motion a series of actions that tightened the security in each muster assembly area. The terrorists closed down two of the smaller areas and herded all the men into the larger rooms. They pulled the guards from there and doubled up their presence in the larger facilities. Unfortunately, there weren't enough seats for the additional captive men. They were told to take up the floor space wherever they could find it, adding to the stress already running rampant through the ship.

Inside the Centrum, it was now a packed house. Ace knew that the resistance by the two passengers was only the beginning. Beyond the men being crammed into the room, worry about their families was escalating as no information was being passed on their condition or whether they were safe. Food consumption was also now being limited both in what they were given and in how little time they got to eat it. Now with the death of two passengers, tensions would continue to rise, and when that happened, people did crazy things they might not usually do.

Ace thought of one upside to the situation.

THOMAS BELISLE

"Flamer, with these crowded conditions, it's actually going to make it more difficult for these dudes to keep an accurate count of us. This may be the break we were waiting for."

"What do you mean, *we*?" He looked at Ace. "I know, I know. Look, we can't just sit here and end up like the two guys that got shot. That may be the intention of our captors regardless of whether we resist or not."

Ace didn't answer Flamer. He was too busy formulating a plan.

Later in the evening, around dinnertime, the men were escorted in small groups to the buffet area. As he went through the line, Ace saw Aleksandra handling the small, meager salad bar. She saw him about the same time and gave him a slight nod to approach the bar.

Ace wasn't sure what to think. He'd suspected all along she was part of the group that had taken control of the ship, especially after her intense questioning of him earlier. When he came over to the lettuce bowl, she picked up a large plate and loaded it with lettuce, tomatoes, carrots, and cucumbers. She reached across the bar to hand it to him, but Ace hesitated.

She gave him an intense look and asked him to raise his tray in order for her to put the plate on it. He complied and then walked away. He found the burger tray and grabbed a couple of buns and two large beef patties. He quickly doctored them up with mustard and ketchup and headed for a table. Ace was ready to wolf down his food in the few minutes left for him to eat.

She seemed pretty intent on me taking this salad plate, he thought. As he picked the plate off the tray, he saw something underneath. A piece of paper. He looked around to see if anyone was watching, then slid his hand under the plate and removed the small note. He looked around again and then slipped the paper into his pocket.

When he got back into the Centrum, he headed toward his buddy. Flamer had kept his seat secure from the overflow that had joined them. He sat down, and Flamer headed out to get his meal. As carefully as he could, he pulled the note from his pocket. He wasn't sure why this woman would be passing anything of use to him. He read it.

Ace was stunned at the note's message. His daughter, Claire, was missing. She had left her stateroom to go see her grandparents but had never gotten there. Ace wasn't sure how this woman knew that his daughter was missing. But she did know who Claire was from the morning breakfast ritual. Aleksandra's note said that she would try to find out where the child had been taken. Contrary to Ace's original thoughts, the note was intended to help him. His anger swelled as he thought about what might have happened to his daughter. Then he thought about what Khalil had said to him. That he would suffer. That it would be very personal. Ace seethed with anger and simmered in silence until Flamer returned.

He told his buddy what had happened. "That bastard, Khalil, has taken Claire—I know it—I feel it. All because of me! I pissed him off and he's trying to pay me back for that and probably for all the other things he thinks I've done to him. Now *he's* gonna pay with his life!"

Flamer's face turned almost white with shock. It then reddened, his own anger building.

"Can you trust this waitress?"

"Why would she risk passing me this information, especially when I'm being held captive? There's no point in doing it unless she's trying to help us out."

"Ace, we've gotta do something."

"Roger that. I've got a plan."

Chapter 36

Day 7

A ce hadn't slept well the night before. It wasn't the upright Centrum stadium seat that had kept him awake. It was Claire! He worried about how frightened she must be, still hoping she was unharmed. His mind spun with potential ways he could get to her once he found out where she was being held—it would be a formidable challenge. He also thought about the rescue that was likely being planned by his government to take back the ship.

The *Dream Spinner* was massive. The fourteen decks were supported by over three miles of hallways, breezeways, and staircases accessible to passengers, along with fifteen hundred staterooms. Beyond that, there were an additional two miles of passageways, a couple hundred crew quarters, and functional service rooms that were only accessible to the ship's staff.

Doing some quick figuring, Ace began to understand the difficulty facing the band of hostile captors to control such an expansive territory. The twisting hallways, corners, closets, rooms, and other small enclosures provided ample cover for anyone wishing to conceal themselves. That concealment would be essential in order to have any opportunity to gain even a small advantage over the terrorists.

He needed to understand how many of them were on the cruise ship. If he knew that, he could make an educated guess on where they had positioned themselves. He already guessed that the muster stations had at least two guards in each one, and there were eight muster stations.

Then there would likely be guards on each main deck at each end of the ship. He had gotten this indication during his daily guarded march to the dining area. Also, there had to be militants in the bridge, and perhaps the engine control room.

Knowing where the gunmen were located would increase the likelihood of success in any meaningful resistance they might initiate. Ace had one opportunity to possibly obtain the information he needed. The woman that had passed him the note on his daughter. Maybe she could find out where the terrorists were positioned on the ship. And where Claire was being held. Aleksandra was probably the only way he could find out what he desperately needed to know.

At breakfast, Ace carefully passed a note to the dark-haired Ukrainian woman, shielding his actions from the guards watching the passengers get their food. She took the small folded piece of paper and stuffed it in her uniform pocket. Their actions took no more than a few seconds.

"You," one of the guards yelled at Ace.

His heart sank as he thought for a minute that he had been discovered, that the guard had seen him pass the note.

"Move along. Get to your table and finish."

Ace nodded at the guard and quickly grabbed some toast to go with the eggs Aleksandra had placed on his plate. As he walked toward the table, he breathed a bit easier. For now, he believed his actions had not been observed by the guard, and he hoped the young lady behind the food counter would be able to get the information he needed.

At this point, he had no idea that a certain CIA operative on board the *Dream Spinner* was already working to get that very same information.

While still at breakfast, Ace had a short conversation with a man who had been listening to his conversation with Flamer in the Centrum. Ray Cook had been sitting a row behind Ace. He'd figured out what they were talking about and was interested in the possibility of putting together some form of resistance.

What he said to Ace was even more meaningful. His wife was Martha Cook, the CIA operative. He mentioned very quietly to Ace that his wife had a means of communicating outside the ship, even though all normal communication capability had been shut down. Ace was keenly interested, to say the least. He told the man that they would talk more when they got back to the Centrum.

The conversation they had while sitting in the large auditorium was hushed. They kept their voices almost at a whisper.

"Ray, are you sure about this? Do you think Martha has already tried to use her satellite phone to let our country know what's going on here?" Ace asked. He quickly looked around for the guards to ensure he wasn't being watched.

"There's no question about that. I'll bet Martha was on the phone minutes after she got back to our stateroom. I'm sure the CIA knows about the *Dream Spinner*'s capture. And I'm pretty sure they've passed that info up the chain."

The plan was coming together in Ace's head. He had two key elements. He had a possible means *on* the ship—Aleksandra—of getting the critical information about the terrorists—their number, their location, maybe their weapons. And he had a means *off* the ship—Martha Cook—of passing that information to the people who were hopefully, already putting a rescue attempt together. He didn't realize yet how quickly all of these actions had to occur. He was also not aware of the SEALs who were preparing to execute their assault mission.

Ace knew Aleksandra was the key to the plan. If she was able to tell him about Claire, that his daughter was being held captive, then she might be able to get around the ship without being challenged by the terrorists. He suspected that there were quite a few crew members doing their daily jobs, like her, moving around freely. He thought briefly that maybe the whole "Aleksandra" engagement was nothing more than a trap for him. Maybe something Khalil had dreamed up to uncover any activity among passengers to put up resistance to the hijackers. But he had a good feeling, a gut feeling, about the young Ukrainian. He made the choice to trust his instinct, and trust her.

He thought about the CIA operative. If Martha Cook could securely communicate with her handlers at Langley from the *Dream Spinner*, the ship's hostages could pick up a small advantage over their captors. But it would depend on what Aleksandra was able to provide to him. Could she produce the information he requested—the number and locations of the militants on board? If she could, would she be willing to provide the information to Martha Cook? The CIA could use that to solidify any rescue that might be planned. If there was an assault plan already in the works to free the *Dream Spinner*, could the information about the militants reach the American military in time to be useful?

This was a major breakthrough in Ace's mind. He knew he would be back in the dining area for lunch. Hopefully, Aleksandra would be there. Maybe she would have the information that might help free the *Dream Spinner*. Most important to him was getting the location of his daughter. He hoped Aleksandra would provide that to him as well.

And if he found that Khalil had actually taken her, the Syrian would reap the ultimate price for his actions.

Chapter 37

There was a flurry of action in the White House Situation Room. The president had given the order to prepare to assault the *Dream Spinner* the night before. Luckily, the timing was perfect for gaining as much concealment as possible. The night's darkness worked in President Foreman's favor—tonight would be the last phase of the lunar cycle, with the final glow of light coming from the waning crescent.

Lieutenant Commander Shorty Robinson was ready. The two squads of Navy SEALs were eager to get on with what they were trained to do. Find the enemy—kill the enemy. And free the hostages from the grip of the militant cell. Hopefully with minimal loss of innocent lives.

Tonight, one squad would quietly disembark the aircraft carrier and board the USS *Grayback III*. Once the sub was in position at periscope depth near the ocean surface, Alpha Squad would transition to the two small submersibles secured to the topside rear deck of the sub and remain there until the pre-coordinated execute time.

Bravo Squad would launch from the flight deck of the USS *John F. Kennedy* on the CV-22 Osprey when the time was right. When they reached the prescribed location and altitude over the Caribbean, they would exit the Osprey, pop their chutes, and guide themselves to the *Dream Spinner*'s top deck.

The element of surprise would be paramount, coupled with powerful silenced weapons to minimize the likelihood that the assault teams would be heard as they began eliminating the ship's captors.

President Foreman had bought some time with his ruse on Chernov's illness. Asmaradov had agreed, and now the time set for the release of the terrorist was less than eighteen hours away. The assault would be planned to occur shortly after midnight, a few hours before the deadline.

Meanwhile, the other two terrorists held captive at Guantanamo had been released to Cuban authorities. With great reluctance, the president had acquiesced to Asmaradov's demands. Foreman knew that the bomb maker and the money broker would surely be absorbed quickly into Asmaradov's radical cause. But they would then be hunted men again, and eventually recaptured by the U.S. military's deadly, global reach.

———————•———————

Captain Zoyatov was beginning to worry. At this point in the ship's takeover, he'd expected there to be some progress in bringing things to closure. He'd thought that, by now, the United States would have released the three prisoners at Guantanamo. After that, he would have been on his way to Caracas, Venezuela, where he and the rest of the militants would disembark. He knew that once there, all of them would be out of reach from the Americans.

Venezuela was, at least for the time, sympathetic to anyone who opposed the United States and their policies. Asmaradov had assured Zoyatov and the entire band of militants that they would be warmly welcomed by the dictator who ran the bankrupt country. Once the ship was safely moored there, either the cruise ship company would need to get a qualified captain to sail the boat back to Port Canaveral or the passengers could make their own travel arrangements to fly back to the United States.

The captain couldn't contain his nervousness about how things were going to play out. Zoyatov asked Khalil, Cho Lee Kwan, and Drako Kratec to come to the bridge as soon as they could. The captain was looking for some reassurance that Asmaradov's plan was still on track. And he was smart enough to know that the longer it took to execute, the more likely it was that the United States would try to take back the ship by force. And Zoyatov was not excited about that particular prospect.

Cho and Kratec left trusted colleagues in charge of their respective areas and headed for the bridge. The entrance was guarded by one of the heavily armed Tajik radicals who picked up the phone and called Zoyatov. The lock clicked, and the guard pushed the door open.

"Have any of you heard from Asmaradov?" Zoyatov asked.

He got a strange look from Khalil. "How do you think he's going to communicate with the ship with all incoming and outgoing signals shut down," he remarked sarcastically. "You are not going to hear anything from him."

Khalil looked at Kratec and Cho, who both nodded. They both knew about Khalil's means of communicating with the Viper. Then he continued. "The mission we have is not dependent on any communication from Asmaradov. We have our tasks to carry out."

Zoyatov didn't seem too convinced.

"Just continue to pilot this ship along the same random course that you have been doing. Maintain twenty knots." Khalil paused, then continued. "Have faith, brother, in Farad Asmaradov. He is very wise and trusts us all to carry out our responsibilities."

The three of them knew that Zoyatov had not been completely read in on every part of the mission. While the captain had been told about a final stop in Venezuela, that stop would very likely never happen.

Chapter 38

I t was approaching the lunch hour, and the passengers held captive in the large auditorium were long past being just restless. While they were still getting fed three times a day, the smell inside the Centrum was beginning to become intolerable. No showers for two days, overcrowding of the facility, and profuse sweating by many of the hostages due mainly to stress had made the air offensive to even the least sensitive nose.

Sitting shoulder to shoulder, Ace and Flamer contemplated their budding plan to do something positive about the desperate situation they were in.

"Flamer, I'm telling you, people in this auditorium are going to explode at some point. You can only subject folks to so much before they go nuts."

"Roger that. I'm surprised that the stink in here alone hasn't already set somebody off."

"Yeah. Let's hope they can keep calm for a bit longer. I gotta believe that something big is going to happen soon. Our country isn't going to just sit around waiting for this hijacking to resolve itself," Ace said. He looked across the tired, frustrated faces of the men in the Centrum auditorium.

"I'm eager to see if we've made any progress with the information that Aleksandra was going to try to get for us," Ace whispered to Flamer.

"You know, buddy, she hasn't had much time to react. I hope she was able to get it as well. Or at least some of it. Anything will help."

THOMAS BELISLE

"If she got it, we've got to figure a way to get it to Martha Cook. We certainly can't walk down to her cabin and hand it over. It's going to have to be Aleksandra. I wonder if she'll do it if we ask?"

"Well, I'll tell you. If she was able to walk around the ship and make mental notes on where the militants are, she pretty much has the run of the place." Flamer looked at Ace, who nodded back in agreement.

"Maybe as a Ukrainian, she's considered as more of a trusted crew member by the militants. If these terrorists are truly from Tajikistan, it kind of makes sense. That country has had some pretty heavy Russian influence over the past years," Ace remarked.

The two friends watched as small groups were ordered, by row, to head for the dining room under their armed escort. It looked like they would be next.

When their row was called, they began to file out, but Flamer was stopped, along with all the men behind him. For some reason, the guards didn't want any more in that group to eat together. The men were escorted from the Centrum to the dining area for the noon meal. They were led in single file, like prisoners—which in fact they were.

When he arrived, Ace looked across the different buffet areas. The person he wanted to see had been at the salad bar before. He didn't see Aleksandra there. Maybe she had moved to another food service area. He looked carefully at each one as he grabbed a plate and silverware, sans the knife—all of those had been removed early on in the hostage crisis. He had to keep moving or risk being shoved by one of the guards, or not getting any food.

He began to think the worst. What if Aleksandra had been discovered with his note? Perhaps she'd asked too many questions about the militants? Maybe she wandered into parts of the ship in her quest for information and had been detained by the gunmen? What if she really wasn't who she appeared to be—a sympathetic crew member hoping to help in some way? Maybe she had turned him in and Khalil would be sending armed guards to drag him off.

He was relieved when he saw her appear from the kitchen with a tray of vegetables and walk over to one of the food bars. Ace made his way to that location and stood behind two other men waiting for food. When it was Ace's turn to ask for a serving of summer squash, he looked into Aleksandra's eyes. Her nod was almost imperceptible as she passed a small dish toward him. A note was taped to the bottom. He took the dish, thanked her, and headed to his table.

When he was done eating, he pulled the note from the bottom of the plate and slipped it into his pocket. After he got back to the Centrum, he quickly looked at the list. His near-photographic memory cemented the information into his brain—over thirty separate parts of the ship were identified. It also included the location of his daughter. She was being held in the ship's communications center. He quickly passed the note to Flamer, after he scrawled the name "Martha Cook" and her stateroom number on it.

Flamer was escorted to the dining area with another small group, and when he arrived there, he quickly found Aleksandra. He requested vegetables, and she handed him a dish full. He pushed it back to her and shook his head. He took his dinner plate and extended it towards her. He held the small note against the plate bottom, and as she took the dish, the note fell to the counter. She quickly grabbed it and put it in her pocket. She added the squash to his plate and gave it back to him. He smiled and headed to his table to eat his meal.

When she was back in the kitchen, she walked into the vegetable storage room. There was nobody nearby, and she quickly looked at the note. It was the same note she had provided to Ace. But she noticed on the back of it the words "Martha Cook, room 8132. Now." Aleksandra knew what she must do. Get the note to whoever Martha Cook was. She didn't understand why, but she suspected it was extremely important.

When Flamer got back to the Centrum, he gave Ace a nod as he took his seat. His buddy acknowledged the meaning—the message had been delivered. His plan was hopefully coming together.

THOMAS BELISLE

But he couldn't get his daughter out of his mind. He strongly suspected that Khalil was behind Claire's abduction from her stateroom. He didn't really believe the Syrian would harm her. He had to at least tell himself that to keep from going crazy, from imagining what might happen to his daughter. He resolved to himself that if it took the last breath in his body, he would find Claire, soon. And he would finish the job he should have completed years before. To send Khalil on his way to meet his maker.

Martha Cook had not been *that* successful in coming up with what the CIA had asked her to provide. She had managed to estimate where at least some of the terrorists were positioned as she transited the hallways and stairwells to get to the dining area. And she presumed, based on the small ship's diagram on the door, where all the muster stations were listed, that militants occupied each one of those areas as well. But, at best, it was still incomplete.

She was surprised at the soft knock on her stateroom door. When she opened it, she saw a young female crew member.

"Yes, what is it?" asked Martha.

"This is for you," Aleksandra replied. Then the young lady quickly walked away.

Martha looked down both sides of the hallway. Other than Aleksandra, no one else was there. She closed her cabin door and sat down by the sliding glass balcony door, carefully opening the note that had been handed to her. As she read it, her analytic mind quickly determined what she was looking at. At the top of the note, the word *captors* was written. Beneath it was a listing of locations on the ship.

Martha stared at the list, almost in disbelief. *This is a list of where the terrorists are positioned,* she thought to herself. Why had the young crew member given this to her? She quickly put the pieces together in her mind. Her husband, Ray, knew that with her sat phone, she was the only conduit for getting information off the ship. He had to be involved, and perhaps some others. Ray likely sent her to their stateroom.

She wondered briefly if there was anything brewing among the captive men about taking back the *Dream Spinner*. If there was, it might clearly complicate things if an assault by the U.S. military was getting ready to happen.

Martha wasted no time. She needed to immediately pass the information to Langley, to the CIA headquarters, to her handlers. They would know precisely what to do. Pass it up the chain to those military forces who, at this point, had to be planning on taking back the captive ship.

Time was of the essence. She removed the sat phone from its secure hiding spot and stepped onto the balcony. She quickly obtained a signal. Minutes later, the information had been passed to her handlers. She shut the transmission down and replaced the communications device in its hiding place.

At Langley, the information was immediately assessed as extremely relevant. It was passed to DoD minutes later. Within one hour from the time Martha had made the call, the potential locations of most of the terrorists on board the cruise ship were in the hands of the SEAL team aboard the USS *John F. Kennedy*.

Lieutenant Commander Shorty Robinson finally received the critical information he had hoped for. Knowing the positioning of the terrorists, at least at the time the information was gathered, was crucial to the elements of his assault plan. He quickly correlated the information against the ship's deck layout. He pulled his SEALs together and they adjusted their strategy to take back the *Dream Spinner*. After two hours of detailed planning, they were prepared to take action when given the president's execute order.

Chapter 39

A board the *Dream Spinner*, the hostage situation continued to deteriorate. After days of being cooped up in overcrowded, rather pungent holding areas, passengers were growing more desperate, in spite of what had happened to the two men who had been shot after they'd attacked a guard the previous day. The captain's warning had apparently faded from their memories as their level of stress and discomfort rose.

It was just after the noon meal when a man from the Centrum visited the restroom at the rear, but his actual intent was getting out of the large holding area in a desperate but futile attempt to see his family. He couldn't take the confinement anymore. As he left the restroom, he noticed the guard had moved away from the rear exit door to talk with his militant partner on the stage. He turned, ran to the door, pushed it open, and raced down the hallway.

The guard on the stage flashed by Ace as he ran toward the fleeing man. Both Ace and Flamer turned to look back at the exit door. They heard commotion coming from just outside the Centrum.

"Stop!" screamed an angry gunman on the foyer staircase outside the Centrum. The militant vaulted down the last few steps and then ran in the direction of the passenger. "Halt!" he shouted and then leveled his rifle. A shot rang out. The fleeing passenger fell violently forward from the impact of the high-velocity round that entered the center of his back. He was dead before he hit the carpeted hallway floor.

The gunshot echoed back through the opened door of the Centrum. Ace knew that another *Dream Spinner* guest had been executed.

"This shit is getting bad, Flamer. Most normal people have a pretty high breaking point before they start doing crazy stuff like that."

"I know, buddy. Running out of the room is pretty insane when you have a bunch of nutballs training their weapons on you. Not sure what that dude was thinking racing out of here."

He looked across the Centrum at the men seated around him. Fear and helplessness were evident in many of their tired faces.

"Flamer, when folks get desperate, they do irrational things." Ace thought about what he had just said. He wondered if he would ultimately fall into that category.

Once the Centrum was secured again by the guards, all the captives were again warned about the consequences of any attempt to escape or resist. There would be no more warnings, no mercy. Passengers would be immediately executed for not complying with the directions they had been given.

———————•———————

The piercing report from the automatic weapon echoed through the hallway where Julie Black and her children remained confined in their stateroom. It wasn't the gunshot from two decks below that she heard but the subsequent sounds of militant gunfire in each hallway firing warning bursts. The message was clear. Stay in your cabins!

The twins screamed when they heard the loud bursts from the automatic weapons. They didn't dare look out into the hallway. Nobody would think about opening their cabin doors after the threats made over the loudspeaker to all passengers, and certainly not after the gunshots.

Julie did her best to comfort her boys—a difficult task given that they had no idea where Claire was or whether she was safe. Likewise, they worried about their missing father.

"It'll be okay, boys," she said softly. "We'll find Claire as soon as we can. You know your daddy is probably already looking for her."

"Momma, I want my daddy, now!" shouted Roman.

"I know. I want him too. We'll see him soon. I just know it," Julie responded lovingly.

Two six-year-olds were tough to convince. They only knew that the two people they loved most were gone. The desperate mother was trying to convince herself that things would be okay.

Throughout the ship, in many of the staterooms, the same thing was happening. Spouses wondering about the men who had been taken from them. Parents wondering about their sons who were being held hostage. The control the terrorists had over the ship made them feel helpless. A few passengers, in desperate attempts to let the world know what was happening, had taken bedsheets and hung them from their stateroom balcony rails. Some had the letters *SOS* scrawled on them with magic markers, others the word *HELP*. Of course, there was no one around in the large expanse of the Caribbean to see the messages. Nobody to react to their hopeless plea to do something about their terrible situation.

———•———

Khalil Atta was in the *Dream Spinner*'s communications center, checking and rechecking the status of all systems that he controlled. He verified that every potential signal path used by the passengers and crew was blocked, except for a select few. Even though all the passenger and crew cell phones and iPads had been collected, he knew there was still a small possibility that a hidden device might be used to try and let the outside world know what was going on.

He had activated secure internal lines between himself, the ship's captain, the security chief, the provisioning manager, and the chief engineer. But those lines were essentially useless for any outgoing transmissions from the ship. Khalil's modifications ensured that the only inbound or outbound communications would come from him—*when* and *if* he desired it.

He told himself that he was prepared for any contingency. But the Syrian knew that with every subsequent day that crept by with the ship under siege, the threat of an attack by the Americans increased exponentially. He didn't trust them. In spite of the "negotiation" that the Viper was engaging in with President Foreman, Khalil had little faith that the United States would honor any agreement. He suspected that an assault plan had already been prepared. Perhaps it was already underway and the rescue attempt would occur at any moment.

His skepticism about his adversary prompted him to recheck the systems that would help deny an attack. Rigged along the stern of the ship, an array of electronically networked explosives had been placed from the waterline up to the first accessible deck. He felt that the stern was the most obvious choice for any seaborne assault. It was the easiest place to scale for those combat warriors who were skilled at those kinds of actions. The antipersonnel devices had been silently installed during the night while the ship was moored in Santiago de Cuba. Sensors were also rigged around the ship to detect any intrusion from the waterline to the first open deck walkways. Khalil ran a continuity test and verified the integrity of them all. He smiled to himself, assured that everything was as it was supposed to be.

The mines affixed to *Dream Spinner* below the waterline were armed to function as designed. They were set to explode if boats approached too closely, as in an attempt to board the ship. They could also be initiated by Khalil, either by a timing device or triggered to detonate immediately.

The cameras mounted ubiquitously around the ship, from bow to stern, and literally in every hallway and staircase, were all in commission.

After he finished his checks, he opened the door in the back of the communications center, where the main banks of equipment were located. He looked down at the frightened young girl secured to the bulkhead support mount. She was unharmed, for now. He had kept her hands bound but had given her bottled water and food. Also a blanket and pillow. He thought she looked pitiful. Part of him revolted against what he had done to this child. Khalil handed her another bottle of water.

"Are you okay?" he asked. "Do you have enough to eat? Do you need to use the bathroom?" He had made sure to respond to her requests to use the small bathroom in the communications center whenever she asked.

Claire shook her head. No—she was far from okay. She hadn't known what was happening when she'd been grabbed in the hallway outside her stateroom and brought here. She had done her best to keep the tears from flowing. Up to now, she had been only somewhat successful. Her dad had raised her to handle adversity, even at her tender age, and turn it to an advantage. She stemmed her tears and, drawing upon her anger, lashed out.

"Why are you doing this to me?" Claire demanded.

Khalil thought about how he should respond to the child.

"I know your father. I met him years ago, when he was flying the F-22 Raptor stealth fighter aircraft. You were a very small child back then." He stared at her, looking for any reaction. He saw none.

"He took something from me. Or I should say, his father, your grandfather—who you never knew." Again, no reaction from Claire.

"Your family, you Americans, took everything from me. They took my mother and father, my brothers, and my sister. How would you feel if that happened to your family. Would you be angry?"

Now there was a small flash in Claire's eyes—maybe a flicker of fear that Khalil noticed. A few tears trickled down her cheeks.

"Don't worry, child. I won't harm you," he lied.

Khalil thought about why he had taken the girl—to make her father feel pain. To make him suffer, to make him understand what it felt like to lose someone you loved. Khalil knew it wouldn't be the same kind of pain that he had suffered through. *At least not yet, not until the time is right.*

She didn't need to know what was ultimately going to happen. He would not share with her the fate of all passengers on board the *Dream Spinner*.

Chapter 40

The video transmission from the Viper came through with little notice to the White House.

"This message is a warning to President Foreman. My brothers, Soleimann and Heydar, have informed me of your foolish and reckless ruse regarding Victor Chernov. You have made a big mistake with your lies. It is clear you had no intention of releasing Chernov. You were buying time, perhaps to prepare an assault on the *Dream Spinner*. You have paid a heavy price for your dishonesty."

Foreman was shocked at hearing the accusation from Asmaradov. He wasn't yet aware of what had happened a short time before aboard the *Dream Spinner*.

It had begun in the muster stations. Guards had singled out one or two men from each area. They had not been selected at random. They were among the youngest and most fit. The men had been marched down the long carpeted hallways, up the staircases with their polished banisters, and past the beautiful works of art hanging on the walls. When they eventually reached the top deck at the ship's stern, the ten passengers were lined up against the rail. Their hands were bound behind their backs and blindfolds placed over their eyes. A video camera was propped on a stand, ready to record the subsequent slaughter.

Asmaradov's video transmission panned away from the terrorist leader and then switched over to the *Dream Spinner*. Foreman wasn't prepared for what was coming. He saw the men, blindfolded and bound, lined up on the back deck of the ship. Two gunmen, their faces masked, trained their rifles on them. The president's staff in the Situation Room reacted with horror when, within seconds, the helpless captives were cut down by automatic weapons fire. Their bodies crumpled to the deck, blood pooling from multiple bullet points of entry to their bodies. Foreman witnessed the final bullet shot into the head of one of the still-breathing victims. He watched the lifeless bodies being tossed over the back of the ship like garbage into the cold, dark water below.

The stone-faced appearance of the Viper flashed up on the video again. "You will release Chernov by eight o'clock in the morning. If you delay even one minute, more passengers will be executed. Additionally, if any attempt is made to assault the ship, it will be sunk immediately. As I warned you before, the ship is rigged with high explosives that will crater the hull, breach all key watertight compartments and sink the *Dream Spinner* in minutes."

The video went dead.

President Foreman was stunned. "Oh my God, is this real? Did he really execute ten people on that cruise ship?" He looked across the faces of his staff. They were silent, all clearly shocked by what they had seen and heard. A few shook their heads.

"He can't get away with this," replied the JCS chairman. "Mr. President, I believe we should act now. We have a small window of opportunity to hit that ship before Asmaradov's deadline for Chernov's release."

Foreman turned his back on his staff and began pacing the room. He felt as if he had been gut-punched. When he was urgently requested to leave the Oval Office and head to the Situation Room, he suspected the worst. Now, like the ominous clouds and torrential rain racing into DC, darkness seemed like it was ready to envelope him. Had he made a major mistake in approving the stalling tactic? Was it his fault that the innocent passengers aboard the *Dream Spinner* had been summarily executed. Shot like animals. Dumped like trash. And now he had to make another decision, a major one that could jeopardize additional lives.

"Mr. President, we can't delay for long if we intend to hit the *Dream Spinner* under the cover of darkness. Our window of time is closing fast."

"What if we wait a bit? What if we release Chernov tomorrow at eight? Once that's done, Asmaradov says he'll direct the ship to proceed to Caracas. Once it gets there, maybe then this whole mess will end."

"There's some risk there, Mr. President. Remember first that we're dealing with a terrorist leader. He's already got the blood of innocent people from that ship on his hands. Do we really think he'll hesitate to take more lives? That he won't scuttle the ship as soon as Chernov is turned over to the Cubans? That he didn't simply give us a reason to agree with his demands by indicating that the *Dream Spinner*'s takeover would end in Caracas?" The JCS chairman was clearly promoting an assault by the SEALs in the next few hours.

"We can't lose any more lives here," Foreman responded. "I want assurances that we can pull off this rescue without a major catastrophe happening."

"Sir, our SEAL teams are the best warriors in the world when it comes to situations like this. That's what they are trained to do. They've proven themselves again and again. And their success rate is unmatched anywhere on the planet."

Foreman was torn with indecision. He had the highest confidence in his military forces. They could get the job done, but at what cost in innocent lives? Surely the terrorists aboard the *Dream Spinner* would begin executing hostages once the assault started. Or Asmaradov would detonate the mines and sink the cruise ship. But would the Viper do that with his own men on board?

On the other hand, should he rely on the word of the globe's top terrorist? What was the likelihood that Asmaradov would keep his word once Chernov was released? After all, he had already killed a number of passengers, most of them probably Americans. It would be a gamble either way. But Foreman could better control the odds if his powerful military was in command of the situation.

"Alright. I think this may be the only way to be sure we get our people back and not leave that decision in the hands of that maniac Asmaradov." Foreman waited a few seconds and then turned to the chairman.

"Have our forces ready to assault the *Dream Spinner* the moment I give the order to execute Operation Clean Sweep."

Chapter 41

S hortly after the video had been shown to President Foreman, the passengers aboard the *Dream Spinner* heard a sinister message over the ship's intercom. They were told that a broadcast over the ship's closed-circuit network would be airing momentarily. When Ace heard the announcement, he suspected the worst. The video would confirm his belief that the terrorist demands had been received by the United States. But negotiations, if they were happening, were not going well.

When Ace and Flamer saw the tragic massacre on the Centrum's big screen, they couldn't believe their eyes—the new level of violence was completely unexpected. Nearly everyone in the auditorium reacted with horror to what they saw. Loud gasps—terrified looks—heads hanging down, hoping it wasn't real.

"No!" screamed a man three rows in front of Ace. He recognized his brother as one of those executed. As he doubled over in tears, an older gentleman sitting next to him tried to provide a measure of comfort.

"Holy shit," shouted Flamer. "I can't believe this!"

Ace continued to stare in silence at the now-blank screen, trying to process the savagery. He wondered about what had triggered this action. Maybe a response by the terrorist mastermind to send a violent message to the president of the United States?

Inside the staterooms, the tragic scene was witnessed over the televisions. Screams piercing the quiet hallways from staterooms on multiple decks—families believing their loved ones had been ruthlessly murdered.

Julie and Cathy Black had watched the video, terrified that Matt had been one of them. The boys, fortunately, had been pulled away from the television when Julie saw what was about to happen. She convinced herself that none of the victims had been Matt.

Ace knew that the assassination of the men on the rear of the ship was a major mistake by the terrorists. All that had been done was provoke the rage, the *will* of captive passengers and hopefully, rescuers to defeat those who held the ship hostage—at any cost.

There was no doubt in either Ace or Flamer's mind what was going to happen next. The United States would not let the terrorists' actions go unpunished. The resources available to the most powerful country on earth would be applied forcefully, violently, and effectively. If something was going to happen, it would happen very soon. Perhaps in the next twenty-four hours—maybe earlier.

The American military already had the best information that could be obtained on the number of captors and their location on the *Dream Spinner*. It was securely in the hands of a strike force intent on rescuing the captive cruise ship. All that Asmaradov had done was punch the president in the face with the execution of innocent passengers. The response from the United States was going to be more than a return punch.

The two aviators sat silent for a few moments, both deep in thought. They contemplated their next moves. Thought about the need to do something that they hoped they wouldn't come to regret.

———•———

Khalil had been made aware of the Viper's demands to the U.S. president, and specifically the time for Chernov's release—eight o'clock the following morning. He alone had the coded satellite communication device used to send messages to Asmaradov and receive key instructions. The messages were always brief—ten to twenty-seconds. Just short enough to hopefully avoid interception by American sensors that were surely watching, listening.

Given Asmaradov's order to slaughter passengers hours before, Khalil now expected an American assault at any time. He pulled his key operatives together and briefed them on how he expected the next twenty-four hours would play out. Then he sent them back to prepare to execute the Viper's final plan.

On Deck 10, Cho Lee Kwan gathered the armed militants assigned to that part of the ship he had been told to protect. He gave them their final orders, coinciding with the Gitmo release planned for the next morning. Since the chance of an American assault before that time increased exponentially in the security officers mind, Cho wanted assurances from the Tajiks that they were prepared to prevent the Americans from taking back the ship—at all costs.

In the engine control room, Drako Kratec was going through similar preparations. If Zoyatov failed to execute his responsibilities on the bridge, the chief engineer could take control of the *Dream Spinner* and maneuver the ship in ways that would make it extremely difficult for any assault team to board.

At nearly the lowest level of the ship, the provisioning manager reviewed his defensive plans to stop an assault through the Deck 2 doors. The entry points on the hull would likely be targeted by the Americans to gain access from the water. While the doors could be breached from the outside, they also could be easily defended from inside. Two heavily armed guards had enough firepower ready to either repel attackers, or at the very least inflict significant casualties.

Zoyatov understood what he was tasked to do on the bridge but had serious reservations about how things would eventually end up. He reviewed the scenario in his mind. Once the execution of the passengers had been broadcast, he knew the fate of the ship was sealed. He knew that the United States would act fast and forcefully to stop the carnage. And once they began taking back the ship, anyone who appeared to be a terrorist would be shot.

He had never *fully* committed to the Viper's radical ideas. He'd initially wanted no part of the mission but had been recruited under duress. His family was the leverage that had incentivized his participation. Their lives would have been at stake if he had chosen to defy Asmaradov.

At this point, there wasn't much he could do other than follow the plan. Continue to pilot the cruise ship on a random course, adjusting his speed and keeping a sharp eye on the ship's radar for any vessels that might try to approach.

He waited for the assault he *knew* was coming. His only protection was the pistol on the console. That pathetic weapon would do little to stop the Americans from breaching the bridge door. If he appeared to be a threat, he would surely be shot dead. He picked up the pistol and slid it into the console drawer.

Inside the communications center, Khalil was unexpectedly joined by Kelly. She was shocked to see the young girl tied up in the back room. The child was shaking, curled up in a ball like she was trying to hide. Claire made eye contact with Sayeed.

"What is going on here? Who is she? Why is she in here? What are you doing? What are you thinking?"

"This is not your concern. She is the daughter of Matthew Black. I have my reasons for what I do. Trust me, this girl has nothing to do with our mission."

"Are you crazy? You can't let your personal feelings jeopardize our real purpose on this ship." She scolded him. "You know what is coming. You must stay focused, with no distractions."

"Banu, please," he said angrily. "I am ready to carry out what Asmaradov has ordered. All preparations have been completed. All is ready. Soon, it will be over."

She stared into his eyes, trying to understand how his priorities seemed to have shifted.

"Stay focused, Kahlil. This is your jihad!"

"Do not worry. Just be sure you get to the elevator in the Chop House kitchen when the time comes to escape this ship."

"I know—you don't need to remind me."

With that comment, she left. Kelly headed back down to Deck 4 to monitor the daily meal activities, easily blending in with the rest of the dining room staff wearing the same standard pleasure cruise uniform. Kelly mingled with the men who were trying to rush through the few minutes they were given to consume their meals, chatting with them occasionally. She was on the alert for any sign of resistance that might be building in the captive group. Up to now, nothing she heard or saw had given her any undue concern.

Kelly also watched the attendants serving the meals. Nothing appeared out of the ordinary. Nothing that would raise her suspicions that anything other than normal meal service was being provided. In fact, the only thing that had piqued her interest was the way one particular attendant interacted with the passengers. She had been watching the young Ukrainian, not quite sure if something was off. But she had seen some awkward interactions once or twice between the pretty server and her customers. She would find out what, if anything, this woman was up to. If she was a problem, Kelly intended to quickly remedy the situation.

She talked with a number of the guards who maintained control of the dining area. Had they noticed anything odd about the Ukrainian crew member serving the captive passengers? Had they noticed her doing anything that would indicate she was trying to help them do things *other* than serve their meals? Had they seen her going about the ship in places she shouldn't?

Sayeed picked up enough information, albeit a bit abstract, to build concern about the Ukrainian. *Time to eliminate the problem.*

Back in the communications center, Khalil thought about his angry confrontation with Kelly. He was not distracted by what she had implied—his fixation on punishing Matt "Ace" Black. He was in total control, fully committed to Asmaradov's plan—to send a searing shock wave through the society, the culture that he truly despised. To make the Americans and the Western world realize that they would always be a target. He would succeed in that.

THOMAS BELISLE

His plans to exact pain from his old enemy, Matt Black, was just an added *extra* to his primary objective. Nothing would interfere with what had begun as a glowing ember of hate, now transitioning into a raging fire within him.

Chapter 42

Lieutenant Commander Shorty Robinson was thinking through the upcoming tactical operation, playing out in his head how it would proceed, and tossing around the potential risks to his team. He considered each risk and how he would overcome it. SEALs never worried. They developed concerns, then dealt with them.

Compounding his tactical plans, he had been watching a tropical storm move swiftly across the Atlantic Ocean from the east. It had formed off the coast of Africa, as was typical of the weather patterns this time of year. It wasn't a hurricane-sized cell, but more like a tropical depression that had grown into a small storm. The sustained winds were expected to still be in the neighborhood of thirty-five miles per hour, but with gusts up to fifty. If it kept its course, it would cross the track of the *Dream Spinner* just about the time of the planned assault. His two squads had operated in worse, but there were added risks—especially to the SEALs planning to parachute to the top deck of the *Dream Spinner*.

The SEALs also had a small window of time to make the most effective use of the darkness, while trading off the risk caused by the unpredictable storm. Current projections indicated the strongest winds would be clear of the *Dream Spinner* by three o'clock in the morning. With a little bit of luck, Bravo Squad could conceivably make their jump shortly after that, skirting the absolute ragged edge of the safe wind limits for a controlled descent to the ship while still optimizing the cover of darkness. Their specialized parachutes were designed to enable pinpoint landings in most weather. If they made

THOMAS BELISLE

it safely to the upper deck, their NVGs would quickly highlight any Tajik militant unlucky enough to be there.

The underwater assault would also require a bit of luck. Transiting the gap from the *Grayback III* to the *Dream Spinner* would be no problem under the churning surface of an angry sea. But the close-in work near the big cruise ship's hull was another story. It would take all the skill of the highly trained mini-sub operators to prevent a tragic impact against the cruise ship's steel hull. Once the frogmen departed their small submersibles, they would have to fight the violent, crashing waves to board the ship and begin their assault.

Of course, there was also the issue of an explosive deterrent that Asmaradov had intimated to President Foreman. The U.S. intelligence sources presumed that the Viper *had* actually placed mines on the hull. Given Asmaradov's tight connections and outright sponsorship by Russia, the deadly underwater devices would have been easy to acquire. Shorty's men were well trained to defeat virtually every type of mine while fighting the unpredictable swells pounding the ship. And there was always a chance of encountering something new—something deadly that they had never seen before. If that happened, the SEALs would do as they always did. Improvise, overcome, and complete the mission.

Shorty figured that the Viper had to know a preemptive attack was very possible while he waited for Chernov's release—especially after the brutal execution of passengers. Asmaradov would have made accommodations for that possibility and have his militants on high-alert for an American attack.

Another thought crossed the SEAL commander's mind. If he waited for the storm to pass in order to minimize the risk to his airborne assault squad, it would put the attack in daylight, *after* the release of Chernov. Once the terrorist was released, Asmaradov might do the unexpected. Perhaps sink the ship.

Robinson discussed the options with his squad leaders. They hated to give up the darkness and the advantages that came with it.

The SEAL team's night vision goggles would provide a distinct advantage in the blackness of the night, one that would be lost in daylight. But they understood the power of an angry sea and high winds and what both could do to those who didn't respect the power of nature. Moving at thirty miles per hour, the storm wouldn't be completely clear of the ship until about seven o'clock in the morning. But the storm's strongest winds would likely pass the ship by three o'clock since the central cell of the tropical depression was moving fast.

Shorty had a plan. He believed they could use the storm to their advantage. First, the terrorists holding the ship might believe that an attack was unlikely in a tropical gale. They wouldn't be expecting it nearly as much as during calmer seas. Second, he knew that tropical systems could impart "unintended consequences" on ships, not the least of which were all manner of problems induced by the violent wind and surging sea. Like engine problems. *Like a power outage.* If things like this occurred on the *Dream Spinner* while the storm was raging, the militants might believe it to be a consequence of the gale—*as opposed to a little surprise from the Navy SEALs.*

Robinson knew that he could still maintain some element of surprise. After all, Asmaradov believed he had a deal with the president of the United States. The terrorist leader had already given Foreman a strong, violent message about the cost of resistance to his demands. Farad Asmaradov might believe that the United States would do nothing until after Chernov was released. And Asmaradov had to be aware of the tropical depression in the Caribbean and believe it might keep the Americans from doing anything until it had passed.

Lieutenant Commander Robinson was now betting that the Panja cell leader would not expect the imminent violent attack that was about to descend upon the *Dream Spinner*.

Chapter 43

R etired Colonel Jack Stevens had done his best to comfort those he loved after Claire had been abducted. He hoped that no news was good news. If there was a motive behind her capture, they would likely have heard what it was by now. But he didn't expect things aboard the *Dream Spinner* to degrade so quickly. When he had seen the video simulcast to every part of the ship, including his stateroom, he had not been shocked, having expected that it might come to this kind of violence. The video had made his wife, Gemma, sob almost uncontrollably. All it did to him was make him angry. Very angry.

He had seen plenty of violence, horror, and the worst of what men could do to other men during his military career. Jack knew that to deal with this kind of situation effectively, you often had to reduce yourself to the same level as the perpetrators. He knew how to do that. Jack had been forced to do it thirty-plus years ago—in his distant past, when leading dismounted patrols in Afghanistan.

The former Army Ranger was perhaps the most athletic, young-est-looking sixty-year-old man on the ship. He had kept his physical fitness regimen constant over the years and could still bench-press twice his own weight. Likewise, he controlled his diet in spite of the occasional temptation to consume junk food. He had no real health issues to speak of. He was as limber as he had been thirty years ago. All would serve him well in what was to come.

Jack strongly suspected that at some point in the next twenty-four hours, the United States would initiate action to free the boat from its captors. He knew that the execution of ten passengers had been a major mistake by the terrorists. He knew that the brutal action would not go unchallenged. Jack also knew that, given the number of militants he presumed were on board, able-bodied passengers might need to do their part to help ensure the success of any assault team.

He thought about the first day at sea. The skeet shooting area on Deck 5. The armory. The shotguns. There was a potential opportunity if he could get there, and get inside without being discovered. Maybe he could enlist a few others to help. But after all the passengers had witnessed the ruthless executions, it was unlikely that anybody would voluntarily commit to putting up a fight and perhaps become the next victim.

He thought about Ace and Flamer. Jack knew that both aviators would be all in on a plan to help take back the ship. Also, Buzz Caster, the skeet instructor and former Royal Marine, clearly had the ability to put up a formidable fight against the militants. That would help even the odds just a little in favor of the rescue team he hoped was coming. But how to get the men all together—or even get a message to them? Impossible. Maybe not.

As Jack continued to think it through, he knew that the armory was likely to be guarded. There was no way the terrorists would leave it unattended. He would have to figure out how to get past that obstacle.

Jack was ready to spring into action and began to feel the rush of adrenaline, his heart rate slightly elevated. He had a strong incentive to do something. Not just because of the horrific video of the execution—his granddaughter's life was at stake, and the lives of the rest of his family.

⸻

Khalil received the next coded message from Asmaradov as evening approached the *Dream Spinner* on the sixth day of the cruise. He thought deeply about its contents.

Asmaradov's original ruse after release of the Guantanamo Bay prisoners involved turning the ship toward Venezuela. The intent was to make the Americans believe that there would be a peaceful conclusion to the crisis once the ship arrived in the port of Caracas.

But the message Khalil received reminded him about the final outcome. Nearly all of the Viper's faithful militants would never leave the ship. The slow approach to Venezuela would enable a few key people to escape the *Dream Spinner* on the Venezuelan diesel-electric submarine. Following that, the cruise ship would be sunk with all on board.

He was to be one of the few survivors, as well as Kratec, Cho Lee Kwan and Kelly. They were too valuable to Asmaradov. Too critical to the continuation of the terrorist leader's future plans. If all went according to the extraction schedule, they would be the only ones to escape from the *Dream Spinner* on the Venezuelan submarine. Zoyatov would go down with his ship.

Khalil relished the thought of the explosive conclusion coming to the unsuspecting passengers. And how he would be subsequently remembered for striking a major blow against the Americans and other countries around the world whose citizens had made the unfortunate choice to board the *Dream Spinner*.

As he thought about what was to come, his phone rang. It was Zoyatov, providing an update on the weather. The ship's radar had been tracking the tropical storm for two days. In the last twenty-four hours, it had shifted its path slightly and was now heading directly for the cruise ship. Zoyatov was not especially worried. The *Dream Spinner* could easily handle the small storm. He had previously encountered winds and waves many times greater and never had a problem controlling a ship this size. Regardless, he planned on taking necessary precautions.

When Zoyatov finished his update, Khalil questioned him.

"We need to be at the designated coordinates by eight o'clock tomorrow morning," he said, referring to the specific location he had previously given to the captain. It was his preplanned pickup point for the sub.

"That might not be possible, depending on weather conditions."

"Can't you avoid the storm?" demanded Khalil.

"The system is moving too fast and is still very strong. I plan to maneuver north to avoid a major impact by the winds, but we are still going to feel strong effects. It shouldn't impact getting to that position."

Khalil didn't want any disruption in what was planned to happen the next morning after Chernov's release. He wanted to be sure he could escape from the *Dream Spinner* in spite of the storm and rendezvous with the submarine. The commander of the Venezuelan Navy vessel had just recently left Caracas and begun his trek north to get to the pickup point.

"Why don't we head south? The storm's effects look like they will be significantly reduced if we sail toward Caracas." Khalil knew that a movement in that direction would put him closer to the sub.

"I can't do that. I have my orders from Asmaradov on where I am to operate this ship. I won't leave this zone of operation unless it is directed by him. And we have received no communications from him since the takeover of this ship." The captain was not aware that Khalil had been in regular communication with the Viper.

Khalil thought for a moment before responding, controlling his growing anger at Zoyatov.

"I too have specific instructions from Asmaradov. You may not be aware of all of them."

"Why do I need to proceed to the south, to these specific coordinates? What is the compelling need?"

"Captain, you must trust me. It is imperative that we be at that position before eight o'clock. There are things the Viper told only to me that make this necessary. You will come to understand why Asmaradov wants us there."

He continued, "There will come a time, soon, when I will ask you to do things with the ship's systems you may disagree with. You must react immediately and comply with my directions."

Zoyatov had become silent after Khalil's bold statement.

"I am the captain. I don't take my orders from you, Khalil. I know my job. If you have directions from Asmaradov that are different from what he has required me to do, you need to show me what those directions are, now!"

Zoyatov paused. He wondered what Asmaradov could have told Khalil about the ship's operation that he didn't already know.

THOMAS BELISLE

After all, the Viper had told Zoyatov that *he* was in charge of this mission.

Khalil needed to tamp down the angry rhetoric and reassure the captain a bit.

"Hafez—you have been chosen, like the rest of us, to participate in something greater than yourself. Our leader has provided this opportunity to strike a mighty blow against the United States. There surely are things that all of us have not been equally briefed on. I am trying to ensure our success."

Zoyatov, albeit reluctantly, replied. "Very well. I will move the ship a bit more south as soon as I can, and I will do my best to be at the prescribed coordinates tomorrow morning."

"Rest assured, Captain, we will be victorious in our mission," responded Khalil. He hung up the phone.

Khalil knew that after eight o'clock the next morning, he would have no further use for Zoyatov.

Chapter 44

Martha Cook had successfully passed as much information that she could gather to the CIA. She hoped it would help whoever would carry out the rescue—likely the Navy SEALs. This was their environment. This was what they were trained to do. She was told the assault would come in darkness—perhaps tonight. Martha expected to hear the precise time on her next and possibly last planned call with Langley.

The talented CIA operative thought about warning passengers of the upcoming rescue operation and advising as many as she could to stay in their state rooms when hell broke loose. But she also didn't want the information to be inadvertently leaked to the militants.

She could certainly get the message to everyone on her side of the deck. Cabin-to-cabin word of mouth. Simple enough for rooms with adjoining balconies. With everyone confined to their rooms, most were already on their balconies. That would take care of one side of her deck—a fraction of the passengers aboard the *Dream Spinner*. Beyond that, nobody was willing to step into the hallway for fear of getting shot. It would also be too risky to try to pass the word when they all gathered at mealtime. The possibility of being overheard by militants was too great.

But Martha had to figure a way to get the information to the men in the muster stations. They were the most vulnerable once the assault began—the ones at most risk being shot by their captors. Before the evening meal, she could search for Aleksandra. The young lady had already proven herself to be one of the "good guys." Maybe Martha could somehow get the Ukrainian to pass the information to Ace Black. It would depend on whether Aleksandra was in the dining area used by the women—not very likely since the waitress worked out of a different dining room. But if she *was* there, then at least one muster station, a very large one, would be able to respond accordingly. Surely Ace would know what to do—garner support once the assault started, provide some resistance, and maybe even take out a couple of the terrorists themselves.

One hour before the evening meal, Martha made contact with her handlers. SEALs *would* lead the attack. It was set for early the next morning. The night would be at its darkest at that time. Minimal moonlight was a huge plus, and the storm's violence would have mostly passed. She was told that the power to the ship would be killed at three thirty. That was good news—at that time, nearly every passenger and crew member would be asleep in their cabins. If they stayed put during the assault, there was a reduced risk that they would become casualties during the chaos.

———————•———————

There was something different about the guards. They were not nearly as attentive to their hostages as they had been. Perhaps they believed that the butchery on the ship's stern had sent a strong message both to their captives and to the United States—and that the end of their mission was near and their own freedom was fast approaching. Maybe it was the rapidly moving tropical storm that gave them a sense of security—no attack would occur while a storm raged. And by the time it passed, Chernov would be released.

Ace had already committed to his next actions. He wasn't going to sit in the Centrum until another horrible event occurred. If an attack by the U.S. military began on the *Dream Spinner*, it was very possible the militants would quickly slaughter the men confined to the muster areas and eliminate a potential source of internal resistance. And who knew what might happen to the passengers in their cabins—did the terrorists have a deadly plan for them as well?

Weighing heavily on his mind was his daughter. He had no idea what was happening to her, and it was driving him crazy. It was also making him very angry. In a way, he believed it was his fault that she was taken. He was determined to act, to do things on his terms, not on whatever terms the radicals had in store for him.

The two aviators had a pretty good idea that the next few hours would be the beginning of the end of their ordeal, one way or another. Hopefully, a military assault would happen in the darkness. But they had no way of knowing that—Martha had not yet passed on that information. So Ace was proceeding the only way he knew.

He had shared his thoughts with Flamer, who was all in. The plan was pretty daring, and definitely dangerous. There was a high degree of risk that both of them would be shot during their attempt to resist. Heck, if they did nothing, they might be shot! But Ace knew that everything in life carried risk. He believed he could effectively manage that risk with his wits—and with the knowledge he had gained on his pre-captivity daily walks about key parts of the ship. He knew where the other muster areas were. That was where the guards would be. There and at the ends of each deck, each hallway. He also had plenty of inside information on key areas of the *Dream Spinner* gained from his tour. That knowledge would help in what he planned to do. If things turned badly while he was trying to save his daughter, then so be it. At least he would go down fighting.

"Okay, buddy. Time to get our show on the road. Ready?"

"Yeah. Just hope we can pull this off without taking a bullet."

"Flamer, I'll head to the restroom first. You follow a few minutes later. Then we wait for Ray Cook, sitting behind us, to create some commotion."

Ray would cause the distraction needed to hopefully prompt the rear Centrum door guard to move away from his position, giving the two aviators a chance to slip out of the large room.

"Roger that," Flamer replied. "Let's do this."

Ace left his seat and started toward the back of the Centrum. As he approached the restroom, the guard stopped him. Ace motioned that he had stomach problems. The guard waved him past. A couple of minutes later, Flamer did the same. The guard thought that was a bit strange. He turned toward the restroom and was about to go inside.

About that time, Ray began moaning loudly and then started screaming. He doubled over, holding his stomach, feigning terrible pain. His screams prompted the guard on the Centrum stage to motion to the rear guard to see what was happening. As soon as the rear guard moved through the overcrowded room toward the screaming passenger on the left side of the auditorium, Ace and Flamer made their move. Making sure the guard on stage wasn't observing them, they slowly opened the door. They both hoped there wasn't another militant outside, waiting to blast them both. They got lucky. The foyer was empty as they slipped out. At this point, nobody in the auditorium had any idea that they had escaped.

"This way," directed Ace. Flamer followed him, both men hugging the side wall of the Centrum's entryway, using what little concealment there was to hide their movement as much as possible.

They reached the stairwell, relieved that they had encountered no resistance, and headed down to the next deck. They peered through the horizontal gaps in the colorfully carpeted stair steps, looking for anyone who might be standing guard on the next level. Nobody was there. Moving silently, they turned toward the stern of the ship. The twisting hallway provided them both some measure of comfort and thankfully, some concealment. As they approached the final hallway turn to their destination, they slowed.

"There has to be another guard around the corner. These nutballs would never leave the skeet range and armory unprotected," Ace whispered.

He took a quick peek around the corner and saw a guard, his back turned to them. Per the plan, Flamer groaned loudly and fell forward around the corner. The militant was on him instantly, his rifle pointed at Flamer's head. The Tajik shouted at him, lowering the gun barrel close to Flamer. In that instant, Ace bounded around the corner. Fortunately, Flamer was ready as Ace sprang forward. As the terrorist turned his rifle toward Ace, Flamer grabbed it to keep both of them from getting shot. Ace surprised the terrorist, using the most violent attack he had learned from his South Korean tae kwon do trainer years before. The guard was down for the count.

"He's gotta have keys to the armory," Ace said hopefully. As he quickly checked the unconscious guard, he found them. He opened the door and they dragged the militant inside, along with his assault rifle. They checked back outside the doorway to ensure there was no sign of the struggle that had taken place. Finding none, they closed the door, locked it and got to work.

Ace found some zip ties in one of the cabinets and used them to secure the militant's hands behind his back and bind his feet. Then he gagged the man to keep him quiet once he regained consciousness.

"Okay, Flamer. Grab all the twelve-gauge shotguns and set them over here on the table. Make sure they're all in working order. I want to put the max number of rounds into each one of these. That should be one in the chamber and three in the magazine. I'll grab the ammo."

"Got it." Flamer went over to the rack and removed all six shotguns. He laid them on the counter and checked the serviceability of each. The weapons all appeared in working order. "They look good, Ace."

Ace pulled open every drawer and cabinet door, looking for ammo.

"Great. Here are a few boxes of shells. They're skeet load, number eight shot. Not the best for what we need, but I think that's all that's here." He had a concerned look. "If this is all we have, our targets will have to be the militants' heads. From any distance past about ten feet, a body shot will just piss them off. A head shot will at least incapacitate them."

Ace looked around the armory a bit more thoroughly. In one part of the room, he found a locked cabinet, its steel doors with reinforced hinges clearly designed to keep things inside—a bit more secure.

"Flamer, look for keys that might be for this cabinet. If you can't find any, look for a crowbar, or anything else I can use to pry open this door."

Flamer couldn't find any keys but did find a flat-tipped metal rod. "Try this."

Ace took the rod and worked on the cabinet doors. He finally got them open. Staring inside, he first saw a set of combat knives in leather sheaths. He looked further and then found what he was really searching for.

"Hey, check this out." He held up four boxes of shells that were clearly not designed for skeet shooting. "I'll bet these are for the security guys. Maybe for use in the ship's defense, if they ever needed it. These shells are loaded with buckshot pellets. Perfect for what I intend to use with these guns." He smiled. "These will bring down those pricks pretty quickly."

They quickly loaded all six guns with buckshot. While they were busy, the unconscious guard on the floor began to come around. Ace saw his movement and figured it was time to try to get some information, if possible. He pulled the gag away. Unfortunately, the guard spoke limited English. The gag was put back in place.

Ace shook his head as he looked at the shotguns. They couldn't handle three shotguns apiece. Maybe two. They could rig up some slings and attach them to the shotguns. One carried over the shoulder, the other shotgun at the ready. But now, he also had the AK-47 rifle the captive militant had previously carried. Ace needed a few more recruits—but he didn't expect to find any more volunteers beyond Flamer. The two of them were going to be pretty limited in their armed resistance.

"Ace, what happens if one or two of the terrorists head down here to get to the weapons themselves? Or maybe the security guys?"

"Well, I suspect they may head here once the assault begins. If they do, we let them open the door, presuming they have a key to get in. We stay hidden, let them come in, and then introduce them to their maker." He paused for a moment. "We'll definitely have the element of surprise. And actually, I hope that happens. That will mean we've taken out a couple more of these dudes and improved our odds."

The two fighter pilots stared at each other—both wondering how the next few minutes would play out, and if they would survive their next encounter with death. They both hoped an American assault on the ship would begin soon.

"Meanwhile, we wait," Ace concluded.

Chapter 45

Khalil made his way to the engine control room to meet with Drako Kratec.

"The next twelve hours will be critical in this storm."

Kratec nodded. "I am aware of the storm. It's not a problem."

"If the Americans try to take the ship before morning, I am not convinced Zoyatov will do as he has been ordered. We may have to override his ability to control the ship."

"You believe Zoyatov will not do what is required of him?"

"No, Zoyatov only cares about his own skin. I believe he will do anything to keep himself safe if the Americans attack." He paused. "Remember, we must get to the specific coordinates north of Caracas before we scuttle the ship. Our escape route is the Venezuelan submarine. Nothing can prevent us from getting there. Not even an American assault."

"I understand. Don't worry. Even the Americans would not be foolish enough to attack a cruise ship in a tropical storm."

Khalil shook his head. He knew the Americans pretty well. He believed his own instincts were accurate and that a rescue attempt was imminent.

"Be ready to react with full control of the ship's steering and propulsion if I direct you."

Kratec nodded.

Khalil was satisfied—Drako would respond as needed.

He left and walked through the ship until he reached the security officer's station. At the entrance, he picked up the phone. Cho Lee Kwan answered, then unlocked the door and let Khalil in.

The two men spent the next few minutes discussing the final preparations to end the cruise after Chernov's release. Khalil also shared his worry about an imminent attack.

"I am as concerned as you are that we are at a very vulnerable time," Cho said. "After this number of days, with this many American hostages, it is inconceivable that the United States has not tried to take back this ship. Because of the aircraft we shot down and the ten passengers that were killed per Asmaradov's order, I believe an attack has to happen soon. Like you, I know the Americans very well. We should be ready for them, prepare for their assault. I feel it, I know it is coming."

"We *are* prepared," replied Khalil. "We may have a few hours before that particular threat is upon us. But once the storm is not a factor, be ready for them." He paused. "I believe that will probably be just before dawn, based on the storm's current track and speed."

Cho agreed. Khalil could see that he was still concerned, a worried look on his face.

"Look," Khalil said. "Between your security team, the thirty members of our Panja cell that boarded in Cuba, and our embedded cell members, we have sufficient manpower to thwart an American assault if it were to come. We have plenty of grenades and explosives. And we have shoulder-fired missiles to fend off an unlikely air attack in this weather. Furthermore, our mines attached to the hull are a major threat to the Americans. They would not approach the ship and risk having the mines explode and sink the ship. They know that most of the passengers would perish—a steep price if they tried to take the *Dream Spinner*."

Khalil was doing his best to reassure Cho. "Even if there is an attack tonight, we proceed as planned to our escape location before destroying the *Dream Spinner* and everyone on board. Zoyatov agreed to begin moving toward the coordinates I gave him. If he fails to execute his responsibility, Kratec will take control of the ship and get us there."

Cho agreed with Khalil, but only to finish the conversation. He knew better than to discount the power of the United States.

Khalil left abruptly and began walking back to his communications facility. He stopped suddenly and thought about his exit plan from the cruise ship. He had wanted to check the escape route one last time, the path he would take in the final moments of the *Dream Spinner*'s life. He reversed his direction and headed down to Deck 2.

———————•———————

They heard footsteps outside the entrance, then the sound of the door latch being tested. Someone was checking it—trying to get in.

Ace quietly approached the reinforced steel door. He peered out the small peephole and was amazed at what he saw. He unlocked the door and opened it. The man was ready to throw a punch at Ace, prepared to disable the guard he suspected was inside, but stopped in his tracks.

"Jack. What are you doing here?" Ace asked his father-in-law in a hushed but forceful voice. "Get inside, quick!"

"Looks like I'm trying to do the same thing you are. Put up some kind of fight against this band of militants." He hustled into the room, carrying a couple assault rifles. Ace closed the door, locking it before turning to talk with Jack.

"How did you get here without being shot?"

"Believe it or not, when I got to the end of my hallway, there was just one guard. I played my 'old confused guy' routine, and it distracted him just long enough for me to get up close and personal with him and take him down. Stuffed him in a stall in the men's room. Then I managed to get through two more stairwells before I had to take another one out. He never heard me come up behind him. His neck snapped pretty easily. Slid him behind one of the small credenzas nearby. Picked up a couple weapons while I was at it, since the two militants didn't need them anymore."

"You gotta be shitting me," said Flamer. "Jack, you are one *real* badass!"

"I'm just glad I could still execute my close-combat skills at my ripe old age," he chuckled.

"You took a lot of chances, Jack. Things could have turned out badly for you, considering you were up against two trained, armed terrorists."

"Before you say anything else, I'm pretty glad to see you here too!" he remarked sarcastically. "Thought I was going to be on my own, at least for a while, until the reinforcements got here."

"What do you mean, reinforcements?" asked Ace.

"I got word that there's going to be an assault on the *Dream Spinner* early tomorrow morning. It will be Navy SEALs. We are lucky enough to have a CIA operative, Martha Cook, on board who has been in contact with Langley and the cavalry."

"Holy cow. You know about Martha?"

"Yep. Her cabin is only a few rooms down from ours. She saw us in the dining room and knew you were a hostage. She passed information about what's getting ready to happen."

"It's pretty incredible that I met Martha's husband, Ray, in the Centrum. He told me about her and said he suspected she'd been communicating off the ship for help." He paused. "Ray created the diversion that allowed me and Flamer to slip away from the auditorium."

Jack reached over to shake Flamer's hand.

"We can sure use your deadly aim when it comes time to use these weapons," Flamer commented.

The two walked over to the counter and looked at the six shotguns.

"Ace found some buckshot that we loaded up in these babies," Flamer noted. "Hopefully that'll do the trick when it comes time to use them. I'm guessing our lives might depend on it, considering we're going up against automatic weapons. But I'm glad to see you brought some *real* firepower with you."

"Yeah, courtesy of the two dead bastards that got in my way. These will come in handy."

Jack looked at the shotguns. "The buckshot is great. But six shotguns aren't going to do us much good, except to defend ourselves in the armory. Once we're on the move, we'll need to use the automatic weapons." Jack looked at the two aviators. "I see you made shoulder slings—we can at least carry one shotgun apiece and the extra buckshot shells. They'll work well if we get close to these bastards. We'll even up the odds with these assault rifles. They're limited to what's in their magazines. I didn't waste any time looking for extra mags."

Jack looked over in the corner and saw a bound and gagged man. "Who is that?"

"He's the guy who was guarding the armory door. He's out of the fight for now, maybe for good."

Jack saw the militant's AK-47 on the floor and picked it up. "This makes it three assault rifles. We're now a potent fighting force."

"Wait a minute. How are we going to keep from getting shot by the SEALs when they see us with these weapons?" Flamer asked. "We'll look like just more armed dudes that need to be taken out!"

"I told Martha what I was planning to do. She knows that there's at least one 'good guy' with a weapon that will try to join the fight to free this ship. I let her know that if I could recruit others along the way, our numbers would increase and hopefully we can put up more of a fight. She's relaying that information to her contacts." He paused. "I told her that I'll have to figure a way to identify ourselves as friendlies to the SEALs. We'll use reflective tape if there's any here."

The three men then spent some time trying to figure out the best way they could support the SEALs. Ace explained to Jack where he believed the armed militants were positioned on the ship. Of course, once an assault by the Navy was in progress, the ship's captors might move to where the action was taking place, or hunker down to defend their positions. The militants couldn't very well escape the *Dream Spinner*. They were as captive as the hostages were at this point.

The determined trio had to figure a way to use what they had to their best possible advantage. They collectively agreed that when it came to countering a trained militant armed with an automatic weapon, three against one was the best strategy, presuming they could approach their target without being seen. And, of course, gain an advantage by positioning themselves to use interlocking fields of fire against the terrorist. If they could take out even a couple of them, that would improve the assault team's overall chance of success. And possibly keep themselves alive.

They inventoried their ammunition stash and divided it up. Jack saw some vests that were intended for skeet shooters. The vests had plenty of large pockets for shells. Between the men, they had enough ammo for multiple shotgun reloads. There was also one spare magazine for the assault rifle taken from the bound terrorist on the floor.

All three agreed that Jack would take the lead in their counterattack. He was the former United States Army Ranger and had already proven that he hadn't lost his ability to hit exactly what he aimed at.

"Maybe we should try to increase our odds," Ace said. "The Centrum is just over us on the next deck. What if we head up there, at the right time, and take out the two guards in that facility? We can bring the extra shotguns and ammo, and recruit a few men who know how to use them."

Jack didn't like the idea. "That may be tough once the power is knocked out when the assault begins."

"What do you mean, once the power is knocked out?"

"I guess the SEALs are going to do some magic to put this ship into absolute darkness when they begin their attack. At this point, I think trying to recruit anyone else has a pretty high risk. We're too close to the time when the shit will hit the fan." He paused. "We don't want to be caught in the middle of all that."

Flamer piped up. "I'm a bit concerned that the crazed terrorists will begin shooting the hostages when the attack begins and the lights go out."

"I don't think the militants will be inclined to waste ammunition on hostages if they're under attack. If SEALs are shooting at them, they'll be shooting back," Jack said. "But I also hope the captives don't do anything crazy. Like emptying the auditorium and racing to their staterooms. The casualty count could grow astronomically." Nods of agreement.

"Martha has already spread the word the best she could to let some of the passengers know the assault is coming. She told them to stay in their staterooms. Barricade the doors with anything that they can drag within their rooms. The last thing we need is literally hundreds of passengers in the hallways when the assault is going down." Jack saw the nods from the other two.

"Let's plan to get Claire first. I think we absolutely can reach her quickly in the darkness, and handle any radical gunmen we confront," Ace said. Jack agreed.

Their plan was now set. They each armed themselves with a shotgun slung across their shoulder, one automatic rifle, and a combat knife. Also, each now wore reflective tape on their chest and back. They had crudely fashioned the tape into the letters *U.S.*, hoping that would be enough to assure they would be identified by the SEALs as friendlies and hopefully not get shot.

"Given the time we think the rescue attempt will take place, we should make our move when the power goes out," Jack said, referring to the information Martha had given him. "At three thirty, the *Dream Spinner* will be hit with a power outage. We move at that time."

The three men unanimously agreed on the risky plan.

They felt the ship pitching and rolling a bit more than usual in the stormy seas. All of them wondered about the ability of the SEALs to safely board the *Dream Spinner* and free the ship.

Chapter 46

Captain Zoyatov was doing his best to maintain the programmed random course while trying to move toward the coordinates Khalil had provided. It was becoming increasingly difficult given the fifty-mile-per-hour gusts and twenty-foot swells blasting in from the eastern Atlantic. The storm had grown in size and intensity. Control of a ship in high winds and rough seas was always improved by turning the bow into the wind. Zoyatov ordered the navigator at gunpoint to program a standard racetrack pattern, first heading east into the wind and then, after five or so miles, turning back west. His choice made the *Dream Spinner*'s path much more predictable to those closely tracking his movement.

The gale was now moving much faster than expected. Weather radar showed the center of the approaching storm passing through his location after midnight. At that rate of speed, the ship would be clear of the highest winds and rough seas by about three o'clock in the morning.

His attention was interrupted by the ringing phone. It was Khalil.

"Captain, is everything okay?" he asked. "The storm seems to be upon us earlier than expected."

"Yes," he replied. "I am in full control. There is no problem. But I'm sure the passengers are not too happy with the wind and waves. I'm certain many are already experiencing bouts of sea sickness."

"The passengers' condition is not my concern. Whether they are sick or not, they are just useful tools for our cause. Soon, their health won't matter."

Zoyatov was startled by that response. He had originally hoped that the mission would not cause any loss of life—at least, he had hoped it would be minimized. But that hope had gone out the window when ten passengers were executed. Still, Hafez Zoyatov expected to finish this mission in Venezuela, perhaps as early as two days from now. Once Chernov was released, the ship could chart its course to Caracas. Then he could get off the cursed vessel, fly back to his home, and hopefully join his wife and daughter. The passengers could also try to resume their *normal* lives after what they had experienced.

"Make sure that you alert me to anything unusual on the ship's radar. If there is going to be an attempt by the Americans to take this ship, I believe it will come just after the storm passes," Khalil said to him.

"Perhaps. But nobody would be foolish enough to try anything like that in this kind of gale. It would be a suicide mission," replied the captain.

"Just do what I ask." Khalil hung up the phone.

He looked over at his hostage. Claire was pretty frightened. Although food had been brought to her from the dining room and she had been able to use the small bathroom in the communications center, she was still captive—still chained like an animal. She had not been harmed, but after two days, she was beginning to believe that she had been forgotten by her family—by her father. The tracks of her tears were clearly visible on her freckled cheeks.

Part of Khalil, the piece of him buried deep within his heart, had some sympathy for the young girl. He remembered his sister. Ana. He remembered the pain she had gone through in her life, before it had ended tragically on a Dallas street. The young child reminded him slightly of his sister, when they were youngsters in Syria.

He didn't especially relish *seeing* pain being inflicted on anyone up close. If it occurred out of sight, it became more impersonal. More distant and detached. More tolerable. Even when he'd tried to bring down the most powerful fighter aircraft in the world years before, including Matt Black, he tried to keep death at a distance from him—impersonal. The death of the child would be no different.

"You will not be harmed," he lied. "Just be patient. You will be united with your family soon."

He didn't hate the innocent girl. But he hated the country her father stood for. Since the United States had ruthlessly taken his own family from him years ago, in his mind, they still had a debt to pay. Beyond his own personal loss, the country's reckless behavior around the world had never abated. Invasions, occupations, drone strikes, sanctions—the intervention by America never ceased. *The debt will be paid soon*, he thought to himself. *After Chernov is released from Guantanamo.*

Khalil knew very well that what he was now doing was more personal than it was supposed to be. The real mission had everything to do with supporting Russia's desire to maintain its predominant role in Tajikistan. A role that kept the Americans out of the region. Russia's ambitions would be enhanced by the murder of thousands of people on the *Dream Spinner*. The action would be directly linked to the current leadership of the country—to the Tajik president, and his presumed complicity with a leading terrorist faction. Asmaradov's goal of gaining release of a few terrorists at Guantanamo Bay would be attained as well.

But in Khalil's mind, it didn't matter. If President Mikolayev got the blame, so be it. If the political leadership was influenced to lean heavily toward the Russians, perhaps put in place another regime led by Voitek or maybe a Russian puppet, then okay. It just didn't matter. The only thing that mattered to him was that the United States would pay a large debt, one paid in its citizen's blood.

———————•———————

Lieutenant Commander Shorty Robinson was pretty happy that the storm had accelerated toward the *Dream Spinner*. He and the Alpha Squad had transferred from the USS *John F. Kennedy* to the USS *Grayback III* twelve hours earlier, before the storm winds had gotten out of hand. Now safely on board, he had time to load their gear aboard the SDVs and make last-minute preparations before the submarine slipped beneath the surface of the water as conditions rapidly deteriorated in the angry Caribbean Sea.

The storm's early arrival meant they had only about three hours before beginning their approach to the captive cruise liner. Shorty met with the *Grayback* captain to discuss the final attack plan. The submarine would begin its short trek to the *Dream Spinner* as the tail end of the tropical storm was passing and would silently approach the ship.

The USS *Bainbridge* had moved to a position approximately fifty miles from the *Dream Spinner*. At that distance, the launch of a specialized weapon that, up to now, had only completed testing in the desolate region of the South Atlantic, would not be seen by anyone on the cruise ship. The destroyer was about to operationally employ the newest weapon from the DARPA. It was a modernized version of the missile that had neutralized Iran's nuclear capability in 2018.

Called the Pulsar X, the missile was designed for pinpoint accuracy to disable targets as small as a ship using an advanced low-altitude electromagnetic pulse (LEMP). If it worked as it had in testing, its nonnuclear effects would shut down literally everything run by an electronic circuit. The submarine would not be affected by the pulse, nor the aircraft carrier—both would be well out of range.

As soon as the missile worked its magic, the *Grayback* would race toward the *Dream Spinner*, stopping a thousand yards from the cruise ship. The SDVs with Alpha Squad's frogmen would leave the security of the *Grayback* and move the final distance toward their target.

Shorty was absolutely confident his men could pull it off. They would move fast and board the cruise ship quickly from multiple attacking points. Their forces would violently eliminate every militant wherever they hid. The SEALs counted on finding them quickly based on the *Dream Spinner*'s plans and Martha Cook's information. He hoped that any attempts to scuttle the ship by the terrorists would at least be temporarily held up by the power outage, giving the SEALs time to foil that plan.

In the darkness, well out of range of the LEMP warhead's effects, Bravo Squad would be airborne on a CV-22 Osprey, a tilt-rotor twin-engine aircraft capable of both horizontal and vertical flight.

The squad would fight the storm's winds as they parachuted onto the *Dream Spinner*'s upper deck. The operators would move swiftly down through the ship, sweeping for terrorists, as the Alpha Squad warriors brought their assault team up from the waterline, doing the same.

They would be on the lookout for passengers who might be already resisting the terrorists. The SEALs would do their best to keep them from being shot by friendly fire.

It was a good plan. In fact, it was the only plan at this point. Hopefully the SEALs could surprise the militants in the darkness of the power outage. Plenty of violence, shock and awe would provide the advantages they counted on to succeed.

Chapter 47

The lights were burning brightly in the White House Situation Room, and in spite of the late hour, President Foreman was wide awake. He hadn't gotten much sleep since the *Dream Spinner* crisis had begun. The primary thing on his mind was the safe release of the Americans on board, and for that matter, the rest of the international passengers.

He wasn't terribly concerned about Chernov's release, if it came to that. While he hated to open the jail cell door to the former number one terrorist in the world, he knew that the opportunity to recapture him would present itself in the future. Or simply vaporize him with a high-explosive missile from a Reaper drone, once his location was discovered either by a careless mistake he made or the long reach of America's advanced sensors. He would be found. That was a certainty.

"Are we ready to take back this cruise ship from Asmaradov's grasp?"

"Yes, Mr. President. As you know, the timetable has moved up. The storm system that formed off the African coast has picked up speed. It's going to pass the *Dream Spinner* in a couple of hours."

"Is that going to be a problem for our SEALs?"

"No, sir. They're ready. In fact, Alpha Squad is already on board the USS *Grayback III*," replied the JCS chairman. "Operational control has been turned over to Commander Nash, the sub's captain."

"The other group of SEALs, Bravo Squad, is standing by to board a CV-22 Osprey that will take them to their airborne position for their jump to the *Dream Spinner*. The storm's early arrival actually gives them more darkness to conceal their descent to the ship."

"Are they going to be able to pull that off with the tropical storm's remnants still kicking up?" asked Foreman.

"Yes, Mr. President. They should be *just* within the wind minimums for their parachute approach to the ship."

"Level with me," Foreman said to the chairman and the rest of his staff gathered at the late hour. "What do you estimate our chances for success are? I know our SEALs will succeed, but what do you think, in terms of innocent lives lost, should we expect as a result of the assault?"

"Mr. President, we believe that if our information is correct about the militants' location on board the *Dream Spinner*, we can take them out pretty quickly. The operative words, of course, are *knowing their location*. If they have repositioned themselves, there is a bit more risk."

"We believe the male passengers are still being held in the muster stations, which means that guards must still be there. That would account for maybe half of the total number of radicals on board. Our latest communication from Martha Cook validates that. The men are still being held in the muster areas." He paused and chose his next words carefully.

"But we clearly can't count on having precise locations for all of the radicals. They may scatter once power is shut down. The SEALs will have to flush them out of their ratholes and dispatch them as quickly as they can."

"So, you're telling me that we can expect some casualties? We don't know that, once the assault starts, the militants who might have repositioned themselves won't start executing passengers. Especially the captive men. They're easy targets."

"Sir, our SEAL teams are the best warfighters in the world. They know what's at stake, and how quickly they're going to have to sweep that ship. Eliminate every radical they can before they can do any more harm."

Foreman wasn't satisfied with what he heard. He shook his head, tightened his jaw, and walked slowly around the conference table, deep in thought about the consequences of the decision he would soon make. He knew that there was no way to determine how many innocent lives would be lost.

"Mr. President, are we certain we're not going to get any interference from any other country who might be aware of their own citizens being held hostage? That could throw a real wrinkle into our SEALs' plan." The president's National Security Agency director looked over at the JCS chairman, as if to question whether all potential obstacles in the plan had been accounted for.

Foreman responded, "I've only advised Canada and the UK of what was happening. They're standing down. I don't believe anyone else actually knows what's happening with the *Dream Spinner* given the lack of any communication coming from that ship. Let's hope that holds for a few more hours."

———————•———————

Foreman prepared himself for a decision that could determine his next term as president and make him either a hero or a pariah in the eyes of his critics, the American people, and the world.

"Mr. President, we think our CIA operative only partially got the word out to passengers about the upcoming rescue. Most will be asleep when the assault begins. Hopefully they'll keep themselves safe inside their staterooms until the ship is retaken by our guys."

"That will definitely help. At least the women and children will have some degree of protection," President Foreman commented. "What time is the assault scheduled to begin?"

The chairman looked at his watch. "Less than three hours from now."

The NSA director chimed in. "Mr. President, meanwhile, we're proceeding at Gitmo as if Chernov's release is going to take place. We don't believe that Asmaradov has any eyes inside, but we don't want to take that chance. As far as anyone will be able to tell, Chernov is being prepared for handoff to the Cuban authorities. We've already contacted them, and they will be outside the prison at eight o'clock in the morning."

"Good. Let's make sure that we don't give the Viper any indication that we aren't complying with his demands."

"Also, Mr. President, once the power is shut down aboard *Dream Spinner*, there should be no way that Asmaradov will know that an assault on the ship is in progress." The chairman paused. "When we've secured the ship, we'll shut down the faux Guantanamo prisoner release."

"Sounds like we're ready," President Foreman exclaimed. "May God be with our SEALs and all the passengers aboard the *Dream Spinner*."

President Foreman made one of the most difficult decisions a commander in chief can make. He gave the order to execute Operation Clean Sweep. His decision could have significant consequences for over three thousand passengers and the sizable ship's crew. The lives of America's finest, the Navy SEALs, were also in play in a major way.

Chapter 48

Day 8

K halil nervously waited for something to happen—the storm to pass, Chernov's morning release, his escape from the *Dream Spinner*, the scuttling of the ship. He also worried about a preemptive American attack in darkness.

He was somewhat reassured that Asmaradov's Russian benefactor had promised the Panja warriors that they would be well equipped with everything they needed, including night vision goggles—the one item his militants needed to put them on an even footing with the Americans.

Khalil directed one of the militants to report to the provisioning manager and bring a set of NVGs to him. By this time, he presumed that his warriors were all well equipped for night fighting.

At three o'clock in the morning, the storm was still raging outside the *Dream Spinner*. Inside the quiet cruise ship, the Syrian reviewed his plans for every contingency. Each problem could be instantly addressed by his team of Tajik militants and personal collaborators. He was pretty proud of himself at this point. His shameful defeat in Iran years before at the hands of the Americans was going to be overcome by the events of the next few hours. This time, he would not fail. This time, the United States could not stop the inevitable destruction that was only hours away from happening. And the man who had been instrumental in stopping him before was helpless to do anything to save the *Dream Spinner*.

He thought about Black. This was perhaps his last chance to see Ace Black alive before the *Dream Spinner* sank to the bottom of the Venezuelan Basin.

"Bring him to me," Khalil ordered one of the militants. "Go to the Centrum, pull Matt Black from his seat and bring the aviator to me."

He wanted to make sure that his adversary knew he had failed. That there was nothing he could do—that he couldn't even protect his own daughter. He might even divulge the ultimate fate of *Dream Spinner* to Black. Make the American aviator's suffering get very personal.

Khalil thought to himself. *I want to look into the American's face, see the reaction in his eyes when he sees his daughter on the short video recording of my iPhone. I want him to hear her cry for him to save her. And to realize that he can't do anything to rescue her—or himself. Then, Black will understand my suffering and my personal loss at the hands of his country.*

Ten minutes later, the Panja militant was in the overcrowded Centrum, its seats and aisles packed with tired smelly hostages. He stepped onto the stage, and called out for Matt Black to stand up. The captive men looked around, trying to figure out who was being singled out. When nobody stood, the militant yelled the name louder. He made a threatening move with his assault rifle, sweeping it toward the crowd. "If you don't identify yourself, I will shoot one of you. Perhaps then you will comply."

Ray Cook, sitting in the crowded room, smiled. He hoped that Matt and Flamer had made it to the armory and would inflict some reciprocal pain on the terrorists.

When it became apparent that Matt Black was not there, the militant stormed off the stage and ran back to the communications center. He was not looking forward to giving the news to Khalil, and the reaction he received from Atta was expected.

"Where is the American?" Khalil screamed. "Find him, now! Go to his stateroom. He must be there. When you find him, bring him to me. And do not kill him if he resists. I want to be the one who ends his life."

Khalil was about to explode with rage. "And where are my NVGs?" he asked the Tajik who had just returned from the provisioning area.

"Sir, there were none to be had. Only weapons and explosives."

Khalil about had a meltdown as his rage exploded at the hapless messenger. "Get out! Go find Black!"

⸺•⸺

Almost thirty minutes later, the storm system's strongest winds had mostly passed the *Dream Spinner*'s location, and they were now moving quickly to the west. Aboard the USS *Grayback III*, Shorty and Alpha Squad were securely inside the mini-subs, ready to bring the fight to the cruise ship. On the flight deck of the USS *John F. Kennedy*, the twin-rotor Osprey with Bravo Squad on board was already airborne, positioning itself near the drop zone. It had departed the aircraft carrier's flight deck earlier and now remained safely out of range of any man-portable missiles, like the one used to take down the Marine Corps aircraft days earlier. The Osprey crew also trusted the scientists who had provided the range limits of the electronic pulse that was just minutes away. If they somehow got caught in the LEMP warhead's blast, they would fall from the sky like a rock.

"Captain, SEAL Chalk One and Two are ready to execute," Shorty communicated with the *Grayback III* captain through the secure line in his SDV.

"Roger that," came the reply.

He transmitted an encrypted message to both the *Kennedy* and the *Bainbridge*. The attack was about to begin.

The captain of the USS *Bainbridge* gave the order to fire. The fifteen-foot-long missile quickly left its launcher, its solid rocket motor igniting in a plume of orange flame. It began its initial airborne parabolic route toward the cruise ship.

"Missile away. Time to target, forty-five seconds," the weapons control officer announced. Into the heavily overcast sky, the missile followed its programmed attack route, dropping down to one hundred feet five miles out from the cruise ship. Its warhead would emit its powerful pulse as it overflew the target.

———————•———————

The Tajik militant ran down the two staircases, catching up with the other radical at Matt Black's stateroom. They pounded on the locked door, ordering that it should be opened immediately.

Inside the room, Julie and the two boys were hiding behind the bed by the glass balcony door. She had done as she had been told to do, to protect herself and the kids. She had managed to drag the end tables and a small bureau and stacked them against the door. At this point, she hoped it was enough. She glanced at her watch. It was twenty-nine minutes after three in the morning.

The militants continued banging on the stateroom door, threatening to shoot through the lock. Julie grabbed the boys and lay flat on the floor behind the bed, preparing for the worst as the clock struck three-thirty.

Then the ship went dark.

The electromagnetic pulse from the powerful missile warhead had done its job. All power, all lights, including emergency lighting, had been shut down. Now in total blackness, the angry and confused gunmen worked their way back to the staircase that led to an open deck.

The *Dream Spinner* was now not much more than a dark, massive free-floating hotel. The twenty-foot propellers wound down until they stopped. The diesel generators were silenced, their electronic controls now useless. The command Khalil had had over all ship systems, including communications, was now eliminated.

The Alpha Squad frogmen in their SDVs departed the *Grayback III* and were rapidly approaching the *Dream Spinner*, traveling just beneath the surface of the dark Caribbean water. Overhead, the Bravo Squad SEALs had stepped off the open rear ramp of the Osprey and were now fighting the storm's remaining strong, gusting winds, trying to somehow safely reach the top deck of the cruise ship.

As the SDVs approached the ship, the SEALs trusted the LEMP had done its job, and the mines wouldn't detonate as they got close. The underwater operators quickly reached their destination and tied off their mini-subs to the *Dream Spinner*'s propulsion structure. Half of Alpha Squad went to work on the hull of the ship. Their job—check for and disable any mines or other explosive devices. The second group of SEALs began boarding the ship. They counted on the effectiveness of the missile warhead to have also killed the militant's electronic sensors and disable any antipersonnel devices that might pose a hazard as they scaled the ship.

————— • —————

There was chaos on board when the lights went out. While the terrorist cell had been expecting an assault, they hadn't expected it to happen while the storm was still present, and they definitely didn't expect the power to be shut down. A few of the gunmen had flashlights. Most didn't. None had NVGs—a strategic advantage the SEALs.

Inside the muster areas, the guards fired a few rounds from their rifles to retain order—or so they hoped. It worked initially, but for how long before passengers bum-rushed them in the darkness?

Khalil was prepared. He flipped on his flashlight and scanned the darkened displays within the communications center. Everything was dead—all systems, all ship power, even the secure communication lines Khalil had created. Even more significant, the deadliness of the protective array of explosives and sensors surrounding the ship was now impossible to verify. Would they still work to defend the ship from the assault that had certainly begun?

He wondered briefly if this might be the beginning of the end of the Viper's plan.

Chapter 49

When everything went dark in the armory, the three Americans knew that the *Dream Spinner*'s rescue was underway. Ace felt his way to the flashlights on the back counter, grabbed one and turned it on.

"It's begun," stated Jack. "Time to get going. Let's make sure our reflective tape is secure."

The tape glistened when the flashlight beam hit it. But would it do the same when the SEALs used their NVGs?

They were ready to move.

"We've got to get to Claire now," insisted Ace. "She's got to be scared out of her mind. Aleksandra indicated that she was in the communications center with that bastard Khalil."

"In due time, Matt," said Jack. "We've got to move quickly but carefully. It's not going to do us much good if we're shot by militants or the good guys while we try to reach her."

"Jack, it's my daughter we're talking about here. I don't trust a thing that Khalil would do to her, especially now that he's got to know that an attack is in progress."

"Matt, I understand. She's *my* only granddaughter as well. Believe me, we *will* rescue her from that crazed Syrian. We'll move as fast as we can. You've got to trust me on this."

His stomach in a knot, Ace reluctantly agreed. All he could think about was Claire. *She must be thinking I've abandoned her.* It was killing him to think that he should have been able to protect her from this—but didn't.

As the three moved to the armory exit, they heard a noise outside the door. They stayed silent as the door slowly opened in the darkness. Ace put the beam of his flashlight on the figure as Jack prepared to shoot.

The man froze when the light hit him.

"Buzz, what the hell? We almost shot you. It's me, Ace!"

"Thanks, mate. Lucky for me that you're not too trigger-happy. Guess I wasn't the only one with this idea," he said as he nodded to Flamer and Jack. "Looks like we might actually have enough here to put up a little resistance against this group of buggers."

Ace agreed, knowing that Buzz was also a crack shot and an experienced soldier.

"How did you get here without being discovered?"

"Fortunately, in the darkness, the guards are pretty confused. I got here unseen and unopposed."

"Great. Get in here and we'll explain our plan. You know the ship pretty well, so chime in if you have other ideas."

They had plenty of ammunition, and enough firepower to do some real damage to their captors—if they got lucky. Each of them also had a flashlight pulled from the emergency kits in the armory. Buzz grabbed the shotgun from the countertop, checking its ammo load and stuffing extra shells in his pockets. He made sure to apply some reflective tape to his body as well. The men headed toward the stairwell in darkness, keeping the flashlights off, guiding themselves with their hands on the corridor walls. They stopped suddenly. Two men were talking loudly in a foreign language, sounding panicky.

Jack whispered to Flamer, "Stay behind the corner, on your knees. Make sure to keep a low profile. Ace and I will move to the other side of the hallway. It's so dark, those two dudes will never see us. In ten-seconds, shine the flashlight right at them. When they turn to the light, we're going to take them out."

"Just make sure you get them before they blast me," Flamer whispered.

"Stay close to me," Buzz said softly. "I'll cover you if a weapon is turned our way."

When the flashlight came on, the two militants weren't sure what was going on. They turned toward the light, rifles raised. From the opposite side of the hallway, Jack let loose with a short burst from the AK-47 while Ace nailed the other one. The gunshots were nearly deafening, but both found their targets. The ship now had two less Tajiks to deal with. Neither terrorist had gotten off a shot. Buzz grabbed the rifle from one of the dead Tajiks after slinging his shotgun over his shoulder.

"Let's keep moving up toward Deck 10. I'm sure the other bad guys heard the gunfire," said Jack. Surprisingly, they hadn't yet heard any gunfire from the SEALs who were coming aboard the ship, doing what they did best.

———————•———————

Four Alpha Squad frogmen working on the mines just below the surface of the water determined that the deadly devices could not be completely disarmed. The SEALs had heard about these, the latest advanced technology straight out of Mother Russia. The high-tech explosives had anti-tamper mechanisms that would detonate the mines if any attempt was made to remove them. Even though they were still affixed to the *Dream Spinner*'s hull, the SEALs believed they posed no real hazard to their assault force if the electromagnetic pulse had eliminated any means of remotely triggering them from on board the ship.

Meanwhile, the other half of Alpha Squad had scaled the stern and were descending to the lowest decks. They would be joined shortly by their teammates now exiting the water.

On the top deck, the SEAL operators had silently landed after their short parachute descent and dispersed per Shorty's plan. The dark night kept the deck almost completely black, ideal for an attack that hinged on surprise. The NVGs each SEAL wore illuminated anything with an infrared or thermal signature. The squad got lucky. Between the storm and the power outage, any militants who might have been on the top deck were absent. Maybe they believed that there was no threat during the storm conditions. When the power had been killed, they'd likely left seeking answers on the deck below them about the unexpected power outage. Their confusion wouldn't last long, as they would soon meet the frogmen who were moving quickly, silently toward the access points that would take them to the next deck below.

Shorty and his squad raced to the bottom two decks. On Deck 2, the ship's provisioning manager was one of the first casualties there. He had positioned himself to protect the forward entry hatch but had not counted on two things. The SEALs hadn't tried to breach that hatch but had come from a different direction, and their NVGs had highlighted his location and rewarded the terrorist with a bullet.

The SEALs then quickly cleared the crew staterooms. There were no guards there, as the crew members believed what they had been told—that there were sensors in the hallways that would signal their exit from their rooms and trigger a burst from a guard's automatic weapon. All the operators found were scared *Dream Spinner* crew members. The rooms were quickly checked, and the frightened crew were ordered to stay put until the ship was secure.

One of Shorty's primary objectives on Deck 2 was to secure the engine control room. While the ship had no power, the team was taking no chances that it might be quickly restored by a creative *Dream Spinner* engineer under threat by a militant. When they arrived at the door, the American warriors were surprised when a white-overall-clad engineer let them in. The man was not armed and tried to convince the SEALs that the terrorist who had been guarding him had left after the power was shut down. The explanation was not believed—at least for the moment. The engineer was bound with zip ties and gagged, taking him out of any potential action.

Drako had gotten away from the engine control room just after the missile had cut power to the ship. He would have another role to play very soon.

Shorty and his squad moved quickly, eliminating a terrorist approaching them. The Tajik made the mistake of turning on his flashlight and received a bullet for his mistake. Another one was shot on the staircase leading to Deck 3. Alpha Squad checked the rooms on that deck, found the rooms empty, and moved on to Deck 4. Part of Alpha Squad was already on Deck 5, moving in sub-teams of two SEALs each. They had their respective assignments, and were wasting no time executing their assault strategy. They swept the armory next, found the zip-tied terrorist, and then secured the place. They continued their hunt.

------•------

In the total darkness of the communications center, Khalil swept his flashlight beam quickly across the array of now-dead screens, looking for any sign of activity. There was none. The backup power he counted on was also not available. Even the circuit that led to the detonation timer for the ship's explosive mines was dead.

He turned the flashlight beam toward Claire and stared at her in the darkness. She was curled up in a ball, shaking.

"I will be back shortly," he said. He opened the door, but not before arming himself with a high-capacity Russian semiautomatic pistol. The twenty-round magazine it held wouldn't do much if he was confronted by the Americans who he now knew were finally making their move on the *Dream Spinner*. The firepower they possessed would make his pistol not much more effective than a peashooter, but it was all he had.

He hesitated, then opened the door and listened in the dark hallway. There was no sound. If an attack was in progress, he expected that he would hear something. Gunfire, screams, the sounds of death, perhaps coming his way. But he never expected that the SEALs would have suppressors on their weapons to silence the otherwise loud gunshots.

He ran down the hallway, running his hands along the walls to guide his way until he reached the bridge. He had something to take care of. He knew that Zoyatov was weak. And now that the ship was surely under attack, he knew that the bridge would be a prime target for the assault team. Zoyatov could not be trusted and would likely do anything to save himself—including giving up details about where the

Panja militants were located. He banged on the door and got ready to remedy the situation by silencing the captain.

"Zoyatov, open the door. It's Khalil."

The ship's captain heard the sounds of a fist hammering the outside of his protected area. He approached the door carefully. He was about to open it when he paused. Zoyatov thought quickly about his next moves. While he had signed on to Asmaradov's plan, albeit under duress and threat to his family, he strongly suspected that the power loss was the beginning of the end of the hostage crisis. He knew that the Americans were, at this very minute, attacking the ship. It might be time for him to switch sides. The banging on his door became a bit louder.

"Zoyatov, open the door, now! The American attack is underway. I need to speak with you urgently and provide the final plan for our escape," he lied.

"I can hear you. And I already know the plan. One that I presume is now worthless." Zoyatov had no intention of letting Khalil enter the bridge. The captain shouted, "The ship is definitely under attack. I saw soldiers from the bridge window floating from the sky toward the *Dream Spinner*. It is best that I keep the bridge door secure."

"You are a traitor!" yelled Khalil. "I will ensure you meet your maker, soon." Khalil thought about trying to shoot his way in, but the sound might draw the Americans right to him.

Zoyatov moved back from the door. He was safe for now. But he knew it was only a matter of time before the entrance to his secure area was blasted open by the Americans.

Khalil stormed off, now in a race to get back to the communications center before he was intercepted by the assault he knew was underway. He intended to do two things. First, notify Asmaradov about what was happening on the *Dream Spinner*. Khalil strongly hoped he could somehow still send a cryptic message to the terrorist leader. The second thing was to make his escape after somehow initiating the mine's timer mechanism with Drako's help—thus fulfilling his promise to the Viper. *Sink the Dream Spinner.*

Chapter 50

Shorty reached the darkened dining room at the aft end of the ship, his night vision goggles providing him an eerily lit green-and-black glow of the entryway. As he proceeded silently across the foyer, he picked up movement near the door leading to the outside walkway. A figure carrying a weapon was looking in his direction, raising his rifle but unsure about what he couldn't see in the darkness.

Suppressed muzzle bursts from Shorty's M4A1 combat rifle dropped the militant to the floor, dead before he hit the carpet. As the operators swept the dining area clear of radicals, they slowly entered the kitchen. The steel cabinets, ovens and grills provided ample hiding places for an ambush.

Movement just behind the large produce counter. A warm glow in the NVGs. The SEAL waited. No clear shot. Heads of lettuce on the counter blocked his deadly aim. Now! The muffled sound of the high-velocity round barely broke the silence. As the head of lettuce exploded, it did little to slow down the hollow-point bullet from penetrating the Tajiks forehead.

After sweeping the kitchen area for additional radicals, the SEALs split up to cover both sides of the ship, checking the inside hallways and outside perimeter walkways for any other terrorists. They found none.

They moved swiftly through the art gallery and past the darkened shops that had once been full of tourists purchasing jewelry, watches, and other overpriced items. Moving carefully now, they reached the central part of the ship that opened up into a large, circular passenger entertainment arena.

Shorty gazed up, looking for any movement on the stairs and balconies extending five decks up in the massive opening. The glass-sided elevators appeared empty, confirmed by his NVGs.

Suddenly, he detected movement on the balcony two floors above him. By the railing, a figure had his back turned to the SEAL. Shorty deliberately made a sound, hoping the man would turn toward him. As the figure swiveled around, his rifle was clearly visible. One shot by the deadly operator to the Tajik's head dropped him where he stood, ending his all-expense-paid cruise.

The determined frogmen continued to sweep the area. Alpha Squad moved in a half-sprint toward the bow, splitting into groups of two and heading down each hallway, while the rest scaled the stairs to the next deck.

Two armed men stood on opposite ends of the final exit to the staircase leading up to Deck 6. Before they knew the SEALs were there, muffled shots rang out. Two more militant Tajiks had their cruise cards permanently revoked, along with their lives.

"Keep moving," the battle-hardened American frogman said to his fellow operator.

"Roger, moving to Deck 6," he said into his secure-comm microphone.

In the pitch blackness of the Centrum and in all other muster areas, the terrorists suspected an attack on the ship was fully underway. They had no way of knowing their numbers were being progressively reduced by each minute that passed. They struggled with what to do next. It was impossible for them to see any movement in muster areas that had no ambient starlight coming in from a window, like in the window-less Centrum auditorium. They knew if they started to shoot the hostages, some would likely turn on them. The sheer number of hostages was too great to kill them all. Those who weren't killed would be on them, quickly overwhelming them. So the guards positioned themselves by the exit doors, looking for an opportunity to escape. In a twisted way, what they had previously controlled by force now became a prison for them.

They did have a backup plan. Before the power went out, they had rigged the doors with explosives. All that was left for them to do was to arm the devices with a ten-second timer, exit and lock the captives inside. They made their decision. Better to fight it out in the ship's decks and hallways than trapped in the Centrum.

The Tajiks stepped into the hallway, secured the doors and moved down the darkened corridor toward the center of the ship. Their pathway widened as they approached the main administrative area, including the purser, passenger service, and excursion counters. As they passed between them, they were both taken down by short bursts from SEALs positioned silently and invisibly behind the counters.

Back inside the Centrum, several of the nervous hostages approached the exit doors. They could barely see the devices attached to them. There was no visible warning to them to stay away. They had been told not to try to leave the room.

"Come on. We've got to get out of here," shouted someone in the darkness as he headed for the door.

"No! The doors have explosives attached," another captive screamed out.

As the man pushed his way to the door, he yanked it open. The bright flash was instantaneous, followed in milliseconds by the explosive blast that killed six men who had gotten too close to the doors. Many more were injured. Fortunately, Ray Cook was okay.

The SEALs in the administrative area reacted immediately to the explosion. Two of them raced through the darkness toward the Centrum, the smoke from the blast billowing down the hallway toward them. They approached quickly, but cautiously. The entryway was clear of terrorists, but what the two warriors saw was horrific.

Through their night vision goggles, they could see inside the badly damaged entrance as the smoke partially cleared. A number of twisted shapes lay awkwardly against the side wall, a few thrown across the splintered remains of the first two rows of stadium seats. The floor was wet. Blood and bits of flesh were everywhere.

They called out, "Navy SEALs! If you approach the entrance, move slowly with your hands in the air!" Through the darkness and pungent smoke, one man stumbled toward the American warrior, his arm obviously badly injured by the blast.

"They locked us in and left," the injured man cried out. "Then someone rushed the door. We screamed for him to stop, but when he tried to pull the door open, the explosion occurred. There's probably not much left of him."

"I need you to follow my instructions. I want you to stay in the auditorium for now. Try and treat the injured the best way you can," said the SEAL, tossing him a flashlight and one of the first aid kits he carried. "We're taking back the ship, and if you leave here now, you may have a lot more casualties among yourselves. In the dark, it will be tough to distinguish you from the guys we're trying to kill. Stay here!"

"But our families. We've got to get to them."

Shouts of agreement came from most of the others crowded up at the entrance.

"They've all been told to barricade themselves in their rooms until this is over. They're safe." He insisted one more time, "Please stay here. Give us about twenty minutes, and this should be over. We've already cleared this deck of militants, so you should be safe."

The men, still in shock from the blast in the dark auditorium, reluctantly agreed.

The SEAL operator quickly passed the word across the secure comm to all other operators: be ready for booby-trapped doors in the muster areas. He then turned to his fellow frogmen. "We need to move out. We're already three minutes behind schedule."

Chapter 51

Ace, Flamer, Jack and Buzz were on the move after their first kills, and were headed toward the deck stairwells.

Buzz was the most familiar with the ship's layout, being an experienced crew member. Between that and his military training, he knew intuitively where the militants were most likely positioned. He recommended the group follow him, taking the path of least expected resistance. He also knew where valuable cover and concealment existed. As they pressed steadily upward, they managed to eliminate a couple of surprised terrorists. Their primary objective now was Claire.

In the darkness, they used what cover they could while silently climbing the stairs, slowly heading toward Deck 10. They heard sporadic gunfire above them, muffled by the ship's massive bulk, and realized that combat actions were taking place on the decks overhead. They were pleasantly surprised that they didn't run into any more militants guarding the access path to the upper decks. They surmised that when the power had been cut, terrorists guarding the access points had moved outside onto the walkways to figure out what was happening or confront the assault force that they presumed would come from outside the ship.

When they reached Deck 9, they were faced with some added risk. On this part of the ship, the internal stairway stopped. The only way to safely get to Deck 10 was to proceed to the exit door, step outside onto the glassed enclosed walkway, head past the solarium, and then take the outside stairs to Deck 10.

Ace carefully pushed the door open a crack and looked into the walkway. About thirty yards away, an armed militant stood motionless, staring out the glass windows into the dark hallway. His figure was barely distinguishable but was enough to help silhouette his body.

"Jack, can you take him out?" Ace whispered. He knew that the militant was standing in the way of their final access to the next deck, and the communications center.

Jack took a look and whispered back that he could. He slipped carefully out of the door. Jack's Ranger skills with a rifle had been unmatched in his younger days. Even now, his eyes were still perfect, and his hands didn't have the slight tremor that sometimes came with advancing years. His daily fitness regimen and time on the pistol range in Fredericksburg no doubt helped as well.

He leveled the AK-47 at his target. Tough to see in the darkness. Also a difficult shot, with the man standing sideways to him. Jack let out a short whistle, and the dark shadow turned to face the sound. The crack of his rifle subtracted one more uninvited guest from the *Dream Spinner*.

The group raced toward the end of the glassed enclosed area, doing their best to dodge the tables and chairs that on a normal sunny afternoon, would have been packed with passengers enjoying a snack, reading a book, or playing cards.

The entryway to the small staircase leading to the next deck was in the darkness ahead of them. Ace flipped on his flashlight briefly to see the path, then flipped it off. He wanted to minimize any likelihood that they would be seen by militants who might be at the top of the stairway. Both Ace and Buzz strongly suspected that the communications center would have a guard in place, and it was entirely likely that if a guard was there, he had heard the crack of the rifle.

They moved quietly, but apparently not quietly enough. A burst of gunfire peppered the wall of the stairway, narrowly missing Flamer's head. They checked each other—nobody was hit—then slowly picked themselves up off the floor, raised their weapons and waited for the shooter to advance toward them.

Khalil had made a quick detour on his way back from the bridge. He slipped through the darkness toward the ship's security room. Looking down the black-shrouded hallways, he saw nothing, heard nothing. He knocked on the door. "Cho, it is Khalil. Open up."

Cho Lee Kwan pushed the door open and quickly ushered Khalil in. He closed it tightly and turned to him. A small battery-powered lantern provided what little light there was in the room.

"The ship is under attack. Although the cameras are out, my men reported to me that many soldiers were already on board. What few men we have are trying to kill as many as they can." Cho shook his head. "From what they have reported, these attackers must be Americans. *Maybe Navy SEALs!* Their firepower is significant, and there must be plenty of them on this ship."

"They may be Americans, but they will fail in the end," Khalil remarked arrogantly. "You know I have made the arrangements to get us off this doomed ship. But we must be quick. Drako Kratec assured me that he can initiate the backup diesel generator to provide what I need to finish off the *Dream Spinner*. In a few minutes, he will power it up. I will be in the communications center when that happens. Hopefully, the protected circuit I created will work and it will only take a few moments to initiate the timers on the mines."

"So we execute our escape plan now," Cho stated as a matter of fact, not a question. "Is our means of departure ready?"

"Yes. I believe the Venezuelan ship is standing by one mile to our west. An attack submarine. They are prepared for us. That is, if we have not drifted out of position since power was lost."

"And what about our comrades who are fighting off the Americans? We must help get them off this ship."

"That's not going to happen, Cho. They are probably already dead, or about to die. We need them to continue to fight. Give us the time to finish our mission. And to make our escape."

Cho didn't need much encouragement. "What about Zoyatov?"

"He's a traitor. He wouldn't allow me entry into the bridge. He's trying to save his own hide and will die with the rest on this ship."

Khalil was now adamant.

"We need to get to Deck 2 quickly," he said, reminding Cho of what he had previously been told. "Remember, use the elevator shaft in the kitchen of the Chop House dining room. With no power, we can climb down the maintenance ladder. That path is invisible to the attackers. They will be searching the hallways, the rooms. We will be safe using that route."

Cho nodded his understanding. He also knew that they had to dodge the SEALs just to *get* to the Chop House. But he was well armed and could handle a confrontation with them. At least, that was what he thought.

Khalil shook his hand and left quickly, determined to get down the hallway to finish his job in the communications center. He stopped in his tracks, hearing gunshots coming from down the long passageway, then proceeded carefully toward his destination.

———————————

Khalil made it back to the communications center while trying to control his boiling anger, thinking that he had lost the opportunity to inflict the pain he had hoped on Ace Black. But he knew that in the end, the pain would be inescapable. No one on *Dream Spinner* would survive after he made his escape.

He quickly checked his watch. Two minutes remained before Drako Kratec would energize the standby generator for a couple of minutes. It would apply the power needed to one specific shielded circuit. Just long enough for Khalil to do what he needed to do. Send the Viper a quick message and then scuttle the ship.

Drako managed to evade the SEALs in the darkness and made his way back to the engine control room to finish his last task there before heading down to Deck 2. Khalil had briefed him on the contingency plan to sink the ship if all hell broke loose and their primary plan was in jeopardy. When he entered, he saw his assistant tied up in the corner. *Too bad*, he thought. He got ready to initiate the emergency power source, wait for the precise time, and then activate it. He energized the system, which would otherwise be used for another type of crisis. Of course, the kind of crisis envisioned by the ship's builders was more along the line of storm damage, a collision with another vessel, or an internal failure of the main diesel generators—not the result of an LEMP warhead.

Immediately, across the ship, emergency lighting came on. It caught the SEALs temporarily by surprise and interfered with their NVGs, making them useless. Their stealthy advantage was reduced, but the SEALs pressed forward. With their targets now plainly visible in the light, the operators were intent on quickly eliminating any terrorist who exposed himself.

Khalil opened the laptop computer. It had been disconnected from the ship's power when the torpedo had killed most of the circuits. He tried to boot it up and waited. Nothing. He verified that the circuit providing power from the standby generator was working; it was specifically designed to ensure the ship had emergency communications capability in a crisis. It was. But his laptop computer was lifeless. He had to work fast. In the low emergency light, guided by his flashlight, he quickly gained access to the shielded circuit. He grabbed what he needed from the small maintenance drawer and wired the emergency power into his computer.

The laptop screen illuminated. Khalil quickly tapped in the coded message that would warn Asmaradov of the American president's actions. He got an indication that it had been sent. He then linked his laptop to the mine's activation system and sent the signal that would mean the end of the *Dream Spinner*. The timers on all eight mines attached to the hull were activated. The detonations would occur in one hour, and there was nothing anyone else could do to stop it from happening. The specially designed timers could only be disarmed by Kahlil.

Khalil was supposed to wait until after Chernov was released from Guantanamo before he destroyed the *Dream Spinner*. But the SEALs were moving too quickly. Before long, maybe minutes, they would control the ship. Chernov's release time was still several hours away. Khalil had no choice but to execute the contingency plan.

Moments later, the power was killed by Kratec, per Khalil's original plan. When the emergency generator shut down, the ship was again immersed in darkness, much to the chagrin of the SEALs. They repositioned their NVGs and continued their sweep of the ship.

As Khalil prepared to leave the communications center, the sound of distant gunfire startled him. He looked for the pistol he had set on the console, moving his flashlight erratically in an effort to locate it. He grabbed the weapon and moved toward the doorway.

He knew it was now time to make his escape. The extraction plan provided by Asmaradov had its own risks. He needed to get to the Chop House and the kitchen elevator shaft that descended to the provisioning area. The ladder inside was his path to freedom—hidden away from the hunters, the SEALs, who were searching for and eliminating every terrorist they could find.

Khalil and his comrades were to rendezvous on the second deck close to the small doorway used for the harbormaster to enter the ship. From there, they would use the jet propulsion units vacationing snorkelers rented to help them move quickly through the water. The units had been stashed in a locker by Cho two days prior, the gear removed from the dive shop on board.

The propulsion units could get them several hundred yards from the ship before running out of battery power—that was, of course, if the batteries still worked after the LEMP hit. According to the plan, the Venezuelan submarine would pick up the beacon Khalil had been provided and make the pickup.

Before he exited, he took a final look at his captive. Claire was nearly invisible in the darkness. "Don't worry, child, it will be over soon." He removed her gag, believing that, at this point, it was of little use.

Khalil slipped into the darkness, away from the gunfire that periodically echoed through the ship. He moved quickly but silently toward the Chop House restaurant and the elevator shaft that would make his escape possible.

Claire had watched everything Khalil had done with his computer in the dimly lit room. Now, alone in the darkness, she sobbed uncontrollably.

———————— • ————————

As Ace approached the door to the room where he expected to find his daughter, he prayed to God that she was alive. That she was unharmed. He felt that Khalil would be inside, ready for him. When they prepared to breach the door, the men hoped that Claire would be well away from it, safe from what was going to come next.

"Let's do this," Jack ordered. Although the door to the room was likely reinforced for security, it would not withstand a burst from an AK-47. They verified the door was locked. The rifle blast in the confined space of the tight corridor was earsplitting, but it did the trick. They kicked the door open and rushed in with guns raised for action. The four swept the room quickly with their flashlights. No Khalil. But they saw Claire huddled in the corner.

Ace rushed to her. "Baby, it's Dad. I'm getting you out of here. Are you alright?"

Claire's ears were ringing from the piercing blast of bullets. She was confused and crying loudly. Dark shapes around her. When she saw her father's face, she cried, "Daddy, Daddy."

"It's going to be okay, honey. Let's get you untied and out of here."

After he freed her from the straps Khalil had used to secure her, Ace took a quick look around the darkened communications room. He rifled through a couple of the console drawers, not sure what he might find. Maybe some evidence of what Khalil might have up his sleeve. He only found a laptop computer on the counter, wired into the console. Time to go.

They wasted no time in heading down the dark hallway, found the staircase, and were going to start down. "Wait," Jack said. "I think we need to stay on this deck. Head to the fitness center. It's only down the hallway."

"What are you talking about, Jack?" Ace questioned. "I think we should head to our staterooms."

"Matt! Listen to me," Jack insisted. "The passengers were told to barricade themselves in their rooms. The SEALs are right this moment sweeping the ship for terrorists. We don't want to be one of those targets while we try to get to a stateroom. I think the right plan is to go to the fitness center. One way in, one way out. We can hold off an army with what we're armed with until the SEALs take the ship back."

"I have to agree," said Buzz.

"Makes sense." Ace looked over at Flamer, who nodded.

"Hey, I'm not going to argue with the logic of an Army Ranger," Flamer retorted.

With his arm around Claire, Ace followed Jack. As they walked, the body of a militant lay ahead of them, dead in the hallway. He did his best to shield Claire from seeing it. The SEALs had already swept that end of the ship. As they turned a corner in the winding hallway, a bright light shone on them.

"Halt," shouted someone with a Texas twang. The SEAL held his fire for some reason, perhaps noticing the reflective tape on their chests—or maybe the frightened young child. "Put your weapons down," he yelled at the group.

They immediately complied, and the frogman approached them.

"Where did you come from?" the SEAL demanded. "You're supposed to be in your staterooms. I almost shot you all."

"A couple of us were captive in the Centrum and slipped out during some commotion. Made it to the armory and managed to pick these up." Ace pointed to the weapons. "We were joined by my father-in-law and my good buddy from the ship. The bastards took my daughter, and I wasn't letting anything stop me from getting her back."

The SEAL was joined by another squad member. "We need to have these folks hunker down until we finish. We're moving toward the bridge now."

Jack spoke up. "We had the same idea. We were heading to the exercise area. Figured we could wait there until you guys are finished taking out the bad guys. And I believe we could hold off a few of the militants with these weapons if they try to get through the entrance."

"You know how to use them?" the SEAL asked.

"You bet," said Jack. "A Ranger doesn't lose his touch, and these boys with me can hit what they aim at as well."

"Absolutely, mate," replied Buzz. "I played with these toys plenty of times serving with Her Majesty's Royal Marines."

"Good, get going. Lock the door after you go inside, if you can. We already cleared that area. Wait until we come back for you."

"Roger that," said Ace.

Chapter 52

As the rescue attempt progressed on the *Dream Spinner*, President Foreman was wide awake with his staff in the Situation Room. He was looking for some good news. He had given the execution order, and now the United States Navy had its premier fighting force in action. At stake were the lives of over three thousand passengers and nine hundred crew members. He wondered if he had made the right decision. Perhaps he should have bet on Asmaradov keeping his end of the bargain. Foreman would release Chernov, and Asmaradov would release the *Dream Spinner*. He hadn't thought long and hard on that one. Rely on a terrorist? The one who called himself the Viper? Probably not a safe bet. It didn't matter now—the die was cast. He was counting on success. The alternative was too difficult to even think about.

"Admiral, what can you tell me?" Foreman asked the JCS chairman. "Do we have any reports yet?"

"Mr. President, we know that our SEALs have successfully boarded the *Dream Spinner* and are at this moment sweeping the ship to find and eliminate its Panja cell captors."

"Do we have any reports of innocent passengers killed in the assault?"

"Not yet, Mr. President. It's too early. But we should begin to get feedback shortly. It's a big ship, a lot of territory to cover, and plenty of places for the militants to hide. The SEALs will root them out of their holes as quickly as possible," the chairman answered.

"Meanwhile, let's ensure that, as far as Asmaradov knows, we're on track for the release at Gitmo." Foreman ordered. Then he questioned, "There's no chance that the terrorists on the *Dream Spinner* can notify Asmaradov about what's going on, right?"

"Sir, we've knocked out the ship's ability to do anything other than float. The LEMP missile warhead killed power, communications, and every electronic instrument aboard the vessel. There's no chance that Asmaradov knows what we're really doing."

"Even if for some reason he got tipped off on the attack, and I assure you that it's not possible, at this point it's too late for him to do anything about it," the NSA director added.

Foreman thought about that last statement. Was it too late, at this point, for the Viper to essentially execute thousands of people by sinking the *Dream Spinner*? Even with the SEALs taking the ship, what if the mines were somehow detonated? Asmaradov surely had backup plans in the event things went awry.

The Situation Room had a direct link to Shorty Robinson on board the cruise ship. Up to now, the only feedback was that the SEALs were methodically and successfully clearing the decks. Foreman needed more. He prayed that he wouldn't regret his decision to take back the *Dream Spinner*.

———•———

When Ace and the others arrived safely at the fitness center, they immediately looked for a place where Claire could be hidden if the room was attacked. In spite of what the SEAL team operator had told them about the area being cleared, Jack knew that they had to be ready if the militant rats tried to hide from their inevitable fate. Combat warriors like the Tajiks would undoubtedly have recognized the exercise room as a great spot to stage a last stand when all was lost. By now, many knew their end was near.

After a quick survey of the room, Jack picked the spots where he, Ace, Flamer and Buzz could establish some protection for themselves while providing interlocking fields of fire on anyone coming through the doorway. Unfortunately, the door couldn't be fully secured, its glass having been shattered during the SEALs' sweep of the area.

Ace finally got an opportunity to spend a few minutes with Claire and try to find out what she had gone through in her ordeal with Khalil.

"Baby, we're safe here. Are you okay? This is the best place to stay until the ship is secure. And I know it won't take long for the SEALs to finish the job." He held her close to him and gave her the most comforting hug he could.

"I want Mommy," she whimpered. "When can I go see her?"

"Soon, Claire. But we have to wait just a little longer. We'll see her soon."

Ace sincerely hoped he was right about his last statement. This horror show needed to be over.

"I'm sorry this happened to you, baby. It's my fault. The madman that kept you captive knew I was on board with my family. He took you to punish me."

"Dad, why did he want to punish you? He said grandpa did something to him."

Ace was stunned that Khalil had told her that.

"He blames me for what happened to his own family years ago. And blames my father, your grandpa."

"What did grandpa do to him?"

"Back in 2003, long before you were born and when I was just a kid, my father was on a combat mission over Syria. You remember me talking about him, right?"

"He was a pilot, like you. A fighter pilot."

"Right. Well, I never told you about what happened, but his mission was to stop a tragedy from happening to the Syrian people. He was trying to eliminate a horrible terrorist leader who caused incredible pain and death to innocent people. My dad was called on to erase him from the planet, and that is what he did."

"What does that have to do with the man who captured me?"

"Claire, sometimes, in spite of the best efforts to keep from hurting innocent people, bad things happen. The bombs that killed the terrorist in Syria also killed this man's family, except for two of his children. His son was one of the survivors. He was seven at the time. His name is Khalil, and he is the man that took you."

"That's terrible. So, Grandpa killed Khalil's family?"

"Yes, that's right. It was never supposed to happen."

"So Khalil blames you for something Grandpa did?"

"Yes." He wondered about how much more to tell her.

Ace hadn't intended to provide this level of detail to Claire. After all, she was seven! But given what she had been through, she had a right to know. Even if she might not understand most of what he was saying. And he knew that things could still go badly before the SEALs completed their job.

A noise coming from outside the front entrance to the fitness center broke into their conversation.

"Stay quiet," he told her. "Lay flat on the floor. Cover your ears. It's going to be loud."

"Don't leave me, Daddy," she whispered, nearly sobbing as she said the words.

"I'll never leave you again," he assured her.

Claire quickly did as she was told. Then, Ace hustled to his position. The four men could hear two voices, talking in whispers. Barely audible. Not English. The sounds getting louder. Moving toward the entrance.

One of the militants stuck his head around the corner of the door, glancing briefly into the dark room. He entered, followed by another radical.

Jack didn't make a sound. No reason to ask these two if they were friendly. He could see enough to convince himself they weren't SEALs, and they clearly carried weapons.

He had prearranged the kill plan with Buzz. If it was one man, Jack would take him out. If two, Jack would take the one on the left with his AK-47 and Buzz would take out the one on the right. They waited seconds until the two shapes approached, then opened up. The two militant Tajiks never knew what had hit them. Their Pilates appointment had been canceled—permanently.

Jack hoped that these two were the last that they would see.

Chapter 53

Captain Zoyatov had come to grips with the inevitable end to the Viper's now-doomed mission. He wasn't willing to become another one of the mounting casualties aboard the ship and had figured a way out—a path for his survival. He knew the Americans would be on him in minutes.

Zoyatov walked over to the zip-tied, gagged navigator.

"I'm sorry I have to do this. But, you see, I have no choice."

The wide-eyed navigator had a look of terror in his eyes as Zoyatov's flashlight beam swept across his face.

The captain pulled a large-bladed combat knife from the console drawer and approached his bound victim.

The navigator shook his head violently, a muted plea for mercy.

"You know, I can't leave you alive. You know that I am one of them. I can't risk you telling the Americans."

With one quick move, he sliced the defenseless officer's throat. He pulled the gag off the man and removed his bindings, not wanting those who would find both of them to believe the navigator was being held hostage by *him*.

He then summoned the courage to do to himself what most rational people would believe was unthinkable. He stuck the knife into his own side, hoping that he had missed any vital organs. The pain was excruciating, much worse than he had expected. He tossed the knife across the room and slumped to the floor. He hoped the Americans would find him before he bled out.

Meanwhile, Shorty had been getting regular updates from his squad leaders over the secure-comm system used by all SEAL team members. The top three decks had already been cleared of militants by Bravo Squad. When they reached the bridge on Deck 10, they didn't knock. They easily breached the door, the explosive charges tearing it completely apart. As the SEALs entered, they found Captain Hafez Zoyatov on the floor, bleeding badly, barely conscious, but alive.

When Zoyatov was able to speak, he told the frogman who was trying to patch him up that the terrorists had entered the bridge and tried to kill both him and the navigator. He claimed he was an innocent victim, a hostage, just like the passengers.

Hafez Zoyatov hoped that his story was believable. But once the SEAL looked around and saw the discarded gag and bindings and the knife tossed to the side, he quickly deduced that the captain was not telling the truth—and was one of the terrorists. Once the captain's bleeding was under control, he was quickly zip-tied and secured to the rail overlooking the bow of the ship. One of the operators positioned himself on the bridge while the rest moved on.

All the decks from six on down had now been cleared. But the price was high in a few of the muster areas, where terrorists chose to fight it out with the SEALs. In the end, the Tajiks were still quickly eliminated by the laser-accurate shots from the American SEAL team, but not before the radicals had sprayed gunfire into some of the hostage areas. The death count of innocent passengers had risen, but it could have been much higher if not for the speed, shock and lethal force applied by the SEALs. The pincers were closing on the remaining decks as the assault forces moved rapidly. Soon, the *Dream Spinner* would be free of their Tajik captors and the Viper's grasp.

By Shorty's count, from the reports he'd been getting, at least thirty-four militants were dead. That left another fifteen or so, depending on what the actual number really was in the beginning. In any event, the SEAL commander was confident that in a very short time, the ship would be completely swept of terrorists. Using secure voice communications, he assessed the current situation and gave the order to his squads to continue executing their planned mission.

THOMAS BELISLE

The Americans knew they could face a more concentrated defense as they closed around the remaining radical Tajiks. As the bloody combat moved through the ship, those Panja cell radicals still left standing migrated to the last three decks that might give them a chance to live a little longer—or more likely, choose their place to die.

From the central balcony area, the squad leaders signaled each other as they moved outward toward the ends of decks eight and ten. Blocking the path of any militant who might try to escape toward the bow and stern were SEALs positioned at the ends of each hallway.

As Shorty swept through the art gallery and toward the casino on Deck 7, shots rang out. The numbered Picasso print on display was shredded, and the wall behind Robinson's head splintered from the bullets raking across it.

From behind the large array of slot machines, his NVGs picked up the red-hot barrel of an automatic rifle. Shorty motioned to one of his teammates to move left into the foyer in front of the casino. He would move right, flanking the militant, and hopefully put an end to the assailant.

The Tajik's hot rifle barrel began to move forward in the darkness, the Tajik terrorist hoping to rip off another burst, maybe getting lucky and hitting his target.

Before he could get off a round, the pop-pop of the SEAL's suppressed M4A1 rifle sent two hollow-point rounds into the Tajik's forehead. Another casino player had just cashed out.

The team kept sweeping the ship. Hunting deliberately, with deadly precision.

Chapter 54

Khalil managed to get to the Chop House without being seen. He found the door unlocked. He moved slowly through the entryway, looking as carefully as he could for anyone who might be hiding there. He located the kitchen and knew where to find the elevator. The shaft was pitch black, his flashlight providing the only illumination in the six-foot-square elevator passage. He stepped over the threshold and began his descent to Deck 2 on the steel maintenance ladder. The top of the elevator five floors below him was barely visible when he followed the flashlight's narrow beam down into the darkness.

He was glad the power was still off. He didn't need the elevator to be moving while he slithered by its side, the area between the shaft wall and the elevator's side not much wider than a foot. He kept moving.

As Khalil clambered down, he tried to keep as quiet as he could. Any noise might alert the Americans, who by now were all over the ship. He thought about the escape plan. The deal that Asmaradov had apparently made with the Venezuelan leader and his Russian sponsors. The submarine that *had* to be out there waiting for him. He was relieved that he had sent the message to Asmaradov—that he had activated the mines, and they were set to explode soon. He had no choice. The Viper would understand, even if it caused the United States to keep Chernov captive in Gitmo.

He suddenly stopped his descent, realizing that he had forgotten something. A critical item—the laptop computer used to activate the mines. He had left it in the communications center, in his haste to get away. For an instant, he thought about going back to get it.

Not enough time, he thought. *And by now, the Americans will be all over that deck. It's useless to them anyway. I have the only password to initiate the program. And there is no power.*

He reached the bottom. He thought that by now, Drako Kratec and Cho Lee Kwan were probably waiting at the bulkhead door on Deck 2. Hopefully, they had gotten the propulsion units ready. There was no time to waste as the mine detonation timers counted down.

Khalil carefully pushed the elevator door open, emerged from the shaft and listened carefully. He looked into the darkness for any sign of movement. He didn't want to get shot by Kratec, Cho or Kelly, mistaking him for American assault team members.

Two of his co-conspirators were expecting him. Khalil saw the provisioning manager's body crumpled by the right forward bulkhead, a victim of the SEALs who had swept the area earlier.

———————•———————

In the fitness center, Ace was growing anxious for the SEALs to finish the job of freeing the cruise ship. He began to think about Khalil. The terrorist was responsible, directly or indirectly, for the death and suffering on the *Dream Spinner.*

As they waited for the American assault team to return, Jack filled in the details of what he knew. He had explained what Martha Cook had told him. The plot by Asmaradov to hold the ship hostage in order to obtain the release of a terrorist in custody at the American prison in Guantanamo Bay, Cuba. And the terrorist's promise to release the ship and its hostages in Caracas, Venezuela. That was a lie, he was sure of it.

Ace strongly suspected—no, downright *knew*—that Khalil was responsible for all of the communication issues on the ship before the passengers had even known there was *going* to be a hostage crisis. He was a brilliant engineer who had the skills to pull it off, and it couldn't possibly be just a coincidence that he was on the ship.

To top it off, he had kidnapped Ace's daughter. For that alone, the radical Syrian needed to pay a price. He thought about the SEAL teams.

They would hopefully catch him. But if they didn't, if somehow Khalil managed to escape, yet again, from another terrorist attack that he was instrumental in prosecuting, well, that just wasn't right. Justice had to be served. He wondered where Khalil had disappeared to.

"Claire, do you remember anything about the man who kept you captive? Do you remember him saying anything, either to you or to someone else?"

Ace didn't want his daughter to relive her ordeal with Khalil. But maybe there was some clue about what was happening, or what was going to happen.

"Dad, he worked on his computer for a few minutes and then said that you would pay a price for what you did."

"Anything else?"

"He did talk with a lady once. She didn't seem happy that I was there. She told him that he had to focus on the mission. That he had to complete his tasks before they left the boat."

"Wait. She said something about leaving the boat?"

"I think so. It was hard to hear sometimes. But I think that's what she said."

"Tell me about this lady. Did you get a look at her? Did she come to see him when the lights were still on?"

"Yes. She was shorter than him. Black hair. She looked like she was from some other country, not from the United States. He called her Banu, I think. I thought that was a strange name," She paused. "He got angry with her when she seemed to be talking about me."

"What do you mean?"

"She scared me. She told him to take care of his problem, and she pointed to me. I didn't know *what* was going to happen."

"That's very good, Claire. You were brave, and I'm proud of you." He hugged his daughter close to him.

"Oh, and he talked with the lady about the Chop House and an elevator. He told her to make sure she gets there soon."

He thought about what Claire had just said. *The Chop House? The elevator? Wait. The elevators in the restaurants go all the way down to Deck 2.*

If Khalil planned on leaving the ship, how was that going to happen? Was the plan really for the Guantanamo prisoners to be released, and then Khalil and the terrorists were going to leave the ship once it berthed in Caracas? If the plan was to get off the ship in Venezuela, then what did an elevator shaft in a restaurant have to do with anything?

It was a bit puzzling. But then, a thought. *I'll bet there is a contingency escape plan. Asmaradov planned for a possible American assault and likely wants to ensure his main man, Khalil, survives. Maybe others.*

He explained to Jack, Flamer and Buzz what he thought might be actually happening. It made sense.

"Jack, this is going to sound stupid, but there's something I've gotta do. I believe that Khalil is, right now, trying to get off this ship. I think I know how he's planning on doing it. I'm going after him."

"Matt, don't be crazy. Let the SEALs handle him. I'm fairly certain they'll get every last one of these terrorist bastards."

"He crossed a big line when he took Claire. Thankfully, she's okay. But I need to finish what should have happened years ago in Iran."

Jack wasn't keen on the idea at all, nor were Buzz and Flamer. There was nothing to gain, as far as they saw it. Only satisfaction. But Jack also understood the need for that kind of closure as a combat warrior himself. And he knew what Ace was capable of doing. He was a trained fighter.

"Take this." Jack handed Ace the pistol commandeered from a dead militant. "It's already got a round in the chamber and a full clip. Safety is on. Just flip this lever and you're good to go," he said.

"I'll be back," Ace promised. "If the SEALs come back, tell them where I've gone. I may need some help if I run into more than Khalil."

He turned to give Claire a kiss. She was sound asleep.

"Be careful, mate. Sure you don't want a bit of top cover on your personal mission?"

"No, Buzz, I've got this."

It took only a minute to get down the hallway to the Chop House. He carefully went through the door, not certain if Tajik militants had escaped death from the SEALs and taken refuge in the restaurant. He kept his flashlight off for a few moments, walking softly on the carpet, feeling his way in the darkness, moving cautiously past the small reservation desk and into the dining area. With his pistol at the ready, he flicked on the small flashlight and swept it across the room.

The movement from behind hardly made a sound, but it was enough to make him turn quickly in that direction, hoping to get off a shot if he had to. His flashlight beam caught a black blur, his senses knowing that something was coming at him. But it was too late to do anything. Before he could react with his pistol, he was hammered by a body blow that knocked him to the floor.

Banu "Kelly" Sayeed had just introduced herself to Ace Black in a rather violent, very personal fashion. It was sheer coincidence that the confrontation between the two of them occurred at all. She'd realized once the power was out that she had little time to get to her escape point and had made her way to the Chop House elevator.

She hit him again before he could react, this time with a kick to his head that fortunately, due to the darkness, landed only a glancing blow. Then she was on him. As they both tumbled in the darkness, he realized that his weapon was no longer in his hand.

Ace was now in the fight for his life. His Korean martial arts training kicked in, and he landed a fist into her ribs. Kelly responded before he could make another move and hit him hard in the face with a punch that might have immobilized most people. Ace somehow was still in the fight. At least he thought he was. But now she wasn't near him.

The flashlight beam was now on him. The former Iranian commando also had a weapon in her hand. A semiautomatic pistol. It was pointed directly at Ace.

She was ready to pull the trigger but realized who the face belonged to, her flashlight giving her a good look at the man. She would delay his death for just a few moments.

"If you move again, you die," she said.

"Wait. I'm an American. Are you a crew member?"

She laughed. "I am your enemy. You are the man who Khalil hates most in his life. He is obsessed with you and your death. Your time has come to meet your fate."

Ace was still blinded by the light beam, and surprised that she had spoken about Khalil. He wondered who the woman was. How she knew Khalil. What her connection was to him. *She's a terrorist just like him*, he thought.

"Who are you?" he asked, hoping to buy some time.

"It does not matter. All that matters is what will happen shortly to everyone on this ship," she said, the disdain for him and all the passengers clear in her voice.

Ace thought about her words. Again with the inference that something awful was coming to the *Dream Spinner*, beyond the carnage already taking place. He thought about what he could do to extricate himself from this situation. Maybe dive to the side in the darkness, pull his knife, go on the offensive. Perhaps her bullet would not find its mark.

Before he could move, the sound of the gunshots startled him. The dark figure lurched toward him and crumpled to the floor, propelled by the two pistol rounds that entered her back.

Ace wasn't sure what was happening but dove to the floor. He then heard a familiar voice.

"It is okay. You are safe," she said. "It is Aleksandra."

In the adjacent kitchen area, the young Ukrainian waitress had been hiding from the terror happening on board the ship. She was tipped off earlier by other attendants in the dining room that the militant woman was coming for her. Before the power had gone out, she had slipped away, hoping to hide from the hunter who was intent on taking her life.

When Aleksandra had heard the confrontation going on in the dining area, she had peeked out. She had seen the flashlight beam highlight a man. It was Ace. As she'd quietly moved forward, her foot had bumped into something. She had reached down and picked up the gun that had fallen from Ace's hand in the scuffle. She knew how to use it. And her aim was perfect, even in the dark room.

The deadly bullets hadn't missed the center of Banu "Kelly" Sayeed's back—not from three feet away.

Recovering from the floor and his close brush with death, Ace exclaimed, "Boy, am I glad to see you. Your timing couldn't have been better. Thanks for saving my life."

"I'm just glad I hit her in the darkness, and not you!" Aleksandra picked up the flashlight and handed it to Ace, along with his gun. "What are you doing here?" she asked.

"I'm heading below to take care of some personal business with one particular terrorist." He paused. "You need to stay in the kitchen and hide. The U.S. Navy SEALs are on board and in the process of taking back this ship. They'll find you eventually. You'll be fine."

Ace picked up Kelly's weapon and gave it to Aleksandra. "I think you can use this if you're threatened by any militants. You didn't miss your target."

"Yes, it is no problem. I learned how to use many weapons at an early age in my country during all the unrest."

"Okay. Remember, your best strategy for staying alive is to stay hidden until the SEALs find you."

She did as she was asked and disappeared into the darkness. He followed her into the kitchen, his trusty flashlight highlighting the way, and then found the storage elevator near the back wall. Normally, crates of food were lifted from the lower deck storerooms to the kitchen. Today the elevator would be used for a very different reason. It was not visible when he pulled the door open. He shone his flashlight beam down the shaft. He saw the ladder on the side, stepped across the threshold, and began his downward trek into the blackness.

Chapter 55

I t was early in the morning in the Situation Room. Black coffee by the gallon was being consumed by the bleary-eyed occupants as they waited for their next update from Lieutenant Commander Shorty Robinson.

"Mr. President. Comms are up from the *Dream Spinner*. We have Robinson on the line."

"Thanks," President Foreman said to the JCS chairman. He took his seat and hoped to hear some good news.

"Mr. President, Lieutenant Commander Robinson here. I have an update for you."

"Press ahead," Foreman ordered the SEAL officer.

"Sir, we have all but one deck secured. We should have that completed in the next ten minutes. We've eliminated thirty-eight terrorists and taken no casualties."

"What about the passengers?" Foreman demanded.

"There were some casualties in a couple of the muster areas. In one of them, the militants had locked the men in and wired the exit doors with explosives. Unfortunately, someone tried to get out. At least six men were killed in the explosion, and a number injured." He paused. "In one other area, it was much worse. When the power went out, a militant panicked and began shooting into the group of captives. When his gun emptied, a number of men swarmed him and beat him to death. Several of the passengers were killed by the gunfire, and an equal number injured. Fortunately, the captive passengers stayed put rather than try to leave that area—guess they felt they had a better chance staying there with the militant's weapon and his extra clip."

"My God. That's terrible. Is that it?"

"Yes, sir. The passengers confined to their staterooms are okay as far as we know. We're verifying that now. Once we finish clearing the last deck, we'll continue to methodically open each stateroom. We need to verify that there are no militants hiding in any of them."

"That's great to hear. Let me know when you've finished."

"Yes, sir, Mr. President. Will do."

There were plenty of smiles around the room as the president and his staff shook hands and slapped backs. Foreman began to breathe a bit easier now that the violence aboard the *Dream Spinner* appeared to be coming to an end—on President Foreman's terms—or so he hoped.

———————————•———————————

Ace was descending the elevator shaft, nearing Deck 2. As he approached the closed elevator door, he knew that he had to be careful. He wasn't sure who might be waiting for him on the other side of the door. Maybe a terrorist waiting to blast him? Or maybe a booby trap?

There wasn't a handle on the inside to pull the door open. He shut off his flashlight, making sure it didn't cast a beam through the door he was about to pry open.

He reached for the combat knife secured to his waist, found the break between the doors and inserted the blade, prying them about a half inch apart. It was pitch black on the other side. He listened for any noise, anything that would indicate movement by the door. Nothing.

He stowed his knife and slowly pulled the doors open. They stayed in place when he stopped separating them, with no power to automatically close them. He stepped from the security of the maintenance ladder onto the deck. He was hesitant to flip the flashlight on. If Khalil or anyone else was nearby, he would be a prime target—follow the light beam, kill the man.

He heard the movement of feet across the deck. Very close! He heard a click, the sound of a jammed gun. He turned in time to avoid the hand swinging a pistol that nearly took him out. Ace reacted with instinct honed by the combat training that he continued to practice since his assignment in the Pacific. In a sweeping move, he pulled the combat knife from his belt and caught the attacker just under the rib cage as another blow aimed at his head narrowly missed. His attacker was now doubled over. Ace pulled the knife from its buried position in the militant's chest. The man began to utter a muffled moan as his life began to slip away. With his left hand over the man's mouth, Ace brought his blade across the man's throat, slicing it cleanly. No more sound.

Ace lowered him to the floor and then quickly focused his flashlight's beam on the man. The name Kratec was on his uniform.

The chief engineer, thought Ace. *Figures he would be tied in to this operation.* He looked into the darkness for any other signs of movement. It was deathly quiet. Now, where to go? He needed to turn right out of the elevator and move down the wide storage area corridor. About thirty yards ahead, the hallway curved left toward the starboard side of the ship. Just past that, the area opened up even more to allow access to the hull door that led outside the *Dream Spinner.*

He moved slowly. Deliberately. He had been lucky. He had just escaped another very close call. One that could have easily gone the other way in the darkness. Had he not heard the footsteps, he would likely be the one on the floor, dead with a crushed skull.

As he moved along the left side of the corridor toward his objective, he believed, actually hoped, that at this point, nobody had heard him take out the militant that tried to attack him. Even in spite of Kratec's last moan, if they had heard anything, surely they would have responded to the commotion.

He had his pistol out, safety off, extended in the combat assault position. He was ready to use it. The flashlight was off. The low-hanging bulkhead seemed to come out of nowhere in the darkness. When his head hit it, he winced a little too loudly.

The corridor's steel side wall was instantly peppered from the sparkling ricochet of bullets headed in his direction. Ace dropped to one knee and hugged the wall. There was no other cover. He hoped that the darkness was enough to keep him safe from the streaming gunfire coming from up ahead.

The shape came out of the darkness toward him, still firing until the pistol magazine was empty. Miraculously, the spray of bullets missed their target in the blackened hallway. Ace got off two rounds that missed his target before he was tackled to the deck. The impact caused his pistol hand to painfully hit the side wall. The weapon fell from his grip. For the moment, his attacker was not on him. That wouldn't last.

Cho Lee Kwan, the security chief on the *Dream Spinner*, had also been well-trained to fight, learning from some of the best hand-to-hand combat instructors in North Korea and Central Asia.

As the dark shape came flying at him again, Ace threw a straight punch toward what he hoped was his opponent's head. His fist glanced off the side of the man's skull, missing its mark in the darkness. But it gave Ace the time to block the punch coming his way. However, he didn't block the knife strike that his attacker managed to inflict on him. The blade penetrated his side, but not deeply. He ignored the pain and prepared for his next move.

No time to spar with this guy, he thought quickly. Ace could see enough of his opponent that he managed to execute a classic eye strike that temporarily stopped his attacker. He finished the man off with a throat strike that dropped his assailant to the deck, gasping for air. Ace gave him a final savage punch, rendering him unconscious. The fight was over, at least with that particular militant.

While Ace had managed to subdue his attacker, he'd sustained a nasty stab to his side. Fortunately, no vital organs were hit. Holding his wound, he found his combat knife on the floor near his feet, and his pistol as well. As he tried to rise from the floor, a light blinded him.

"Drop your weapon," shouted Kahlil, "or I will kill you where you stand." He leveled his pistol at Ace and fired one round near his feet, to make sure Ace knew that he had a gun. "The next shot will be through your heart."

His ultimate adversary had bested him. He dropped the gun he was holding.

"The knife too," ordered Khalil.

Ace pulled the combat knife from its scabbard, the blade still wet with Kratec's blood. He placed it on the floor.

Shining his flashlight on the unconscious security chief, Khalil demanded, "Take the handcuffs from Cho and put them on your wrist."

He did as he was told. Khalil directed him to walk toward the access door. "Put your hand past the steam pipe and lock the cuff to your other hand."

This is bad. Ace slowly complied. "You know, Khalil, you're not going to get off this ship. The Navy SEALs know all about you. They're headed here right now." He really hoped he was right about that.

Khalil shook his head. "You are lying. I will get free from this doomed ship. The rest of you—including your family—will perish."

"Hey, man, you underestimate the SEALs. They already have control of the *Dream Spinner*. Every one of your terrorist buddies is either dead or getting ready to die. Most likely, they're already dead. The same thing's going to happen to you if you don't give up."

"You are the one who is underestimating things. I'm leaving in a few minutes. I'll get to safety. My exit plan is in place." He smiled at Ace. "And you will meet your maker in about thirty minutes," he said, looking at his watch.

"What are you talking about?"

Khalil laughed. "You don't think Asmaradov was going to let you all live, do you?"

"You may be able to kill me, but that's about it, Khalil. You don't have control of this ship. And you don't have what it takes to do anything else." *Probably shouldn't have said that last part,* he thought.

"How did you find me?" Khalil asked.

"Well, you're not as smart as you think you are. You yapped a bit too loudly about the elevator in the Chop House in front of my daughter. She told me what you and your now-dead female friend talked about in the communications center. She's lying on the dining room floor of the restaurant right now. I put the pieces together."

Khalil stared at his captive, stunned at what he had just been told about Kelly. He tried to control his anger, directing it instead to his escape plan. Khalil began to break out the propulsion gear he would use to help pull him away from the ship once he jumped to the water.

"You know, you made a big mistake taking my daughter. If not for that, I probably wouldn't have come after you." Ace paused. "I'm just sorry I didn't eliminate you years ago. Before you had time to do more harm to peace-loving people."

Khalil swung the bulkhead door open, pulling it inward. The salty sea breeze flowed through the dark opening, propelled by the storm's waning winds.

"You are the one who will be eliminated when the mines detonate in less than thirty minutes and this ship sinks like a rock with everyone on board. Including your daughter."

Ace was stunned to hear that comment. The thirty minutes Khalil referred to dealt with the mines! He must have somehow activated them before heading down to Deck 2.

"Boy, you gotta be pretty stupid. By now, the SEAL team that has taken back this ship has already disarmed them all. They likely did that before they even boarded."

"You are the one who is stupid. I set the timers only a few minutes ago in the communications center. Long *after* the SEALs boarded this ship."

"That's pretty unlikely. There's no power on this ship. You'd need that to have done what you say."

"Again, you underestimate my ability with a computer."

The look on Ace's face, in the glow of the flashlight, delighted Khalil. "You see, you are not so smart. And even if the mines are somehow, miraculously disarmed before they detonate, this ship will still end up at the bottom of the Caribbean Sea."

"What do you mean?" Ace asked.

Khalil hesitated to say any more. But then again, the man he was looking at was not going to survive. He should know the truth about what was to happen to him and his family before the Syrian jumped into the water.

"There is a submarine waiting to take me away from here. Once I am on board, this cruise ship will be torpedoed and sunk."

It all started to come together in Ace's head. The open hatch. The propulsion devices to get a swimmer quickly through the water. At this point, Ace was out of options. He couldn't stop Khalil. He couldn't protect his family, his friends, or anyone else on board. Even the SEALs would take casualties when the mines blew. And if that didn't happen, a torpedo would finish the job.

Ace tried to play one last card. "You know, Khalil, your god, Allah, a god of peace, would not approve nor accept what you're doing. You are evil. A terrorist. The lowest form of life on the planet. You're going straight to hell!" He paused. "Give up while you still can, and maybe you'll be granted some forgiveness from your god for what you have done."

"You know nothing of my god," he shouted angrily. "I will inflict pain that you Americans haven't experienced in decades."

As he seethed at Ace's comments, Khalil changed his mind. He was originally going to let his nemesis live to see the ocean pour through the open hatch. To feel what it was like to drown. A horrible death. And before he drew that last breath, to think about his daughter, his boys, his wife and mother, all meeting the same fate.

But now, a bullet was a better death sentence. He could look into Matt Black's eyes as he died. This one time in Khalil's life, he wanted to see death up close and personal. Watch the American he hated so much draw his last breath. He would exact the final revenge that had been long overdue. He raised his gun and aimed it at Ace's forehead.

Chapter 56

S horty Robinson was ready to report to the president of the United States that the *Dream Spinner* was clear, at least from the SEAL's sweep of all decks. The only thing remaining was to finish checking every cabin for hideaways. There was always a possibility that one or two militants would try to use a stateroom as a hideout. His operators were prepared for it, knowing they might have to pry them out.

It was going to take a bit longer to cull their way through the nearly one thousand crew members. The SEALs knew that the majority, actually nearly all of them, were innocent victims, just like the passengers. They also strongly suspected that once the crew knew that the ship had been secured by the American warriors, any militants trying to remain disguised as crew members would be quickly identified.

The main objective now was to regain control of the vessel and reestablish at least minimal power.

"Go ahead, asshole. Do it. But I promise, you will *never* get off this ship alive!" He quickly prayed to himself that he was right—and for a miracle.

Ace prepared for his execution. He actually believed that his life was about to be brought to a violent end. He briefly thought about his family. He didn't close his eyes. He wouldn't give Khalil the satisfaction of thinking that he feared death.

The piercing cracks of gunfire startled him. He felt excruciating pain in his left forearm, but he was still standing, still chained by the handcuffs to the bulkhead.

"Ace, are you okay?" Buzz shouted from down the corridor. He ran up, his rifle still smoking from the bullet that had penetrated Khalil's head just next to his nose. He looked down at the dead militant.

Although he was in pain, Ace was trying to comprehend what had just happened in the darkness as he'd waited for the bullet he'd thought for sure would end his life.

"I'm glad that this bugger had his flashlight on. In this darkness, I'm lucky as hell to have hit the bloke in the head."

"Buzz. What are you doing here? Boy, am I glad to see you. You just save my life!"

Then Flamer appeared out of the shadows. "We thought you might need some help. Guess we were right about that," he laughed. He aimed the flashlight at Ace, and noticed the blood on his arm.

"Are you injured?" he asked.

"Yeah, Khalil must have gotten off a shot and it hit my arm. Some of the blood on my shirt is mine, the rest from one of the militants—in fact, the chief engineer and security chief almost got the best of me. One is dead, the other is lying over by the other bulkhead. I'm not sure if he's dead, but he left me with this souvenir in my side. I don't think it's too bad."

Flamer walked toward his buddy to check his wounds.

"I still can't believe you came here, but boy, am I glad you did."

"When the SEALs finished clearing the remaining decks, they came back to the fitness center and led us to our staterooms. Jack took Claire to Julie. Everyone is okay," he said. "But then, I started thinking about what you were trying to do. We hustled down here and now I'm just glad we weren't a moment or two later."

"Get me out of these cuffs fast," he yelled. "The keys should be in that terrorist's pocket."

Flamer rolled the security chief over and quickly found the handcuff keys. He handed them to Buzz, who carefully unlocked the cuffs to avoid any more pain to Ace's arm.

"Let me put a compress on that gunshot wound," Buzz remarked as he walked over to Ace. He ripped part of his shirttail off and wrapped Ace's wounded arm tightly. He checked the stab wound.

"Better put something on that as well to stem the bleeding." He pulled a couple pieces of his reflective tape off his shirt and used it to bind a piece of his torn shirt to Ace's side.

Flamer then checked Khalil for anything of value and found a small folded paper in his shirt pocket. He looked at it under the beam of his flashlight and saw a bunch of letters, numbers and characters all jumbled together.

With the cuffs off, Ace said, "I've got to get to the SEAL team. Before you guys got here, Khalil told me about destroying the cruise ship. He said there were mines on the hull that were set to explode. We only have about twenty minutes, according to what he said."

Ace grabbed his knife and pistol, unsure if he would still need them. "What have you got there, Flamer?" he asked.

"Don't know. It was in that dead bastard's pocket. By the way, Buzz, nice shot."

The Brit smiled. "Anything else I can do for you folks from the colonies? If so, just ask."

Ace reached for the paper. "Let me see that." He wasn't sure what it was, but if Khalil had kept it, it must have been important in some way. He stuffed it into his pocket.

Ace began to run down the corridor, his flashlight bouncing beams off the hallway walls.

"Close that service door to the outside of the ship and then get up to the staterooms," he yelled back. "Get ready to head for the lifeboats if we can't stop the mines from going off."

Ace raced to the stairway, figuring it would be quicker than the elevator shaft. He scaled them rapidly, in spite of his injuries. He was abruptly stopped by a SEAL on the Deck 7 platform, his weapon pointed directly at Ace.

"Where's your team leader?" Ace yelled. "I've got to get him an urgent message."

Shorty turned around from across the platform. "What's the problem?"

Ace was shocked by who he was looking at. Even in the darkness, the face was very familiar in spite of the beard.

"Shorty? Is that you?" Ace recognized the frogman immediately as his old friend. A blast from the past when he worked with the SEALs in South Korea.

The frogman looked at Ace closely with his flashlight.

"Well, I'll be damned. Ace Black. What a friggin' coincidence."

Shorty noticed the blood on his shirt and forearm. "Looks like you caught a bit of combat action. Are you okay?"

"Yeah—but I could have done without the injuries."

The two old acquaintances quickly exchanged pleasantries, but this was clearly not the time to celebrate a reunion of two friends.

"The mastermind of this mess was just killed down on Deck 2. He was trying to escape the ship before the mines that are attached to the hull are detonated," said Ace.

The SEAL team leader looked at Ace, seeming to question what he was being told. "How do you know about the mines?"

"I just told you how I know, Shorty. The dead terrorist trying to escape this ship said the mines were on a timer. By his own admission, we've got only about fifteen minutes from right now to figure out how to stop them from going off and sinking this ship." Ace kept the pressure on Lieutenant Commander Robinson.

"This terrorist, Khalil Ruffa, or whatever he may have changed his name to, was the IT expert on this ship. He was the guy responsible for killing the communications capability several days ago. This guy had history with me, and with the United States years ago. He was a technological genius, a software wizard. I suspect whatever he did to activate the mines is inside the communications center, where he kept my daughter hostage."

Shorty couldn't believe the story he was hearing. But if it was correct, the *Dream Spinner* had less than twelve minutes before the mines blew.

The emergency lights came on at that moment, the main backup generator now online. One of the engineers had made his way to the engine control room, accompanied by a SEAL operator, and managed to get limited power restored through the shielded system that had not been fried.

Shorty radioed his IT expert to get to the communications center immediately. He and Ace raced up the stairs to Deck 10 and then ran down the winding hallway. The IT guy was already inside.

"What's up, Commander?" he asked.

"This ship may be rigged to blow in spite of the pulse that silenced every other power source. There may have been some means in here of activating a timer in those Russian mines. See what you can find. And hurry!"

Ace thought about what Khalil had done. How his advanced software skills might have been used to activate the mines. He reached into his pocket and pulled out the folded piece of paper.

"Shorty, I think this has something to do with it. Khalil was a computer genius. He likely built a program on his computer, maybe that laptop over there on the counter, to activate the mines. This was in his pocket. It might be a log-in or password to get into the program. Maybe to deactivate it if his situation changed."

Shorty took the note and handed it to his IT guy, who had already powered up the computer. The laptop screen had the usual icons, and one that was odd-looking. He moved the cursor to it and clicked.

It opened a new window that requested a log-in and password.

"Shit," he said. "We're screwed." He looked at his team leader. "There's no telling what the log-in is."

Ace thought for a minute. "Try his parents' names. Mohammad. If that doesn't work, try Nayifa. Use this set of info for the password," he said, passing the paper to the IT guy.

"We don't have all day here. About another six minutes if you were right about the threat this guy made to destroy the ship." Shorty made a call to all members of his team.

"Be prepared for explosions below the waterline. Alert the crew as quick as you can to prepare to deploy the lifeboats."

The minutes ticked by. The IT expert was getting frustrated as nothing seemed to allow access to the program.

Wait, Ace thought. *Khalil's sister. What was her name? Anna?*

One minute remaining. "Try his sister's name. Anna!"

The name Anna was entered. "Incorrect log-in," said the prompt.

With seconds remaining, Ace said, "Try Anna using just one *n*!"

The IT specialist entered it and the program opened. He quickly typed in the lengthy password written on the paper. Another screen opened. He scanned what he saw, looking for something that would have an Arm/Disarm message. He saw it. He moved the cursor to Disarm and, holding his breath, clicked on it just as the time expired.

The trio waited—listening, hoping, praying they had guessed correctly. They looked at each other. After a few seconds, they breathed easily.

The silence was golden!

"That was too close," Shorty remarked.

Ace had more bad news to share.

"There's one more thing. Khalil told me about a contingency plan if the mines didn't work. I'm sure he wouldn't have said anything about it if he didn't believe he was going to put a bullet in my head."

Shorty was right in Ace's face. "What did he say?" he demanded.

"He said that his escape plan was to be on a submarine nearby. Once he got to it, the sub was to fire torpedoes at the *Dream Spinner* and finish what was apparently the terrorist's intent all along."

"Are you sure you heard him correctly?"

"Absolutely. When you think you're about to die, you listen carefully to what's being said."

"We don't have any time to waste," Shorty said. "It may already be too late." He stepped out of the communications center and headed out to the deck. He needed to make an urgent call that would likely determine whether he and the rest of the people on board the *Dream Spinner* would live or die.

Chapter 57

While Shorty and Ace had been working furiously in the communications center, the SEAL operators from the two squads had been quickly making their way through the staterooms. They worked as fast as possible to verify that each one contained only passengers and that no terrorists were hidden inside. This took a lot of time. Some passengers were reluctant to open their doors, in spite of the reassuring voices of the SEALs.

Doors had to be opened to verify who was inside. Those passengers who refused to open their door had them opened by master keys the crew stewards used, since there had been no power to activate the electronic locks when they had begun their sweep. Up to now, they had encountered no radical Tajiks in any of the passenger cabins.

Inside Julie Black's stateroom, she and the kids were huddled together when they heard the knock on their door. Hearing the SEAL's voice, she slowly opened it and was immensely relieved to see his face.

"Thank God. I thought for a moment that you might be one of the terrorists. I'm so glad to see you. Is it over?"

"Just about, ma'am. But I'd ask you to stay in your stateroom for now."

"Please, have you seen my husband? His name is Matt Black. Do you know about him?"

"Ma'am, I believe your husband is safe. There were also a couple of other men with him. They're all safe."

"Oh my God, thank you, Lord, for that," Julie shouted. "And thank you so much for coming to our rescue. When can I see my husband?"

"As soon as we finish securing the ship, we'll open up the hall-ways for the passengers. It shouldn't be long now."

When the door closed, Julie corralled the kids and hugged them close to her. She began sobbing almost uncontrollably.

"What's wrong, Mommy?" asked Roman. "Are you sad? I thought the soldier said that Daddy was okay."

"Honey, I'm not sad at all. I'm just so happy that they're all safe."

Julie wasn't going to be completely happy until she was reunited with Matt. She didn't know that Flamer was also safe but presumed at least one of the other men the SEAL had referred to was Colene's husband.

For the past twenty-four hours, Captain Raul Vasquez had been sitting silently four miles away from the *Dream Spinner* at a depth of three hundred feet. The Venezuelan submarine had now moved closer to the cruise ship based on the plan that had been approved by Farad Asmaradov and communicated to him by his command-ing officer.

His crew had not detected the large electromagnetic pulse but had noticed that the *Dream Spinner* wasn't underway. Vasquez had initially wondered what was happening. The captain knew the American aircraft carrier was not far off. It was a clear image, along with the *Dream Spinner*, on his sonar screen. Perhaps the carrier had initiated an attack on the cruise liner. Vasquez had not, however, detected the stealthy USS *Grayback III* submarine, nor the mini-subs that had rendezvoused with the *Dream Spinner*.

While the Venezuelan Navy was not nearly as technologically advanced or trained to the same level of skill as their American coun-terparts, Vasquez put two and two together. The assault on the *Dream Spinner* had begun. It was still several hours before the planned release of Chernov from Guantanamo Bay, after which Vasquez knew that he had to be prepared for the extraction of a few key people aboard the cruise ship. The action he presumed was taking place on the *Dream*

Spinner prompted his decision to move inside a mile of the ship, well within the swimming distance for the three men and one woman he believed would be escaping toward his sub.

He released a small buoy to the surface, but he knew there was little chance the swimmers would see it in the darkness and eight-foot waves. The escape had been planned for daylight, in calm weather. The American assault in the darkness now made a successful extraction almost impossible.

Vasquez had another tough decision to make. His orders from the Viper contained a contingency plan in the event that an American attack occurred before Chernov's release. If there was a chance the United States might succeed in an assault to free the captive ship's passengers, he knew the advanced mines secured to the hull of the *Dream Spinner* might be neutralized and never have an opportunity to destroy the ship.

The Venezuelan sub captain had been told to do something that would violate his own code of war. He had been directed to sink the *Dream Spinner* with a salvo of torpedoes. He had no problem, as a member of the Venezuelan Navy, destroying an enemy that threatened his country. That was what he signed up to do—what he was trained for. But sinking a cruise ship loaded with innocent civilians was another matter. He struggled with the final decision. But he also knew the consequences if he disobeyed his orders.

"Prepare torpedo tubes," Vasquez ordered his bridge weapons officer, "and stand by to fire."

———————•———————

Shorty Robinson pulled his satellite phone from his pocket and punched in the number. His call was immediately answered in the *Grayback III*'s communications center. The secure call shocked its captain—he hadn't contemplated the type of threat Shorty described. Aside from all-out war, passenger vessels just didn't get sunk by torpedoes. While the *Dream Spinner* appeared to be secure from the mines' threat, this new threat had to be dealt with quickly.

The *Grayback*'s captain knew all about the Venezuelan submarine. It had been picked up a day earlier on the nuclear sub's sonar. Nash had been informed about the plan to sail the *Dream Spinner* to Caracas after the Gitmo prisoner release. He knew that it wasn't unusual, given that scenario, that the cruise ship might be shadowed by a Venezuelan vessel to its port in the South American country. Perhaps to serve as a threat, albeit a pathetic one, to the U.S. Navy to keep its forces away and prevent them from trying to interdict the final trip to Caracas in order to capture the militants.

The *Grayback III* had already obtained a firing solution on the sub. Once the fire control system was locked on to the Venezuelan vessel, Commander Dennis Nash was ready to eliminate the last threat against the *Dream Spinner*.

"Tubes one and two are ready," replied the weapons control officer.

"Open torpedo doors one and two," ordered Nash.

"Prepare to fire," he stated.

Two stealthy ultra-silent high-explosive torpedoes were ready to engage the Venezuelan submarine. Once they were on their way, their deadly approach to the doomed sub would never be detected. The advanced technology built into the torpedoes would keep them both silent and invisible to sonar.

"Fire one and two."

"Fish one and two, on the way. Time to target, thirty seconds," replied the weapons control officer.

Chapter 58

Captain Vasquez was stalling. It wasn't that he didn't have the authority, as the submarine's captain, to order the attack on the cruise ship. He did, by virtue of his position and rank. But he also knew that attacking a defenseless vessel, a ship that was clearly no threat to him, was a prohibited action in the civilized world. During wartime, ships that were not necessarily a direct *armed* threat were sunk by an enemy because they carried equipment, military personnel, even munitions. Clearly this was not the case here. Although he was a committed warrior in the Venezuelan military, the thought of killing innocent men, women and children weighed heavily on his mind. It was against his Catholic faith and against everything that he, as a Navy officer, held dear.

He also knew about the consequences of his actions if he carried them out. He would join the ranks of others who had violated the International Humanitarian Law, as the rules of war are officially known. Members of those ranks had, over history, been accused of and tried for war crimes for intentionally targeting civilians. Even though civilians were on a cruise ship where a skirmish was underway between Tajik militants and Navy SEALs, the major loss of civilian life would be seen as grossly disproportionate to any argument about killing the small number of military members on board.

But Captain Vasquez also knew that if he failed to carry out his orders, he would likely be shot once he got back to Venezuela. Maybe before then by the Russian intelligence officer on board his sub. There was little chance that he would survive the tight bond that had been built between Venezuela, Russia, and Farad Asmaradov.

"Captain, we must fire on the ship now," stated the submarine's first officer, a loyal member of the Communist Party in Caracas. The first officer had *his* orders as well. He saw the hesitation in Vasquez, the lack of any commitment to fire on the cruise ship.

"Do it now, captain," he ordered.

Vasquez looked into the man's eyes. He saw the Russian intelligence officer behind him. He also saw the first officer's right hand, which had settled on the leather strap securely holding the pistol to his belt.

He turned to the fire control officer. The words that left his mouth were choked, almost inaudible.

"Fire all tubes."

———————————•———————————

Moving at high speed, the *Grayback*'s stealthy torpedoes quickly homed in on the unsuspecting Venezuelan submarine. Their warheads hit its hull nearly simultaneously, the explosions ending the lives of all on board the sub. Captain Vasquez's torpedoes had not yet left their tubes when the American weapons hit.

"We have two detonations," replied the USS *Grayback III*'s weapons control officer. "Target destroyed."

"Good shooting," Commander Nash stated. "Bring us up to the surface, XO. Let's see if there are any survivors on the sub we just killed."

"Aye-aye, Captain."

———————————•———————————

Shorty Robinson walked back toward the fitness center with Ace, Flamer and Buzz as the morning sun rose from the east and burst through the glass windows.

"It's over," he said to Ace.

Those were the sweetest words Ace had heard since the terrorist hijacking of the *Dream Spinner* had begun.

"Thanks, Commander," Ace responded, formally acknowledging his friend's rank. "Did your SEALs have any casualties?"

"No sir," Shorty acknowledged his friend's rank in return. "We managed to avoid any injuries while taking out these terrorist bastards. We were fortunate, but, then again, we're pretty damn good at what we do. Failure is not an option"

Flamer jumped into the conversation. "How many militants were there? Are you sure you got all of them? And what about the rest of the passengers in the staterooms? Are they all okay?" Flamer was looking for some assurance about the *Dream Spinner*'s status.

"Whoa, slow down. We can talk about all that later on. But, yes, all the passengers in their staterooms appear to be safe. For now, I'll bet you want to get back to your families. My guys will escort you to your cabins, if you're ready."

"I can't thank you guys enough," said Ace.

He reached out to shake Shorty's hand, and the SEAL reciprocated.

"I still can't believe our rescuers turned out to be a SEALs led by an old friend," Ace remarked.

"Yeah, pretty weird after all these years. A hell of a reunion!"

Buzz walked over to Shorty and they both exchanged a fist bump.

"You frogmen are one tough bunch of dudes," Flamer remarked. "I don't know what might have happened if you hadn't shown up."

"The only easy day was yesterday, sir. No thanks are needed. Besides, from the looks of things, you all seemed to handle yourselves quite well. We're just glad we pulled this off as quickly as we did. This is a massive ship!" Shorty paused.

"My team has some cleanup to do, and at some point, we'll turn the security of the *Dream Spinner* over to the Marines who are standing by to board." He looked at Ace's wounds. "Let's have one of my guys do some triage on your injuries. Get them checked soon by the ship's medical staff."

"What happens next? When will we be able to get off at our home port?" Ace suspected that his question might not have an immediate answer.

"For now, there's no *full* power to the ship. I'm not sure that full power can be restored after the massive pulse fried all the electrical systems, except for the shielded circuits. We'll see what the engineers say. Hopefully the limited power will allow some minimal services to support the passengers and crew. I suspect you will all transfer off, possibly to the aircraft carrier nearby."

"Holy shit," retorted Flamer. "Are you talking about transferring several thousand people off this boat while floating around the Central Caribbean?"

Shorty smiled. "That's not for me to decide. But with mines secured to the hull, I don't think anyone is staying on board except perhaps for a skeleton crew. My guys will get you back to your staterooms." Then he warned them. "You're going to see some nasty things on the way. Dead terrorists, plenty of blood. We haven't had the chance to take care of that particular problem. But I guess by now, that's really not going to bother you guys much after what you all have been through."

Chapter 59

Aboard the *Dream Spinner*, the battle was over. The SEALs were confidant they had accounted for every Tajik militant on board. The only survivors among the terrorists who had hijacked the ship were the *Dream Spinner*'s captain, Hafez Zoyatov, the zip-tied gunman who Ace had left in the armory, and surprisingly, Cho Lee Kwan, although he was in serious condition. The young engineer tied up in the engine control room had been released after questioning.

The cruise ship's captain had hoped that his story about being a hostage himself had been believed by the SEALs. But it was not to be. Several of the crew members would eventually come forward and identify Zoyatov for the terrorist he was and earn him and the other surviving militants a first-class all-expenses-paid, one-way trip to Guantanamo Bay—courtesy of President Foreman and the United States government.

Meanwhile, the SEAL frogmen had reentered the water to take a closer look at the mines. They were able to at least verify that the proximity systems had not been reactivated once power had been partially restored to the *Dream Spinner*. But, given the type of Russian mines and the potential unpredictability of an internal design they didn't really know enough about, a decision had been made to transfer the passengers and crew to the aircraft carrier USS *John F. Kennedy*. It was safer than to risk continuing to a port in a boat with high-explosive mines attached.

At this point, getting lights and water flowing to the cabins and kitchen areas was going to be essential to buy a little time until a passenger transfer took place. It had been only a short time since the *Bainbridge* missile had knocked out power to the cruise ship. If at least a bit more electricity could be generated, then the foodstuffs in cold storage could still be eaten, and the ship's diesel generators could begin running. The two senior electricians from the machine shop on Deck 2 set about restoring as much power as they could to make things a bit more comfortable for the passengers and crew.

It was approaching eight o'clock in the morning at Guantanamo Bay, Cuba. Victor Chernov was excited. He had been told earlier about his upcoming release when he was allowed to recover from the medicated state he had been placed in. The other two captives had been handed over to the Cubans two days earlier, thanks to the Viper.

Victor had plans for his immediate future. First, a change of clothes and a good meal in Havana. Then a flight out of Cuba, and back to doing what he did best—executing terrorist actions on soft targets, without warning, against Americans and their pawns. Asmaradov awaited his arrival.

He wondered why no guards were coming for him. Perhaps there was a problem? He saw an American soldier approaching. *Time to get out of this horrid place*, he thought to himself. The man did not stop at his cell.

"Hey. What's going on here? I am supposed to be leaving."

The guard stopped, turned to Chernov and smiled. "You're not going anywhere. You'll spend the rest of your days here until we execute you for your crimes."

"No. The arrangement has been made. Your president has agreed. You will face the consequences for your failure to release me. Asmaradov will never forget."

"Enjoy your breakfast," the guard said, laughing loudly as he walked away.

While the president of the United States had energized his tactical military forces to execute the *Dream Spinner*'s rescue, another action had been taking place on the other side of the world. It had begun the day the first video about the *Dream Spinner*'s capture had been broadcast to President Foreman. The effort had gone into overdrive when ten passengers had been executed.

The bounty President Foreman had placed on the man known as the Viper, Farad Asmaradov, would hopefully bear fruit. The amount would make a banker salivate with excitement. It didn't matter whether Asmaradov was captured or killed—either was acceptable. Twenty-million dollars might be enough to spur widespread criminal elements that occupied much of Tajikistan and the surrounding Central Asian countries to reveal what they knew about the radical leader's activities and likely whereabouts.

When Asmaradov became aware of the bounty, he wasted no time bolting from his hideout on the outskirts of Dushanbe and fleeing to where he believed he would have more protection. He headed to the city of Vanj, near the Afghanistan border. It would be a bit more difficult for Americans or anyone else to attack him there. Deep within the mountainous area surrounding Vanj, the Viper believed he had some degree of safety. His new hideaway in northwest Gorno-Badakhshan was close to an Islamic State hotbed of activity, and by virtue of that fact alone, kept Farad somewhat insulated from the Americans whom he assumed were now hunting him.

He was not a nervous man. He had established a broad communications network that kept him apprised of both threats and opportunities. He also possessed a multilayered defensive army of well-armed and skilled Tajik and Uzbek fighters. They had served him well for years, and not one had ever been disloyal. They had fought and died for Asmaradov's causes. But the bounty made him a little more cautious, a bit more concerned. Twenty-million American dollars could turn the most loyal person into an instant traitor.

He didn't know it, but one particular criminal element in the Gorno-Badakhshan Autonomous Oblast region had decided not to pass up President Foreman's offer. Actionable information was passed on the Viper to warrant another American-led counterterrorism operation.

————————•————————

At first, President Foreman had believed that the Tajik president had been complicit in the cruise ship attack. When the reports of Tajik militants on board had been confirmed by the Navy SEALs, Foreman had been ready to bring down the hammer on Mikolayev. He had talked with him on the phone and accused him of being involved in the attack, but the Tajik leader had vehemently denied it. In fact, Mikolayev had, just days before, uncovered a plot within his government to stage a coup, backed by Russian operatives and General Voitek. He had already arrested the perpetrators and had established their link to Asmaradov. The Tajik militants aboard the *Dream Spinner* were a means by Putonov to frame Mikolayev, and enable Voitek to take control of the country.

The Tajik president was now more than ready to help President Foreman go after Farad Asmaradov. In spite of the Collective Security Treaty that required the approval by all member countries before any outside military could engage on their soil, Mikolayev gave the United States president the go-ahead. It had taken less than a day to move the American Special Forces team from Europe into Uzbekistan, with agreement from that country's president. Then the team moved forward to their current location in Kyrgyzstan, with the Kyrgyz leader's concurrence. Some nice incentives by President Foreman had sweetened the request. In the end, all three Central Asian presidents stood to gain by the Viper's elimination.

In spite of the sovereign territory it was flying over, the Global Hawk surveyed the craggy terrain over the Vanj Valley, looking for signs of America's most wanted terrorist. The high-flying unmanned reconnaissance aircraft was focusing on one particular area in Tajikistan, near the Afghanistan border. Besides the Global Hawk, the extensive communications intelligence apparatus of the United

States sifted through thousands of information shreds—intercepted phone conversations, emails, texts, and feet-on-the-ground word of mouth—that might be used to pinpoint Asmaradov's whereabouts.

The speed with which the United States had gone from a concept to being ready to execute a strike had been unprecedented. Only days had passed since the hijacking on Dream Spinner had begun. Now, sources on the ground near Vanj had pinpointed the Viper's location, and the long reach of the American military's might was about to be demonstrated.

On the ground in Kyrgyzstan, the Special Forces assault team was making last-minute preparations while staging in the town of Daraut-Korgan, just a few miles from the Tajik border. The distance to their target was less than one hundred miles—a flight time of thirty-five minutes aboard the helicopter that would insert them.

Now, with the *Dream Spinner* in the trusty hands of the SEALs, the last part of President Foreman's plan was ordered to proceed.

Chapter 60

The walk down the *Dream Spinner* passageways was as nasty as the SEAL commander had described. Mainly in the stairwells, the dead terrorists still lay crumpled on the bloodstained carpet where they had drawn their last breaths. Their weapons had been taken and secured by the SEAL squad members.

Ace did his best to keep from looking at the bloody bodies, but they were hard to miss.

When they arrived at their staterooms, it was a spontaneous celebration. Neither Julie nor Colene had any idea that their husbands were on their way back. Between the laughter and sobs of joy, the happy families reunited after an ordeal that nobody should ever have had to endure.

Julie was stunned at the bandages on Ace's forearm and the blood on his shirt, a pressure bandage evident underneath.

"My God, what happened? Are you alright?"

"I'm okay. Just a few scratches."

For Ace, it was one of the best moments of his life. Tears flowed from them all. There had been a few times during the hostage crisis when he hadn't been very sure he would ever see *any* of his family again.

After their joyous reunion, Ace knew he needed to get to the medical bay to get patched up. Fortunately, Shorty had already freed the captive *Dream Spinner* medical staff and they were already doing what they could for the injured passengers.

Ace made his way there and was stunned at the number of wounded passengers being treated. The most critically injured were triaged and efforts were already being made to transfer them via helicopter from the *Dream Spinner*'s small deck to the USS *John F. Kennedy*.

One of the SEALs saw Ace and waved him forward.

"Doc, see what you can do for this man," the SEAL directed the *Dream Spinner*'s medical team.

Thirty minutes later, Ace was on his way back to his stateroom, his wounds cleaned, stitched and bandaged. A shot of antibiotics had also been provided to stem any infection, and he had been given some pain medication that would surely come in handy in a few hours.

As the crew members were allowed to leave their cabins, they were encouraged to get back to serving the *Dream Spinner* guests as quickly as possible. Reports from the engine control room indicated that a slight increase in electrical power should be restored within the next thirty minutes.

Juan showed up at Ace's door, the stateroom steward happy to serve his passengers again.

"Sir, I extend my most sincere apologies for what happened on the *Dream Spinner*. I will do everything in my power to take care of you for the rest of the cruise." He smiled broadly. "You are a hero! Everyone knows what you did. And of course, the SEALs."

"Juan, no apologies are necessary. You were a captive too, just like we were. The terrorists that captured this ship had no regard for human life, and we're all lucky to have survived. I know that there are some passengers that didn't make it. I'm no hero. I just helped do what needed to be done."

"Sir, many crew members were killed as well. It is a sad day for our *Dream Spinner* family."

Ace had not been aware of the casualties among the crew. "I'm sorry to hear that, Juan. Hopefully, we can all get back to the port safely and put this trip behind us."

He thought about something he needed to do.

"Juan, can you find a kitchen attendant by the name of Aleksandra? She helped us, and me in particular, more than anybody knows. The rescue attempt by the SEALs might not have been as successful without her involvement. I'd like to talk with her and personally thank her. She worked in the dining area, but the last time I saw her was in the Chop House."

"Yes sir. Right away. I will try to find her and send her to your cabin."

Ace also wanted to thank Martha Cook. Without her, the SEALs would never have known the locations of the terrorists on board. The results might have still been the same, but her information had definitely prevented American military casualties.

He knew her room number from the conversations he'd had with her husband, Ray, in the Centrum. He headed down the hallway and knocked on their door.

Martha opened it, Ray standing behind her. She knew it was Ace immediately. She had never met him, but there was no doubt in her mind.

"Hi, sorry to bother you. I'm Matt Black. I just wanted to tell you what a hero you are. What you were able to do likely saved the ship," he said.

"I know who *you* are," she said. "Do you mind if I give you a big hug?" They shared a quick embrace.

"Martha, all I know is that your skill and bravery helped get critical information to the SEALs. That alone limited the number of casualties on the *Dream Spinner*."

"You're no slouch yourself, Major Black. The SEAL commander has already been by here. He told me what you did. Without you, we would never have been able to stop the mines attached to this vessel from detonating. Without you, we likely would also have been hit by torpedoes and sunk. You are quite the warrior—a credit to the United States military."

Ace wasn't used to that kind of praise. He blushed a bit and then thanked her. He also shook Ray's hand and expressed his appreciation for all he had done. He headed back to his stateroom to rejoin his family.

One hour later, there was a soft knock on his stateroom door. Ace opened it and saw a familiar face. The beautiful Ukrainian woman, Aleksandra, stood there with a broad smile.

Ace gave her a big hug and asked her to step inside to see the rest of his family for a moment.

"This beautiful woman saved my life," he explained to his family.

She blushed and shook her head.

"It was nothing."

"My family, and all the passengers and crew on this ship, owe you more than anyone knows. Your bravery and willingness to risk your life made the difference between us all dying on this boat and surviving to enjoy our lives in the future. I'll never forget you."

Chapter 61

nside Tajikistan, just outside the northern city limits of Vanj, America's most wanted terrorist was hiding. In the rugged mountains and glacial valleys, amidst the sparse ground cover and numerous caves, he plotted his next move.

He had waited for the reports he was routinely receiving from Khalil Atta. Everything had appeared to be proceeding on track to the Viper's plan. But in the last few hours, there had been dead silence from the *Dream Spinner*. The message Khalil had sent to Asmaradov about the ongoing American assault on the cruise ship had never gone anywhere. It had been intercepted and blocked by the United States Navy.

The Viper had instead found out from the Venezuelan president that things had not gone well. He had been told about the silent cruise ship engines and the sonar images of the American aircraft carrier. The information meant only one thing to Asmaradov. The Americans had attacked the *Dream Spinner* and were in the process of taking it back from his Panja militants.

But the Viper knew that there was a final card to play. He trusted Khalil Atta to execute the final conclusion of the *Dream Spinner's* fatal journey. Khalil would detonate the mines and sink the cruise ship with all on board. If that failed, he trusted the submarine to finish the job.

At this point, Asmaradov didn't know if the cruise ship had been sunk or was still afloat. Nor had he received any more reports about the American military's assault on the ship. If Foreman had given the order to begin the attack, surely Khalil would have notified him.

But there was no word from Khalil Atta. Little did the Viper know his Syrian genius was dead, lying on the steel deck by a hull door, an extra hole in his head. And the Viper's backup plan had been scuttled by the USS *Grayback III*'s torpedoes—the remains of the sub were now littering the Caribbean seabed, about 4,600 feet deep in the Venezuelan Basin.

The final call he had gotten from Cuba had prompted him to make immediate plans to leave Tajikistan. Victor Chernov had never left his jail cell in Guantanamo Bay. Asmaradov presumed that the other two terrorists released the day before were still in Cuba but likely being actively hunted by the American military. The U.S. president had gotten the best of him. But there was always another day, another opportunity. The Viper would make sure his next strike on America would be successful—and very deadly.

Farad Asmaradov would not stay in Vanj for long. In light of the attractive bounty on his head, he was not going to wait for someone to sell him out for the cash. Tonight, he would rest. Early tomorrow morning, he would depart his hideout, and head east, just across the border into Afghanistan.

------------ • ------------

The helicopter lifted off early in the morning and headed south. The flight was expected to take less than forty minutes as the chopper streaked across the Kyrgyzstan border and, after a short time, descended into the Vanj Valley beneath the Pamir Mountains. Thus far, the weather, which could be pretty nasty at this time of year, was cooperating with the mission, at least for the moment. Unless something very unusual happened, the helicopter would offload its cargo precisely as planned.

The Special Forces team aboard had information from a hopefully reliable source—the local constable in Vanj. For years, the lawman had watched the corruption and terror inflicted on his village. His president had tried but failed to restore the rule of law to his country due to Russian influence and interference, significant numbers of criminal factions, and of course, the likes of Farad Asmaradov. Days before, he had made a phone call, passing key information to Dushanbe. It had then been quickly up-channeled to President Mikolayev. That had triggered the mission that was now in progress.

The Viper's current location had been pinpointed to a small village at the base of a rocky glacial outcrop. The warfighters expected to hit the ground north of the village and proceed on foot to their target. The darkness would provide some degree of cover for them.

When the helicopter was five miles away from their intended landing zone, they encountered heavy morning fog. It was so thick the pilot diverted to his nearest alternate landing area. Unfortunately, that put the Special Forces team over ten miles from their target and, making things even more complicated, the rugged terrain they had to traverse would add several hours to reach their destination. They proceeded regardless, betting they could still nab the Viper.

It was approaching nine o'clock as they emerged from the small draw in the steep valley terrain. The target house did not appear to have any activity around it. They cautiously approached. It was empty. As they looked around the small village, a man walked toward them. He was wearing a woolen smock, a small badge pinned to the front. The translator with the team had a brief conversation with the lawman and determined that the Viper had left only a short time before. The constable indicated the route he had used—west on the Vanj Valley Road, paralleling the river toward the Afghanistan border. Asmaradov was in a black luxury sedan with three other men, accompanied by a pickup truck modified to carry a mounted heavy machine gun in its bed—commonly referred to as a *technical*.

Sergeant First Class Jeffrey Spader made two calls. The first one was to the Special Forces communications center to advise them that the Viper was on the move. Spader needed an overhead asset to try and pick up the car as it fled Vanj. A second call was made to the helicopter pilot ten miles away. The Blackhawk quickly lifted off and raced to the small village, the fog now completely burned off. Minutes later, after picking up the team, the armed helicopter streaked west, following the two-lane highway.

There was little if any traffic on the road as the Blackhawk searched for their target. A few trucks carrying vegetables and fruit. One dilapidated bus that had once carried schoolchildren, now filled with all manner of men, women and children. Then nothing for a few miles.

The Blackhawk pilot saw the road end up ahead, intersecting with a north-south road. Up to now, he had not seen any evidence of the black Mercedes carrying the number one terrorist in the world.

"We've gotta make a decision. Did the Viper head north or south?"

"Any word from our eyes-in-the-sky asset?" asked Spader.

The pilot made another call. He was surprised when he was told that an UAV had picked up the two vehicles. The suspected terrorists had turned south following the Pyandzh River, again tracking along the Afghanistan border. The helicopter needed to be careful not to stray too close to the border, particularly in this area, which was known as a hotbed of radical activity—mostly Islamic State. The propensity to pop off shoulder-fired missiles at those who got too close was always there. Especially if the target was an American aircraft.

The Blackhawk banked hard to the south and followed the winding road.

"Believe I've got a technical in sight up ahead," the pilot said. "There's a black sedan about two hundred yards ahead of it."

"Take us a bit lower. I want to make sure we have Asmaradov," said Spader.

As they drew closer and descended in altitude, the two vehicles made a right turn toward the Afghanistan border. They were headed for a river crossing that would take them into the rugged Afghan countryside toward the town of Jamarj-e Bala. That area was apparently the Viper's destination.

"If that's our target, we've got to do something before he crosses that river," stated the pilot.

As they dropped lower in altitude, the copilot saw movement in the bed of the pickup truck.

"We've been seen by that technical. Looks like he's swinging the gun our way."

"Light him up," responded Spader. "I've seen enough."

The APU-4's quad 14.5mm guns mounted on the technical belched out a stream of bullets toward the Blackhawk, the tracer rounds bending the path of the deadly explosive projectiles toward the helicopter.

The pilot launched a Hellfire missile in response. It streaked down toward the vehicle, and seconds later, the truck erupted in a violent ball of flame.

The detonation did not go unnoticed by the black sedan. It rapidly accelerated toward the small bridge ahead, trying to get to what they presumed was the relative safety of Afghanistan.

"I believe that's our guy," stated the pilot.

"Roger that. Hit him."

A second Hellfire missile leapt from the stub wing, its plume designating the track it was taking toward the doomed black car.

The Mercedes was now only a hundred yards from the small bridge that would take the Viper across the river. Two men by the bridge entrance had seen the exploding truck and had already started running for their lives.

The Blackhawk pilot couldn't see Asmaradov's wide eyes staring out the back window of the car as the Hellfire missile streaked toward the car.

Moments later, the missile's warhead found its target. It decimated the automobile and killed everyone in it, an orange-and-black ball of flame marking the kill just a few feet from the bridge.

"Take us down to what remains of that car," Spader asked.

They landed as close as they could to the flaming hulk. Spader walked toward the wreckage. There was no way to discern whether the Viper was one of the victims. But the car had been identified by the Global Hawk, and it fit the bill. Four people in a now-shredded black sedan, followed by a technical. It had to be Farad Asmaradov. The Viper was dead.

On the other side of the river, there was a flurry of activity. Two vehicles were racing towards the bridge.

"Grab some DNA samples from the bodies, or their parts," Spader directed. "And then let's get the hell out of here."

He got no argument.

Chapter 62

"We've got to take every precaution with the passengers aboard the *Dream Spinner*," President Foreman directed his staff. "Since our military forces can't safely remove the mines from the cruise ship, I see no other way to proceed than to carefully transfer them by helicopters and CV-22s to the *John F. Kennedy* or another one of our ships."

"Mr. President, I agree. Our Navy is ready to safely handle the movement of everyone, with help from a few trusted crew members. Once we get the passengers transferred, we'll get the crew members off as well," replied the chairman of the JCS.

"We're also moving a hospital ship into the area to make sure we can handle any injuries that already exist on the *Dream Spinner*, and to address any other health issues that might arise if needed."

"I presume that the cruise line owner is going to concur with pulling all their folks off the ship? And then scuttling it?" asked the president.

"We've been in contact with them. They're trying desperately to figure out an alternative to scuttling it. Like maybe taking a chance with a limited crew to sail the ship to a place where they can dock—not sure who would ever let them approach a pier with those mines attached. They may be thinking that if they do that, they can strip out as much from the ship as they can salvage. Regardless, it's going to be a very expensive loss to them," the JCS chairman answered.

"Have there been any repercussions from the Venezuelans?" Foreman asked.

"Nothing yet, Mr. President. There has been some chatter that we picked up. Their navy has been trying to communicate with the sub. They surely knew the mission it was on. And knowing that, they likely know about the possible consequences," replied the chairman.

"I'm not sure what they'll do, other than scream about our aggression against their country. Taking out one of the few subs he has is likely to make a big dent in their military. And they are pretty unpredictable to begin with, so who knows how they will react?"

He continued, "Our information about what we think that sub's skipper was about to do came from a terrorist who's now dead. After all, do we *really* know the sub was ready to take a shot at a cruise ship and kill a bunch of our citizens? If the Venezuelan president was secretly complicit in the Viper's plan all along, he'll deny any involvement, and probably claim his sub was operating in international waters on some kind of training mission."

"I also hear that we got the Viper. Has that been verified?"

"Yes, Mr. President. He was tracked by one of our UAVs as he tried to escape across the Afghanistan border. We got him just before he crossed. Our Special Forces guys landed right after they took him out. There was little left of Asmaradov to make a positive identification on site, but they grabbed some samples for DNA verification. We'll know soon enough."

"Great. I want the results as quick as we can get them. As soon as we know for sure that the Viper is dead, I'll want to make a tele-vised address to the nation to explain just what happened to the *Dream Spinner* over the course of the last week. Word has gotten out about our SEALs taking back the ship, and about the innocent passengers who were killed. The press is already making wild claims about what they think they know."

"I think the American people—and in fact the world—need to understand what really happened here. And that terrorism is never going to succeed. The radical bastards may think they can win, but in the end, we'll hunt them down like rabid dogs and terminate them."

"Oh, one other thing. I presume we have our eyes on the two militants we released from Gitmo. Let's not waste any time finding out where they are and bringing them back to their prison cells."

"We've been tracking them since they were released. They left Cuba, but we've got eyes on them. As soon as we can grab them, we will," replied the chairman.

"Well, for now, the crisis appears to be over," commented a much relieved and very tired commander-in-chief.

————————•————————

The SEALs had successfully accomplished their dangerous mission with no casualties to any member of the elite military unit. After they had returned the SDVs back to the Grayback, Lieutenant Commander Shorty Robinson was ready to pack it up, head back to the carrier, and hitch a ride home to Little Creek, Virginia.

A contingent of United States Marines had boarded the *Dream Spinner* to provide the ship's security and careful overwatch of the passenger and crew transfer from the previously hijacked cruise ship. They would direct the crew's actions to clean up the bodies that still littered the decks, dining areas, and everywhere else where the militants had drawn their last breath. Additionally, arrangements would have to be made for the passengers and crew members who had lost their lives.

The three surviving militants in the Viper's nest of terrorists, Hafez Zoyatov, Cho Lee Kwan, and the combatant in the armory, were turned over to Navy security personnel on the carrier, given medical treatment as needed, and quickly confined to the ship's brig. They didn't know it yet, but they were going to be airlifted from the USS *John F. Kennedy* to a secure location, where their interrogation would begin. President Foreman was intent on finding out just how far Farad Asmaradov's deadly network had spread.

It took another two days for the passenger and crew transfers to take place until only a skeleton crew of a few *Dream Spinner* officers was left. They would remain on board until the parent company, Pleasure Cruise Lines, made a decision on the future of the ship. Hopefully they would find a port that was willing to take the mine-ladened cruise ship. If they were successful, the company could salvage as much as they could before the inevitable—moving the ship to a deep water graveyard and sinking her.

Major Matt "Ace" Black was ready for the fun to end. The rest of his family and friends were right in there with him. Their cruise of a lifetime had been more of a nightmare adventure, one that they would not soon forget. It would take a couple of days for the big aircraft carrier to get them back home. It would disembark them at Naval Station Mayport in Jacksonville, Florida, where the Navy's deepwater port was ready to service the *Kennedy*. A fleet of buses would get all the passengers back to Port Canaveral—and hopefully, a return to some sense of normalcy after their ordeal.

————•————

As the USS *John F. Kennedy* pulled into the harbor at Naval Station Mayport, the *Dream Spinner* passengers were ready for their "vacation" to end. That is, of course, all except three children. Claire, Roman and Nick had been treated like royalty on the big floating city and had been given personal tours of the ship. Word had gotten out about the role Major Matt "Ace" Black had played in bringing the disaster on the cruise ship to an end. The carrier skipper made sure that the Black family, in particular, got first-class treatment back to their home in the United States.

Their great adventure was about to end, and Ace, for one, was ready to go back to work. He knew that Julie and the kids would need some time to adjust after what they had been through. He thought to himself that no one, especially children, should ever have to go through that kind of experience. He committed to get them all whatever counseling they needed, especially Claire. He was in no hurry to take another family adventure for a while, and especially not one that involved a cruise ship.

He thought briefly about his ordeal, and the tragic consequences that might have happened aboard the hostage vessel. They were lucky. Many people hadn't survived, and an equal number had received significant injuries. At least, he believed, the threat by the militants had been eliminated. He hoped that the long, persistent reach of his government would take care of any other terrorists linked to the disastrous voyage.

As they boarded the buses to take them back to Port Canaveral, Ace took a deep breath of the warm, humid Florida air.

"Well," he proclaimed, "this has been one hell of a vacation."

⸻

One week later, off the coast of Tunisia, a freighter slowed to allow two men to board from the approaching small boat. It had not taken the two freed terrorists from Gitmo very long to covertly make their escape from Cuba by way of South America and then catch a flight to Algiers. The freighter planned to eventually take them into the Black Sea and offload them into the waiting arms of another radical Central Asian cell.

Overhead, the deadly Reaper UAV wasted little time passing video to its operator sitting in the air-conditioned ground control station at Creech Air Force Base in the Nevada desert. Once the identities of the small boat's passengers were confirmed, two Hellfire missiles streaked down from the cloudy Mediterranean sky. They found their mark.

The two Gitmo terrorists who had been released would not be receiving a return trip to the American prison in Guantanamo Bay, Cuba. The lives of Ismail Soleimann and Zafir Heydar had been violently snuffed out, putting an exclamation point on the final closure of Farad Asmaradov's reign of terror.

THE END

ACKNOWLEDGMENTS

My personal thanks go out to many key people who helped bring this novel to completion. As with my first novel, this second effort required a range of talent to help me craft a story that was filled with realism and intrigue. As always, my technical skills have limits, much like everyone. This story plunges the reader into an area that clearly goes beyond my personal, technical experience. In order to keep things realistic, I relied on experts to keep me pointed in the right direction.

One of my old friends, John Olson, was instrumental in the early days when I was putting the concept together for this story. While on a cruise vacation, I spent plenty of time bouncing ideas off of him about how the ship's takeover and subsequent rescue might play out. Thanks, John, for the help.

My wife, Cathy, helped provide ideas for the story. Additionally, her memory was much better than mine when it came to key aspects of vacationing on a cruise ship—we've been on plenty over the years. Thanks, dear, for your valuable input.

My friend and military veteran Lieutenant Commander Amir Pishdad Jr., U.S. Navy UDT/SEAL (retired), was incredibly helpful. A plank owner of SEAL Team FIVE, Amir provided me first-hand knowledge about one of the most potent American fighting forces in the world, the Navy SEAL teams. They are the best! Thanks for taking the time to open a new world of action to me.

Two distinguished senior military officers who served their country admirably provided key input. Lieutenant General Sam Angelella, USAF (retired), gave me some critical insight into Pentagon and White House operations, helping me keep a semblance of realism in how our government might respond to a crisis on the high seas. My brother Rear Admiral Ken Belisle, USN (retired), was integral in helping describe how the United States Navy might operate in a cruise ship scenario like the one described in *Taking the Dream Spinner*. The insight you both gave me was invaluable. My sincere thanks.

LT Malcolm E. Baird, USN (retired) and CWO4 Dan McIntyre, USCGR (retired) provided insight on submarine operations and nautical issues, subjects that I had limited knowledge of prior to writing this book. Thanks for your superb support.

My son, Lieutenant Colonel Matt Belisle, USMC (retired) was essential to getting my facts and terminology correct when it came to the scenario involving the tragic aircraft shoot-down. I really appreciate the help. Additionally, my daughter Kelly, and my daughter-in-law, Monica, helped me keep the medical-related aspects of the story within the realm of accuracy.

Once my manuscript was complete, I relied on several people to give the novel a thorough read and provide me critical feedback.

Colonel Dick Higbie, USAF (retired), an avid reader of action novels, did a thorough scrub of the novel and helped point out disconnects in the flow and story logic. Your input was greatly appreciated.

Several friends and siblings were helpful in reading the near-final version and providing feedback. Reg Fox, whom I met during a book signing, agreed to take a critical look at the story and look for any escapes. His inputs were on target. My sincere thanks. My friends Laurie Watkins and Linda Dorling gave me valuable input as well. I really appreciated it. Reviews by my brother, John Belisle and my sister, Maureen Powell helped keep me on track with their contribution. My thanks.

From a purely editorial standpoint, there are two people I'd like to thank.

First, early on in the construct of *Taking the Dream Spinner*, my sister-in-law, Ginger Belisle gave me detailed editorial feedback. Thanks for your dedication and perseverance.

My professional editor, Eliza Dee, was invaluable in getting my novel ready for publication. I really appreciate your effort.

Finally, thanks to all my readers for your confidence in my writing, and taking the plunge by buying my book. I will try never to disappoint you in your search for interesting, action-packed thrillers.

Lightning Source UK Ltd.
Milton Keynes UK
UKHW011432310521
384684UK00007B/781/J